Annihilation

Origins and Endings

RICHARD T. BURKE

Books in the Decimation series

Book 1 – Decimation: The Girl Who Survived
Book 2 – Termination: The Boy Who Died
Book 3 (this book) – Annihilation: Origins and Endings

Other standalone books by Richard T. Burke:

The Rage
The Colour of the Soul
Assassin's Web

Annihilation:
Origins and Endings

Richard. T. Burke

First published: August 2021

First Printing: 2021
ISBN: 978-1916141728

www.rjne.uk

For Theo

My silent companion during the writing of this book. You didn't offer any suggestions, but you sat beside me throughout.

It is always easier to see the beginning from the end, than the end from the beginning.
Julia McNair Wright

Part One: Retaliation

Monday 23rd March 2037
Compton Majestic Hotel, Northstowe

Antimone Lessing drew back the curtain and peered down onto the street below. The clamour of voices rose to greet her, only partially muted by the one-way glass.

"Bloody vultures," Jason Floyd, her partner, murmured from behind her. "How are you feeling?"

She flinched as his hand touched her shoulder. Ever since their escape from the Tripoli Infectious Diseases Hospital in The Republic of North Africa, she had felt tired and irritated, a condition not aided by her family's constant questions about her state of mind. She knew they meant well, but she wanted to scream at them to leave her in peace.

"I'm fine," she muttered between clenched teeth.

Jason let out an exasperated sigh. "Clearly you're not. I wish you'd just talk to me about it."

She spun the wheelchair around, scowling at him. "All right, if you really need me to spell out what's bothering me, I haven't had a good night's sleep since we were rescued. I murdered a man by injecting him with acid for Christ's sake. Every time I close my eyes, I hear his screams, and I see the smoke rising from his arm. How am I supposed to move past that?"

"It wasn't your fault," Jason replied gently. "Max Perrin got everything he deserved."

"Don't you think I'm aware of that?" Antimone snapped. "That bastard was going to kill us all. I thought he'd killed you. Unfortunately, none of that makes the slightest difference to how I feel. He taunted me, and I lost control. I allowed my anger to get the better of me. There isn't a minute that goes by when it's not on my mind."

She paused and drew breath. Her voice rose again as she ploughed on. "Then there's Paul. I can barely function myself, let alone give a four-year-old child the love and attention he needs and deserves. I understand that everybody's only trying to help, but sometimes I wish you'd all just leave me be."

"Look, I know it's hard," Jason said, "but we'll get through this."

"Will we, though? Now, there are paparazzi camped outside on the pavement. I can't even go to the toilet without worrying that some arsehole is watching me through the camera lens of a drone.

"And if that's not enough, we've been cooped up in a hotel room for the past two months. I haven't been able to get down to the track for fear of all the nutjobs and lunatics who might want to hurt me simply because I was the first woman in twenty years to survive childbirth. It's the one thing I love doing, and I can't even train at the moment, let alone compete. Everywhere we go, we have to be accompanied by a bodyguard. I feel like a prisoner with our bloody warders camped out in the hall." She waved a hand towards the door.

Finally, the dam burst. Tears flooded down Antimone's face. "I've had enough," she sobbed. "Now tell me, how could this get any worse? I just want it all to end."

Jason grabbed a box of tissues from the nearby table and crouched down beside her. "Here," he said, handing them to her. "There's something you need to remember. We all love you. Me, Paul, your parents; we're all looking out for you. One day, everything will go back to normal. But you can't bottle it up. You have to talk to us about it. Isn't that what the shrink with the caterpillar eyebrows told you?"

Antimone let out a sound between a sob and a laugh. The psychiatrist appointed to help with her recovery had advised her to discuss her feelings with close members of the family—and he *did* have bushy eyebrows that seemed to move with a life of their own.

"Yes, you're right," she said, drying her tears. "But it's far harder to put into practice."

"I'm here for you."

"I know."

A silence descended, punctuated only by the sniffles as Antimone dabbed at her face. Paul was spending the afternoon with his grandparents. The press interest in them had waned over the past few months, and earlier that day, a car had whisked him the short distance across town to her parents' house.

A light knock came at the door. Jason rose and took a step towards the heavy wooden frame. "Who is it?" he called.

"Derek Walker, sir. Could we have a chat? Today's codeword is dinosaur."

Somebody from the Prime Minister's office had assigned Walker the task of ensuring their safety. Every morning he selected a new password that progressed by one letter from the day before. If any member of the protection detail failed to provide the correct security code, his clients were under strict instructions to stay well away from the door and raise the alarm. It was a simple precaution, but Walker insisted they follow his directive.

3

Jason twisted the handle.

"Hello, sir," Walker said. "May I come in?"

"Yeah, sure."

The tall figure stepped inside the room and performed a quick surveillance of the interior. Apparently satisfied with what he saw, he turned to Antimone. "Good evening, madam."

She rolled her eyes. Ever since taking on the role and despite numerous attempts to get him to use their first names, Walker had clung to the practice of using formal terms of address when speaking to the family.

"Evening, Derek," Jason said with a slight smile. He knew addressing their protector in this way would irritate the man, but he couldn't help himself. "What can we do for you?"

"You've probably noticed members of the press occupying the pavement outside," Walker replied, his face an impassive mask. No trace of colour remained in his hair, leaving it almost totally white, but his skin displayed few signs of ageing, making it hard to estimate his age. His everyday work attire comprised a grey suit with highly polished, lace-up shoes.

He carried himself with military precision, was immensely organised and took no nonsense from his subordinates. To cap it all, he appeared to lack any sense of humour; none of his clients had ever witnessed a single smile from him, let alone a laugh. When asked, he always deflected questions about his career or background.

"Yes, we had spotted that," Antimone said. "How did they find out?"

"I imagine one of the hotel staff must've talked. I intend to discover who it was. They're all signed up to a strict non-disclosure agreement."

"What does it mean for us?" Antimone asked.

"I'm afraid we're going to have to move you. It'll take a few days to sort something out. In the meantime, we'll strengthen the security detail. You'll have to stay in your room."

Jason released a deep sigh.

Walker carried on regardless. "The glass at the front of the building is fitted with a reflective film, so nobody can see inside, and the mesh fence will block any drones. Even so, I advise you to keep away from the windows."

The thin netting had been developed a few years earlier to protect privacy. It was extremely durable, almost invisible and designed to be impenetrable to the small flying machines frequently used by the paparazzi to capture footage of unsuspecting victims. Even if they managed to sneak a drone through this barrier, the interference emitted by the material blocked the outward transmission of any unauthorised radio signals.

"Where will you take us?" Antimone asked.

"We haven't decided yet, but it'll be somewhere we can keep you safe."

4

"Sounds like another prison," she muttered under her breath.

If Walker heard her comment, he gave nothing away.

***

On the pavement outside, a figure stood apart from the other journalists. He held a pair of high magnification binoculars, which he pointed at the reflective windows. He might not be able to see inside the building, but at last, he had discovered where they were hiding. Earlier that day, he had watched as a man escorted the wheelchair bitch's four-year-old son to a waiting car. He and his team had tracked the family down once and would do so again wherever they hid. And the next time, they would get to them before the press.

Max Perrin lowered his hands. A loose component rattled as the servo motors in his left arm moved the limb. He could have asked the scientists to rectify the problem before the start of this mission, but he had chosen not to. The irritating noise served as a constant reminder of his new goal in life.

The familiar surge of hatred flared in his chest. He would make her pay for what she had done to him. He would make them all pay.

Tuesday 24th March 2037
New Dawn Immigration Centre, Dover

Major Ibrahim Halim lay on the single bed, watching the television screen: a current affairs programme about the political situation in the Middle East. He wasn't listening to the bearded male reporter as he spoke to camera—the sound was turned down low—but the dusty backdrop in the three-dimensional image filled him with a sense of nostalgia. He desperately missed the country of his birth. This place he found himself in was comfortable enough, but the featureless room, the bland, functional architecture of the facility and the perpetually grey skies left him yearning for home.

He had been held with the two surviving members of his team in the New Dawn Immigration Centre since leading the operation four months earlier to free his old commander, General Shaladi. In doing so, he had ended any chance of returning to his birthplace. The leaders of The Republic of North Africa had long memories and would never pardon somebody who had so blatantly opposed their brutal regime.

And that single factor was what made his appeal to remain in Britain so vital. Despite rescuing four British nationals including their celebrity Olympic wheelchair champion, Antimone Lessing, the immigration authorities had yet to decide whether he could stay. If they deported him, he would almost certainly die within a few days; if he was unlucky, his life would extend for much longer under the tender ministrations of the torturers in his former homeland.

His court-appointed lawyer had assured him the authorities would allow him to stay, but a niggling worry never left his mind. The second hearing wasn't due for another fortnight, and in the meantime, he remained a guest of the British government.

The immigration centre lay somewhere in the spectrum between prison and refugee camp. Living standards were higher than he had expected, and he maintained a modicum of freedom; he could come and go from his bedroom whenever he pleased, and he had free access to the communal facilities, including a canteen and well-equipped games room. But the tall metal fence topped with razor-wire that surrounded the facility left little doubt as to his true status.

The inmates, as he thought of them, originated from a variety of trouble spots around the world. Rising temperatures and a shortage of fresh water had rendered vast tracts of land across the globe uninhabitable, triggering a rapid increase in the flow of immigrants to more temperate climes. As far as he knew, none of the other refugees were fellow countrymen, but new people arrived all the time.

Many had travelled in dangerously overcrowded boats, only to be picked up by the fast patrol vessels off the British south coast. A significant proportion of those who set out either drowned or ended up being deported to their countries of origin. And of course, there were no refunds. Despite decades of trying to stop the traffickers, it was still a lucrative business that attracted the criminal fraternity like pigs to a trough.

A tapping sound drew him back from his thoughts. He slid off the bed and padded across the room in bare feet. He hauled open the door to discover a solidly built man he didn't recognise, blocking out the view of the corridor.

"Yes?" Halim said in English, his gaze running up and down the muscular figure standing before him. The man scratched at the armpit of his plain yellow T-shirt. Halim's eyes shifted to a rust-brown stain around the neck. A second, slightly shorter man stood to the side and behind his colleague.

The visitor lowered his head in greeting. "As-Salaamu Alaikum."

"Wa-alaikum As-salaam," Halim responded automatically.

"May we come in?" the first man continued in the major's native Arabic. The speaker's familiar accent identified him as a fellow countryman and placed his origins somewhere in the region between Tripoli and Misrata.

Halim gestured the men inside. "Where are you two from?" he asked.

"We are from The Republic of North Africa, just like you."

"It is a pleasure to see some new people from our beautiful country. When did you arrive?"

"They intercepted our boat and brought us here yesterday," the newcomer replied. "We have travelled a long way to meet you, Major Halim."

The mention of his rank and family name triggered a spike of adrenaline in Halim's bloodstream. Nobody at the immigration centre outside the members of his team knew his true identity. He instantly transitioned to a state of high alert. His attention switched momentarily to the second shorter man who hadn't spoken yet. The major's gaze drifted down to a dark patch on the left knee of the visitor's jeans. *Is that blood?*

Their eyes met, but there was no friendship in his countryman's hard expression.

"I have a message from Mullah Awad," the taller man said.

Too late, Halim spotted an object protruding from the man's clenched fist. The man lunged. The major swerved sideways to avoid the weapon's trajectory. Despite evading the main force of the surprise strike, he sensed the slightest of impacts.

There was no pain yet, but his fingers came back tinged with red when he dabbed them against the site of the contact, just above his right kidney. His eyes darted across the room, desperately searching for anything with which to defend himself. *Nothing obvious.* His only chance was to get out and call for help.

As if reading his thoughts, the two men stepped forwards and closed the door behind them. Each grasped a wooden handle with a protruding shaft. Halim immediately recognised the objects as narrow-bladed screwdrivers. And the way the pair bounced lightly on their feet advertised their training in close-quarters combat.

The shorter man bared his teeth in a snarl. "You are a traitor to your country. You deserve to die."

Halim backed up. "Punish me if you must, but my men had nothing to do with the mission. Leave them alone. They were only following orders."

"It is too late. They are already dead. They squealed like pigs."

A surge of anger burned in the pit of the major's stomach. Bellowing in rage, he hurled himself at the taller of his two assailants. He locked his grip on the man's wrist as they tumbled onto the floor. The sole of a boot slammed into his chin, dazing him. A sharp pain in the back shocked him out of his momentary disorientation. He scrambled to the door on all fours and reached for the handle.

A heavy weight hammered into him from behind, sending him crashing face-first into the solid panelling and closing his only avenue of escape. He staggered upright, shaking his head to clear the dizziness. As he did so, the shorter of the two darted in from the side, stabbing him once again with the makeshift weapon.

Halim groaned and lowered a hand to cover the new wound. The taller man feigned to his right, jabbing his blade in the air to drive him away from the door. The major backed along the wall. Behind him, the display continued to show images of a region he had once called home. A sudden idea burst into his brain.

He moved a little further, then whirled around and seized both sides of the screen. One sharp tug and the fixings gave way, leaving a bulky rectangle of plastic in his hands, still attached to the plug socket by a length of wire. He could feel his strength waning. In a few seconds, he would no longer have the ability to resist.

Holding the display panel under his left arm, he wrapped the electrical cable around his right hand and yanked it free. Without releasing the white cord, he once again grasped both sides and held the screen out in front of his body as a shield. He waited for his nearest assailant to move a step closer, then flung the chunk of electronics at his opponent's head.

The man raised an arm and ducked. The television narrowly missed its target and smashed into the wall behind. Several components detached during the impact and scattered over the carpet. The assassin advanced another pace, focusing his gaze on the face of his victim in quiet concentration.

Halim waited until the distance separating them was less than a metre. Then he lunged. The bared ends of the electrified wire touched the taller man's skin, causing him to yelp in pain and drop his weapon. The major dived to retrieve it. But the smaller of the two was on him in a flash. The thin shaft penetrated Halim's back three more times. He rolled over and raised his arms to protect himself, but the jabs rained down on him.

Finally, one struck him in the neck. The blood welled between the major's fingers. Now the assassins backed away, their job done, watching as the life ebbed from their target.

Major Halim's chest rose for the final time. He let out a final juddering breath and was still. A crimson stain soaked into the fibres of the carpet beneath his body. The two killers tossed their weapons on the floor as the shorter man leant forwards and spat on the corpse.

"That is what happens to traitors. You will pay for your sins in hell."

Wednesday 25th March 2037

Acorn Guest House, Northstowe

Mohammed Abadi pushed the wafer-thin screen towards Max Perrin. "Have you seen?" he said. "They killed the traitor Halim and his two men. There is a news article here about it."

Max didn't respond. He stared into space, scratching absent-mindedly at his prosthetic left forearm.

A puzzled frown materialised on the forehead of the North African. "Are you not pleased? It was your plan to get the killers into the immigration centre. It worked perfectly."

"Huh? What?" Max's gaze transferred to the diminutive figure with the sun-bronzed skin and tightly curled black hair.

"I said the traitors are dead."

"Yeah, good, Mo," Max replied distractedly.

The man exchanged a glance with the third member of the team, Omar Hijazi. If Mo was a featherweight and the brightest person in the room, Omar was more of a heavyweight and provided the brawn. At just over six feet in height, he carried himself with a gracefulness that defied his sturdy frame. He kept his head shaved, the stubble forming a dark ring on his polished scalp. The material of the black T-shirt he wore showed off the pronounced muscle structure of his arms and chest.

"Unfortunately, there is nothing about the Shaladi girl," Mo added. "It seems they must be keeping her somewhere else."

"Hmm," Max replied. "That's not much of a surprise. She may have helped the British prisoners to escape, but she and her father played a huge part in the attack at the Olympics. He's lying in an unmarked grave in Tripoli, so they need somebody else to prosecute. He led the mission, but as far as the authorities here are concerned, she was a crucial member of the team. She's all they've got. They'll be holding her in a high security location while they decide what to do with her. It shouldn't be too hard to track her down, but we won't be able to reach her until they release her, and I can't see that happening anytime soon."

"And that traitor, Kubar?"

"The intelligence from higher up is that he's working at Porton Down. I expect he'll be under close guard with his background and what he knows, but we have more chance of getting to him. I want you to find out where he's staying."

"What about the Baxter woman?" Omar asked.

Max's breath caught in his throat at the mention of the person he had witnessed murdering his father. "We know exactly where that bitch is, but we're not the only ones who'd like to see her dead. It's no secret she's being held at Bronzefield prison. There's no way we can reach her in there. Normally, I'd suggest the same approach as at the immigration centre: arrange for somebody on the inside to do it. But they're bound to be keeping her in solitary, so nobody would ever get close enough."

Omar rose and paced backwards and forwards, rhythmically clenching his fist. "So, at the moment, there is nothing we can do about the traitors from our country or the woman who started this disease. How will we kill the wheelchair girl and her boyfriend?"

Max raised his head and studied the weapons expert. "I'm thinking about it."

"I admit your plan for the immigration centre was effective, but sometimes there is a simple answer to a problem."

"In that case, there was an obvious solution. You don't have to be a genius to work out that they send most immigrants they pick up crossing the channel into a nearby detention facility. The only challenge was to make sure our assassination team got sent to the same place. By now, the British authorities will probably be on high alert."

"This time, we should just go in and shoot them all."

Max rolled his eyes. "That's why I'm the one planning this mission. If they went to the trouble of hiding them, don't you think they'd also arrange protection? It's not like we have an army at our disposal. There are only three of us."

"Blow them up, then. That worked well at the Olympics."

"And how do you propose to get close enough to plant a bomb? No, this requires careful thought. We can't just blindly rush in."

"So, what *is* your master plan?"

Max bit down on his irritation. The team had been selected for their specialised skills and aptitude at speaking English, not their ability to organise a mission. Mo was there for his expertise in Information Technology, and Omar for his proficiency in killing people. They had travelled separately on fake Algerian passports, arriving in the UK on different days and only meeting up the day before at this guest house, where they had rented all the free rooms for the next week.

"We know where they're staying," Max said, forcing himself to speak calmly. "The only problem is so does everybody else. They're bound to move them to another location. We have to track them down and complete our mission before the press find them again."

"How do we do that?"

Max turned to Mo. "That's where you come in. Mullah Awad told me you were the best hacker in Africa. I need you to use your skills to discover where they're taking them."

The IT expert puffed out his thin chest in a show of pride. "Don't worry. I'll get on it right away. I have a few ideas."

Thursday 26th March 2037

Solitary Isolation Wing, Bronzefield Women's Prison, Near London

The bolts shot back with a metallic clank. The door swung open to reveal the stocky figure of the female prison guard. A second male warder remained in the corridor. The all-in-one blue uniform did the woman no favours, emphasising her bulging waistline. Her lank, greasy hair hung down in a basin cut. A kink on the bridge of her nose told of some past altercation with a belligerent inmate. She carried a cloth in her hand.

"Not feeling hungry?" she asked with a malicious grin.

Rosalind Baxter's gaze rose to the newcomer, but she remained silent. She pushed the barely touched plate of food across the scuffed surface of the moulded plastic table.

"What a shame," the woman continued. "The chef worked hard on that." She poked a finger into the centre of the grey-coloured mashed potatoes. "Who knows what he puts in to make it so creamy?"

Rosalind's eyes narrowed. "You'll be hearing from my lawyer."

"Ooh!" the guard cooed. "I'm really scared." Her tone hardened. "You might have been able to threaten people when you ran that big company of yours, but things have changed. In here, I'm the one setting the rules."

In truth, Rosalind's threat was worthless. Her lawyers were far too busy fighting to uphold the terms of the amnesty document she had negotiated with Andrew Jacobs four years earlier to be concerned with the conditions of her incarceration. That and the numerous requests for extradition from foreign governments.

Rosalind rose from the table and perched herself on the edge of the narrow bed. The thin mattress provided little cushioning. Whenever she lay down, she could feel the lumpy padding through the stained material of the covering.

But that wasn't the only thing to keep her awake at night. In addition to the persistent bangs and clanks during the hours of darkness—many of which she believed to be deliberate attempts to deprive her of sleep—her mind continually played back Max Perrin's last moments. Her subconscious mingled the vivid images with those of her own agony as she had pushed the tip of the pen into her eye. Most nights, she would throw off her blankets, unsure whether the screams that woke her were real or just part of her dreams.

Not that she had any regrets about Max's demise. It was only what he deserved. Apart from anything else, he had tried to murder her adopted son. What mother wouldn't do the same to her son's would-be killer? The irony that she had also threatened Jason's life was not lost on her. But that was just the heat of the moment; she would never have gone through with it. At least that's what she kept telling herself.

"Don't get too comfortable," the female guard said, jamming the plastic knife and fork into the mountain of mash. "You've got an important visitor. I'll be back in a minute."

Rosalind raised her head sharply. Other than her lawyers, visitors were rare. "Who is it?"

The woman ignored the question. She placed the paper plate on the bolted-down chair and wiped down the metal surface of the table with the damp cloth, filling the cell with the acrid stench of disinfectant. When she had finished the task, she scooped up the remains of the meal and headed to the door.

Moments later, she returned with her male colleague, carrying a clinking bundle of cuffs and chains. Dressed in the same style of blue uniform, the man was an inch shorter than the female warder and probably weighed a third less. He had a narrow face and thinning brown hair. He carried a second chair, which he deposited on the opposite side of the table to the other.

Rosalind groaned. "Is this really necessary?"

"It is if I say so," the woman replied. "Come here."

Rosalind rose stiffly and ambled towards her.

"Put out your hands."

Rosalind complied. The guard slipped the handcuffs over her wrists and ratcheted them down tightly.

"Now, sit."

The female warder lowered herself to one knee and fitted a set of ankle restraints. Next, she looped the chain through the loop in the floor beside Rosalind's feet, then both sets of cuffs, before securing the arrangement with a bulky padlock. She checked the bonds, then invited her colleague to repeat the inspection.

"All secure," he agreed.

The woman grinned down at the prisoner. "It's a shame we can't shackle you like this all the time." She turned to her fellow warder. "Come on. We better not keep them waiting."

The cell door clanged shut behind the two guards. Rosalind stared at the wall, wondering about the identity of her surprise visitor. Several minutes passed, and her fingers lost feeling as the cuffs restricted the blood supply to her hands.

Eventually, the clang of bolts signalled the wait was over. The solid steel barrier swung open, and two men wearing dark suits entered. Rosalind had never seen the pair before, but she immediately recognised the body language as they surveyed the room for threats. They finished their inspection, and one of them returned to the man waiting in the shadows outside. Andrew Jacobs stepped forwards, confirming Rosalind's suspicions. The bodyguards took up position by the wall behind her.

She rolled her eyes. "I might have guessed. As you can see, I can't shake your hand—not that I'd particularly want to. Is it really necessary to keep me trussed up like this?"

The Prime Minister raised an eyebrow. "Unfortunately, Rosalind, you have past form. You murdered your partner in front of several witnesses. My people insisted you remain under lock and key during my visit."

"What's wrong with an interview room? If you're so worried about what a danger I am to you, why not talk to me from the other side of a Perspex screen?"

"I wanted to see the conditions they're keeping you in." Jacobs surveyed the cramped surroundings and the narrow bed. "Not exactly the Ritz, is it?"

Rosalind scowled back at him. "Have you come here to gloat? Because this is unlawful imprisonment. Need I remind you that you signed an amnesty four years ago. Why am I stuck in this hole?"

The British leader shook his head. "We're keeping you in protective custody for your own safety. If I let you out, you'd be lynched in five minutes flat. The taxpayers would strongly object to footing the bill for your protection on the outside. Unpleasant though it is, you're far safer here than anywhere else."

"Surely, that's my decision to make."

"Maybe, but then there're the dozens of extradition requests we've received from around the world. Several of those countries still have the death penalty, so you should be grateful I haven't handed you over to any of them yet. Even those bastards from The Republic of North Africa had the gall to ask for you back, if you can believe it."

"What are you doing about those savages? I've heard nothing on the news about any retaliatory attacks."

Jacobs sighed. "It's complicated. I shouldn't really be telling you this, but there's been a lot of debate at cabinet level about a suitable response. We submitted a report to the United Nations. Getting the Europeans, Chinese, Russians and Americans to agree on a course of military action is like herding cats, so I don't expect much progress there. The US are thinking about going it alone, but Congress is very nervous about being drawn into another ground war. The best we've been able to achieve is a strengthening of sanctions. Needless to say, nobody wants to be associated with a terrorist state, so they're holding for now."

Rosalind lifted her arms as far as the chains allowed. Immediately, both the Prime Minister's bodyguards placed their right hands inside their jackets and took a forward step. "Relax," she said with a sigh. "I'm just trying to get some blood flowing. How's my grandson?"

Jacobs blinked in surprise. "He was traumatised by the whole affair, but all the members of the family have been receiving counselling. Miss Lessing is taking it the worst. The experience affected her badly, coming so soon after the last episode. But then, you'd know all about that. That girl has been through a lot in her life."

Rosalind strongly suspected Antimone's current state of distress derived more from the part she had played in Max Perrin's final moments than any carryover from their incarceration in Tripoli. Only four people knew about Max's fate. During the journey back to England, Rosalind and Antimone had agreed to keep the details to themselves, telling anybody who asked that a stray shot had killed him in the gunfight while they were trying to escape.

"It's been hard on the entire family," Jacobs continued. "They've gone into hiding to avoid the press and the lunatics who still think she had something to do with the virus."

"What happened to the rest of the people who escaped with us?"

"The young African boy has been adopted. Unfortunately, last week somebody murdered Major Halim and his men in the immigration centre where they were being held. They'd all requested asylum, and we were processing their applications. We booked them in under false names on the paperwork, but sadly it seems that wasn't enough to protect them. We caught the killers; they said they were from Algeria and claimed they got into a fight when one of Halim's group insulted the prophet, but the Algerian authorities have no record of them. Our people suspect they're actually operatives from The Republic of North Africa.

"We can't decide what to do with Aya Shaladi. We're holding her somewhere secure, much like this. Her father led the operation, and there's no doubt she knew what was going to happen. She's claiming she took no part in the planning. According to her account, the Reponan authorities threatened both of them with death if they didn't follow orders. I don't suppose you can shed any light on matters."

Rosalind met his gaze and held it. "I'm sorry. All I know is that she helped with the escape, but by then she was a prisoner, just like the rest of us. From what I heard, the only part she played in the original attack was getting the Lessing girl out of the stadium after the blasts. What happened to Dr Kubar?"

"Ah, yes. The good doctor. He brought details of the drug he developed for this new strain of the virus with him."

"You mean *we* developed, Andrew. He didn't do it alone. It was a joint effort between the two of us."

"If you say so. He used the formula as a bargaining chip. It seems he learned that trick from somebody else I know. We agreed to grant him immediate asylum. He's now working at one of our government research labs. The first human drug trials started a week ago."

"Let me correct you again, Andrew. I think you'll find the first trial took place in Tripoli. My grandson was among the test subjects. Why did you decide to stop quarantining people with the new strain?"

Jacobs stood and paced a few steps in each direction. "It must have been about six weeks back. By then, it was clear there was nothing we could do to halt the spread. We couldn't afford to implement strict social isolation. The last occasion we tried that, it practically bankrupted the country. We took the decision that it was easier to isolate all expectant mothers from the population. I won't disagree there have been some unpleasant incidents—it's not a good time to be overweight and mistaken for being pregnant, for example—but it seemed like the lesser of two evils."

Rosalind tried to stretch her legs but found her movements restricted by the chains binding her ankles to the floor. "Look, Andrew, nice though it is to have somebody vaguely intelligent to talk to, these cuffs are cutting off my circulation. I'm sure you didn't come here just for a chat or to tell me how generous you are in not handing me over to the countries requesting my extradition. Why exactly are you here?"

Jacobs stopped pacing and sat down again. "Vaguely intelligent: that was almost a compliment. But you're correct. I have a proposition to make to you."

Rosalind leant forwards. "I'm all ears."

"My scientific advisors tell me it's only a matter of time before there's another mutation of this virus."

Rosalind tilted her head in agreement. "They're probably right."

"And the next one could be far worse. Nothing actually kills this thing inside the body. The best we can hope for with current treatments is to prevent the activation phase."

"Unfortunately, also correct."

"So, I've attended a series of high-level discussions with other world leaders, and we've reached an agreement to set up an international research effort with the brightest minds we can bring together. Unlike previous initiatives, we plan to collocate the team at one location. As you can imagine, arranging all the equipment and facilities will be very expensive. While the other countries have agreed to help with some of the funding, they feel we are responsible for creating this mess and should pay more."

"What do you want from me, Andrew?"

"After much debate, we have reached consensus on establishing this research centre in Britain. Specifically, at your old company, Ilithyia Biotechnology. They recently went into receivership, and we're keen to retain a major interest in the global pharmaceutical industry. I'd like you to join the new team."

"What's in it for me?"

Jacobs made a point of staring around the small cell. "Well, for a start, we'd move you out of here. It would also delay any extradition arrangements. You'd have to live on site under lock and key, but that would be more for your protection than anything else. You wouldn't receive any salary, only food and board."

"And if we succeed in beating this thing?"

Jacobs's eyes locked onto Rosalind's face. "I'm not making any promises, but let's just say I might oppose any attempts to extradite you."

"No, that's not enough. I want your personal guarantee that you'll deny any extradition requests."

"I'm sorry, Rosalind. I can't give you that assurance. In any case, I won't remain in office forever. I'm thinking of retiring before the next election."

Rosalind continued to stare back at the British Prime Minister.

Finally, she conceded with a sigh. "All right, you have a deal. When do I start?"

Friday 27ᵗʰ March 2037
Ilithyia Biotechnology, Northstowe

The man stopped in the open doorway and turned to Rosalind. "I'll be back to pick you up in half an hour. I expect you to be ready"

He had informed her he was responsible for security at the Ilithyia site, but she had already forgotten his name. Before she could reply, the door closed behind him, and the lock clicked home. "That doesn't exactly give me long," she called anyway.

In a supreme act of irony, her new custodians had allocated her the room which was once her own office. During her absence, they had converted the area her secretary previously occupied into a bathroom, as she discovered when she pushed the door open.

They had come for her at five o'clock that morning, allowing her to change into the garments she wore during the escape from The Republic of North Africa before bundling her into a prison van. A pair of guards sat up front as the autonomous driver whisked them from Bronzefield on the west side of London to the site of her former company in Northstowe, a few miles north-west of Cambridge. The journey took the better part of ninety minutes. By the time her escorts guided her through the security gates and inside the chrome and glass building, another hour had passed.

Upon entering the foyer, she had stared around at the sweeping arch of the ceiling. Until recently, she and Nigel Perrin had owned everything she saw. It was a far cry from the poky little two-storey unit she and her business partner rented on the Cambridge Science Park during the first few years of the company's existence.

Between them, they had built the organisation into a multi-billion-pound enterprise. The British Prime Minister had forced her to sell off her stake as part of the deal for her immunity from prosecution, and she received only a fraction of its true worth. Even then, she pocketed a staggeringly huge sum of money, not that there had been much chance to benefit from her burgeoning bank balance over the past eight months.

The early start combined with a sleepless night, had left her with a headache, pulsing at the back of her skull. She rubbed her temples, then returned to the narrow hallway and entered what was now the bedroom. A single bed lay along one wall, and a simple wooden desk, a quarter the size of the massive expanse of wood she had previously sat behind, rested against the opposite side. A small wardrobe butted up to the desk.

She strolled to the floor to ceiling plate-glass window and looked down. The neatly tended flowerbeds were as she remembered them, but a high metal fence, topped by razor wire, marred the aesthetic qualities of the grounds. Another recent addition was the presence of the man in the dark uniform, patrolling the barrier alongside the large German Shepherd guard dog, which he kept on a short leash.

Perhaps sensing the movement behind the glass, the man glanced upwards. Rosalind stepped back out of his view and surveyed the rest of the room. A cream-coloured towel, a toiletry bag and a small suitcase lay on the bed. She undid the zip of the case, lifted the lid and studied the contents: several sets of plain underwear, a supermarket-branded pair of jeans, a white blouse and a thin, pale-blue jumper.

She checked the labels; at least they had bought the right sizes for her. A click drew her attention to the dial of the wall clock. In a little over twenty minutes, somebody would come by to introduce her new colleagues. If she was going to freshen up, now was the time.

She had brought nothing with her apart from the clothes she stood in. She raised an arm and sniffed the back of her hand: a musty, faintly metallic odour, overlaid with a hint of sweat. Before meeting her new colleagues, she wanted to remove the prison smell from her skin. It would come as a welcome relief to shower without a warder carefully watching her every movement.

She grabbed the towel and sponge bag and headed to the bathroom. The light and a fan came on automatically as she entered. Moments later, she was standing under the shower. She felt the soul-sapping crust of prison life washing off as she luxuriated under the stream of hot water. Even though she remained a prisoner, she could at least avail herself of a few home comforts.

She emerged from the cubicle feeling refreshed and towelled herself dry. A quick search of the sponge bag turned up a plastic toothbrush and a tube of mint toothpaste. She wrapped the towel over her chest and hummed to herself as she brushed her teeth in front of the misted over mirror.

A metallic thunk interrupted her musical interlude. She rinsed the brush head under the tap and opened the bathroom door. The same man who had escorted her to the room stood in the open doorway to the corridor. He was in his mid-fifties with short-cut grey hair. A cheap suit hung off his trim frame. His face carried a frown. Try as she might, she couldn't remember his name.

"I thought I told you I'd be back in half an hour, Mrs Baxter," he said.

Rosalind self-consciously checked the overlap of the towel. "Yeah, sorry. I lost track of time."

The man's scowl deepened. "May I remind you, this isn't a holiday camp. If I had my way, you'd still be rotting in prison."

Rosalind glared at the man, then looked away. "I'll be ready in two minutes. Tell me again, what did you say your name was?"

His eyes lasered in on her as if he could determine simply by staring at her whether her words intended a lack of respect. "My name's Nick Butler, and when I ask you to do something, I expect you to follow my instructions. Is that clear?"

"Yes, sir." Rosalind couldn't resist putting a slight emphasis on the second word.

Butler glared at her for a moment longer, then said, "Two minutes."

"I take it you don't plan to stand there and watch me get dressed."

A vein pulsed at the man's temple. He spun around and stormed out of the open door, slamming it behind him.

Rosalind padded back to the bedroom in bare feet. "Windows, darken," she commanded.

The outside world took on a darker shade. It seemed the previous owners had retained the same system from her time in this office. One of her last acts before leaving the company was to update all the executive offices to use voice control. "Windows, opaque."

The overhead light turned on, and the view disappeared as the glass transitioned into a matte black. She allowed the towel to drop and quickly slipped on a pair of knickers and a bra. She was pulling on the jumper when the outer door opened again.

"Christ," she muttered. "Is there no privacy in this place?"

"Time to leave now, Mrs Baxter," Butler announced, marching into the room.

"Don't you know it's rude to enter a lady's bedroom without knocking?"

Butler ignored the question and studied the band on his wrist. "We're already late. Do I have to carry you out of here?"

"All right. Calm down. Just lead the way."

Butler spun around and marched towards the corridor. Rosalind had to jog a little to keep up. "Where are we going?" she asked.

Once again, the man refused to answer. She followed him to the lift. He pressed the button and entered as soon as the doors parted. He jabbed the letter G before Rosalind was even inside.

"You're not really one for conversation, are you?" she said.

Butler's eyes narrowed, and the muscles of his jaw spasmed. He raised a hand, grabbed her by the neck and pushed her back against the metal side of the compartment. He thrust his face within a few inches of hers, so close that spittle flecked her skin when he spoke.

"This might not look like a prison, but make no mistake, you're still a prisoner. For my sins, I'm responsible for you in here. You may have run this place once, but as far as I'm concerned, you're just a mass murderer, who should be made to suffer for your crimes. My wife died from the virus you created. I can't for the life of me understand why anybody would choose to let you out. If it was up to me, I'd put you against a wall and shoot you."

Rosalind tried to inhale, but the fingers around her throat prevented her from breathing. A gurgle escaped her mouth. Just when she thought she was about to pass out, the panels slid apart. With a grunt of disgust, the man released his grip.

"Now, no more talking," Butler growled. He marched ahead without checking to see whether Rosalind followed. She stumbled along the carpeted corridor behind him as she tried to catch up, the breath rasping in her throat as she filled her oxygen-starved lungs.

"Here," Butler announced, slowing as they approached the door of what had once been the boardroom.

A man stood outside, leaning against the wall with a coffee cup in his hand and seemingly deep in thought. He raised his eyes and stared at the two newcomers, but his gaze focused on Rosalind as they drew closer. "Mrs Baxter?"

Butler greeted the man with a nod. "Good morning, Dr Hendrick."

Rosalind blinked in surprise. She hadn't recognised her former employee. She had last seen him about twenty years ago when Ilithyia Biotechnology was still a fledgling startup on the Cambridge Science Park. His face was rounder and his sandy hair thinner, but now she clearly remembered the scientist she had let go two decades earlier.

"Martin, it's been a while," she said.

"I take it the pair of you know each other," Butler said.

"Yes, we met in a previous life," Hendrick replied. "I can escort Mrs Baxter in and introduce her to the others."

Butler stepped away from the doctor and beckoned Rosalind closer. He lowered his head to her ear and spoke in a hoarse whisper. "I'll be along later to take you to your room. If any of the people in there ask you to do something, you follow their instructions immediately and without question. If you fail to do so, I will personally drag you back to prison before your feet can touch the floor. And don't even think about trying to leave this building—it wouldn't be good for my career, but it would give me great pleasure to see one of my men taser you and send several thousand volts arcing through your body."

He spun on his heel and marched back the way he had come without a backward glance.

Rosalind rubbed her throat and glared at the departing figure. "What are you doing here?" she asked, turning to her former employee.

"The same as you, I imagine. Christine mentioned that somebody else would be joining the team. I had no idea it would be you."

"Are you talking about Christine Harris?"

"Yes," Hendrick replied. "Do you know her?"

"We've met a few times over the years. She's a fairly competent virologist."

"More than competent. One of the best, I'd say."

"So, what have you been working on for the last two decades, Martin? I haven't seen your name mentioned in any of the journals."

"I've become something of an expert in cross-species viral transmission, but I've stayed out of the limelight for the past few years. They've pulled together a pretty diverse group here. Let's go in, and I'll introduce you."

Hendrick's hand stopped halfway to the door handle. He turned back to his former boss. "Just one last thing: I haven't told anybody that I worked at Ilithyia. I'd prefer they didn't know."

"Fine. I won't mention it."

Hendrick's blue eyes locked on Rosalind's. "You have no need to worry," he said with a glint. "I don't hold anything against you. In fact, I'm looking forward to working with you once again."

Part Two: Disinformation

Friday 14th August 2015

Ilithyia Biotechnology, Cambridge Science Park

Twenty-one years ago

Martin Hendrick swallowed, then raised a hand and knocked on the office door.

A female voice from inside shouted, "Come."

He twisted the handle and stepped into the small room. A window in the back wall looked out onto a car park. Behind the solitary desk sat the CEO and co-owner of the company, Rosalind Baxter. Nigel Perrin, who formed the other half of the company's ownership, stood beside her.

Several frames adorned the walls. They held a variety of certificates, awards and group photographs. From a preliminary inspection, they gave little personal information away about the occupier of this space.

Hendrick focused his attention on the woman. She was elegantly dressed in a dark skirt, white blouse and matching jacket. Her straight blonde hair fell to shoulder length and framed an attractive face. From his research into her background before joining the company, he knew she was in her early thirties. For all her good looks, there was a coolness about her, a barrier through which little emotion leaked, and which made her hard to like.

Her partner was more approachable. Dr Nigel Perrin was a year or two older and held the title of Chief Scientist. His appearance—the thinning hair, dark-rimmed glasses and white medical coat—combined with his earnest manner gave him the air of an eccentric professor, but beneath the stereotypical exterior lurked a razor-sharp brain. His infectious enthusiasm helped him to motivate the twenty members of the science team who worked under his management.

Mrs Baxter also came from a scientific background, having studied Biochemistry at Cambridge University, but had gravitated towards the commercial side of the business. Both had to be convinced if the company was to take on a new project, but ultimately, the CEO held the purse strings. And releasing them was Hendrick's motivation for calling this meeting.

"Good morning, Martin. Please sit." Rosalind gestured towards one of two empty chairs on the opposite side of her desk. Perrin moved around and took the remaining vacant seat.

"Now," she continued, "you mentioned in your email that you have a potential new project you wanted to discuss with us. I'm not sure why you felt you couldn't document your proposal like everybody else, but here we are. So, what's this all about?"

Hendrick had spent a lot of time preparing his pitch, but under the attentive gaze of the company owners, he suddenly couldn't remember how he planned to start. He took a calming breath, then cleared his throat. "Ah, right."

Perrin pulled a ballpoint pen from the top pocket of his medical coat and clicked the point in and out. Most of the staff joked about the boss's nervous tic, but rather than distracting the Belgian scientist, the repetitive action helped him to focus.

"Do you know what the most common notifiable disease is in the West?" Hendrick began.

"Measles?" Rosalind said.

"Mumps?" Perrin suggested.

"No," Hendrick replied. "It's actually Chlamydia trachomatis. It's also the most prevalent of all the sexually transmitted diseases. In America alone, over one and a half million cases were reported to the CDC last year. In the UK, the figure is around a third of that. Across the developed world, the average notification rate is somewhere around one in every three hundred people."

"That's a lot of cases," Rosalind said, "but aren't antibiotics commonly used to treat that sort of thing? Azithromycin and doxycycline as I recall."

"Correct," Hendrick replied, getting into his stride, "but they're typically only ninety-five per cent effective."

Perrin wrinkled his forehead in concentration. "So, if we took just the US and UK together, that would be around one hundred thousand patients per year who don't respond to conventional treatments."

"Yes," Hendrick said, leaning back slightly as his message hit home. "But I'm thinking bigger. Much bigger."

Rosalind rested her chin on her left hand. "What do you propose? I take it you don't have a miracle cure up your sleeve."

The Belgian researcher let out a low chuckle. "Well... no. That's true." He hesitated. *Would they take the bait?*

Perrin clicked the pen in and out faster. "What if we could develop a vaccine?" he asked. "The market would be colossal."

Hendrick waited a moment in silence to allow the words to sink in. *Good.* The Chief Scientist had taken the first nibble. "My thoughts exactly. The main problem would be generating adequate levels of mucosal T-cell and antibody responses to provide long-term immunity." Once again, he paused.

Perrin returned the pen to the top pocket of his medical coat. "You'd need a vector to target the right cells—like a virus."

Hendrick recalled something he had heard at university; if you want something approved, allow the boss to think it's at least partially their own idea. *Time to attempt the strike.* He had stacked the deck by leaving printouts of an article around the office and in the printer output tray. The paper described the work of a research group, who had used flu viruses for exactly this purpose.

"Yes," he said, gaining momentum as he reached the critical part of his pitch. "I was reading a paper only last week about using an attenuated influenza A virus to target specific cells."

Perrin jumped to his feet. "Yes, I saw something about that recently. That's a fantastic idea. I'll need to do some reading, but the potential is huge. We should definitely look into this one, Rosalind."

Hendrick released the breath he had been holding. *Hook, line and sinker.*

Rosalind drummed her fingers on the desk. "I'll admit it sounds promising. The only problem is we'd require a lab with biosafety level two to work with a live flu virus, whether attenuated or not, and I don't need to tell you that cash is tight at the moment. We couldn't afford to update the facilities in this building without a considerable cash injection. And who would perform the research? It's not as if we have a spare team sitting around twiddling their thumbs."

Hendrick's face flushed. Just as this was looking like a done deal, it was slipping away from him. "We could rent space at another lab with the facilities we require."

Rosalind shook her head. "Didn't you hear what I said? We don't have the capital to engage in unfunded research, let alone what it would cost to hire lab space from a third party. We can barely make ends meet as it is."

"I could do the research here," Hendrick blurted out.

A stunned silence greeted his statement. Eventually, Perrin spoke in a hushed voice. "You know as well as we do that this building is only suitable for biosafety level one. We'd lose everything if anybody ever found out."

Rosalind let out a humourless laugh. "That may happen anyway the way things are going."

Perrin grabbed the pen from his top pocket, subconsciously clicking it in and out at a furious rate. "Mrs Baxter and I could end up in prison if the authorities ever got wind of something like that."

"I'll be careful and take all the right precautions." Hendrick could hear the wheedling tone in his voice. "You can trust me to keep quiet about this."

"And what about the jobs you're already working on?" Rosalind asked. "They bring in the revenue that we need to survive."

"I'd continue with the paid contracts during the day and work on this in my own time during evenings and weekends. If it's the money that's the problem, you don't need to worry about paying me overtime; I'm happy to do this unpaid. I could do the preliminary tests here. If everything pans out, we could rent the external lab space to confirm the results. We'd have to repeat everything, but we'd already have all the answers."

"Dr Perrin and I will think about it," Rosalind said. "A professor of mine once told me you should never perform an experiment when you don't already have an expectation of what the results will be. I'm not sure he had this sort of thing in mind though."

Perrin turned to Rosalind, his face tight with shock. "You aren't seriously considering doing this work here, are you?"

Hendrick stood. It was time to try to land the fish. "This is something I'd really like to explore. If I can't do it here, I'll have to seriously consider finding somewhere else I can pursue this avenue of research."

Friday 14th August 2015

Ilithyia Biotechnology, Cambridge Science Park
Twenty-one years ago

The door to the small office closed behind Martin Hendrick as he left. The CEO and Chief Scientist sat on opposite sides of the desk without speaking. The only sound came from the clicking of the pen in the latter's hand.

"For Christ's sake, Nigel, will you stop that?" Rosalind snapped.

"Right, sorry." Perrin returned the ballpoint to his top pocket.

Rosalind's brown eyes locked onto Perrin's. "So, what do you think of Dr Hendrick's proposal?"

"I can't believe you're considering this. It's a fantastic idea, but like I said a minute ago, the authorities could shut us down if they ever found out we were working with live viruses without the right biosafety precautions. We might even end up in prison."

"Come on, Nigel. I'm not for one moment suggesting that we wouldn't enforce sensible safety measures. All I'm saying is that we can't afford to upgrade the labs to pass a level two assessment. We both know the rules are set by a bunch of old men who are afraid of their own shadows. Didn't you hear him say that he proposes to use an attenuated influenza virus? We all take far greater risks when we venture outside our homes. You're a lot more likely to pick up a dangerous bug in a shop or a pub."

"I'm more worried about being caught. Even if we don't end up in jail, the company would be finished."

Rosalind tapped the desk with a manicured fingernail. "Clearly you haven't been looking at the spreadsheets I send over every month. It's time to face facts; if nothing else changes, we'll be forced into administration in around twelve months, eighteen at tops. The rent on the building is due in three weeks, the overdraft is close to its limit, and we're on hold with a significant proportion of our suppliers.

"Our purchasing people are using the company credit card to pay for the essentials. We have a couple of outstanding customer invoices, but most of those funds will go to paying the salaries. We're operating hand to mouth and have been doing for the last year. It's possible we may be able to find another investor, but we both know it dilutes our shares every time we bring somebody new on board."

"Yes, but—"

Rosalind cut him off before he could continue. "Dr Hendrick is on one month's notice. If he resigns and leaves, we'd never get anybody else up to speed on his projects quickly enough. Both would miss the deadlines, and the late delivery penalties would leave us even shorter of cash."

Perrin shot his partner an angry scowl. "I was against accepting those terms in the first place. Anyway, how does letting him take on more work help us?"

Rosalind's expression softened. "You know I didn't want to accept those penalty clauses, but we discussed it at the time, and it was either that or lose the contracts. As for increasing Martin's workload, he said he's happy to put in the extra hours for no additional salary. And what if he manages to pull it off?"

"Don't get me wrong. I'd love to start researching this area, but doesn't it worry you, gambling on the company's future?"

"Look, I'll be honest. It would place both of us in a risky situation, but we could take a few precautions. We'd have to make sure that any work he does on this project is off the books: no emails about it, no research notes on the company file servers, no meeting minutes. Absolutely everything would have to be stored offline. That way, it's all deniable. If the Health and Safety Executive ever caught wind, we could claim we knew nothing about it. It would be Martin's word against ours."

"Bloody hell, Rosalind. You'd throw him under the bus?"

"I'm sure he'd do the same to us. But think about the upside. This could be worth billions."

"Where would we even get a live influenza virus from? It's not as if you can just walk into the local chemist and buy a bottle off the shelf."

"We'd have to keep that off the books too. I'm betting the good doctor has a way of getting hold of a sample. He seems to have thought of everything else. If not, we could probably obtain some off the dark web from a part of the world where the regulations are somewhat less strict."

"Christ, Rosalind. I can't believe what I'm hearing." Perrin's hand moved towards his top pocket again, but a scowl from Rosalind stopped him before it reached the pen. "I still find it hard to understand how this is going to improve our cash-flow problem. Approval for a new vaccine takes years. From what you've said, we'll run out of money long before then."

"We don't have to get it approved ourselves. Hell, we don't even have to complete the research. Once we have something solid, we rent some lab space and repeat the work. Then all we need to do is show the results of early tests to one of the big pharma companies. We license any vaccine to them and arrange for them to rerun the trials.

"Alternatively, we sell them the company. They're not stupid; they'd offer a fortune to own the rights for a treatment to eradicate Chlamydia. It would be worth looking into who owns the antibiotics commonly used today; they might even pay us big money to drop our research."

Perrin shook his head. "I'm pretty sure you'll find the patents for azithromycin and doxycycline both expired a long time ago."

Rosalind forced a tight smile. "I bow to your superior knowledge, Nigel, but it doesn't really matter. A vaccine for the most common sexually transmitted disease on the planet is a pharmaceutical company's wet dream."

"I'm not sure about this, Rosalind."

"Do you have any other bright ideas to increase funding over the next few months? Because if you don't and you say no to this, we may as well cut our losses and fold the company right now. Who can tell what chance Martin has of delivering, but surely it's better than nothing? If we decline his proposal, there's a strong possibility he'll leave and find somebody else who will allow him to pursue this research. They'll reap the rewards, and it'll bring about the end here even sooner. I know you're not comfortable with all this, but I think we should take the gamble and go for it."

Perrin closed his eyes and took a deep breath. He remained still for a few seconds, then exhaled and met Rosalind's questioning stare.

"All right," he said. "You win. We've put too much in to give up now. Let's do this."

Friday 14th August 2015
Ilithyia Biotechnology, Cambridge Science Park
Twenty-one years ago

Eileen Floyd sat on the toilet seat, staring intently at the white strip. *Five minutes*, the instructions said. She had planned to take the pregnancy test when she got home, but her impatience to know the results whittled away at her resolve throughout the day. Her manager's request to work late again had finally cracked her resistance. He could hardly begrudge her the short time required to learn whether such a life-changing event lay in her near-term future.

Is that a line? Her heart beat faster as she moved the plastic closer to her face. Yes, there was definitely something there. As she watched, the thin band grew darker. It was as she suspected; she was pregnant.

Her immediate reaction was to call her husband, Daniel. Two things prevented that: first, company rules prohibited employees from bringing mobile phones onto the premises, and second, the father of the recently conceived child was on the other side of the Atlantic and occupied in a series of business meetings.

She performed a quick calculation in her head; five hours behind, so that would make it one o'clock in the afternoon over there. Daniel had told her he expected a long day with his potential new customers. The earliest she would be able to share her news was at least ten at night UK time.

They had been trying to start a family for the past six months, mainly at Daniel's instigation. She was more than happy to wait a while, but he claimed he wanted to be a youthful parent as their offspring grew up, unlike his own father, who had been in his mid-forties when his only son was born. Sadly, Eileen's child would never get to meet their paternal grandfather; the man had passed away five years earlier from a heart attack.

Anyway, this wasn't the sort of information to send in a text message. She wanted to see her husband's face when she told him. A smile formed on her lips as an idea occurred to her. When he arrived back home the following morning, she would tell him she thought she *might* be pregnant without revealing that she already knew the result. Then she would repeat the test with him present to watch his reaction.

Pleased with her decision, Eileen pulled up her panties and flushed the toilet. She took one last look at the strip of white plastic to confirm the presence of the solid line, then tossed it in the bin together with the packaging. The face that stared back at her from the mirror as she washed her hands glowed with happiness.

Eileen pushed through the swing door and followed the corridor to the laboratory in which she worked. As she entered, she spotted her boss, Alan Hastings, bent over a computer screen alongside the third member of their small team, Natalie Stevens.

The former was in his mid-thirties and, according to the office rumour mill, still single. His thick-framed glasses accentuated his narrow face. He was the only researcher to wear a shirt and tie to work every day. The latter was an attractive black woman who had only been with the company for a few weeks. She was quick to find humour in a situation and possessed a bright and bubbly personality.

"You need to reword this sentence," Alan said, jabbing a finger at the display. "Oh, and this one, too. Um... if you don't mind."

The door closed behind Eileen with a click. Her manager spun around. "Ah, there you are. I was beginning to think you'd gone home already. We have to get this report submitted tonight, and there're still some results to format. Apologies for keeping you late again."

Eileen hid the huge grin that threatened to burst out. It wouldn't be appropriate to reveal her exciting news to her co-workers before telling her husband.

Alan misread her facial expression. "Is everything okay?"

She felt sorry for the poor man. He really wasn't cut out for leadership and struggled to set the right tone managing the two women who worked for him. It was clear that members of the fairer sex made him deeply uncomfortable. He would certainly have no idea how to react if she told him what was on her mind.

"I'm fine. Better than fine actually."

Natalie stopped typing and shot a curious glance at Eileen before resuming her work. The pair had become friendly after being thrown together on their latest project, although they had never met up outside the workplace.

"What can I do to help?" Eileen asked.

Alan thrust his hands in his pocket. "Those graphs aren't good enough for a printed report. Would it be possible to include the units on the axes and export them as JPEGs at a higher resolution? If that's okay with you."

"Sure." As Eileen moved towards her workstation, she spotted a reagent bottle perched on the edge of her desk. "Do you want me to put that away?"

"Uh... yes, please. There's no room in our refrigerator at the moment though. Could you ask Dr Hendrick if we can store it in his lab just for tonight? I think he's working late again. I'll rearrange everything tomorrow to make more space."

Eileen picked up the chemical container. Natalie turned sideways in her chair and flashed a brief smile.

A sudden impulse came to Eileen. She could do with some company while her husband was out of the country. She didn't plan to discuss her pregnancy, but it would be good to share some girl talk. "Hey, do you fancy going out for a drink after we finish tonight?" she asked.

Alan's gaze jerked towards her. He turned away, embarrassed, as he realised she was directing the question at Natalie.

"I'd love to," the woman replied, "but I've arranged to go into Cambridge with my boyfriend. Definitely some other night though."

"No problem. I'll take this over now, then I can sort out those graphs."

Eileen headed across the room. Her boss rushed to get the door for her. "Thanks," she murmured as she entered the corridor. Hendrick's lab was three doors down on the right. As she drew nearer, she spotted a square of light coming through the small window. She peered inside and saw the doctor sitting at a workstation with his back to her. Good. He was still working.

Eileen rapped on the glass with her knuckles. He didn't move, continuing to stare intently at the screen. At that point, she noticed the pair of thin white wires leading up to his ears.

She turned the handle and stuck her head through the gap. "Excuse me, Dr Hendrick."

Once again, he failed to acknowledge her presence.

"Dr Hendrick," she said a second time, raising her voice.

Eileen entered the room and took a tentative step towards the seated scientist. Unaware that he was no longer alone, Hendrick reached a finger out and tapped a key.

The screen contents changed. Eileen advanced another pace, now close enough that she could read several words. Two immediately caught her attention: *virus* and *influenza*.

"Hello, Dr Hendrick," she called, practically shouting.

The doctor jerked his head around at the unexpected intrusion. His hand shot out. Moments later, the display went blank. He tugged the right earbud out.

"What the hell are you doing in here?" he yelled angrily.

Eileen took a backward step at the vehemence of his reaction. "I'm sorry," she replied, her voice shaking. "I knocked and called out several times, but you didn't hear me."

"Yeah, I had the music on." He gestured towards his ear, then offered her an apologetic smile. "Look, I didn't mean to shout. You gave me a fright. So, what can I do for you?"

"Um... we don't have enough room in our fridge. Alan wanted to know if he could store this in yours until tomorrow."

"Okay, no problem. Just put it on the bottom shelf."

As Eileen approached the glass-fronted cabinet, a flash of yellow caught her attention. On the workbench to the side of Hendrick's desk rested a sealed metal flask with a bright triangular label. Beside it sat a petri dish.

Hendrick spotted the direction of her gaze. He leapt from his seat and stood in front of the bench, blocking Eileen's view. She studied his face, but he retained an impassive mask. Her eyes lowered to the slight tremble in his left hand. The Belgian doctor thrust his fingers under his armpit.

"Right, I'll just put it in," Eileen said, mystified by his nervous reaction. She pulled the handle, releasing a puff of condensation as the door swung towards her. Her knees creaked as she knelt and placed the bottle in the empty space.

She rose to her feet and was about to close the cabinet when a second identical flask marked with a yellow triangle drew her eye. The breath caught in her throat at the biohazard symbol of four overlapping rings and the text below: *Danger Biological Hazard*. Another word stood out in smaller black letters on a white background: *influenza*.

What the hell is something like that doing in here? She opened her mouth to ask Hendrick the question, then thought better of it. The doctor watched her carefully as the seal closed with a gentle thud. Still, he blocked her view of the workbench.

"Thank you," she muttered. She crossed to the door and shut it behind her. When she turned and stared through the small glass windows, Hendrick remained stationary, his gaze fixed upon her.

As she made her way back to her boss, all thoughts of her pregnancy fled her mind, leaving one abiding question; why was Martin Hendrick working with what appeared to be an influenza virus with no evident safety precautions?

Friday 14th August 2015
Ilithyia Biotechnology, Cambridge Science Park
Twenty-one years ago

Nigel Perrin frowned as the phone on his desk rang. The caller ID signalled the call originated from Alan Hastings's laboratory. He wasn't expecting the report to be finished for at least an hour, so it probably meant yet another problem had arisen. And he certainly didn't need anything else to deal with right now.

"Yes," he snapped, picking up the handset.

"Um... good evening, Dr Perrin. It's Eileen Floyd. I wonder if you could spare a few minutes. There's something I'd like to discuss with you."

Perrin stifled a groan. In his experience, when an employee asked for a meeting late in the day, it normally played out in one of two ways: they either demanded a salary increase or handed in their notice. Or sometimes one followed the other.

"Yes, fine, Eileen," he said despondently. "I plan to be here for at least the next thirty minutes."

"Thanks, Dr Perrin. I'll come up in a second."

Perrin lowered the phone to its cradle. What could this be about? Another thought occurred to him: perhaps she planned to tell him she was pregnant. He knew she was married with no children, and she was around the right age to start a family. That was all they needed when cash was tight and the workload heavy. But surely she would discuss something like that with her manager first. He sighed. There was no point trying to second guess the subject of her request. All would become clear shortly.

Moments later, a gentle tap came from the door. "Come in," he called.

The handle turned, and Eileen Floyd's head appeared in the gap. A worried expression clouded her face. "Can I...?"

"Yes, take a seat," Perrin replied impatiently, gesturing towards the empty chair on the other side of his desk. Her demeanour suggested whatever she planned to reveal wouldn't be good news. He studied her carefully as she crossed the carpet. Up close, he saw she wore little makeup, not that she needed any. She was an attractive woman, with dark wavy hair, flawless skin and an open face. At around five feet six in her flat-heeled shoes, she carried herself with a precise elegance. She sat and folded her hands on her lap.

"How's the report going?" Perrin asked.

"Oh, fine," she replied, glancing down. "It should be done tonight."

He waited for a second to allow her to speak, but she remained silent. It seemed he would have to tease out the reason for her meeting request.

"Well, thanks for staying late. What can I do for you?"

She looked up and met his gaze for a moment before looking away. "Um... I don't know if I'm doing the right thing. I wasn't sure who to talk to."

"What's the problem, Eileen?"

She raised her head slowly. "Is this company working with a live influenza virus?"

Oh, God! That's what this was about. Perrin feigned ignorance. "I don't understand what you're asking."

"I saw a colleague with a flask on his bench. It appeared to be a viral sample. There was a biohazard sign on the container. I didn't think we were set up to perform that sort of research."

"Are you sure it wasn't something else? There's no way anybody here is authorised to undertake any work like that."

Eileen scowled at Perrin's attempt to brush off her question. "There was also an article about viruses on his monitor."

"Do you mind if I ask who it was?" he asked.

"I'd rather not say."

"But Eileen, this is a serious accusation. There must be a good explanation. Are you certain it wasn't a hazardous substance label?"

Her chin jutted out. "Yes, I am aware of the difference between a biohazard and a hazardous substance label."

Maybe she wasn't quite as meek and mild as he had thought.

Perrin placed his palms flat on his desk. "I'm not sure what you expect me to do if you won't tell me who it was."

"What's the procedure if I want to take this further?"

The first real sense of alarm sent Perrin's pulse racing. "You're thinking about taking this further?" His eyes locked onto hers.

"I haven't decided yet."

Perrin let out an inner sigh of relief. There was still hope she would drop the matter. "I guess you'd need to consult the whistleblower policy, but I have to say, that's a big step to take. Once you set the process in motion, it becomes very hard to stop. People end up losing their jobs."

"I know that. I'll sleep on it and let you have my decision in the morning."

"Great. I'm sure it's all just a misunderstanding."

Eileen stood, then crossed the room and stopped in the doorway. She turned back to Perrin. "Thanks for your time. See you tomorrow."

"Goodnight."

When the latch clicked into place, Perrin rose from his desk and padded across the carpeted floor. He placed his ear to the door for a few seconds, then pulled the handle and stuck his head into the corridor. She had gone. His next act was to return to the phone and dial a three-digit internal number.

Martin Hendrick answered after two rings. "Hello, Dr Perrin."

Perrin's voice trembled with barely suppressed fury. "What the hell did she see?"

"Sorry, what are we talking about?"

"Eileen Floyd," he spat. "She spotted the virus in your fridge. For heaven's sake, why did you even let her in your room?"

"Ah, that. There was no refrigerated space in their lab, so she asked whether she could store some chemical solutions in mine."

"Well, she saw enough to ask me about the whistleblower policy."

A pause. Then Hendrick whispered a single word: "Shit."

"Yes, shit indeed. She hasn't decided what to do yet. She said she's going to sleep on it. I need you to remove anything that shouldn't be there immediately. And delete your browser history. She also spotted something related on your screen."

"Sorry, I had my headphones in when she came in. I'll get on it right away."

"Let's hope she doesn't take it any further. I should never have agreed to let you do this research."

"I'm making good progress. In a few weeks, I should be ready to start some trials with mice."

"It better be worth it. Just make sure there's nothing in your lab that will incriminate anybody."

Perrin slammed down the handset.

He tapped in the sequence of digits for his next call from memory. The ringing tone repeated twice before a female voice answered.

"Yes, Nigel."

"Rosalind, we have a serious problem."

Friday 14th August 2015
Ilithyia Biotechnology, Cambridge Science Park
Twenty-one years ago

Rosalind Baxter returned the mobile phone to her handbag. *Bloody typical.* The one night in the week she left work early to eat at a decent restaurant, events conspired to drag her back to the office. Not that she was overly worried. Eileen Floyd was no match for her, except perhaps in the affairs of the heart.

Rosalind knew Eileen's husband, Daniel—intimately—having dated him whilst both were students at Cambridge University. The sex had been good, but she realised fairly quickly that they weren't compatible enough for a long-term future together. The relationship drifted along for a while, but after six months, they agreed to separate. Until relatively recently, they hadn't talked for over ten years.

When Eileen joined Ilithyia, Rosalind had been unaware that her new employee was married to her onetime boyfriend until they became reacquainted at last year's company Christmas party. Everything remained amicable, but Rosalind couldn't help wondering how much Eileen knew about her husband's previous love life. Maybe this was nothing but a fit of jealousy.

She took another mouthful of the tuna steak, then summoned the waiter and asked for the bill. While she waited for him to return, she picked up the half bottle of red wine and inspected the label: a twenty-thirteen Bordeaux. She had certainly tasted better. She raised her glass with the other hand and drained it.

"Was everything all right, madame?" he asked, speaking with a slight French accent as he eyed the remains of the meal on her plate.

"Yes, fine thanks," she replied, handing him her bank card. "Although the vin rouge left a little to be desired."

"Oh, I'm sorry," the man said, any trace of his alleged heritage now missing from his voice. "Would you like me to fetch the manager?"

"No, don't bother. I'm in a bit of a hurry."

She inserted her card in the reader and entered the PIN. His eyes tracked her movements as she removed a ten-pound note and placed it on the crisp, white tablecloth.

The note disappeared into his back pocket within seconds. "Thank you, madame," he said, the accent returning. "Bonsoir. Have a good evening."

Rosalind strode down Bridge Street to the car park on Castle Street. There, she climbed into the driver's seat of the white, year-old BMW three series. Ten minutes later, she rolled up in front of the squat, two-storey Ilithyia building. Lights blazed from both the ground and first-floor windows. Despite the relatively late hour—just after eight o'clock—half a dozen cars remained in the marked spaces outside. She rummaged in her bag for her access card.

She looked around as she passed through the empty reception area. It was strange to think she had invested her financial future in such an ugly structure. At the top of the stairs, she knocked on the door of Nigel Perrin's office and entered without waiting for a reply.

Perrin glanced up from behind his desk. "Thanks for coming back in, Rosalind."

She lowered herself into the chair opposite. "What's this all about?"

Perrin peered over his glasses at her, a worried frown creasing his forehead. "Eileen Floyd saw something she shouldn't have in Martin Hendrick's lab."

"What the hell was she doing in there, anyway? I thought we told him to keep the door locked while he was working on his secret project."

"Well, obviously he didn't. She also spotted some related virus research material on his screen."

Rosalind shook her head. "It never ceases to amaze me how somebody, who is so intelligent in some ways, could be so stupid in others. Has he left yet?"

Perrin turned and peered out of the window. "His car's still down there. Let me call him."

Rosalind stood and paced over the worn carpet while they waited for their errant employee to arrive. A sharp knock signalled the doctor's arrival. She pulled the door open. Hendrick failed to hide the worried expression on his face as the CEO directed him to the second chair opposite the Chief Scientist. He glanced anxiously from one to the other.

Rosalind stared down at him for a moment, then took the remaining free seat. A red spot formed on each of her cheeks. "What the hell do you think you're playing at?" she yelled.

Hendrick shrank back at the ferocity of her words.

"Well?" she continued. "I wasted an expensive meal because of this. I'd like an explanation."

The researcher swallowed, then spoke in a subdued voice, refusing to meet her gaze. "I was wearing my earphones, so I didn't hear her come in. She caught me off guard. I totally forgot about the virus samples in the fridge."

"You know she asked about the whistleblower policy?"

Hendrick raised his head sharply. "Yes, Dr Perrin mentioned that earlier. Is she planning to go ahead with a complaint?"

Rosalind ignored his question. "I hope you've hidden away anything that shouldn't be in your lab. There better not be any incriminating files on the server either."

"Um, yeah. There's nothing to find."

"If she takes this further, deny it all. Tell her she was mistaken, that it was just hazardous chemicals."

"She seemed pretty insistent to me," Perrin said in a low voice. "She made a point about knowing the difference between a hazardous material label and a biohazard one."

Rosalind's head snapped towards her partner. "I'm sure I don't need to remind you what might happen if this escalates, Nigel. They could shut this place down. We could all go to prison. At the very least, the company will be prosecuted and fined. We'd become pariahs. Nobody would even consider putting more work our way. I've put in far too much to let it fail now, and that's not to mention losing my house and every penny of the money I— make that we—have invested in this business."

Perrin removed a pen from his top pocket and started clicking the tip in and out. "I think you're forgetting that I was the one who argued against this project. We all knew the risks. Anyway, none of that matters now. The big question is what we do next."

The sound of the ballpoint was the only noise to disturb the silence. Perrin glanced down at his hand as if seeing the pen for the first time, then placed it on his desk.

"Perhaps we should go on the attack," Rosalind said after a few seconds.

"What do you mean?" Perrin asked.

"We inform her she was breaking company rules. There's something in one of our policy documents about entry to unauthorised areas. What if we put a sign up on the door to Dr Hendrick's lab? Nobody ever reads those things, so we could claim it was there all along. From what you mentioned before, she never received permission to enter. We can always get Anders to play bad cop and raise the subject of disciplinary action."

Anders Grolby had joined the company a year earlier. The blond-haired Swede led the IT team and doubled as the head of security. His background in the Swedish military had given him a unique blend of skills. Amongst his initiatives was a ban on the use of mobile phones and memory sticks inside the premises. He argued that both posed a severe risk to the protection of intellectual property, which provided a core part of the company's value.

"I'm not sure that'll work, Rosalind," Perrin said, a look of uncertainty etched on his face. "If we get all heavy-handed with her, it might push her the wrong way."

"So, you're suggesting we play nice? She shouldn't have been there in the first place. She'll probably change her tune if we threaten her with the sack."

The worry lines on Perrin's forehead deepened. "I really don't think that's the right approach."

Rosalind stood. "If all else fails, remind her she signed a non-disclosure agreement. Let me give Grolby a call and brief him."

Hendrick followed her lead. "If there's nothing else, I'll get back to my work."

Nigel Perrin sat, absent-mindedly clicking his pen.

"See you both tomorrow," Rosalind said, brightly, but she wasn't smiling.

Friday 14th August 2015
33 Willow Drive, Cambridge
Twenty-one years ago

E ileen Floyd arrived home shortly after eight o'clock. She had completed the tasks assigned to her but found it hard to concentrate on work after the discovery in Dr Hendrick's laboratory. She shoved all thoughts of her recently confirmed pregnancy to the back of her mind. What could he be working on? The biohazard warning labels, combined with his angry reaction when he realised what she had seen, set the alarm bells ringing inside her head. Dr Perrin's attempts to downplay her concerns were equally baffling.

She felt fairly sure of her ground but decided to check the guidance on biosafety anyway. Using her phone, she pulled up a search window and browsed through the results. Her findings confirmed her original suspicions; influenza viruses fell under the Hazard Group two classification, which meant any work should be carried out at Containment Level two or higher.

All new employees received a safety briefing during induction, but she was certain there had been no mention of working with potentially dangerous pathogens. Neither did she remember any reference to viral materials during the audits many of the company's customers demanded before placing a contract. Even if she was mistaken, what was the flask doing out on the bench and not inside a biosafety cabinet?

Dr Perrin had mentioned a whistleblower policy. She didn't want to get anybody in trouble, but if Dr Hendrick wasn't taking the correct safety precautions, she owed it to her colleagues to escalate the matter. If he was recklessly endangering his fellow employees, she had a duty to act. And it no longer just affected her; she now had another life, growing inside her, to think about.

Eileen performed a second search using the words biosafety and whistleblower. The topmost hit pointed to a page at the *hse.gov.uk* domain. She opened the link to discover an article about whistleblowers on the Health and Safety Executive website. It advised employees with a serious concern to take the issue up with a senior manager in the first instance. But hadn't she already done that?

She followed several more links. From what she read, if an employer didn't deal with the complaint to the employee's satisfaction, the recommended next stage was to contact the Advisory, Conciliation and Arbitration Service, otherwise known as ACAS. She strongly suspected the owners of the company would try to sweep her concerns under the carpet.

Daniel would know what to do. She glanced at her watch and performed a quick calculation in her head. It was still only mid-afternoon in the States. Perhaps the meeting had finished early, and he was free to give her advice.

She selected his name from the recent contacts list and pressed the dial icon. Several seconds of silence went by, then her husband's familiar voice emerged from the speaker. "Sorry, I'm not available. Leave a message."

She hesitated for a moment, unsure what to say. She needed time to organise her thoughts, and answer machines always flustered her. Should she tell him first about the pregnancy or her worries at work? *Damn.* She lowered the phone and stabbed the disconnect button.

Maybe a text was the right approach. She tapped at the screen with her thumbs.

"Please call when free. E xxx."

***

Daniel Floyd pulled back the sleeve of his jacket below the table and glanced at his watch. The purchasing director of the electronic measurement equipment distributor they were visiting droned on in his brash New York accent: something to do with volumes and profit margins. Daniel turned off; this was the domain of his colleague, Trevor Taylor, who had joined him on this trip to cover the sales side.

"That's great, Trev," the large American sitting opposite said, eventually. "Let's do this deal. If you can update those figures, I'll send the order through tomorrow."

Daniel breathed a silent sigh of relief. *Finally.* It had taken an entire morning discussing the technical details and most of the afternoon on the commercial side, but at last, they had reached an agreement. The long hours on the plane in economy class might be worth it after all.

The four men in the spacious boardroom stood. Trevor rounded the expanse of polished wood and grasped his new customer's hand. "Thanks, Randy. I look forward to receiving your business."

Daniel stifled a smirk. He could never understand why anybody given the name Randolph would abbreviate it to Randy. Perhaps the word didn't have the same connotations on the other side of the pond. Moments later, he found his own fingers crushed by the American's meaty paw. As if that wasn't

45

punishment enough, he received a hearty slap on the back from the man. "I want you technical guys to keep talking to each other, Dan."

"Sure thing," he replied in an American accent, suddenly worried that the new clients might think he was parodying their way of speaking. Randy didn't seem to notice as he turned to Trevor and resumed an enthusiastic conversation.

The fourth meeting attendee and the more subdued of the two customers came up and also shook hands. Mike Peters headed up their technical sales support team. Daniel found himself liking his opposite number. They had established a good rapport over the phone, but this was the first opportunity to meet in person.

"Great to finally get together," Mike said. "You should come for longer next time. We could see a few of the sights. It's quite a city."

"I might just do that," Daniel replied with a smile. "I'm sure we'll be seeing plenty more of each other if this deal is as successful as we both hope. Let me know if you're visiting the UK anytime, and I'll show you around Cambridge. London's less than sixty minutes away by train too."

"Thanks. What time's your flight?"

"Seven fifty."

Mike consulted his watch. "You probably need to get moving. You've got over two-and-a-half hours before take-off, but traffic is hell during rush hour. What time do you land?"

"That's easy. Exactly twelve hours later."

"A real red eye then."

Daniel laughed. "You're right. Travelling cattle class doesn't help either. I better go and drag Trevor away."

***

Mike Peters hadn't been lying about the trip to the airport. After a journey that combined long stretches of sitting stationary in traffic with an adrenaline-filled dash at the mercy of a lunatic cab driver, Daniel and Trevor Taylor arrived at JFK with seventy minutes to spare before take-off.

They rushed through passport control and reached the gate just as boarding started. Finally, they sank into their cramped seats near the back of the plane, a quarter of an hour ahead of the scheduled departure time.

Daniel pulled his mobile phone from his jacket pocket and remembered he had set it to silent to avoid being disturbed during the meeting. Half a dozen emails, two missed calls and a text message awaited him. He started with the calls, checking the caller ID: both from Eileen. The message also originated from his wife. "Please call when free."

He did a quick calculation. The UK was five hours ahead, making it close to one o'clock in the morning. Would she really want him to wake her? She had called him twice, so he reasoned she probably wouldn't mind being woken in the middle of the night. He selected the contacts and was about to click the call button when the stewardess came down the aisle, checking that everybody had fastened their seatbelts and placed their seats in the upright position. The embossed name tag identified her as Barbara.

Her gaze landed on the phone in his hand. "Excuse me, sir," she said, speaking in a clipped British accent. "I'm afraid passengers need to turn off all electronic devices for take-off."

Daniel hesitated for a second. Five minutes still remained before departure. He was about to ask whether he could make a quick call, but the stern expression staring back at him signalled it would be a pointless request.

He pulled down the settings menu and set the phone to flight mode. "Okay, Barbara."

She flashed a false smile in return and waited until he returned the device to his pocket before continuing her journey down the aisle.

Daniel turned sideways in his seat to Trevor, but his colleague already had his earphones in with his eyes glued to the video on his laptop screen.

Friday 14th August 2015
33 Willow Drive, Cambridge
Twenty-one years ago

The harsh jangling of the alarm clock jolted Eileen from a deep sleep. Reaching out a hand, she slapped the mute button. She lifted her wrist and checked the time on her watch through bleary eyes: six-thirty.

She had lain awake most of the night, only drifting off around four in the morning. A pounding headache throbbed at the base of her skull. Her body felt like she had spent the previous evening drinking heavily, but not a single drop of alcohol had passed her lips.

She threw back the covers and lowered her feet to the carpet. A wave of nausea washed over her. *It couldn't be morning sickness already, could it?* She sat with her face in her hands for several seconds, waiting for the sensation to pass. A sudden thought penetrated her sluggish brain; had Daniel tried to call?

She staggered upright and crossed to where her mobile lay on the dresser, connected to the mains charger through a coiled black wire. She pulled the cable free and unlocked the screen: two junk emails but no missed calls or texts and nothing from her husband.

Cursing silently, she tossed the phone on the bed and padded to the en suite bathroom. After standing under the jet of hot water for over ten minutes, she felt vaguely human again. She brushed her teeth, then returned to the bedroom.

What time had Daniel told her the plane was landing? She wracked her brains: around eight o'clock if she remembered correctly. It would be at least another half hour before he cleared passport control, but she planned to be at work long before then. She would leave the building during a coffee break and call him from the car park—unless he called her first on the office line.

She hurried down a breakfast of tea and toast and was on the road before seven-fifteen. At this time of the morning, the drive would be much quicker than her usual forty-minute commute. She rolled into a parking space twenty minutes later, remembering little about the journey. A final check of her phone confirmed no recent messages before she locked it in the glovebox.

Despite the early hour, she wasn't the first to arrive, judging by the three cars parked near the entrance. The two-year-old blue Toyota Prius belonged to Nigel Perrin. She immediately recognised the new Ford Focus with red metallic paint as Dr Hendrick's. Had he been here all night? Whatever he was working on, he was certainly putting in long hours. Her heart lurched in her chest at the prospect of jeopardising his career if she decided to proceed with her complaint.

The last car, a battered white Saab 93, took longer to identify. She glanced inside as she passed and spotted a paperback on the passenger seat. The cover depicted an armed man holding a machine gun. The title, in a foreign language, contained several accented letters. Of course; the vehicle had to belong to Anders Grolby.

She recalled hearing about the man's background in the Swedish military. He was perfectly friendly around the other employees, but something about him made her uncomfortable in his presence. She had tried to place the cause of her uneasiness but failed. The closest she came was a sense that he was weighing her up as a potential opponent.

She raised her identity card to the reader and pushed through the front door into the building. She headed past the empty reception desk and down the corridor towards her workplace. Her footsteps slowed as she approached Dr Hendrick's laboratory. Unconsciously, she inhaled deeply and held her breath as she drew nearer the doorway. A piece of white paper covered the small window, preventing a view of the interior. Beneath it, a laminated notice in inch-high letters read, *No Unauthorised Entry*.

Neither had been there yesterday. Their presence sent a shiver of apprehension deep within her core. She quickened her pace and shoved through the door into the area she shared with her two colleagues. On any other day, she would have brewed herself a cup of tea before settling down at her workstation, but her mind was on other things.

Her boss, Alan Hastings, had spent most of the previous night watching over her shoulder as she corrected the graphs, making it impossible to study the whistleblower policy. She navigated the network to the company folder and pulled up the document on her PC screen. On the first pass, she scrolled down quickly, skimming through just the headings: *Introduction*, *Scope*, *Safeguards* and *Procedures for Making a Disclosure*. Two pages in total.

She started again at the top. Ten minutes later, she had digested the contents. The process obligated the company to treat any complaint in a sensitive and confidential manner. It made the directors responsible for investigating any grievance unless they were the target of the allegation, in which case they would nominate a senior manager as the investigative officer. In the final stage, the assigned investigator was required to acknowledge the issue in writing and keep the complainant apprised of any progress.

Eileen closed the file and leant back in her chair. The new notice outside Dr Hendrick's laboratory implied that somebody must have already discussed the issue with him. That meant confidentiality was now a moot point. The Belgian researcher would have little doubt as to the identity of the whistleblower if she chose to go ahead.

She cursed her stupidity. Why hadn't she waited to discuss the matter with Daniel before raising it with Dr Perrin? Her husband would know what to do. She checked her watch: still five minutes until the plane's scheduled landing time.

***

Seventy miles away, a British Airways Boeing 747 completed the long flight from New York as its wheels touched down on the northernmost runway at Heathrow Airport.

The captain's voice came across the tannoy. "Would all passengers please remain seated until the aeroplane reaches the gate and the seatbelt signs are extinguished."

Despite the instructions, frantic movement broke out around Daniel Floyd. Unlike many of his fellow flyers, he remained in his seat. A wave of exhaustion swept over him. The man sitting in the row behind had sneezed and coughed throughout the flight, not only spreading his germs throughout the cabin but also ensuring nobody in his vicinity got any sleep.

Daniel removed the phone from the top pocket of his creased white shirt. After unlocking the screen, he navigated to the settings menu and cancelled flight mode. Almost immediately, his mobile added to the hubbub, pinging as a flurry of emails arrived in the inbox. He brought up his contacts and selected Eileen's name from the list. The ringing tone repeated eight times, then his wife's voice spoke in his ear. "Sorry, I'm not available now, but if you leave a message, I'll try to get back to you as soon as I can."

Daniel waited for the beep. "I've just landed. You're not still in bed, are you? I'll ring again later."

Next, he selected the text message icon and tapped in a few words. "Arrived in the UK. Will call when through customs."

He put the mobile away and sat patiently as the stewardesses urged the passengers to remain seated. After what seemed an age, the plane eventually stopped moving, and the seatbelt lights turned off with an accompanying ping.

Daniel watched his fellow travellers leap back to their feet and haul their cases out of the overhead lockers as if their lives depended upon it. "Cabin crew, doors to manual," came the captain's voice over the tannoy.

Five minutes later, a mechanical whirring sound set off a fresh frenzy of movement as the occupants of the plane packed closer together to get nearer to the exits. When the crowd began to disembark, he collected his overnight case from the locker above and followed them down the aisle. His colleague, Trevor, had already departed in the first crush after a hurried farewell. The stewardess named Barbara waited by the rear door.

"Goodbye," he said.

She flashed an insincere smile at him. "Thanks for flying British Airways. Have a safe onward journey."

It took another fifty minutes before he had cleared customs and stood on the pavement, waiting for the airport shuttle bus to arrive. As he stared along the road, the familiar notes of his ring tone emerged from his shirt pocket. Caller ID told him the call originated from Eileen's work number.

He tapped the green answer icon. "Hello, gorgeous. Have you missed me?"

"Thank God, you're back." Her voice sounded breathless. "Where are you?"

"I'm at the bus stop for the car park. Ah, here it comes now."

"How long will it be until you get home?"

Daniel consulted his watch. "I don't know. It's rush hour, so probably anything between two and three hours. Why?"

"There's something I need to discuss with you. I'll tell them I'm feeling unwell. Hang on."

A bang in the background. She stopped speaking. The faint sound of a man talking came down the line. Eileen's reply was also severely attenuated, but he picked out the word "see".

"I'll be back around eleven—"

A click cut off his wife's voice.

He lowered the mobile and checked the signal strength: three bars. His fingers tapped the screen as he selected the recent contacts option and returned the call. The phone rang six times before an automated female recording took over. "You have reached the number of..." A pause, then a man spoke. "Alan Hastings." Another brief delay followed by the computerised voice. "Please leave a message after the beep. To re-record your message, press the hash key."

The bus door remained open. "Are you getting on, mate?" the driver called.

Daniel returned the phone to his pocket and climbed the steps. If it was important, she'd call him back. But when he slumped into a free seat, he couldn't put the sense of uneasiness out of his mind.

Friday 14th August 2015
Ilithyia Biotechnology, Cambridge Science Park
Twenty-one years ago

Anders Grolby logged into the administrator account and pulled up the activity history from Eileen Floyd's workstation. His actions fell into a grey area; the standard contract of employment at Ilithyia contained a clause which gave the company the right to monitor computer usage but tracking an employee's access to network files probably crossed the line between reasonable and excessive behaviour.

If circumstances dictated, he could also activate the keylogging software installed on all the company's computers, but the current situation didn't yet warrant that level of intrusion. Not even the senior management knew about this capability. In addition, there was no mention in the terms of employment, making it illegal.

Dr Perrin had warned him she was considering invoking the whistleblower policy. He had been half tempted to remove the file from the server but decided that doing so would probably have a detrimental effect and only raise her level of suspicion. A brief inspection of the log from her computer confirmed she had opened the document.

Next, he downloaded her internet browsing history. Her mobile phone and desktop machine both used the Chrome browser, and she had set the options to synchronise data. A quick check informed him she had recently viewed several pages related to whistleblowing and consulted the Health and Safety Executive site.

It seemed she was intent on going ahead with a complaint. Dr Perrin had explained the possible repercussions. In the worst case, the company could be closed down. Alternatively, the authorities might issue a fine, resulting in the loss of most of their customers. If that happened, the inevitable closure of the business would follow shortly afterwards.

Grolby needed this job. Opportunities for an ex-soldier with a dishonourable discharge from the Swedish army were few and far between. There had been insufficient proof to convict him of murdering the Iraqi family of four—not that they didn't deserve it—but he had stayed out of prison only due to the skill of his lawyer.

While on tour in Iraq, Grolby's unit had come under attack during a routine patrol. During the battle, he recognised one of the attackers, a local shopkeeper, who it turned out doubled as an insurgent outside business hours. The army arrested him at his shop the next morning but released him after several days of intense questioning, believing it to be a case of mistaken identity. After all, didn't the locals all look the same?

But Grolby possessed a knack for remembering faces and knew what he had seen. A few days later, he followed the man home and gunned down the entire family, including the wife and two teenage sons. No eyewitnesses to the slaughter came forward, but several neighbours reported seeing a tall, blond Westerner fleeing the scene. At the court-martial, Grolby's alibi had been exposed as a lie, but the defence lawyer successfully argued there was insufficient evidence to return a conviction.

Fortunately, the directors at Ilithyia had been satisfied with his recently gained IT qualifications and omitted to request references from the Swedish military, thereby failing to uncover his chequered past. But the chances were slim his luck would hold for a second time if the closure of the company forced him to seek new employment. Anything that threatened the future of Ilithyia Biotechnology was also a threat to Anders Grolby—and that included Eileen Floyd.

If his army career had taught him one important lesson, it was to take the fight to the enemy. Rather than sitting back and waiting for an attack, the better approach was to go on the offensive and strike aggressively. And that's what he intended to do.

He logged off his machine and moved to the window to check the car park. *Good. Only four cars present.* He descended the stairs leading to the ground floor laboratories at a jog and strode along the corridor to the door at the end.

As he entered the room, she sat with her back to him with the telephone to her ear. She spun around in her seat. "Hang on," she said, raising a finger.

"Mrs Floyd, there's a serious matter we need to discuss," Grolby said.

She tried to mask the consternation on her face. She placed her left hand over the mouthpiece. "Can't you see I'm on the phone?"

She carried on speaking to the person on the line. "I'll be back around eleven—"

He crossed the floor in two strides and pressed the button to end the call. "This is more important. Who were you calling?

Her mouth dropped open in shock for a moment before she regained control of her facial features. "Uh... my husband. Anyway, what's that got to do with you?" She rose from her chair and glared at him. The ex-soldier stepped half a pace closer, towering over her.

"A disciplinary issue has come up," Grolby said. "We should go somewhere more private. Please follow me."

The first sign of fear flickered in her eyes.

The head of security returned to the door and marched down the corridor without checking to see whether she was following. The sound of hurried footsteps trailed after him. He smiled inwardly. *Good. Keep her off balance.*

He proceeded up the steps and into the boardroom. Six chairs lined the opposite sides of the long table. A projector hung from the ceiling, aimed at the large screen affixed to the end wall. A variety of framed certificates broke up the monotonous pattern of the striped wallpaper.

Grolby waited in the open doorway and gestured to a chair where she would have her back to the only door. She stood uncertainly for a moment but followed his lead when he lowered himself into the seat on the other side.

"What's all this about?" Eileen asked, unable to hide the quiver from her voice.

"Are you aware of the company's health and safety policy?"

"Um... well, I know it exists, and I have a rough idea of the contents."

Grolby clasped his hands together and leant forwards. "Yesterday, you committed a serious breach of that policy by entering an area you weren't authorised to go into."

"This is about Martin Hendrick's lab, isn't it? A better question might be why he's working on an influenza virus when we aren't set up to deal with materials of that kind."

"What takes place in Dr Hendrick's laboratory is highly confidential, and you had no business going in there without prior authorisation."

Eileen folded her arms. "Really? Firstly, I was told to go there. My manager, Alan Hastings, suggested I ask Dr Hendrick whether we could use the fridge in his lab. Secondly, there was no notice on his door yesterday. Somebody must have put that up last night after I talked to Dr Perrin about what I'd seen. I asked him about the whistleblower policy, which *you* should be familiar with. There's a clear statement in there that all complaints should be handled confidentially. But the new sign and your presence here suggests that isn't the case, is it?"

Grolby leant across the table. "I am well aware of the whistleblower policy, and it clearly states that the complaint must be submitted in writing. To the best of my knowledge, you haven't actually done that, have you? And if that's true, the confidentiality clause is irrelevant, don't you think? When I came in, if I'm not mistaken, you were engaged on a personal call. Need I also point out that discussing company business with another person contravenes the terms of your employment contract."

Eileen's eyes blazed with fury. "I was trying to talk to my husband who's been away with his work until this morning, but I didn't get the chance to say anything much before you so rudely ended the call."

Grolby's voice took on a conciliatory tone. "Look. I don't want to go to all the trouble of instigating disciplinary proceedings, and I guess you'd rather not have the stress of going through that either."

"What are you saying?" she asked, barely above a whisper.

"If you drop the whistleblower complaint, we'll forget the other thing."

Eileen pushed the chair back and jumped to her feet. She slapped the table with her palm. Her face flushed with anger. "I'm not the one in the wrong here. Do you think you can intimidate me? Dr Hendrick is performing dangerous research without adequate safety precautions. If the people at this company aren't prepared to take my complaint seriously, then you leave me no option but to discuss my concerns with somebody else."

Friday 14ᵗʰ August 2015
Ilithyia Biotechnology, Cambridge Science Park
Twenty-one years ago

Nigel Perrin sat at his desk, the pen clicking furiously in his hand. Anders Grolby occupied the seat opposite.

"I'm sorry," the Swede said. "I may have misread the situation."

"Where is she now?"

"She's still in the boardroom. I don't think we can change her mind. If anything, she seems more adamant than before. Perhaps you should try to talk to her again."

"What am I going to say? Yeah, you caught us doing something we shouldn't?"

Grolby grimaced. "Apologise and tell her you had no knowledge of what Dr Hendrick was working on. Let her know you plan to start disciplinary proceedings against him."

Perrin gave an exasperated shake of the head. "We can't afford to lose him. He's vital to at least two different projects. Damn. I should never have allowed Rosalind to talk me into this."

Grolby splayed his fingers on the desk. "You don't have to fire him. Tell Mrs Floyd you issued him with a final warning. She has no right to see his records. How many people know about this work on the flu virus?"

"Only Rosalind and me. And whomever Eileen has talked to. Why do you ask?"

"Just an idea. Anyway, I'm fairly sure she hasn't discussed the matter with anybody else. From what she told me, her husband has been away on business and only landed a few minutes ago. They were on the phone together when I went into her lab."

"Okay," Perrin said. "Maybe I'll have another chat with her. See if I can salvage the situation."

"Do you want me to come in with you?"

The doctor bit his lip, mired in a moment of indecision. "Yeah, why not?" he replied eventually, returning the pen to his pocket. The two men rose from their chairs and headed down the corridor.

Perrin pushed open the door to the boardroom and entered first. Eileen Floyd paced backwards and forwards at the far end of the room. She whipped around to the new arrivals.

"Good morning, Eileen," Perrin said, lowering himself into a seat. Grolby dropped into the chair beside him.

Eileen took up a position on the opposite side of the table to the men but remained standing. She shot back an angry reply. "Is it?"

Not a great start. This was clearly going to be a difficult sell. "Look, I'm sorry if you don't think we're taking your concerns seriously."

"I came to see you yesterday evening to discuss a serious matter in confidence. It's obvious you relayed our conversation to Dr Hendrick because I arrived at work this morning to discover new signs outside his lab. And then he..." She jabbed a finger towards the Swedish ex-soldier. "... threatens me with disciplinary action for entering an unauthorised area. You're treating me like I'm the one in the wrong when in fact you should be investigating Dr Hendrick."

Perrin forced a reassuring smile onto his face. "You're absolutely right, Eileen. I had a long conversation with Dr Hendrick last night. I wasn't aware he was doing research with a flu virus, but he assures me it's perfectly safe. He's an experienced researcher, and he would never consciously do anything to endanger his colleagues or anybody else for that matter."

Eileen raised her eyebrows, incredulous. "You're telling me you don't know what your own employees are working on? I find that hard to believe. Aren't you supposed to be the Chief Scientist here? Dr Hendrick's reaction when he realised what I'd seen only confirmed that my concerns are valid. And what about the threat to discipline me for not following our health and safety guidelines? You've admitted the signs weren't even there yesterday."

Perrin nodded sympathetically. "It was a mistake to mention disciplinary action. Mr Grolby wasn't aware the notice was only recently put up. I can assure you we'll take any complaint seriously. In fact, after our discussion and my chat with Dr Hendrick, I've started an internal investigation."

Eileen leant forwards and placed her hands on the table. "Why should I believe you? I reckon you already knew about Dr Hendrick's work. And as for you." She glowered at Grolby. "I don't appreciate your attempts to intimidate me. And I certainly don't respond well to threats."

The Swede stared at her, stony-faced.

"So, where do we go from here?" Perrin asked.

Eileen sat and folded her arms. She opened her mouth to speak, then closed it again.

"Look, tensions are a little high at the moment," the doctor said. "We don't want anybody to say something they'll regret later. I suggest we all take some time to calm down. I'd just like you to consider that your actions could have severe repercussions for the future of this company and its employees. We're already on a financial precipice, and it wouldn't require much to push it over the edge."

Eileen's fierce gaze bored into him. "What? Now you're applying the emotional blackmail as well to keep me quiet?"

Grolby stood. "Dr Perrin, may I have a word outside?" he asked.

The Chief Scientist followed the head of security into the corridor, pulling the door closed behind him. "What is it, Anders?" he whispered.

"She's not going to back down. You shouldn't have pushed her at the end."

"Christ, what a mess," Perrin said. "What should we do?"

"That depends upon how badly you want this problem to go away."

The doctor regarded him hopefully. "What do you have in mind?"

Grolby explained the outline of his plan.

When he had finished, Perrin stared back at the door of the boardroom in horror. "You've got to be joking."

Grolby's eyes glittered with venom. "Believe me. This is not something I would joke about."

"But... but you can't expect me to make a decision like that."

"In that case I suggest you either kiss goodbye to this company or call somebody who can give the go ahead."

"I'll need to speak to Mrs Baxter," an ashen-faced Nigel Perrin replied. "There has to be another way."

"Well, you better hurry. There isn't much time. The office will soon start filling up. Actually, may I make a suggestion? Do we have any chemicals in stores that would keep people out of the building?"

"What do you mean?"

"Perhaps something that smells bad and would deter them from coming in."

"Oh... I see. Ammonium hydroxide is very unpleasant."

"Good," Grolby said. "Get a bottle and drop it as close to reception as you can. Pretend it was an accident. Dr Hendrick's here, isn't he? Put him in charge of keeping everybody outside while we organise the clean-up. Tell the employees to go home for the day."

"I'm not sure—"

"Time is running out, Dr Perrin. Soon, we'll be out of options."

"Um... right." Perrin hurried down the stairs and headed to the chemicals storeroom, situated in a secured area off the corridor on the ground floor.

Despite the relatively cool temperature, beads of sweat rolled down his forehead. His mind roiled in turmoil.

This is a total nightmare. What I have got myself involved in?

Friday 14th August 2015
Ilithyia Biotechnology, Cambridge Science Park
Twenty-one years ago

R osalind opened the car door and stared at the small group of workers standing outside Ilithyia Biotechnology. She clicked the button on the key fob and marched towards the entrance. Dr Hendrick stood with his back to the doors, explaining something to the gathering. *What the hell is going on?*

Hendrick's expression brightened at her approach. "Ah, Mrs Baxter. I was just saying there's been an ammonium hydroxide spillage, and it isn't safe to enter. Dr Perrin asked me to close the building and tell everybody to go home."

Rosalind glowered at the researcher. "Where is he?"

"Upstairs. He told me to let you in. He wants to see you as soon as possible."

She turned around. "You heard the man. We can't allow any of you inside until we get this sorted. We'll let you know when it's safe to come in. Watch your email."

"We won't have to book it as holiday, will we?" a woman asked. Laura Brewer. She worked in accounts.

"No, of course not," Rosalind snapped. She waited until the group dispersed and she and Hendrick were alone. "Lock the doors and put a sign up. You better add something for any deliveries that arrive. Get the drivers to call reception. Now, what happened?"

"Dr Perrin dropped a bottle of ammonium hydroxide in the corridor outside my lab. We've shut the door into the reception area to contain the smell, but I'm not sure what good it's doing."

"Damn. We could do without losing another day with all these bloody deadlines looming. Has anyone been brought in for the clean-up?"

"Ah... I don't know. I've been standing here since the accident."

"Okay. Put the notice up and for Christ's sake open all the windows. Then you can go home too."

Hendrick's face creased in worry. "We've already opened the windows, but I'd still hold my breath in there if I were you. It's pretty unpleasant."

Rosalind applied her card to the reader, then inhaled deeply and pushed inside. Despite the precaution, the harsh stench, reminiscent of decaying fish, still invaded her senses. She hurried up the stairs and barged through the door at the top before exhaling. Even here, the pungent reek permeated the air.

The agitated figure of Dr Perrin waited in the corridor. He spun around at her arrival. He greeted her with an anxious frown.

"Christ, Nigel. What the hell have you done?" she asked.

"We need to talk—urgently."

She followed in silence as he led her to his office. He dropped into his chair and covered his face with his hands.

Rosalind closed the door behind her and sat on the opposite side of the desk. "I hope you're about to explain what's going on."

Perrin glanced up with haunted eyes. "It was Anders's idea. We needed to clear the building."

"Whoa, slow down. Are you saying the spillage wasn't an accident?"

"She's sitting in the boardroom. I don't know what to do."

"Who's—? Oh, this is about Eileen Floyd, isn't it? You better start at the beginning."

Perrin met her gaze for a second, then looked away. His hands shook as he placed them on the wooden surface. He seemed to notice the trembling and lowered them to his thighs. It was a measure of his distress that the pen remained in his pocket.

"Anders had a talk to her this morning, but she took it the wrong way. I wasn't there, but it sounds like he tried to threaten her. He told her she'd breached our health and safety policy by entering Hendrick's lab without permission. Then he said he'd forget all about it if she dropped the complaint against Dr Hendrick. Needless to say, she didn't respond well."

"Go on."

"I went in and apologised to her. She accused me of breaking her trust by talking to Martin about her concerns. I tried to reassure her by telling her he wouldn't do anything to jeopardise the safety of his fellow employees, but she didn't believe me. I may've mentioned that she could bring the company down if she decided to go public with her accusation. She responded badly to that too, told me it was emotional blackmail."

"Right," Rosalind said. "None of this sounds good."

"It gets worse." A shiver ran through Perrin's body. For a moment, it seemed he was about to burst into tears. "Anders offered to make the problem go away."

A frisson of dread rippled down Rosalind's spine. She had a strong premonition this was the key factor that had her partner so rattled. "And how did he propose to do that?"

"He said he could arrange for her to disappear."

The two partners in Ilithyia Biotechnology stared at each other in silence for several seconds.

Rosalind lowered her voice when she spoke. "Disappear? How?"

"He didn't say, but that's when he told me to drop the ammonium hydroxide to keep people out of the building."

"Where are Anders and Floyd now?"

"He's still with her in the boardroom."

Rosalind stood. "I better try to sort this out."

"Would you like me to join you?" Perrin asked. The pleading look in his eyes gave away his preferred response.

"No, I can manage by myself."

Perrin's body sagged with relief. "Okay. I'll be in here if you need me."

"If you want to be useful, you could start by finding somebody to clear up the spillage. And send a message to all staff telling them not to come in."

"Leave it with me," he replied enthusiastically. "I'll get right on it."

Rosalind stepped into the corridor. The stench hit her again. No doubt the building would reek for weeks afterwards. *Why did that bloody idiot Hendrick not keep his laboratory locked? And what the hell was Grolby proposing?*

She pushed into the boardroom. The Swedish ex-soldier stood by the large projector screen, leaning against the wall. Eileen Floyd paced anxiously at the far end.

"Can you give us a minute, Anders?" Rosalind asked. She waited for the door to close behind him before continuing. "I have to apologise," she said. "Mr Grolby likes to follow rules. I guess it's his army background."

"He wouldn't let me out of this room," Eileen replied, folding her arms.

"Yes, I'm afraid there's been a spillage as you can probably tell from the smell of ammonia."

"But you still came into the building. If you're allowed to come in, why can't I leave?"

Rosalind pointed to a chair. "Why don't you sit down? I wanted to have a chat, just between the two of us. This whole thing has been handled very badly, and I want to stop it blowing up out of all proportion. What can I do to resolve the situation?"

Eileen reluctantly sat. "I think it's too late for that. Dr Perrin seems more concerned with protecting Dr Hendrick than he does about taking me seriously. I mean he had a flask containing an influenza virus just sitting there on his bench. You know as well as I do that we're not set up for that kind of work. But when I told Dr Perrin what I'd seen, he went straight to Dr Hendrick and discussed it with him. When I came in this morning, there were signs outside his lab, and that arsehole Grolby threatened me with disciplinary action for entering an unauthorised area."

Rosalind offered a sympathetic smile. "That was all a mistake, and I can only apologise again. You have my word; we'll investigate Dr Hendrick's activities. The safety of the workforce is our primary concern."

Eileen shook her head. "I'm sorry, but I just don't believe you. Dr Perrin brought up the financial security of the company. If it comes to a choice between doing what's safe and preserving the company's future, well... I have no faith you'll do the right thing. And I have to consider others as well as myself now."

Rosalind maintained a calm exterior, but her pulse rushed in her ears. To which others was she referring? "It's a shame you feel that way. If I may ask, what do you propose to do next?"

Eileen lowered her eyes to the table for a moment, then looked up to meet Rosalind's gaze. "I don't see any option but to raise my concerns outside the company. Both you and Dr Perrin are too involved to be objective. It's not something I want to do, but it seems to me you've left me with little choice but to escalate the matter."

Rosalind stared at her employee as a flurry of conflicting thoughts tumbled through her head. "What if we were to offer you a substantial pay rise? You're on what? Forty-five thousand a year? What if we raised it to sixty? That's more than generous."

Eileen sat back. "You've tried threats and emotional blackmail, so now I get the bribery angle."

The blood drained from Rosalind's face, pooling in a pink spot on each cheek. Her voice trembled with suppressed fury as she spoke. "I've made every attempt to be reasonable, but it seems you're intent on this foolish course of action. Have it your way. We'll begin an immediate internal investigation into your flagrant disregard of the company's health and safety policy. Until we reach a conclusion, you'll be suspended on full pay. I'll arrange for a formal letter of suspension to be sent today."

"Then we have nothing more to say to each other," Eileen said, rising to her feet.

"And may I also remind you about the strict non-disclosure agreement you signed when you joined this company. If you discuss anything you have seen while working here with an outside entity, you will be in breach of that contract. Let me assure you, we treat such matters with the utmost gravity and won't be shy about using the courts to protect the company's interests."

"Can I go now?"

Rosalind stood. "You better remain here until I check whether it's safe for you to leave."

Friday 14th August 2015
Ilithyia Biotechnology, Cambridge Science Park
Twenty-one years ago

Nigel Perrin rushed up to Rosalind as soon as she emerged from the boardroom. "Did you manage to convince her to drop this thing?"

"No," she said, "quite the opposite, in fact. I told her she's suspended while we investigate her breach of the health and safety policy."

"But I thought you were going to—"

"She made her decision. I tried to be reasonable, but she wouldn't change her mind. So, now she'll have to suffer the consequences."

Perrin's gaze left Rosalind's face and drifted to Anders Grolby, who stood by the door to the stairs, just out of earshot. "What do you mean?"

"Okay. Let me explain. The legal aspects of her case don't worry me in the slightest."

His eyes snapped back. "I don't understand."

"If she takes it to an industrial tribunal or the Health and Safety Executive, it'll look like sour grapes. We instigate disciplinary proceedings against her, so she retaliates with a claim of unsafe practice. There's no documentary evidence of her complaint, so she has no proof whatsoever. It's her word against ours."

Rosalind paused for a moment, then continued. "But what does give me serious cause for concern is the potential damage to our reputation. We need to win new contracts to survive. If there's the slightest whiff of a scandal, our customers will run a mile. She'd lose if she brought a case against us, and we could also sue her for damages, but by then it would be too late."

Perrin frowned in puzzlement. Why was his partner so calm when everything they had worked so hard for rested on the edge of a precipice? "Why can't we just pay her off?" he asked.

"I tried that approach. I offered her a substantial salary rise, but she threw it back in my face and accused me of bribery. Even if she were to drop her complaint now, there's a risk she might use any documented financial incentive we offer her as proof we have something to cover up."

"So, what happens next?"

"I plan to talk to Anders about his thoughts on the matter."

A cold flood of terror swept over Perrin. "You can't seriously..."

"I don't have the details of what he's proposing yet, so the first step is to ask him."

Perrin's eyes followed her as she approached Grolby, who waited impassively, blocking the only way out. The doctor watched on while they spoke for several minutes, their voices low enough not to be heard. Then the Swede turned away, opened the door and trotted down the stairs, an arm over his mouth to fend off the vile stench. Meanwhile, Rosalind retraced her steps.

Perrin thrust his hands deep into his trouser pockets to stop them shaking. "What did he say?" he asked.

"He's going to deal with it."

"What? How?"

"It's probably best you don't know."

"Christ, Rosalind. You can't be serious. You're not really... Just let her go. We've survived worse situations in the past."

"No, Nigel. She's brought this on herself. Did you arrange for somebody to clean up the mess downstairs?"

Perrin stared at her for a second. "Yes," he replied weakly. "I found a company that specialises in chemical spillages. They told me they'd be here around ten o'clock. And I sent an all-staff email telling them not to come in today." He swayed on his feet, his face deathly pale. "Actually, I think I'm going to be sick."

He turned and bolted for the entrance to the toilets. There, he barged into a cubicle and emptied his stomach into the white porcelain bowl. After tearing off a few sheets of toilet paper to wipe his mouth, he staggered to the sinks and inspected his reflection in the mirror. He had joined the medical profession to save lives. Was the face of a murderer staring back at him?

Out of habit, he rinsed his hands under the cold tap, dried them under the hot air dryer and stumbled to the exit. Perrin emerged into the corridor at the same moment as Grolby returned from downstairs. A second pungent smell accompanied the Swede, merging with the stench of ammonia. He held a cloth in his left hand as he shoved open the door to the boardroom. A cry followed by the sound of a brief struggle escaped from inside the room.

Perrin almost fled straight back the way he had come. Instead, he forced himself to approach Rosalind and grabbed her by the arm. "He's not..."

His partner turned to him, her complexion pale. "No, he wanted to know where we stored the chloroform we use for euthanising the laboratory animals. He told me he's just going to knock her out."

"For the love of God, Rosalind, you've got to stop him. I didn't sign up for this."

"So, you'd rather be bankrupt and in prison?"

"Prison? I haven't done anything."

"It's too late to back out now, Nigel. What would we say to her? 'Oh, sorry, we never meant to drug you. It was all a big mistake.' Somehow, I don't think she'd believe us."

"I never agreed to any of it. We could call the police. Tell them it was all Grolby's doing."

"No, Nigel. Anders assures me he can make her disappear without leaving a trail."

"So, you're happy to commit murder?"

Rosalind blinked at the question. "Of course not. But like I said, she brought this on herself."

"She's not dead yet. There's still time to call it off."

"Pull yourself together, Nigel. We're committed now."

The ringing of the telephone interrupted the conversation.

"I better answer that," Rosalind said. "It might be a delivery."

"Are you two just going to stand there arguing?" Grolby called. Neither of the business partners had noticed him emerge from the boardroom. "Perhaps one of you could help me."

Perrin took a tentative step towards the tall Swede. The terrified expression on his face signalled he'd rather be sprinting in the opposite direction. "What do you want me to do?" he croaked.

"We'll hold her in here for the moment. The police will be suspicious if they find traces of chloroform on her, so we need to leave sufficient time for it to wear off. And there are some questions I want to ask her. Have you got anything I can use to restrain her, like duct tape or something?"

"There's some Sellotape in the stationery cupboard. I'll fetch it now."

Perrin turned towards the open plan office, but Grolby shot out a hand and grabbed him by the upper arm.

"One other thing," he said. "I couldn't help overhearing your little conversation with Mrs Baxter. Just so we're absolutely clear, if either of you gets cold feet and confesses to the police, I'll let them know it was all your idea. If I go down for this, you can be sure I'll take you both with me."

Friday 14th August 2015
Ilithyia Biotechnology, Cambridge Science Park
Twenty-one years ago

Daniel Floyd applied the handbrake of the BMW 1 series, turned off the engine and leant back in the driver's seat with his eyes closed. A sudden bout of dizziness greyed the edges of his vision. He never slept well on aeroplanes, and the sneezing man sitting behind hadn't helped. The lack of rest, coupled with the stress of navigating rush hour traffic, had pushed him to the point where his main goal was to fall into bed for a few hours and catch up on his lost sleep.

A hint of worry nagged at the back of his brain. He had called Eileen's number twice from the shuttle bus at the airport, receiving an automated response on both calls. He knew her company prohibited the use of mobile phones on the premises, so it didn't come as a big surprise when she failed to answer. But several times in the past, when she wanted to talk during working hours, she had slipped out of the building and sat in the privacy of her car. He had sent a text message, asking her to contact him when she was free, but his phone remained silent during the entire journey home.

He had also tried her work number several times, recording a request to return his call on the third occasion. Eileen often joked with him about her manager, Alan Hastings, and his struggles to be assertive with his team, but from her description, he didn't seem the type to disregard a message.

Daniel levered himself out of the car and pulled open the rear door to retrieve his overnight case from the back seat. He dragged it up the short drive and let himself into the house. The familiar smell of Eileen's perfume lingered in the air. He dropped the bag in the hall and slumped onto the sofa in the lounge. Once again, he called her mobile and office line, receiving the same machine responses to both. *Strange.* It was now over two hours since she had broken off her call in mid-conversation.

He pulled up a browser window on his phone and performed a search for Ilithyia Biotechnology. The details appeared on the screen. He clicked the listed number to dial the company switchboard. Surely a human would still be there to answer incoming calls.

He was about to give up after six iterations of the ringing tone when a woman's voice answered brusquely. "Yes."

Great telephone manner.

"Hello. This is Daniel Floyd. I wonder if it would be possible to put me through to my wife, Eileen."

"I'm afraid she's not available at the moment. We've had a chemical spill on site, and we sent everybody home for the day."

"So, she isn't at work?"

"No, in fact I don't remember seeing her today."

"Well, she called me from her lab earlier this morning, around eight o'clock."

"I'm sorry, Dan, but I can't help you. There's nobody here."

Wait. Dan? The woman's voice suddenly sounded familiar. "That's not you, is it, Rosalind?"

"Yes, but we're very busy, trying to organise the clean-up. I haven't really got time to chat at the moment."

"Okay, it'd be good to catch up at some point. One last thing: when did this accident occur?"

"I... um. I'm not sure. Earlier this morning. Why?"

"Eileen's not home yet. I just wondered where she is."

"Oh. Well perhaps she did some shopping or went to see a friend or something."

"Possibly, but she's not answering her mobile."

"Look, I'm sorry, Dan. I don't know where your wife is. I've got to go now."

A click signalled she'd hung up. Daniel lowered the phone, a puzzled frown creasing his forehead. If Eileen wasn't at work, where was she? Perhaps she was stuck in traffic. But her car was fitted with a hands-free set. Why didn't she answer? Maybe it was turned off.

Another possibility sprang to mind; had she been injured in the spillage? No. Surely Rosalind Baxter would have let him know if that was the case. He hadn't thought about his former girlfriend for years. It came as quite a shock to bump into her at last year's company Christmas party and discover she was Eileen's overall boss. Eileen hadn't mentioned her before. She told him afterwards most of her dealings at senior management level were with the other partner, Nigel Perrin.

What if his wife had been involved in a car crash? An escalating series of wild thoughts spun through his brain. He clamped down on his panic. *No, she's fine. There has to be a logical explanation.* They'd have a good laugh about his overreaction when she arrived home.

Daniel forced the uneasiness from his mind. The exhaustion engulfing his body made it hard to think rationally. He rubbed his Adam's apple absent-mindedly at the first hints of a sore throat. A cold was the last thing he needed in his current state of fatigue. Maybe he would feel better after a short lie-down. He trudged up the stairs and along the hall to the master bedroom, then threw himself down onto the king-sized bed. He lay on top of the covers, still in his shoes and fully clothed.

Minutes later, he succumbed to the tiredness tugging at his eyelids and fell into a dreamless sleep.

Friday 14th August 2015
Ilithyia Biotechnology, Cambridge Science Park
Twenty-one years ago

nders Grolby grabbed the roll of Sellotape from Nigel Perrin and re-entered the boardroom. The co-owner remained outside. The ex-soldier ran a hand over the back of his neck as he analysed the situation. *The Chief Scientist might become a liability.* He would need to maintain a careful watch on that one. The first doubts crept into his mind. Could he hold all the strands together? Perhaps he had allowed his worries about the company's future and the threat this woman posed to cloud his judgement. But it was far too late to turn back now.

She lay on her side, still wearing the white lab coat. Beneath the laboratory-wear, a dark skirt and a cream-coloured jumper were visible. One black shoe had come off in the brief struggle before she had succumbed to the chloroform-soaked cloth. A strand of hair partially obscured her face. Her chest rose and fell in slow, even breaths.

He knelt beside her, checking for anything about her person she could use as a weapon or to free herself. Now was not the time for carelessness. A quick search of her pockets turned up nothing of interest.

He pulled off a long strip of tape and bound her wrists together behind her back. He repeated the process with her feet, wrapping multiple layers around her ankles. Finally, he taped several shorter segments over her mouth, taking care to ensure she could still breathe. Despite the absence of people in the office, he couldn't risk a passerby hearing her screams if she regained consciousness before he explained the consequences to her of making any sound.

Now that his prisoner was secure, he turned his attention to other priorities. The presence of her car in a parking space outside the building would serve as a big pointer for anybody trying to find her. He would have to move it somewhere else as soon as possible.

Her black leather handbag lay on the table where she had been sitting. He opened the clasp and rummaged inside: a set of keys including one bearing the Mini logo, some loose tampons, a pen, a small pack of tissues and a fluorescent-blue packet with a pink stripe. He pocketed the car key, then grabbed the brightly coloured box: Clearblue Pregnancy Test. The seal was broken. He studied the cardboard box. A pink rectangle in the corner contained the words '5 tests' in white letters. A quick inspection of the contents confirmed only four remained.

Shit. Was she pregnant?

Grolby snapped his head up as the door opened. He let out a sigh of relief: Rosalind Baxter.

"Where's Dr Perrin?" he asked, his heart still racing in his chest.

"He's sitting in his office. I have to say he's not taking this at all well."

"Is he going to be a problem?"

"No, I don't think so. If it hasn't already sunk in, he'll soon realise he's in this as deep as we are."

"I hope so. I made the situation quite clear to him a few minutes ago."

"He won't like it, but he'll come round in the end," Rosalind said, staring down at the unconscious researcher. "Is she still alive?"

"Yeah," Grolby replied. "I think she'll be out for a while."

"I just spoke to her husband on the phone. He wanted to know where she was."

"What did you tell him?"

"I told him there was a chemical spill, and that I haven't seen her today, but he knows she was here. Apparently, she called him from her lab this morning."

"That's right," Grolby agreed. "They were talking to each other just before I brought her up here. She mentioned that he's been away on business, and his flight only landed a few hours ago. It won't be long before he comes here looking for her when she doesn't arrive home."

"So, what do we do when that happens?"

"To start with, we have to move her car. We can use the spillage as an excuse to keep him out of the building."

"There's something else you should be aware of." Rosalind slumped into a chair. "There's some past history between us. He and I were students at the same university. We even went out together for a bit until I dumped him. I hadn't seen him for years, and I didn't realise they were married until I bumped into him at last year's Christmas party."

"I don't see how that changes things."

"Maybe it doesn't. I was just making sure you knew."

"Okay. Thanks."

Rosalind's gaze slipped to the blue and pink packet in Grolby's hand. "What's that?"

"It was in her handbag," he replied, holding the small box up and showing her the label. "It only contains four strips. There should be five."

71

"So, she might be—"

"Yes, it's possible she's pregnant."

"Oh. That might explain her comment earlier today about considering others."

"I'll find out from her when she comes round."

"And if she is?" Rosalind's question hung in the air, unanswered.

After a long pause, Grolby spoke again. "When the police realise she's missing, they're bound to come here and ask you a lot of questions. We need something to throw them off the scent. What if we provided them with a readymade suspect?"

"I don't follow."

"I saw this true crime documentary. It stated that in around fifty per cent of female homicides, the culprit is a close relative of the victim. That means the investigating officers always take a good look at the husband. If we make him the target of their investigation, it'll focus attention away from us."

"How do you propose we do that?" Rosalind asked.

"We frame him for her murder. I assume you have syringes here to draw blood?"

"We have cupboards full of them down in the laboratories."

"Okay," Grolby said. "I want you to fetch one and take a sample from her."

"How much do you need?"

"I don't know. Enough to fill a test tube. We're running out of time. You better get on with it."

The Swedish ex-soldier watched her leave, a plan forming in his head. If everything played out how he hoped, the police would soon be looking in the wrong direction.

Friday 14th August 2015
33 Willow Drive, Cambridge
Twenty-one years ago

Daniel Floyd jerked awake. Bright light streamed through the open curtains. A grainy fuzziness filled his head. His throat ached from the onset of a cold, gifted him by the ill passenger sitting in the row behind on the plane. For a moment, his brain struggled to catch up with his body. He rubbed both hands across his face. As his gaze roamed over the familiar surroundings, the events of the previous twenty-four hours tumbled into place.

He lifted his wrist and studied the dial of his watch through bleary eyes: half-past one. Was it morning or night-time? He cursed his stupidity. The sunlight streaming through the window told him all he needed to know. He had only intended to close his eyes for a few moments. He performed a quick calculation in his head. Despite his unintended sleep, he had still gained less than four hours' rest.

"Eileen," he called. A distant click from the boiler was the only sound to break the silence. He repeated her name, louder this time, and listened carefully. Nothing. The house had a stillness about it that suggested he was alone.

He swung his legs off the bed and onto the bedroom carpet. He tried to stand, but a bout of wooziness drove him back to a sitting position. His head throbbed, and his sinuses felt like they were filled with cotton wool. Shuffling sideways along the mattress, he scooped up his phone from the bedside table: no calls, no messages, just three unread emails. He unlocked the screen and clicked the mail icon. The first was a memo from the human resources team at his workplace; the other two were clearly spam.

Where the hell was Eileen? Why hadn't she contacted him? Hadn't she seen his missed calls and texts? He pulled up the contacts and selected her name. Several seconds of silence passed without a ringing tone, then his wife's familiar voice asked him to leave a message. That had to mean she had either turned off her phone or there was no signal.

"Uh, Eileen," he said, "I don't know where you are. I heard there was an accident at your work, some sort of chemical spillage. They told me everybody's been sent home. I'm really worried. Call me when you receive this."

Maybe she was downstairs or in the garden. He pushed himself upright a second time. He swayed a little but soon recovered his balance. Running one hand along the wall to support himself, he shuffled across to the window. A quick glance down to the short drive confirmed the absence of her car. He descended the stairs and checked all the rooms. No signs of his wife.

Perhaps she had broken down, but that didn't explain why she wasn't answering her phone. An accident then? Once again, his mind ran wild, considering all the mishaps that might have befallen her.

Eileen often teased him about the way he always feared the worst outcome in any situation. Three months earlier, he had received a terse email from his boss, requesting a meeting the following morning. Despite Eileen's reassurances, he didn't sleep at all that night, convinced he was about to receive a redundancy notice. It turned out his worries were groundless; his manager had in fact offered him a promotion and a pay rise.

He forced himself to calm down. There was probably a rational explanation, but he couldn't just sit at home and wait. He had to do something. He started by redialling the switchboard at Ilithyia Biotechnology. The ringing tone sounded eight times before an automated response told him his call was important and requested that he leave a message. He hung up without speaking.

Who could he phone to check whether she had been involved in a road accident? Addenbrooke's Hospital provided the only emergency department in the city. He looked up the number and dialled.

After navigating several multiple-choice options, he eventually selected one that led to a human operator.

"Good morning," a cheery female voice greeted him. "Addenbrooke's Hospital. How may I help you?"

Daniel hesitated. He hadn't thought through what he planned to say.

"Hello," the woman said, her tone becoming more impatient.

"Ah, yes. I'm worried about my wife. I wondered if perhaps she might have been transferred to—"

"If you could provide me with a name, sir, I can check the system."

"Floyd. Eileen Floyd."

The rapid tapping of keys came down the line. The receptionist asked him to confirm the spelling of his wife's surname. Another tap.

"I'm sorry, sir. There's no patient with that name in our care at the moment."

A faint click, followed by silence.

"Is it possible she—?" Daniel trailed off as he realised he no longer had an audience.

What next? It seemed premature to dial 999. He pulled up a browser and searched for a non-emergency number for the police.

After a brief message, informing him that all conversations were recorded, an automated man's voice said, "Thank you for calling one oh one. We are connecting you to..." A slight pause. "... Cambridgeshire police."

Several seconds of another ringing tone. "Parkside Police Station, Cambridge," a man answered. "What can I do for you?"

"I'm concerned about my wife," Daniel replied. "She left work over five hours ago and hasn't come home yet. She's not answering her phone either. I didn't know who to contact."

"Right, sir. Let me start by taking your name and address."

Once again, Daniel provided the details. He had half expected the call handler to tell him to wait until at least a full day had elapsed since Eileen's disappearance, but the man seemed unconcerned by her relatively short period of absence.

"Now, you say your wife is missing. What's her name?"

"Eileen Floyd."

"Her date of birth?"

"Twentieth of June, nineteen eighty-eight."

"And the last time you had any contact with her was five hours ago?" The note of scepticism in the call handler's voice came through loud and clear.

"Yes. The journey shouldn't take more than twenty minutes. I was abroad, and I spoke to her just after I landed early this morning, but she hasn't been answering her phone since."

"Right, sir. I understand. Can you describe her appearance? What was she wearing?"

"Um," Daniel said. "I have no idea what she had on. As I told you, I've been away on business, and I haven't seen her today. As for a description, she's around five foot six, brown hair, brown eyes, slim build, attractive."

"And does she share the same address with you?"

"Yes."

"This may seem obvious to you, sir, but have you carefully checked your home? Are you absolutely certain she's not there?"

Daniel bit back on his irritation. "Her car's not here and neither is she."

"And are you sure she hasn't left you a message or voicemail?"

"Yes, I'm positive."

"You mentioned she was working. Have you called her place of work?"

"I did that four or five hours ago. They told me there was a chemical spillage this morning, and they'd sent everybody home. And no, she wasn't injured in the accident from what they said. I tried again a few minutes back, but nobody's picking up."

"Was that her last known location?" the man asked.

"Yes."

"The address?"

"Ilithyia Biotechnology on the science park."

"And that would be the Cambridge Science Park, right?"

"It is," Daniel replied.

"May I take her car registration?"

Daniel dictated the number plate. The distant sound of tapping keys came through from the background.

"So, the records are telling me that's a red Mini Cooper? Is that correct?"

"Yes."

"Does she have a mobile, sir?"

"Yeah. Like I said. She isn't answering. Do you want the number?"

The call handler responded affirmatively, and Daniel read out the digits.

"Just a few more questions. Are there any relatives she might have visited?"

"Nobody who lives anywhere near here."

"Have you noticed any recent changes in her behaviour? Has she been withdrawn? Worried by something maybe?"

"No."

"Does she have any medical problems?"

"No."

"What about financial issues?"

"No, nothing at all like that."

"I know this is a sensitive question, but is it possible she's been seeing somebody else?"

"You mean an affair? Not as far as I'm aware. We've been trying to start a family, so I think that's very unlikely."

"And what about you, sir?"

"Are you asking whether I've been unfaithful?"

"I'm sorry, but we have to ask these questions." The man's voice sounded apologetic.

"The answer's no."

"Has she suffered from depression in the past? Drugs or alcohol dependency? Suicidal thoughts?"

"No to all of those."

"Is there any reason you can think of why somebody might have abducted her?"

"Christ. Abducted? Absolutely not."

"Do you have any other information that might help to find her?"

"No, nothing."

"Right, sir. I've got everything I need. Let me give you a reference for the case. Do you have something to write this down?"

Daniel reached out and snatched a pen and a magazine off the coffee table. "I'm ready." He recorded the details as the man read out the ten digits, then repeated them.

"One final thing. Is this phone number the best to reach you on, Mr Floyd?"

"Yes."

"That's everything. I'm sure there's no need to worry. It's rare for people to go missing for more than a day; the vast majority turn up within the first twenty-four hours. I'll be in touch if we receive any news. And of course, if you hear from Mrs Floyd, please let us know."

Daniel ended the call and blew out his cheeks. The man had said nothing to assuage his fears and had, in fact, provided him with several more possibilities to add to his over-active imagination.

As he tried to decide what to do next, another avenue of approach for tracking down his wife sprang to mind. The last time he spoke to her, she was at work, but now nobody was answering the phone.

Hopefully, if somebody was still there, they could provide him with more information about his wife's whereabouts.

Friday 14th August 2015
Ilithyia Biotechnology, Cambridge Science Park
Twenty-one years ago

Anders Grolby sank down on his haunches beside Eileen Floyd. Her chest rose and fell in a regular rhythm. He leant over and gently tapped her cheek. Her skin felt warm to the touch.

"Come on," he said. "Wake up."

She groaned, and her eyelids fluttered. Her eyes blinked open. Her gaze wandered to the ceiling in confusion, then locked onto his face. She attempted to move and bucked as the sudden realisation hit that both hands and feet were bound. She tried to talk, but the only noise to emerge was a series of grunts. Her nostrils flared rapidly as her respiration rate increased.

Grolby moved closer so that his head filled her vision. "Mrs Floyd," he said. "I need you to remain calm. Can you do that for me?"

Eileen nodded, but the panic in her eyes told a different story.

"Now, I'm going to remove the tape over your mouth. If you scream or make any other sound, I'll put it straight back on. Then I will hurt you. Badly. Is that clear?"

She made a noise that could have been either a yes or a no.

He reached a hand out. She flinched as he picked at the edge of the strip of adhesive material. With a single sharp tug, he ripped it free.

Eileen let out a cry of pain.

"Ah-ah. Remember what I said, Mrs Floyd."

"Where am I?" she croaked.

"You're in the boardroom at Ilithyia."

"What did you do to me?"

"I knocked you out with chloroform."

Silence greeted Grolby's admission.

"But why?" Eileen continued after a long pause.

"I'm afraid we had to stop you from talking to the authorities and risking the future of this company."

Confusion clouded Eileen's face. "What?"

"You threatened to raise your concerns about Dr Hendrick's work with people outside this organisation. We can't allow that to happen."

"So, you drugged me and tied me up? What the hell is wrong with you?"

"You brought this on yourself."

Another long gap while Eileen processed his words. "So, what are you going to do to me?"

"Well, that depends upon whether you cooperate or not."

"I promise if you let me go, I won't tell anyone."

Grolby chuckled. "Unfortunately, I don't believe you. Now, it would make things easier all round if you answer some questions for me. There was an open pregnancy kit in your handbag. Are you?"

"Am I what?"

"What do you think? Pregnant of course."

Eileen stared at him.

"Do you want me to hurt you, Mrs Floyd?" Grolby asked in a low voice.

"No. I mean yes. I only discovered this morning."

"How far along are you?"

"I... a month, maybe six weeks."

"Good. That wasn't so hard, was it? Now, who have you spoken to today?"

"My husband, but you already know that. You cut him off when you came into my lab downstairs."

"Anybody else?"

"Nobody apart from you, Mrs Baxter and Dr Perrin."

"All right," Grolby said. "What did you discuss with Mr Floyd? Your husband's name is Daniel, isn't it?"

Eileen hesitated.

He could almost hear her brain whirring. "Do you remember me warning you about what would happen if you don't cooperate?" he asked. "Or perhaps I could turn my attention to your partner instead."

"Leave my husband out of this. He told me his flight from America had just landed. That's as far as we got before you ended the call."

"Did you discuss your concerns about this company?"

"No. I said I'd be home early, but I didn't tell him why. I wanted to ask for his advice."

"And you haven't talked to anybody else about Dr Hendrick's work?"

"No. Who would I talk to?"

Grolby's expression tightened. "I don't know. That's why I'm asking."

"I already told you. I haven't spoken to a soul."

"Okay. I believe you."

Eileen shifted her position and winced in pain. She twisted her head sideways and lifted her arm as far as the knots would allow, only now spotting that her sleeve was rolled up above the elbow. "What else did you do to me?" she asked, studying the site from which Rosalind Baxter had drawn blood a few minutes earlier.

"Not your concern. I have one last question. Do you have a mobile phone?"

"Yes."

"Where is it?"

"In the glovebox of my car."

"And what make is it?"

"A Microsoft Lumia."

"What's the unlock code?"

Eileen glared at her captor. "Why do you want to know?"

"I'm told it's a very painful experience when somebody crushes a finger with a pair of pliers. Would you like to find out how it feels?"

"All right. Two, zero, zero, six, eight, eight."

"Thank you. See. You can be helpful when you try."

"Now what?" Her gaze focused on his face as she whispered the words, "Are you going to kill me?"

Grolby didn't answer. He grabbed the roll of tape from the table and tore off a strip. She tried to avert her head, but his left hand held her jaw in a vice-like grip as his right taped over her mouth. He added a couple of extra layers for good measure. Her eyes jittered in panic. A series of frightened squeaks emerged through the muzzle. Her breathing whistled through her nose.

"You'll find it far easier to breathe if you stop struggling and take long slow breaths," he said.

Gradually, her panicked expression faded as it transitioned to one of despair.

Grolby stood. "I'm going to leave you alone for a while now. Don't do anything stupid. Stay still and keep quiet." He leant forwards and stroked her cheek, but there was no warmth in the gesture. "Follow my instructions, or I'll punish you."

The ex-soldier opened the boardroom door and followed the corridor to the Chief Scientist's office. He raised his hand to knock but thought better of it and turned the handle. Perrin sat behind the desk, his face in his hands. Rosalind stood on the other side, looking out of the window. Both stared at him as he entered.

Grolby pointed to the vial of dark red liquid resting beside the keyboard. "I assume that's the blood sample you took from her."

"Yes," Rosalind replied. "Is it enough?"

"I'm sure it'll be fine." He snatched up the glass tube and dropped it in his trouser pocket.

"What will you do to her?" Perrin asked, a pleading look in his eyes.

"She has to disappear. If we let her go now, we'll all be arrested and end up in prison on charges of kidnap and false imprisonment. That's probably a sentence of between ten and fifteen years."

"God. You mean you're going to kill her?"

Grolby folded his arms. "Unless you can think of another way of making somebody vanish indefinitely without killing them. But frankly, I can't."

"What about the pregnancy test?" Rosalind asked.

"She reckons she's somewhere between four and six weeks."

Perrin's mouth dropped open, aghast. "You're planning to murder a pregnant woman? I haven't told you yet, Rosalind, but we're expecting our first child in a few months. Whatever she's done to bring this on herself, you can't take her child's life."

"Yes, on this occasion I'm inclined to agree," Rosalind added, pacing between the walls of the small room.

Grolby's gaze alternated between the other two. "Seriously? Women have abortions all the time, and many are far more advanced than just a few weeks."

"It's not the same thing," Perrin replied. "I can't let you do this."

"So, what do you propose we do instead?" Grolby asked.

Silence greeted his question.

"You won't have to be involved in the..." the Swede continued. "I'll handle all that by myself."

Rosalind stopped moving and turned to face him. "What if we wait until she has the baby?"

"Where the hell would she stay?"

"We could keep her here. I'm sure we could create a soundproof space somewhere. What if we adapted the storage room? If we moved the mice nearby, that would help to mask any sounds. They're noisy little buggers."

Grolby shook his head. "That's a crazy idea. What if somebody hears her? We'd have to feed her and provide toilet facilities."

Perrin raised his chin. "I'm with Rosalind on this. We can make it work."

"What happens after the child's born? Who'll look after it?"

"We drop it off at a hospital or something."

"And what do we do with her?"

"Whatever you were planning on doing before. If you don't agree, I'm going to the police to confess."

"It seems Nigel and I are in agreement," Rosalind said. "Are you with us, Anders?"

"It appears as if I don't have a choice in the matter," Grolby replied. "It would be far simpler just to dispose of her now."

"So, what next?" Rosalind asked.

"You can start by giving me a pay rise. If you're going to ignore my advice, it comes at a price. Unless you'd prefer me to be the one making the confession."

Rosalind scowled at her employee. "How much?"

"What did you offer her? Fifteen grand, wasn't it? Let's say twenty grand then."

"There's no way we could go that high," Perrin said.

"Agreed," his co-owner snapped, glaring at the Swede. "Now what else?"

Grolby forced his face to remain impassive. *Perhaps I should have requested more. But that could always come later.* "First, we need to make sure the police have a suspect. If you insist on keeping her alive, we can't have them searching too hard for her here. I'll take her car and set it up." He stared belligerently at the two company owners. "If that's all right with you." His voice dripped with sarcasm.

"By the way," he continued, "if anybody comes looking for her, make sure you don't let them inside the building. Tell them it's unsafe. Whatever it takes. And you better inform the staff the place is closed for another day or two if you seriously plan on keeping her here. I'll be back in an hour or so."

"Right," Rosalind said. "Got that. Basically, don't allow anybody in."

"Exactly. And just so we're clear, neither of you can breathe a word of this to anyone else. That includes close family. Do you understand?"

"I get it," Rosalind replied with a frown. Her partner stared down at the surface of the desk.

"Do you understand, Dr Perrin?"

The doctor looked up sharply. "Yes, I heard you."

"Good."

Grolby left the room and strode to the main entrance. He unlocked the door, then relocked it behind him, glad to see no other employees loitering outside. He jogged across the tarmac to his own car and grabbed a pair of thin driving gloves from the side pocket before pressing the button on the key fob to let him into the red Mini Cooper. *Not exactly inconspicuous.*

Fortuitously, despite the security cameras on the side of the building, none directed their gaze at the car park. He lowered himself into the driver's seat and pushed the lever to slide his seating position backwards by a few inches. The faint smell of her perfume permeated the interior.

He opened the glovebox. Her Microsoft Lumia phone lay on top of the car's service booklet. Within moments, he had prised the back off the mobile and detached the battery. He dropped the parts into his pocket. A further search uncovered a loose pair of sunglasses. *Good.* He slipped them on. They were slightly too small, but they would hide his face from any prying eyes.

He started the engine and followed the grid of roads out of the science park. He could have taken the main road to his destination and saved time, but there was a chance a traffic camera might pick up and record his progress. Instead, he navigated the narrow country lanes, avoiding any busy routes. Twenty-five minutes later, he parked on a patch of scrubby grass beside a gate leading into a field. The distinctive smell of running water reached his nostrils from the nearby river.

After checking for potential observers, he removed the parts of Eileen Floyd's phone from his pocket and reattached the battery. The screen flashed the manufacturer's logo. After a few seconds, the display showed the time. He swiped up and entered the six digits she had given him. Next, he tapped the texts icon and selected Daniel Floyd from the list of contacts.

He thought for a moment, typed in a brief message and hit send, then tossed the phone in the glovebox. After a final survey of the interior, he locked the car and returned the keys to his pocket.

The plan was in motion. The countdown had begun. Everything was at stake.

Friday 14th August 2015
Ilithyia Biotechnology, Cambridge Science Park
Twenty-one years ago

D aniel Floyd rolled to a stop beside the Ilithyia Biotechnology sign. The summer cold he had picked up on the plane was getting worse. The scratchiness at the back of his throat had worsened. He sneezed and wiped his nose on a handkerchief before exiting his vehicle.

Only three cars, a blue Toyota Prius, an almost new white BMW 3 series and a battered Saab 93, occupied the spaces in front of the building. He twisted in his seat but could see no trace of Eileen's red Mini. He hadn't expected to find her here, but a surge of disappointment at her absence still hit him in the stomach.

Where was she? Hopefully, somebody inside would help him answer that question. He left the car parked sideways across two parking bays and strode to the entrance. A hand-written note was attached to the inner surface of the glass.

Building closed today due to accidental spillage. Check email for more details. All deliveries, please ring the bell.

A shiny metal box occupied a space on the wall to the left of the door. The top half contained a square of black plastic etched with the image of a hand holding an access card. Beneath that sat a call button and a speaker.

He pressed the button. Several seconds passed with no response. He repeated the action. Still, nothing happened. He glanced up and spotted a small camera, mounted high up on the red bricks above the reader and directed downwards at the entrance.

"Come on," he shouted, waving his arms at the lens. "Open up." He jammed his thumb against the pushbutton and held it down.

Perhaps the switch was broken. He switched his attention to the door on his right. The rectangle of paper masked his view, and the reflections of the blue sky flecked with white clouds made it hard to see inside. He cupped his hands and peered through at the interior: an empty reception desk, lights off, two doors leading elsewhere. Raising both fists, he hammered on the glass.

Rosalind Baxter had answered the phone. She had to own one of the three cars.

"I know you're in there, Rosalind," he shouted, increasing the intensity of his banging.

A strong sense of being observed tickled the base of his neck. He spun around. A woman stood in the centre of the road outside the entrance to the car park, staring at him. She held his gaze for a moment, then continued over to the pavement, casting a single sideways glance in his direction.

Daniel directed his focus back to the building. The pattern of light shifted inside. Somebody emerged through the doorway behind the reception desk. The person masked their face with an elbow as they hurried to the entrance. Fumbling fingers twisted the lock. Daniel stood aside to allow room for the door to open. A wave of foul-smelling air, carrying the stench of rotting fish, washed over him. He sneezed as the stink made his eyes water. Clearly, they hadn't been lying about the spillage.

"Christ, what the hell happened?" he asked.

The woman lowered her arm: Rosalind Baxter.

"Hello, Daniel," she said. "Somebody dropped a bottle of ammonium hydroxide. I think you can see—or should I say smell—why we sent everybody home."

"I'm looking for my wife, Eileen."

"Yes, I gathered that from your earlier call. Unfortunately, I can't help you. She was here, but she left."

"What time that was?"

Rosalind's eyes lifted to the right, returned to his face, then looked away. "I don't know. Maybe eight o'clock. I wasn't actually in the building myself when it happened."

"But Eileen was here this morning?"

"Yes, I already told you that on the phone. She must have gone shortly afterwards."

"So, she wasn't injured in the spillage or anything?"

"No, she was in her lab. She came in early to finish a report that's due today. That'll probably be late now with all this going on. I was rather hoping she'd complete the work at home."

"Well, she isn't there. You're sure you have no idea where she could be?"

"Sorry, Daniel. All I can tell you is she's definitely not here. Look, nice as it is to chat, I really have to get back to sorting out this mess."

A slight movement drew Daniel's attention. A muscle in her jaw twitched rhythmically, and she refused to make eye contact. Something was making her nervous.

"I want to come inside and check for myself," he said.

85

A flash of anger clouded Rosalind's face. "We evacuated the building immediately after the accident and then swept it to make sure nobody was left behind. I can assure you there's no chance we missed her. Anyway, even if she was here, why isn't her car in the car park? She has a red Mini, doesn't she? I don't see one. Do you?"

Daniel turned. Only the other three cars and his own. But now a yellow delivery van, emblazoned with the red DHL logo, swung off the road outside. He watched as it sped across the tarmac towards them. A man, wearing a T-shirt in the same colours as his vehicle, jumped out and hurried to the rear doors. Moments later, he approached the pair, carrying a parcel.

Daniel refocused his attention on Rosalind. "I'm really worried about her. Just let me have a look around inside, so I can confirm with my own eyes she's not here."

"That's not going to happen," she replied. "I've already told you she's not there. Now, please leave."

The delivery man's gaze switched from one to the other and back, clearly uncomfortable at having intruded upon an argument. "Um... I have a package for a Dr Hendrick at Ilithyia Biotechnology," he said. "I need a signature."

Rosalind held out a hand. "Give it to me."

The man handed her a terminal with a plastic stylus attached by a short cord.

She scribbled on the screen and returned it to him, then accepted the cardboard box. She turned away, extended the lanyard hanging from her neck and lifted her card to the reader. The lock clicked. As she grabbed the handle, Daniel placed a hand on her shoulder.

"Get your hands off me," she yelled, spinning around in fury.

He released his grip and took a step backwards. His gaze shifted to the delivery driver, watching through the windscreen of the cab.

Daniel raised his palms to Rosalind in apology. "Sorry, I'm just—"

The phone in his pocket pinged, announcing the receipt of a text. He grabbed the device and inspected the screen. A band across the top of the display displayed a speech bubble icon, the sender's name and the start of the message. Any thought of entering the building to search for his missing wife dissipated as the first two words registered on his brain.

Eileen Floyd.

Friday 14th August 2015
Fen Ditton village, Cambridge
Twenty-one years ago

Anders Grolby jogged down the country lane. Luckily, few people were about. He passed a church to his left and continued along the road into the village of Fen Ditton, then turned right. He had done his research in advance and headed down a side street to the offices of a small taxi company. Streaks of rust ran down from the two screws affixing the dilapidated sign to the brick wall.

He pushed through the door and found himself in a cramped room containing a pair of brown plastic visitor chairs. A variety of framed certificates and a photograph of the outside of the building adorned the tatty walls. A woman sat behind the solitary desk. She wore a headset and tapped at the keys of an ancient computer as she peered at the screen.

She looked up in surprise at his entry. "Oh. Can I help you?"

"I need a taxi into Cambridge."

"Right. Um... most people just phone."

"I saw your sign and thought I'd save myself the trouble."

"Okay. Hang on a sec, I've got another call. Fenn Ditton Taxis."

Grolby sank into the scratched chair. The woman listened for a few seconds then said, "So that's Mr Evans on Milton Road, Cambridge, by the Church, to Histon. A car will be with you in around a quarter of an hour. Thank you for your business." She tapped on the keyboard, then turned back to Grolby. "You were saying. Whereabouts do you need to go?"

"The Science... actually, make that Cowley Road."

"It'll be about twenty-five minutes. Is that all right?"

"Fine. I'll wait outside." He would have preferred to return to Ilithyia sooner, but he didn't want to raise attention by making a fuss. He pulled the door handle and stepped into the warm afternoon air. A billboard advertising fresh ice cream occupied the pavement alongside the entrance to the newsagent shop thirty yards down the road.

It was good to be involved in something exciting again. Information Technology paid better than a career in the Swedish army, but he missed the occasional adrenaline surges that accompanied life in the military. This job would provide the first genuine excitement he had encountered in the past three years.

His only worry was whether his accomplices would hold together under the stress. Dr Perrin was the greater liability of the pair. In some ways, it would be easier to dispose of him like the woman, but he reminded himself that without the Chief Scientist, the company would fold even quicker than if he had allowed the whistleblower to proceed. And two disappearances among the company's workforce would raise far too many suspicions. No, he would simply have to keep the man in check.

He strolled down the street to the newsagent and bought himself a can of Coke. After taking a long chug, he crossed to a wooden bench on the opposite side of the road. There, he sat, jingling Eileen Floyd's car keys in his pocket as he pondered the next phase of his plan. It was a shame his co-conspirators wanted to keep her alive. Far simpler to dispose of her now, but they were adamant she should live, at least until after she gave birth.

Was it feasible to imprison her on the premises? If everything worked out as planned, the police would be searching elsewhere. The only risk lay in somebody discovering her by accident. He would have to ensure the room in which they kept her was soundproof, but it could work. Thanks to his quick thinking, at least they had the perfect opportunity to keep the building closed while they prepared a place to hold her.

He checked his watch. The damned taxi was late. He rose and crossed the road. He was about to re-enter the office to ask where it was when the sound of an approaching engine reached his ears. The small white sign on the roof identified the car as the one he was waiting for.

As soon as it pulled over to the kerb, he grabbed the rear passenger door.

"Did you order this, mate?" the driver asked through an open window.

"Yeah. I booked it from the office. Cowley Road please."

"That's all right, then. Jump in." The lock clicked, and Grolby settled himself on the back seat. A floral air freshener scent overlaid the lingering smell of fresh cigarette smoke. He debated whether to say something but chose to stay silent; today of all days, he needed to blend in.

Fifteen minutes later, they drew up fifty yards from the turning into the Science Park. He paid the cabbie and added a ten per cent tip. After a five-minute walk, he arrived back at Ilithyia. Besides the three cars he expected to find, a white van sat in a space by the entrance. A large sign on the side identified the owner as *Chem Response*. The second line read, "24-hour Chemical Spill Clean-up".

He used his card to enter the building, holding his breath so he didn't have to inhale the foul-smelling fumes as he jogged up the stairs.

Rosalind Baxter greeted him as he emerged into the corridor on the first floor. "Thank God you're back. I was beginning to worry."

"Nothing to be concerned about on my end. Is everything all right here?"

"Yes, she's still in the boardroom. I assume you saw the cleaners' van when you arrived. They're sorting out the spillage now, but they did say it would take a few days for the smell to go altogether."

"That may not be a bad thing. If you really want to keep her here, we'll need a day or two to set things up. Did anything else happen while I was away?"

"Her husband came by. He tried to get in the building to look for her."

Grolby jerked his head towards her in alarm. "You didn't—"

"No. He received a message and rushed off. I take it that was your doing?"

"Yes. I'll do a quick check on her, then I need to go out for another hour. Can you give me her home address? I suggest one of you stays with the workmen so they don't come up here."

"I'll send Dr Perrin to keep an eye on them. He's not handling this well."

Grolby lowered his voice. "Has he mentioned going to the police again?"

"No, but he's driving me mad clicking that damned pen like his life depends upon it."

"Perhaps you could have another chat with him. Explain the situation to him once more."

"Leave it to me. I'll just get her address for you." Rosalind headed to her office. The sound of low voices carried into the corridor. Moments later, she returned and handed him a folded piece of paper, which he placed in his back pocket.

Grolby opened the door to the boardroom. Eileen Floyd's frightened face greeted his entry. He leant over her and checked that the tape binding her hands and feet remained intact. She emitted a series of muffled grunts through the adhesive strips across her mouth.

"I have to go out again," he said. "I have just one question before I leave. Does your house have a burglar alarm?"

Eileen's eyes widened in fear.

"Don't worry, I'm not planning to hurt your husband, but I may have to if you won't answer me."

She studied his face for a moment, then shook her head.

"Okay. We'll talk when I get back. If you've lied to me or you try to escape while I'm away, there'll be serious consequences." Satisfied that everything was under control, he headed down the stairs and out to his car.

Fifteen minutes later, he pulled up at the address Rosalind Baxter had given him. The short driveway was empty. *Good.* The husband was still following the false trail. He withdrew the pair of leather driving gloves from the glovebox and slipped them on. After checking that no neighbours were watching, he used Eileen Floyd's keys to let himself in through the front door. No alarm. The same brand of perfume he had detected in her car greeted him. He found what he was looking for almost immediately and dropped the item into his pocket.

Only one task left to complete. That would have to wait until it was dark.

Friday 14th August 2015

St Mary The Virgin Church, Fen Ditton, Cambridge
Twenty-one years ago

Daniel Floyd's white BMW coasted to a stop beside the church at the edge of the village of Fenn Ditton. He pulled his mobile phone off the screen mount and switched to the text application. Once again, he read the brief message.

We need to talk. Meet me at St Mary The Virgin Church in Fen Ditton.

That was it. No explanation, just the two sentences. The last thing she had said before their conversation ended earlier that morning was that she would be back around eleven o'clock. But that was presumably before the spillage. Why on earth did she want to meet here? For the life of him, he couldn't think of any good reason for this meeting place. He had called her several times since receiving the text, but every time the call went straight to voicemail.

He got out of the car. The church lay at the junction between two narrow country lanes. If she was nearby, surely he would spot her red Mini, but the only vehicles he could see occupied private driveways.

He pushed through the gates and followed the gravel path towards the building. Several worn gravestones sat on the short-cropped grass. He passed through an arch into a stone porch set in the long edge of the structure. At the solid wooden door, he twisted the brass handle. It swung open with a metallic clank, accompanied by the squeal of ancient hinges.

A wave of cooler air washed over him, carrying a faint, musty odour infused with the scent of hot candles. Benches carved from a dark wood sat on either side of the aisle beneath a vaulted ceiling. Stained glass windows added a colourful hue to the darker shades of the pews and the tiled floor. But the only occupant was a man scraping excess wax from around the edges of a large candle. As he drew nearer, Daniel spotted the white dog's collar encircling the man's neck.

A sneeze erupted from Daniel's mouth.

The vicar looked up and flashed a warm smile. "Bless you. It sounds like you might be getting a cold. I always find summer colds are the worst."

"Sorry to bother you," Daniel said, "but I'm looking for my wife. She sent a message to meet here."

"Well, your wife has excellent taste in meeting places," the man replied, "but unfortunately I haven't seen anybody here for the last hour or so. Are you sure you've got the right place?"

"This is St Mary's Church, isn't it?"

"Yes, indeed. Perhaps she's in the grounds somewhere."

"Okay."

"What's her name?"

"Eileen. Why do you ask?"

The vicar grinned. "Well, if someone called Eileen comes in looking lost, I can tell her that somebody by the name of, uh…"

"Daniel."

"Right. That Daniel was trying to find her. It's been nice meeting you. If I have the good fortune to meet your wife, I'll let her know you were here."

"Thanks."

Daniel's eyes performed a quick scan of the interior before he retraced his path into the bright sunlight. He completed a route around the perimeter of the church but found no sign of his wife. Where could she be? He pivoted on the spot. Feeling slightly foolish, he shouted her name. No reply.

He returned to the gate by the entrance to the grounds. An elderly man wearing baggy dark trousers and a too-large beige jumper limped along the pavement.

"Excuse me," Daniel called.

The pensioner stopped and, without rotating his neck, shuffled his whole body around. "Yes."

"Um… my wife sent me a message asking me to meet her here, but there's no sign of her. You haven't spotted a woman about my age, looking lost, have you?"

A pair of rheumy blue eyes studied him through thick lenses. "No, can't say I have."

"She's driving a red Mini. Maybe you've seen that."

The man adjusted his glasses. "Now you mention it, I did see a car like that down the lane near the footpath leading to the river. I always try to walk for at least an hour a day to keep fit. At my age, I can't move too fast anymore. It's not really a parking place. Sometimes at weekends, there're two or three cars there."

"How far is it?"

The man stuck out a gnarled finger. "Oh, just a short distance that way. Go to that junction and turn right. It's on the corner where the road bends sharply to the left. It's a dead end. If the car's still there, you can't miss it."

"Thanks."

Daniel was already running in the direction his guide had pointed. The tarmac narrowed to the width of a single vehicle. Up ahead, the lane curved leftwards. He slowed as he approached the bend. *There!* A red Mini sat on a gravelly patch of ground beside a black waste bin. His heart thudded in his chest as he studied the number plate. It was definitely hers.

He performed a circuit of the car. "Eileen," he called. The only sound was the rumble of a tractor in the adjacent field. He cupped his hands and peered through the glass. No sign of her bag on the seat or in the floor well. Perhaps if she was somewhere nearby, he would hear the ringing of her phone. He selected her number from the recent contacts list. The ringing tone repeated eight times, then his wife's voice asked him to leave a message.

He ended the call without speaking and hit the redial button. The clattering of the tractor engine suddenly stopped, and the faint strains of an old-fashioned telephone ringtone reached his ears. He lowered the handset and blocked the speaker with a finger. Was the sound coming from the interior?

When the voicemail prompt repeated, he placed his ear against the window and dialled a third time. Her mobile was definitely inside the car, but where was she? Surely, she couldn't have gone far. He tried the doors but found them all locked.

He jumped over the metal barred gate beside the layby and yelled, "Eileen!" After twenty metres, the path opened out onto a patch of grassland bordering the river. He jogged across the meadow, the grass swishing against his legs as he ran. No trace of his wife.

Once again, he called her name. The only response was the gentle gurgle of running water. He retraced his steps, following the darker band of flattened greenery back to his starting point. *This makes no sense.* Why would she ask to meet him at the church, then abandon her car nearby and disappear?

The narrow lane turned into a gravelly track as it continued around to the left, past a high brick wall. He covered the distance in a few strides and discovered a footpath sign. He passed through a wooden gate and followed the path to the riverbank, calling her name as he went until his voice was hoarse. Two hundred metres later, he came across a footbridge that spanned the slow-moving water.

What now? If she had reached this spot, she could have continued in at least three different directions. *This is hopeless.* Perhaps her phone contained a clue to her whereabouts. He navigated back the way he had come until he arrived at the red Mini. It would take over an hour for him to drive home and return with the spare keys. What if he broke a window to get in?

He rolled the idea around inside his head. Eileen would be furious if he damaged her precious car. But he was seriously concerned about her wellbeing. Better he should incur her wrath than risk her safety. He lowered his gaze to the ground, searching for a suitable implement. All the nearby stones were far too small.

He walked back along the grassy verge, eyes downcast. Eventually, he spotted a potential candidate. He levered the rock out of the soil and brushed off a layer of mud. It fit snugly in the palm of his hand. He would have preferred something weightier, but it would have to do.

"Eileen," he yelled one last time. He strained his ears to pick up any sound above the rattle of the tractor's engine, which had started up again. Nothing.

He returned to the car. After a furtive glance at his surroundings, he stood to the side of the passenger door. He looked away and swung his fist at the window. A shockwave rocketed up his arm, but when he inspected his handiwork, the only evidence of his endeavour was a small chip in the otherwise flat surface.

He put more effort into the second swing. This time, an inch-long crack formed. The third attempt had the desired effect as the glass frosted into a patchwork pattern, and a sizeable chunk fell in onto the passenger seat. He reached inside and felt around for the door handle. The moment he operated the mechanism, the ear-splitting screech of a car alarm filled the afternoon air.

Ignoring the deafening noise, he pulled open the glovebox and retrieved the phone. As he turned to head back to his own vehicle, he spotted a figure. The man, wearing a helmet and garishly coloured cycling gear, stood astride a mountain bike, twenty yards away. He held up a mobile with one hand and tapped the screen with the other.

Then, without a word, the cyclist spun in a semi-circle, stepped on the pedals and raced past the church.

Friday 14th August 2015
Ilithyia Biotechnology, Cambridge Science Park
Twenty-one years ago

Anders Grolby pulled up outside the main entrance to Ilithyia Biotechnology. A quick survey confirmed only two cars in the car park, one belonging to Rosalind Baxter, the other to Nigel Perrin. It seemed the company hired to sort out the spillage had completed the job.

He unlocked the front door with a key, used his access card to operate the electronic mechanism, then locked up once again behind himself. Despite the clean-up, the foul stench of ammonia still lingered in the air as he jogged up the stairs. At the top, he found the corridor empty. A quick check of the boardroom confirmed that Eileen Floyd remained trussed on the floor. She tried to say something through the tape, but he ignored her. He hurried to the CEO's office. Rosalind whipped around as he entered.

"Is everything all right?" he asked.

"Yeah. They cleaned up the mess. They left half an hour ago."

"You wouldn't know judging by the smell."

Rosalind let out a humourless laugh. "They said it would take a few days for the stink to die down. Nigel's having a meltdown, but apart from that, there've been no additional problems. How about you?"

"It's nearly all set up. I have one more task to complete, and it'll be done."

"So, her husband..."

"By the time I finish, all the evidence will point to him as the prime suspect. You told me earlier he came here. Did anybody else see him?"

"Yeah, a van driver dropped off a parcel while he was talking to me outside the building. Daniel Floyd was insistent on getting in and was becoming quite aggressive. He only left when he received a message on his phone."

"And the delivery man saw all this?"

"I think so."

"Good," Grolby said. "We can use that. The police will still want to talk to you. You mentioned earlier that you went out with him at university. I want you to inform them that he came onto you, but that you rejected his advances."

Rosalind's face paled. "But then he'll know I'm lying."

"That doesn't matter. It'll be your word against his. The best lies contain an element of truth. When the police question you, make sure you tell them you were a couple in your student days. You didn't realise his wife was an employee. When you met at the Christmas party, he had too much to drink and tried to kiss you. He became obsessed and attempted to rekindle the relationship, but you rejected him. He came here today, telling you that he was planning to finish with her. You told him you weren't interested, and he got aggressive. Do you think you can carry that off?"

"I suppose."

"I'll get an unregistered phone and send you some text messages. Show them to the police, but only when they ask. Appear reluctant to divulge the information, as if you're still fond of him. Don't seem too eager to drop him in the shit. Did anybody else see her this morning before the spillage?"

"No, only Nigel, you and me as far as I know."

"Right. It's probably best if you keep it quiet that she came in earlier."

"I already told him she was here," Rosalind said. "And what about the phone records? Didn't you say she rang her husband from her lab?"

"Good point." Grolby scratched his cheek. "She was working on an important report, wasn't she?"

"Yes."

"Okay, so you lie. She promised to come in early but didn't show up. You—actually it's probably better if we make that Dr Perrin given the story we're trying to sell—called his number to see if he knew where she was."

A worried frown creased Rosalind's forehead. "Nigel's in no fit state to have a conversation with the police at the moment."

"Hmm. Do you think we can settle him down?"

"I'm not sure."

"We could tell them Mrs Floyd's disappearance coupled with the spillage has left him so shocked and upset that he's in no condition to do an interview, but he'll have to talk to them in the end. If you don't believe he's capable of holding it together, it may be time to consider other options."

"What does that mean?"

Grolby's piercing stare cut through his employer. "If we can't trust him to keep his mouth shut, we could resolve the situation through alternative means. It's not something I want to do, but he may leave us no choice."

"No, he's vital to the future of this company. Let me have another chat with him."

"Okay. And you're still determined to let the woman live until she gives birth?"

Rosalind took a deep breath, then nodded. "Yes."

Grolby sighed. "I think that's the wrong decision, but if you insist. So, we'll keep her at the back of the storeroom. We have to get that set up quickly. We'll need some builders."

"I'll sort that out."

"The building will have to remain closed until the work is done. Ensure they use some top-quality sound-proofing material. Tell whoever does the job it's because of the noise made by the test animals. We'll have to make sure the room is totally secure and that none of the employees can get in."

"Assuming the police search the premises for her, how do we stop them from searching there?"

Grolby rubbed the back of his neck. "Put some shelving in front of the area where we keep her so they can't see it. Stick a big biohazard sign on the doors outside. That way, they won't want to go in. Hopefully, they'll be looking hard at Daniel Floyd by then, anyway."

"Okay, so what happens next?"

"I'm feeling hungry, and our prisoner probably needs something to eat and drink. Oh, and she'll need a toilet break. You'll have to accompany her."

"Me?" Rosalind asked.

"Unless you plan to untie her and wait outside, but I wouldn't recommend it. I suggest we free her legs but keep her hands tied and the gag on. Why don't we do that now, then I'll go out and get some sandwiches and the new phone?"

"Right."

Rosalind followed Grolby as he returned to the boardroom. He knelt and loosened the knot around their prisoner's ankles.

"We're taking you to the toilet," he said.

Eileen made a muffled grunt through the tape binding her mouth.

Grolby grabbed her by the arm and hauled her upright. She almost toppled over, but he tightened his grip and half dragged her along the corridor to the ladies' washroom. When they reached the door, he turned to Rosalind. "Go in with her. If you need help, just shout."

Five minutes later, the two women emerged. Eileen's frightened gaze focused on Grolby's face. He ignored her silent pleas, placed a hand on her shoulder and guided her back to the boardroom. As he grabbed the handle, Nigel Perrin burst from his office and rushed towards them.

"There's a police car outside," he said, his eyes wide with alarm.

Grolby shoved Eileen through the open doorway. "Stay with her," he barked to Rosalind. "Tie her up again and keep her quiet. I'll deal with this."

Moments later, the doorbell sounded. He slipped a cotton facemask over his face, then took a calming breath and descended the stairs. A middle-aged policeman in a dark uniform stood outside with hands cupped around his face, peering in.

Grolby crossed the reception area, unlocked the door with the key and pressed the access button. "Yes, can I help you?"

The man opened his mouth to speak, then stopped and held a hand over his nose. "Christ, what's that smell?"

Grolby pointed to the sign. "We had a spillage and had to close the building while we sorted out the mess. If you think this is bad, you should have been here earlier. Why don't we talk outside?"

The policeman stepped back, and Grolby followed him out.

"We're looking for an Eileen Floyd," the man said. "Her husband reported her missing this morning. I understand she works here."

Grolby folded his arms. "Yes, she does, but I haven't seen her in the office today. We sent everybody home after the accident, but luckily there were only a handful of people here at the time, and she wasn't among them. We followed our company procedures, and I personally performed a full sweep of the building after the spill. I can assure you she's definitely not inside. I hope she's all right."

"Do you have any idea where she might be?"

"Sorry, I'm afraid not. What do you think has happened to her?"

"It's probably nothing," the policeman said. "I'm sure she'll turn up soon. What's your job here?"

"I head up the IT department and look after site security."

"Well, thanks for your time Mr..."

"Grolby. Anders Grolby."

"We'll be in touch again if we can't track her down. If you hear from her, could you please call me on this number?" The policeman handed over a business card.

"No problem," Grolby replied, pocketing the card. He watched as the man returned to the white police car. He raised a hand as the car swept out onto the main road. When he glanced back at the building, the silhouettes of two people stared down at him from an upstairs window.

"Damn," he muttered to himself. "We don't have as much time as I first thought."

Friday 14th August 2015
33 Willow Drive, Cambridge
Twenty-one years ago

Daniel Floyd navigated the quiet residential road and approached the small three-bedroom semi-detached property where he and his wife had lived for the past two-and-a-half years. He parked on the short driveway and got out.

He knew it was irrational, but his spirits sank at the sight of the empty space normally occupied by his wife's Mini. Perhaps she was inside. Maybe she had abandoned her car after breaking down and taken a taxi to get home. But why would she leave her phone in the glovebox? And why hadn't she called to tell him?

He had checked her mobile before returning to the house. They both used the same system for their unlock codes: the date of the other's birthday. The list of emails contained nothing of interest. When he switched to texts, the only item of any note was her message requesting the meeting. She had sent no other messages that day. Neither had she made any outgoing calls, and the only entries in the incoming calls log were his own unanswered ones.

He twisted the key in the lock, strode inside and called her name. Silence greeted his shouts. He climbed the stairs and checked the upstairs rooms. More in hope than expectation, he opened the back door and stepped through into the compact garden. No sign of her there, either. *Where the hell could she be?*

He re-entered the house, made his way to the lounge and sank onto the sofa. The faint trail of his muddy footprints led towards the kitchen. Eileen would have been furious with him for tracking in mud across the beige carpet. He would have gladly traded a few moments of her anger for the relief of discovering she was well.

He pulled out his own mobile and checked for messages. Other than a few work-related emails, nothing. Without thinking, he selected his wife's number from the list of contacts and tapped the dial button. For a moment, hope surged at the old-fashioned ring tone. Just as quickly, despair returned at the realisation the sound originated from his back pocket. Of course. He cursed his stupidity.

Perhaps the police would have some news. Apart from anything else, he needed to tell them about the strange message and finding her car. He dialled 101 and waited for the call to connect to the police station. When a man with a deep baritone voice replied, he gave his name and quoted the reference number he had been given.

"One second, sir," the call handler said. "Right, yes. A Mrs Eileen Floyd, missing since this morning. What can I do for you?"

"I received a text from her, asking to meet me at the church in Fen Ditton."

"So, you've found her then?"

"No, she wasn't there. I discovered her car a short distance down the road. Her phone was in the glovebox."

A keyboard tapped in the background. Several seconds passed in silence. Eventually, the man spoke again. "We've received reports of a theft from a vehicle matching your wife's."

"Yes, that was probably me. I heard her mobile ringing inside, and the doors were locked. I didn't have a spare set of keys, so I broke the window. A cyclist saw me."

"Okay, I'll make a note of that. But there was no sign of your wife?"

"No. The car was in a layby by the entrance to a field. I searched around the area, but she wasn't there. Has there been any other news? Do you have any leads?"

More tapping sounds. "I checked the road cameras and spotted her vehicle on the A14 around seven-thirty, but we have no coverage from junction thirty-three to the science park. We visited her workplace, but apparently nobody has seen her today."

Daniel's breath hitched. A shiver ran across his scalp. "That can't be right. She called me from her lab this morning."

"I'm sorry, sir. I can only tell you what it says here."

"None of this makes any sense. I was talking to her when the call cut off, so she was definitely there. She said she'd see me around eleven o'clock. And why would she send me a message to meet her in Fen Ditton? I don't think either of us have ever been there before. Something's happened to her."

"I'm sure it's just a misunderstanding, sir, but I'll get somebody to check out her car."

"Right," Daniel replied. "Thanks."

"If you hear from her, please contact us on this number. Are you at home now?"

"Yes. I arrived back a few minutes ago, but like I said, she isn't here."

"It's probably best if you stay there for the moment," the man said. "We'll let you know if we find anything."

"I'm really worried. Please find her."

A click signalled the end of the call.

What the hell was going on? Why did the person at Ilithyia claim she hadn't been there that morning?

He searched for the company name and clicked the link to dial the number. After a few seconds, a female voice answered. "Yes."

"Is that you, Rosalind?" he asked.

"Look, Daniel. Like I told you earlier, I'm sorry, but I have no idea where your wife is."

"I've just finished talking to the police. They claim they spoke to somebody at Ilithyia who said she hadn't been in today. She called me using a company phone number while I was at the airport, so I know she was in the building. And when we talked this morning, you told me she'd recently left."

The line went quiet.

Daniel moved the handset away from his face and checked the status. Still connected. "Are you there?"

"I didn't say anything about your wife being here. I haven't seen her today. Now, please stop calling. I can't help you."

A click. The call had ended.

Saturday 15th August 2015
33 Willow Drive, Cambridge
Twenty-one years ago

Anders Grolby lifted his wrist and glanced at his watch: just after two o'clock in the morning. He raised his eyes to the curtained upstairs window. No lights. *Good.* Daniel Floyd's white BMW sat on the drive. A quick survey of the quiet residential neighbourhood confirmed nobody else was about. He had parked his own vehicle a quarter of a mile away and walked the short distance to his target's address. One couldn't be too careful; people tended to remember unfamiliar cars when questioned.

Grolby slipped on his leather gloves and removed from his pocket the spare set of car keys he had taken from the house the previous day. He tapped the unlock button. A loud click echoed through the stillness of the night. He held his breath, but nothing stirred. He moved to the back of Daniel Floyd's vehicle and pressed the BMW badge. The rear door swung upwards with a quiet hiss of air from the struts.

Withdrawing the vial of blood from his pocket, he removed the stopper from the glass tube and sprinkled several drops over the coarse carpeting. The burgundy liquid quickly seeped into the material, leaving barely visible, darkened spots where it landed. He reached up and carefully pulled the tailgate down, taking care to close the mechanism with the minimum of noise.

Next, he withdrew the cheap mobile phone from his trouser pocket and pressed the power button. His fingers tapped out the PIN: 1234. Obvious, but he wanted the police to have no trouble unlocking the device when they discovered it later. He opened the text application and selected the sole contact, Rosalind Baxter. He scrolled down the list of sent messages, all just a few words long.

I love you. Please call me. D x
I told her about us. She didn't take it well.
I'm free of her. Now we can be together. D xxx
I need to see you.
You know I can't live without you.

One more couldn't hurt. Grolby deliberated for a moment, then hit the compose icon and typed in the message.

I'm sorry I lost my temper earlier. Let me make it up to you. D xxx

He tapped the send button, opened the passenger door and dropped the phone in the side pocket. A second low clunk disturbed the silence as he locked the car with the key fob. He listened for a few seconds, but the only sound to emerge from the darkness was a dog barking in the distance.

One task remained. He shrugged the rucksack off his back and withdrew Eileen Floyd's housekeys. After another brief survey of his surroundings, he approached the house and let himself in through the front door. He stood in the hallway, inhaled a deep breath, then released it slowly.

Grolby returned Daniel's car keys to the same hook from which he had removed them the previous day. As he turned to leave, a handle rattled upstairs. Footsteps moved across the landing. He backed up to the open doorway. A pair of bare legs appeared, coming down the stairs.

Grolby eased the door closed behind him, then sprinted over the grass and flung himself to the ground on the far side of the low hedge surrounding the property. He lay on the hard pavement, desperately trying to control his laboured breathing. A quick glance through the dense foliage confirmed a figure in a white T-shirt and dark shorts, standing on the doorstep.

"Eileen?" a man's voice called.

If Floyd came out as far as the road, he couldn't fail to spot Grolby.

The Swedish ex-soldier remained stock-still. He watched as the man looked left and right, then turned and re-entered the house. The loud whoosh of exhaled breath accompanied the sound of the front door closing. *Christ, that was close.*

He maintained the same position for several more minutes. The decision to move was a balancing act; if he broke cover too soon, there was a risk Floyd would spot him. If he stayed where he was, a car might drive past and raise the alarm at his suspicious behaviour. Finally, he rose to a low crouch and cast an anxious glance towards the house. Nothing moved. Nobody called out. He set off, hunched over until he was out of sight of the upstairs windows.

He jogged back to his Saab and sank into the driver's seat. A wry grin formed on his face. The past few moments had been stressful, but it was a long time since he had experienced the adrenaline rush and nerve-jangling thrill of surviving a close encounter with the enemy.

Even though he wouldn't know it yet, Daniel Floyd was well and truly caught in the snare. Later that day, the next phase of the plan would begin.

All it would take to spring the trap was one anonymous phone call.

Saturday 15th August 2015

Daniel Floyd threw back the bedcovers and swung his legs onto the thick carpet. He glanced at the bedside clock: six forty-five in the morning. It didn't feel right to sleep while Eileen was still missing, but he had been unable to keep his eyes open as his body fought off the cold and struggled to recover from the jet lag of his transatlantic trip. Overnight, his sore throat had developed to the point where it felt like he had swallowed a roll of barbed wire. The previous night's disturbance had certainly done nothing to aid his recovery.

He cast his mind back. A noise had woken him just after two o'clock. For a hopeful moment, he wondered if it was Eileen returning home. He could swear he had heard the click of the latch, but when he descended the stairs, he discovered the front door unlocked but nobody there. Try as he might, he couldn't recall whether he had locked up before going to bed. Lack of sleep and the effects of his cold had turned everything from the previous evening into a blur. Perhaps a gust of wind had made the sound.

A quick search of the house confirmed she hadn't returned. Afterwards, he had lain awake until exhaustion dragged him back to a succession of disturbing nightmares featuring his absent partner. Normally, Saturday mornings were filled with reading in bed—or if she was in the mood, activities with his wife of a more intimate nature—followed by a late breakfast. Today, he desperately missed their normal routine.

He snatched up his mobile and checked for messages. Nothing other than the usual emails. A sense of helplessness overwhelmed him. What could he do to find her? Maybe he should search again around the area where he had discovered her car. Perhaps she had been injured or collapsed from some undiagnosed illness. She might be lying somewhere nearby, unable to move and desperately waiting for help to arrive. A spiral of increasingly morbid thoughts spun through his brain. No matter how ill he felt, he couldn't just sit here, waiting for her to come home.

He padded to the en-suite bathroom in bare feet and slipped into the shower cubicle. He raised the water temperature, twisting and turning under the jets until his skin turned a shade of pink. After brushing his teeth, he dressed in a short-sleeved shirt and beige chinos before descending the stairs to brew the first coffee of the day. He needed a powerful jolt of caffeine to survive the coming hours, so heaped twice the usual quantity of grounds into the cafetiere.

While he waited for the water to boil, he strolled aimlessly from room to room. Was there a clue here? Was he missing something? His mind turned to Rosalind Baxter. Her reaction puzzled him. The first time he called the switchboard, she seemed unsure whether Eileen had arrived for work earlier that day. But later, when he visited the company in person, she told him his wife had left following the spillage. During his final call, she contradicted herself by flat out denying Eileen's presence in the building that morning.

The ring of the doorbell interrupted his thoughts. Was it her? Perhaps she had lost her keys. He rushed to the front door but slowed as he drew nearer. The blurred outlines of two figures stood silhouetted on the other side of the frosted glass. He pulled the handle and held up a hand to shield his face from the harsh glare of the early morning sun.

A pair of policemen stared at him with serious expressions.

His heart sank. "Oh, God. Have you found her? Where is she? Is she all right?"

"Mr Floyd?" the taller man asked.

"Yes. What is it? Why are you here?"

"Please stay calm. We haven't discovered your wife's whereabouts yet. May we come in?"

Daniel stepped back and beckoned them inside. Conflicting emotions raced through his brain: relief that the policemen weren't there to report what he feared most, but despair that they hadn't located Eileen either. He led them into the lounge, lowered himself into an armchair and perched on the edge. The two men sat at opposite ends of the sofa.

"When did you last see your wife?" the man sitting nearest asked.

Daniel shook his head in confusion. "As I already told the person at the police station, I've been abroad for a couple of days. I haven't seen her since I left on Wednesday morning."

"Okay. Would you tell us about finding her car?"

"I'd been calling her all day yesterday with no success. Then, out of the blue, I received a text message from her, asking me to meet her at St Mary the Virgin Church in Fen Ditton."

"Did you speak to her?"

"No, she wasn't there when I arrived."

The scratch of a pen on paper drew Daniel's attention to the second policeman. He scribbled something in a notebook.

The other man cleared his throat and leant forwards. "What I meant was, did you try to call her?"

"Yes, of course, but she didn't answer."

"Okay, so you drove to the place she identified, this church, but you didn't find her there. What did you do next?"

"I went in and talked to the vicar. He told me he would let her know I'd been there if she showed up looking for me. Then I searched the grounds. When I came out, an old man was walking up the road. I asked him whether he'd seen my wife. He said he hadn't, but he had noticed a car matching hers in a nearby layby. I followed his directions and discovered my wife's Mini. Anyway, I spoke to the call handler yesterday and mentioned all this to him. Why are you asking me again?"

The policeman ignored Daniel's question. "What happened after that?"

"Her phone was in the glovebox."

"How did you know that?"

"I heard it ringing. So, I searched in the adjacent field and along the footpath, but I couldn't find any trace of her."

"Are you sure about that, sir?"

Daniel jerked his head towards his questioner. "What's that supposed to mean? Of course I'm sure."

The policeman studied him with suspicious eyes. "We received an anonymous call last night. The caller told us they saw a couple having a violent argument by the river bank. The man was yelling the woman's name. It was a very distinctive name: Eileen. The man's description sounds very similar to yours. So, I'll ask you again. Did you or did you not meet your wife at Fen Ditton yesterday?"

A prickle of apprehension rippled across Daniel's scalp. "How many times do I have to repeat myself? We never met. Yes, I was shouting her name, but that was because I was trying to find her. But if she was having an argument with another man, you should be looking for him instead of wasting time asking me questions I've already answered."

"Let us worry about that, sir. Now, tell me about the car."

"Like I said, she wasn't there. I knew the phone was inside the glovebox because I could hear it ringing through the glass. I thought it might give me a clue where she was, so I found a stone and broke in."

"Or perhaps you were so angry with her, you wanted to get back at her by damaging something she valued."

Daniel gasped. "What? I love my wife. I'd never do anything to hurt her."

"And did you find any useful information on her mobile?"

Daniel's head lowered. "No. There were no outgoing messages other than the one asking to meet me."

"Where is it now?"

Daniel pointed to the coffee table where he'd put the phone the previous night.

"Do you mind if we check it ourselves, sir?"

"If you think it might help to find out where she is, go ahead, but I didn't see anything to explain her disappearance on there."

The policeman with the notepad pulled a clear plastic bag from his pocket and nudged the mobile inside, using the top of his pen.

"I take it you know the unlock code then?" his partner said.

"Yes." Daniel dictated the digits. "It's the date of my birthday," he explained.

"We'd like to have a look around the house, if that's okay with you."

"Do you have a search warrant?"

Both men studied him carefully for a moment before the nearest officer spoke. "No. Do we need to arrange one?"

Daniel gave a brief shake of the head. "Sorry, of course not."

The policemen stood. As Daniel followed their example, the taller man raised a hand. "It's probably best if you remain here, sir. This shouldn't take long. Is it all right if we check inside your car too? While we're at it, do you have the keys for your wife's car?"

Daniel gestured towards the door. "The spares for both our cars are hanging on hooks in the hallway." The two men left him alone. He leant back in his chair. His hands tapped out an irregular rhythm to accompany the jiggling of his legs. Floorboards shifted above as somebody moved about upstairs.

After a few minutes, the stairs creaked as the policemen descended. The familiar click of the door-latch followed. A gust of air blew in from outside, shifting the lounge door slightly on its hinges. A short blip from the car alarm. The distant clunk of opening car doors. Several seconds of silence. Hurried footsteps.

The two police officers burst into the room.

"Daniel Floyd, we are arresting you for the suspected murder of your wife, Eileen Floyd."

The nearest officer pulled a set of handcuffs from the pouch on his belt.

"What did—?" Before Daniel could finish his question, the second policeman grabbed him by his upper arm, hauled him out of the chair and yanked his hands behind his back. The cold metal embraced his wrists.

"You do not have to say anything," the other man intoned, "but it may harm your defence if you do not mention when questioned, something that you later rely on in court. Anything you do say may be given in evidence."

Monday 17th August 2015
Ilithyia Biotechnology, Cambridge Science Park
Twenty-one years ago

Rosalind Baxter stared through the glass at the two people waiting outside. Their visit wasn't unexpected. Detective Sergeant James Roberts had called an hour earlier, requesting an interview. Beside him stood his female boss, Detective Inspector Veronica Turner. Rosalind pressed the access button to open the door.

Both police officers turned away in disgust as the faint lingering stench of ammonia washed over them.

"Christ, what the hell is that smell?" Turner asked, placing a hand over her nose.

"Yeah, sorry about that," Rosalind replied, stepping back to allow them to enter. "We had a chemical spillage a few days ago. We called in a clean-up company, but it will take a while before all the fumes dissipate. It was far worse last week. It's slightly better upstairs. Please follow me."

She led them up to the boardroom.

"How do you work in these conditions?" Roberts asked, lowering himself into a chair.

Rosalind sat on the opposite side of the long table. "To be honest, I've become acclimatised. I don't really notice it anymore. Now, you mentioned on the phone this was about one of our employees. What can I do to help?"

Turner withdrew a file from the briefcase she had been carrying. "I believe an Eileen Floyd works here."

"Yes. Has something happened to her?"

The policewoman ignored the question. "When did you last see her?"

Rosalind shook her head. "Do you mean me personally, or anybody here? I vaguely recall seeing her on Tuesday or Wednesday, but she spends most of her time in the labs, and I don't go down there every day. I can check with her manager when she was in."

"If you wouldn't mind, Mrs Baxter."

"Now?"

"We'll wait."

Rosalind rose and covered the short distance along the corridor to her office. Anders Grolby waited inside.

"They want to know when she was last in the building," she said.

"Obviously don't tell them she was here on Friday," the Swede replied. "Have they asked any other questions?"

"Not yet. I'll give it a few minutes, then I'll go back. Can you print out the attendance logs in case they ask?"

"No problem. I've already been in the system to modify the records for that day. May I use your computer?"

Rosalind nodded. She paced backwards and forwards while he tapped at the keys. Eventually, the printer unit by the wall spat out three sheets of paper. She scanned the report. "Thanks," she said, heading back into the boardroom.

The two detectives occupied the same positions as when Rosalind had left them. "Here we are. She was last in on Thursday, but we told everybody to stay at home on Friday after the accident. This data comes from the key cards the employees carry to get through the front door." She placed the printout on the table.

"Is it possible she followed somebody else in and didn't actually use her own card?" Turner asked, picking up the sheets of paper.

"I suppose so, but one of our conditions of employment is that everybody has to present their ID on entry to the building. It's a serious disciplinary offence if they don't. The information is used to check who's here in case we ever need to evacuate, for example during a fire drill."

"Or a chemical spillage," Roberts added.

"Yes, exactly."

Turner studied the report. "So according to this, the only people here last Friday morning were Martin Hendrick, Nigel Perrin, Anders Grolby and Rosalind Baxter—you."

"That sounds about right. May I ask what this is about?"

"Eileen Floyd's husband reported her missing on Friday. He claims she called him from here, and his phone records support that. But now you're telling me she wasn't here that day."

"No, I don't remember seeing her, but I didn't arrive until after the spillage."

"So, it's possible she was here."

"Only if she didn't use her card, and all the people you just mentioned are senior members of staff who know better than to let somebody else bypass the system."

"How do you explain the call, then?" Roberts asked.

Rosalind feigned a look of puzzlement. "Maybe it was Dr Perrin. He's my partner by the way. We had an important report to deliver on Friday. Now you mention it, he was complaining to me earlier this morning that she hadn't shown up. Perhaps he was calling to find out where she was."

"In that case, why would he call her husband's mobile instead of hers?"

"You'd have to ask him that—if it actually was him. We keep several phone numbers on record for each employee. Whoever it was probably chose the wrong one. Or it's possible they tried hers first and called his when nobody answered."

"All right. Can you bring Dr Perrin here? While you're at it, we'd also like to talk to the other people who were present last Friday morning."

Rosalind stood. "I think they're all in today. I'll just go and fetch them." She felt the suspicious stares of the two police officers on her back as she crossed to the door. Moments later, she barged into her partner's office.

Perrin sat at his desk, his head in his hands. He looked up as she entered, revealing the pair of dark half-crescents beneath his eyes.

"They've asked to see you," Rosalind announced without preamble.

The expression of fatigue on his face morphed into one of panic. "What do they want to know?"

"They have Daniel Floyd's phone records, which show a call made from this building to his mobile on Friday morning."

"Christ, what do I say to them?"

"Tell them you needed her to complete an important report. She didn't turn up as promised, so you wanted to track her down. You dialled the first number you came across, which happened to be his."

Perrin's shoulders slumped. "I can't do this, Rosalind."

"You can and you will... unless you want all of us to spend the next ten to fifteen years of our lives in prison. I have to fetch the others, so you've got a few minutes to pull yourself together. The police are in the boardroom."

Rosalind left the room and crossed to her own office. Grolby stood at the window, looking out at the cloudless blue sky.

"What's going on?" he asked, turning around.

"They want to see you, Nigel and Martin," she replied. "Can you fetch Dr Hendrick from his lab? And make sure he doesn't mention anything about the work he's been doing. They know about the outgoing phone call. I told Nigel to say he was the one who made it."

"How's he holding up? He's not about to drop us in it, is he?"

Rosalind let out a sigh. "It's impossible to tell. I had a few words with him. Perhaps you should have a quick chat too."

"Fine. I'll do that. Give me a couple of minutes."

Rosalind turned and headed back to the boardroom. She returned to her seat. "Somebody's just getting them. They'll be here in a minute." The tension grew as she and the pair of police officers waited in uncomfortable silence.

Eventually, the door opened and the three Ilithyia employees trooped in. When everyone had taken their seats, Rosalind introduced her colleagues.

Turner, the female DI, spoke. "As you're probably already aware, we're trying to trace the whereabouts of Eileen Floyd. Nobody has seen her since last Thursday night. Her husband claims she made a call from here on Friday morning. The attendance records show she wasn't in the building that day. So, first of all, did anybody see her?"

A series of head shakes greeted the question.

"Is it possible she didn't use her access card?"

Nobody responded immediately. Grolby filled the silence. "The only way that could happen is if she entered with somebody else. I know for a fact it's impossible that she came in with me."

"Me neither," Hendrick added.

"What about you, Dr Perrin?" Turner asked.

No reply.

"Doctor Perr—"

"No, I don't recall seeing her at work at all that day," Perrin replied.

The detectives both studied the bespectacled scientist for a moment.

"Okay," Roberts said. "Did anybody call her husband?"

Again, an uncomfortable silence.

"I think it was probably me," Grolby said.

"Probably? Surely you would know whether or not you called him."

The Swede cleared his throat. "Dr Perrin mentioned that Mrs Floyd had promised to come in early on Friday morning to finish an important report. When she didn't show up, I offered to talk to her and find out why she wasn't here. I pulled up her file but must have selected the wrong number."

"So, you spoke to her husband, Mr Floyd, then?"

"I assume it was him. He told me his flight had just landed, and he didn't know where she was. I quickly realised my mistake, so I ended the call."

"But after that, you tried her mobile?"

"No," Grolby replied. "The chemical spillage happened before I had the opportunity. My chief priority was keeping people out of the building until we could clean up the mess."

"What exactly is the process when something like that happens?"

"We respond in the same way we would to a fire alarm. We evacuate the premises and perform a name check to confirm everybody present is accounted for. There were only four of us here, so that was quick. After that, I did a room by room sweep to make sure nobody else was still inside."

"So, if she had been in the building, you would have known?" Turner said.

"Yes."

"What exactly is your role in the company, Mr Grolby?" the female detective asked, consulting her notes.

"I head up the IT team, and I also look after site security."

She scribbled a few words in her notepad. "How did this spillage happen?"

All eyes turned to Perrin. "I... I accidentally dropped a bottle of ammonium hydroxide in the corridor downstairs. It was a stupid mistake."

"And what about the report?"

"What report?"

"The one Mr Grolby just mentioned. Apparently, it was of high enough importance to call Mrs Floyd about when she didn't turn up."

"Oh, that. I ended up finishing it off by myself."

"Okay. Have you tried to locate her today?"

Perrin glanced at his watch.

"I'm sorry, Dr Perrin," Turner said, her voice laced with sarcasm. "Do you have somewhere more important to be?"

"No, no, it's not that," he replied hurriedly. "I was just checking the time. Employees have to phone their manager before ten o'clock if they can't work. It's ten fifteen, so she should've called in by now."

"And I take it she hasn't?"

Perrin shrugged. "I don't know. She doesn't report directly to me."

The two police officers exchanged a glance. "Okay," Roberts said. "I think that's all for the time being. Mr Grolby, perhaps you could show us where Mrs Floyd worked. We'd also like to speak to her manager. The rest of you are free to go although we'll probably need you all to make a statement at some point. Thanks for answering our questions."

Nigel Perrin and Rosalind Baxter remained seated while the remainder of the group left the room. Rosalind waited several seconds after the door closed before speaking.

"It's over for now, Nigel. I think that went as well as we could have hoped."

The Chief Scientist raised his elbows onto the table and lowered his face into his hands. The sound of low sobs emerged from between his fingers.

Monday 22ⁿᵈ February 2016

Belmarsh Prison, Thamesmead, London
Six months later

The only sound inside the cramped cell was the scrape of plastic on plastic. Daniel Floyd sat hunched over on the bottom bunk. He held a tray on his knees as he picked at the unappetising fare. This was officially his first day as a convicted felon, although he had spent the past six months behind bars here awaiting trial. The case had been high profile, catching the attention of the public for obvious reasons: a well-educated man murders his beautiful wife and refuses to identify the location of her body.

Another prisoner with short-cropped grey hair and wearing the ubiquitous drab prison clothes occupied the sole chair in the small room.

Daniel looked over at him. "Food all right, Victor?" he asked.

"Same crap as usual," the man replied in a Russian accent. "You enjoy your first day as a convict?" That morning, the two men had become cellmates following Daniel's sentencing.

"Things could be better. Somebody abducted and murdered my wife. Meanwhile, I'm stuck in this place for the next fifteen years at least, paying for that crime."

"You should probably not tell people you are innocent. Many here say this, but nobody is interested. It only marks you as weak."

"You may be right," Daniel replied, "but some bastard set me up. They found her blood in the boot of my car. I've no idea how it got there, but it was certainly nothing to do with me. I'm sure those bastards she used to work with had something to do with it. My wife called me from there the day she disappeared, for Christ's sake, but they claimed it was somebody from the company, trying to find out where she was. That bitch, Rosalind Baxter, also lied. She told the court I came onto her. I was happily married. She and I went out together for a while years ago, but I wouldn't sleep with her now if she was the last woman on earth."

"There is nothing you can do," Victor said. "Once they convict you, it is too late."

"I could always appeal."

"Perhaps you get lucky, and they find new evidence. But I advise you to accept your situation. You will go mad if you do not adapt."

"Thanks for the advice," Daniel replied, piling his plastic fork with peas. Their consistency bore more resemblance to green ball bearings than anything edible. The two men ate in silence for a moment. "How did you end up in here, Victor?" he asked.

The Russian let out a low laugh. "This is something else you should not say to people." He turned serious. "But now we live together, so for you, I will answer. For many years, I work in Soviet army. Much equipment goes missing. Everybody takes it. Pay is bad, but I have good business, and I make much money. When Soviet Union break up, I come to England for new life. Work is hard to find, so I do what I know best; I sell things on the black market."

"What sort of things?"

Victor frowned at the question, then relaxed his features. "Oh, anything a person cannot buy easily: weapons, drugs, women. Anyway, soon others think I take sales from them. They interfere. They hurt my people. So, I do something else I am good at. I start war."

"War?"

"Yes, not like tanks and rockets, but guns and knives. After a short time, nobody messes with me. Most are dead." Another chuckle. "Everything is good for a few years, but then things go wrong. I make too much money. The men who work for me want more. They get greedy and try to take my place."

"So, what happened?"

"Somebody betrayed me. I receive order for weapons. Good money. Very good money. When we deliver to buyer, armed police are waiting. They arrest us all. But I find out who it is. He is already dead along with his close family."

"Um... All right. I appreciate you telling me."

A wide grin cracked the Russian's face. "But perhaps I just tell you this story so you fear me, yes?"

Daniel laughed uneasily.

"Do not worry. They will not bother you in here if you stay near to me. Nobody messes with Victor Yahontov. I see you are good man. We become friends."

"Sure. I'd like that. How much longer have you got inside?"

Victor shrugged. "I don't know. Eight years, ten years maybe. It makes no difference. It is long time in future. I try to make the most of my life even though this is not palace." He gestured towards the discoloured walls.

Daniel resumed his meal.

After a few seconds of silence, the Russian spoke again. "I continue business in here. If you need anything, you come to me. For you, I give good discount. I get whatever you request. But maybe not girls. This is too difficult."

"Cheers, Victor."

"And when we are both out, if you want weapons or drugs or other illegal things, you know who to ask."

"Thanks, I appreciate it, but I don't think that's ever likely to happen."

Daniel Floyd smiled politely at his new cellmate, but a part of him wondered whether he would ever have cause to take up the Russian's offer.

Monday 22nd February 2016
Ilithyia Biotechnology, Cambridge Science Park
Twenty-one years ago

Eileen Floyd stared listlessly around the cramped room. Barely ten feet square, it contained a narrow bed, a washbasin, a toilet, a solitary bare lightbulb dangling from the ceiling and nothing else. No windows, just a single locked door. She would have lost count of how long she had been here were it not for the marks she scratched every day on the beige walls with a fingernail: a little over six months.

She ran a hand over her belly. The rounded bump of her baby pushed out the material of her T-shirt. That bastard, Grolby, had brought her a variety of clothing during the first week, but she had quickly resorted to the cotton top and baggy jogging bottoms as her standard attire. Every few days, one of her three jailers—the Swede, Baxter and Perrin—took away her used clothes and returned them a short while later, cleaned.

Food came only twice a day, once early in the morning—although she could only discern the time from the yawns and tired expressions—and once at night. She had learned to save some of her breakfast to stave off the hunger pangs at lunchtime. The only visitors she received were Rosalind Baxter, Nigel Perrin and Anders Grolby. Presumably, they were the only ones who knew she was here—wherever here was.

Six months earlier, they had drugged her again. When she regained consciousness, she found herself in this tiny space and hadn't been out since. She guessed she was somewhere on the Ilithyia premises, but the soundproofed walls gave no clues as to her whereabouts. For the first few days, she had screamed and hammered her fists against the sides of her prison, but nobody came to her rescue. After a while, they threatened to keep her tied up and gagged if she didn't stay quiet.

As the weeks turned into months, her resolve wavered. The initial fury at her imprisonment transformed into grim acceptance. Now, she almost relished the twice-daily human contact as a respite from the crushing boredom. At her request, they had brought her books and even a handheld gaming console, but neither source of entertainment did anything to drag her from her hopeless lethargy.

She had considered trying to end it all. On at least one occasion, she had removed the bulb and, in the absolute darkness that pressed on her like a physical force, debated whether to plunge her fingers into the exposed pins of the socket. But every time, her thoughts turned to her unborn child. The only reason they were keeping her alive was to allow her baby the gift of life. She couldn't bear to think about what that future might entail, but neither could she bring herself to take it away.

As she lay on the thin mattress awaiting the arrival of her evening meal, she tried to picture her husband's face. What was he doing now? He had to be sick with worry. A few days ago, Grolby let slip that they had framed Daniel for her abduction. At the thought, a surge of molten rage ran through her veins. She couldn't give up. She had to make them pay for what they had done. *I have to get out of here. But how?*

For the past three months, she had been docile and followed her captors' instructions to the letter. Perhaps they had become complacent. She sat up. For the umpteenth time, she surveyed the small room. As on every previous occasion, no obvious weapon caught her eye. She placed her bare feet on the floor. They wouldn't be expecting her to resist after so long. Was there a chance she could catch whoever came tonight by surprise?

Her gaze rose to the lens of the infrared camera. She had to act her usual lethargic self or they would be prepared. At the first click of the lock, she lowered her head and placed her face in her hands. The door swung inwards a few inches.

"I've brought you some food, Eileen," a voice called.

Good. Perrin. The doctor was probably the least physically capable of her three captors. He pushed into the room, carrying a plastic tray holding a pack of garage sandwiches and a can of coke. He approached the bed and placed it beside her on the mattress.

"Are you okay?" he asked.

Still, she maintained the same position.

"Eileen?"

Slowly, she raised her head. With a sudden yell of fury, she launched herself at her captor. He staggered backwards and collided with the wall. His hand reached down for the baton tied to his belt, but she was already past him. Her bare feet slapped against the cold tiles as she sprinted through the doorway. She emerged into another narrow room and, in her haste, barged into a stack of mouse cages with wire mesh fronts. A flurry of movement greeted her arrival as the occupants sought whatever cover they could find inside their own prisons.

She swore under her breath and scrambled along the row towards the only way out. Already her breathing was becoming laboured; six months of confinement had left her unaccustomed to physical exercise. She slipped through the open door and found herself in a storeroom. Locked cabinets filled all the available wall space. Just a few feet away lay the exit. A large yellow sign displayed a prominent message:

Remember to lock up when you leave

She lunged for the handle and twisted. It refused to turn. With increasing desperation, she rattled it up and down.

"Help," she screamed. "Let me out of here."

Footsteps rushed up behind her. A hand landed on her shoulder and spun her around.

Nigel Perrin stood, holding a black baton, hair dishevelled and glasses askew. A bead of sweat rolled down his right temple.

"I don't want to hurt you, Eileen," he said, "but I will if you force me to."

"Please let me go. I won't say a word to anybody." She sank down on her haunches with her spine against the wall. Tears of despair stained her cheeks.

"Come on, back to your room. I'm not going to ask again."

With weary resignation, she forced herself upright and trudged past the caged rodents. She hesitated as she neared the threshold to her cell, but a shove between the shoulder blades pushed her inside. The door slammed shut behind her with a heavy thud. The rattle of the lock followed a moment later.

She crossed to the bed and curled up on her side in the foetal position.

***

In the corridor, Nigel Perrin ran a trembling hand through his hair. If he hadn't locked the door to the storeroom, she would have escaped. How could he have been so careless? The others would be furious if they found out. It was probably for the best if he kept the incident to himself.

After six months, he had finally come to terms with their actions in keeping her a prisoner, but he still dreaded what was to follow after she gave birth. Grolby had said he would be the one to deal with her, but that didn't make it any easier to accept.

He drew a shaky breath and headed back towards the reception area. A square of light leached around the sign, filling the window to Dr Hendrick's laboratory. Perrin failed to notice as the door behind him opened.

A pair of curious eyes tracked his progress.

Wednesday 30th March 2016
Ilithyia Biotechnology, Cambridge Science Park
Two days later

Martin Hendrick glanced at his watch. Five minutes to eight in the evening. If tonight followed the normal pattern, somebody would come down the corridor and enter the storeroom shortly. Ever since the ammonium hydroxide spillage six months earlier, access to the chemical storage cupboards had been restricted to three people: the two company directors, Rosalind Baxter and Nigel Perrin, and the head of IT and security, Anders Grolby.

It made no sense. Why were these senior members of staff performing the role of storeman? What did they do in there every night? Perhaps he should just ask one of them. But that was a problem to solve later. For now, he turned back to his computer screen.

For the past few months, Hendrick had been using CRISPR technology to edit the RNA of the influenza virus. The technique enabled him to alter the building blocks of the organism and insert fragments of modified genetic material. After several ups and downs, his research was finally nearing completion of the first stage. The next step would be to trial his creation on laboratory animals. He had deliberately downplayed the level of progress to his bosses, but the early signs were that he would achieve his goals.

The sound of footsteps in the corridor outside dragged his attention away from the display. *Right on time.* He crossed the room and peeled back the edge of the sign that blocked the small square window. It seemed it was Anders Grolby's turn tonight. Hendrick eased open the door a fraction and watched through the gap as the Swede withdrew a set of keys from his pocket and let himself into the storeroom.

Hendrick waited a moment, then crept after the security chief. If past form was anything to go by, it would be several minutes before he emerged. The scientist placed his ear against the cold, white plastic and strained his ears to pick up any sounds from within. Silence.

With slow, deliberate movements, he twisted the handle. To his surprise, the mechanism turned, and the door clicked open. He hesitated for a second, scanning the interior, then stepped through the doorway. The room seemed much smaller than he recalled. Locked cabinets butted up against the walls. A narrow passageway led off from the right side of the opposite wall. That hadn't been there before.

The characteristic, musty smell of laboratory animals hung in the air. A flurry of movement rattled the bars of their metal cages. So that's what Grolby was doing here. It still didn't make sense why the senior management had taken responsibility for feeding duties, but it did explain the nightly visits.

Hendrick turned away and retraced his steps. He reached for the handle and pulled it towards him. The door was an inch from closing when a new sound emerged from the other side of the room. Were those voices? Had more than one person come in? Surely, he would have noticed.

Caught in a moment of indecision, he stood stationary and strained to hear the words. He was too far away to understand what was being said, but it sounded like a man and a woman. Taking a deep breath, he re-entered the storeroom. He moved cautiously, treading carefully to avoid making any noise.

Grolby's voice rose above the scurrying of animals. "I don't care whether you hate cheese and onion or not, that's all they had. You should be grateful we feed you twice a day."

"Yeah, thanks a million."

Definitely a female, but who could it be?

"Somebody will be back tomorrow morning. It's Rosalind's turn, I think."

"Can't wait."

The sound of a door slamming emerged from the narrow passageway, followed by the rattle of keys. Hendrick turned and sprinted across the floor, counting on the renewed scuttling of the caged animals to mask his retreat. He slipped through the open doorway, pulling the door shut behind him. He raced along the corridor back to his workspace. Once inside, he slumped against the wall and sank down on his haunches.

The click of footsteps drew nearer and stopped outside his room. Hendrick froze. After a few seconds, they resumed. There could be no doubt; only one person had passed by. As the scientist returned to his workstation, a single inescapable conclusion rattled through his head.

Grolby, Perrin and Baxter were holding a woman prisoner somewhere behind the storeroom.

***

Martin Hendrick had been unable to concentrate for the past half hour. His mind kept wandering; who were they keeping in the room? He flinched as a tapping sound came from the corridor.

He rose from his seat, twisted the latch and pulled the door open.

120

Grolby stood outside. "Everything all right?" he asked.

Hendrick could barely meet the man's gaze. "Yeah," he mumbled.

"Everything's locked upstairs. You only need to lock up here and set the alarm when you leave."

"Fine."

"See you tomorrow. Don't stay too late."

The scientist shot him a weak smile. "I'm just wrapping things up. I won't be much longer. Goodnight." He closed the door as the head of security headed down the corridor.

There was no point trying to continue. Hendrick shut down the computer and tidied his work surface. He grabbed his bright-green winter jacket from the coat stand and strolled towards the reception area. Only one car remained in the parking spaces outside: his own red Ford Focus. He approached the beige box on the wall beside the entrance and reached out a hand to tap in the arming code.

His finger hovered over the first digit. Who was the woman? He had to try to find out. With a surreptitious backward glance, he tramped up the stairs. At the top, he turned on the lights at the master switch and followed the corridor to Rosalind Baxter's office. He pushed the door open, stepped inside and crossed to the window in darkness. After peering down at the solitary vehicle, he flicked the light on, squinting against the sudden brightness.

The desk drawers were unlocked, and he spent a fruitless two minutes rummaging through the contents. Maybe he would have more luck in Nigel Perrin's office. He rearranged the items and pushed the drawer closed.

The Chief Scientist's room was the same size as the CEO's, but the interior was fastidiously neat and uncluttered. He lowered himself into the swivel chair and tried the right side first. A desk tidy held an assortment of pencils and several identical ballpoint pens. He lifted the tray out, but nothing occupied the space beneath.

Next, he turned his attention to the left drawer. A pile of post-it pads in a variety of fluorescent colours lay stacked neatly towards the front. At the back was a jam jar filled with paperclips. He picked up the container and peered at the contents. Two silver keys on a ring stood out against the brass colour of the clips.

Hendrick reached in and retrieved the set. Could these be the right ones? He hurried down the stairs, turning off the lights behind him. At the bottom, he barged through the swing doors and jogged to the storeroom door. With trembling fingers, he fitted the first key in the lock, but it wouldn't turn. He removed it and inserted the second. This time, the mechanism rotated with no effort. He pushed his way inside.

Once again, the distinctive odour of laboratory animals assaulted his nostrils. He switched on the light, triggering a sudden bout of activity. His heart mimicked the behaviour of the frightened rodents as he crossed to the narrow passageway. A small amount of illumination penetrated an area approximately three feet wide. A variety of cages lay stacked against the left wall. To the right was a solitary door.

This was where they must be keeping her. His gaze settled on a tiny circle of glass at head height: a peephole. He placed his face up against the white plastic surface and peered inside.

An involuntary gasp of shock escaped his lips as he identified the sole occupant: Eileen Floyd.

Part Three: Relocation

Friday 27th March 2037
Compton Majestic Hotel, Northstowe

Antimone was half-watching an animated film about a baby giraffe when a light knock sounded at the door to their room. "Pause TV," she said.

Paul shifted impatiently on her lap. "Oh, Mummy. I want to watch this."

She ignored her son's complaint. "Jason, somebody's here. Can you get it?"

Jason put down the e-book reader. After a moment, the screen automatically dimmed as the device's sensors detected the focus of his eyes were no longer on the words. He swung his legs off the bed and ambled across the carpeted floor. "Yes, who's there?"

"An important visitor would like to see you, sir," a muffled voice replied from the opposite side of the thick layer of wood.

Jason shot Antimone a worried look and backed away.

"Ah... sorry, sir, I should have said, today's password is hamster."

Jason breathed a sigh of relief and turned the handle. A flustered looking Derek Walker waited in the corridor. A pair of men in dark suits stood behind him. One placed a finger on his left earlobe and muttered a few words.

"If you could just step back, please," the other said.

Jason moved to the side as Walker led the group of three into the room.

The man who had issued the command crossed to the bathroom and peered inside. "Clear."

Moments later, the smartly dressed figure of Andrew Jacobs, the British Prime Minister, appeared in the doorway, flanked by another two sombre-faced men.

"Good afternoon," he said. "Sorry to turn up unannounced like this. I hope I'm not disturbing you."

Jason glanced down at his bare feet. "It's no problem at all, sir."

"I'll catch up with you later," Walker said, retreating from the room and closing the door behind him.

"So, how are you all?" Jacobs asked. "Oh, and please call me AJ."

"We're fine, um... AJ," Jason replied.

"You're probably wondering what I'm doing here," the Prime Minister continued. "You must have noticed the members of the press outside, so clearly your presence in this place is no longer a secret. It's not safe for you to stay here anymore. I have a proposal to make, and I wanted to put it to you in person."

Antimone wheeled her chair closer. From his mother's lap, Paul stared open-mouthed at the four men accompanying the leader of the country.

"Well," Jacobs said after a brief pause, "my advisers tell me there's a high chance another dangerous mutation of this virus will take place before too long, so we've agreed to set up an international research effort. We're bringing in scientists from around the world to try to beat this thing once and for all. Given the original source of this pandemic, it was the least we could do."

He cleared his throat. "Now, as you may have heard, Ilithyia Biotechnology has recently gone into administration. We plan to establish this new science centre on the site. The building already has all the facilities we need, so it's perfect from that perspective. You're probably asking yourselves what this has to do with you. Well, we'd like to move you there too. I know you've been through a lot, and I'm sure it'll bring back some bad memories, but it would be a big help to the team if you could spend some time with them."

Antimone scowled at the Prime Minister. "Let me get this straight. You're proposing to return us to the place where they held me prisoner and where we all nearly died."

"Look, I'm aware it's not ideal from that point of view, but it does have some major advantages. For starters, the location is secure. What's more, it happens to be close to where you used to live, so if you want to pick anything up from home, it won't take long to make the trip. And your parents can visit whenever they like. Not only will you be safe and away from the press, but also the researchers would really appreciate your presence there to assist with their work."

"What help could they possibly need from us?"

Jacobs offered a weak smile. "You're still the only person to survive childbirth without taking drugs to prevent the activation of the virus."

Antimone folded her arms. "Yeah, sometimes I wish that wasn't the case. I don't mind helping, but I'll be the one to choose what tests they run on me and my son."

"Of course. I wouldn't expect anything less."

"Where would we stay?" Antimone asked.

"They've already converted some of the old office space to luxury apartments so the scientists can live on site. I've seen photographs, and it's really quite comfortable. On top of that, you'll be well protected."

"Will anybody else we know be there?"

"I forgot to mention. Dr Kubar has joined the team. He was very enthusiastic about seeing you again."

"So, you've already discussed our situation with him?" Jason said.

"Yes. He and I spoke last week. In fact, he was the person who suggested it would be a good place for you to stay."

"What aren't you telling us?" Antimone asked.

Jacobs glanced anxiously from one to the other. "Right, well I suppose I should mention beforehand that Mrs Baxter will also be on site—not that either of you need to see her if you don't want to."

"What?" Jason said, raising his eyebrows in surprise. "You're going to release her from prison?"

"Yes. In fact, she's already moved to the Ilithyia building. We kept it out of the press for obvious reasons. She wants to help undo some of the damage she has caused. I know the situation may be awkward for you, and I can't force you to go, but I honestly think it's the best solution all round."

"I'm not worried about her," Antimone said. "She's still not my favourite person, but she did save Paul's life in Tripoli. Will there be armed guards? I don't want my son living around people carrying guns."

Jacobs's face cracked in a wry grin. "I'm afraid some of us have to put up with that all the time." His smile faded at the impassive response from his audience. "Given the company's history and the high-value individuals staying on-site, hopefully yourselves included, we need to maintain a significant security presence. It's a balancing act, but we're keen the place doesn't feel like a prison, so we're trying to keep everything low key. The compound is protected by an electrified fence, and we've provided the team with a variety of non-lethal weapons, such as tasers, and sonic cannons, that sort of thing."

"And what about schooling for Paul?"

"How old is your son now? Four? I'm sure we can arrange for somebody to come in and teach him."

"If we do agree to go, how long would we have to stay?" Jason asked.

"Unfortunately, that's a question for which I don't yet have an answer. I have experts to advise me on subjects like that, but my guess is that after we've defeated this virus once and for all, people will be less interested in you and your family. I don't want you to feel that I'm applying undue pressure, but your presence on site may reduce the time needed to come up with a solution."

Jason turned to Antimone. "What do you think?"

She met his gaze for a moment before replying. "It seems there aren't many other options."

Jason refocused his attention on the Prime Minister. "Okay, AJ. We'll do it."

Friday 27th March 2037
Ilithyia Biotechnology, Northstowe

Rosalind Baxter followed Martin Hendrick into the boardroom. A thin woman with shoulder-length brown hair stepped forwards. "Welcome, Mrs Baxter. Glad you could join us."

Professor Christine Harris spoke with a precise British accent. Her clothes, a matching navy-blue jacket and skirt, were clearly expensive and clung to her slim body. Rosalind knew this scientist was over fifty years old, but she could easily pass for somebody a decade younger. She might have the appearance of an ageing model, but she possessed an incisive mind and was a world-renowned expert in viral science. "Obviously, we've met many times before, so I don't need to describe my background," she said. "I'll be leading the team and coordinating the different work packages."

Harris extended an arm to introduce the next scientist. "This is Herr Professor Jacob Fischer. Once again, I'm sure you're already well acquainted." The man with the open-necked, flowery shirt, stood and bowed. As he did so, his floppy white hair fell across his face. He swept it back with his right hand. Fischer, like the woman who introduced him, had established himself as one of the foremost experts in viral research.

Harris moved on to the next team member. "You may have less familiarity with the work of Professor Armand Allard."

"No, I don't think we've met before," Rosalind said, studying the overweight man in the dark suit. She estimated he was in his early sixties, although his hair remained jet black. *Probably from a bottle.*

"Bonjour, Mrs Baxter," he replied, speaking with a heavily accented French accent. "My expertise lies in the subject of nanomachines. I look forward to discussing my research with you."

Rosalind flashed a brief smile.

"That brings me to Dr Rachel Miller. Rachel joins us from Johns Hopkins University in Baltimore. She has spent many years in the biomedical field and is an authority in drug synthesis." The woman on the other side of the table rose from her seat, displaying her full height. Rosalind estimated she stood at least an inch over six feet tall. Her hair was tied back in a ponytail, and she was dressed casually in blue jeans and a white shirt. She tilted her head at Rosalind without smiling.

"I know you are well acquainted with our next team member, Dr Naeem Kubar. He has made quite a name for himself by developing a treatment for the new strain of the Orestes virus although he is very modest and claims you should receive much of the credit. It is mainly down to his insistence that we have asked you to join our group."

Kubar jumped up from his chair, grinning from ear to ear. "It is so good to see you again, Rosalind. I hope we will have another successful collaboration."

"And it seems you've already met, Dr Martin Hendrick. Martin joins us from the Oslo Medical Research Centre and is an expert in the field of cross-species viral transmission."

Rosalind nodded to her former employee. If he wanted to keep his past association with Ilithyia secret, she would play along—for now. Nine months earlier, an employment history at the company that developed the first treatment for the Orestes virus would have been considered a positive, but ever since the revelation about the source of the outbreak, she imagined it counted as a significant black mark within the scientific community.

Harris pointed to an empty chair. "Would you like to take a seat, Mrs Baxter?"

Rosalind headed around the large circular table to the only unoccupied space.

"Right, now that everybody's here, let's begin. I appreciate you joining me on this vital project. You are all world-renowned experts in your chosen field. In the past, we have all worked in our separate groups, and to some extent, in competition with each other. From this point forwards, we have to work together. It's no coincidence that you come from diverse backgrounds. Hopefully, the different skill sets you bring will help us to be more productive and generate innovative solutions to the challenges we face.

"Now, several of you have brought your teams with you. I expect those of you who are alone—that includes Mrs Baxter, Dr Hendrick and Dr Kubar—to spread your time between the specialities. Your experience and insights will help to engender the cross-functional cooperation I believe we need to make a difference and find a solution where we have previously failed. In essence, you will be the glue that binds the separate work packages together. Are there any question so far?"

Allard, the French nanomachine expert, raised his hand. "Madame 'Arris, what is our budget?"

"I have been assured by the people who hold the purse strings that they will not refuse any reasonable request," the professor replied. "If you can justify the expenditure, I'll ensure you get the funds."

Kubar spoke next. "You propose that I spend my time across the groups. May I also perform my own research?"

"Of course. If you would prefer to establish your own group, provided it aligns with our goals, I will do my best to make it happen. Now, if there are no more questions, I suggest each of you gives a fifteen- or twenty-minute synopsis of how you plan to address the problem facing us."

Rosalind listened as each of the scientists described their area of expertise and their thoughts on how to tackle the challenge. She was familiar with the work of most of the attendees other than the Frenchman, Armand Allard. His team of researchers had developed microscopic machines that could be programmed to perform operations at the molecular level. Despite her lack of knowledge, she found herself fascinated by his radically new approach.

When he ended his short presentation, she raised her hand.

"Oui, Mrs Baxter," he said.

"What you've told us is really interesting, Monsieur Allard."

"Thank you. And please call me Armand."

"Okay, Armand. What's stopping your nanomachines from ignoring their programming and running out of control? What would happen if they malfunctioned, and you couldn't stop them?"

The French scientist rolled his eyes.

"I'm sorry if that sounds like a stupid question," Rosalind said, glancing around at the other meeting attendees.

"I blame science fiction," he replied. "They call this the grey goo scenario, or to use a more technical term, ecophagy."

"I don't understand."

"Many writers have written stories about self-replicating microscopic machines that multiply uncontrollably to the point where all matter on this planet is broken down to produce more and more copies until nothing remains other than a sea of nanomachines. The so-called grey goo."

"Right."

"But this cannot happen here. Firstly, my devices do not have the capability to self-replicate. We use specialised machines to manufacture them in a separate process. Secondly, in order to function, we must first send them a signal. This can take several forms, such as light or magnetic fields, but they will not turn on until they are instructed to do so. Thirdly, they are all programmed to shut down upon receipt of the appropriate command. This uses a similar mechanism to the one used to activate them. Finally, the power source contained inside each device has a limited life. When it is exhausted, they stop."

"So, you have no worries about them malfunctioning in a dangerous way?"

Allard clasped his hands over his stomach. "No, Madame Baxter... Rosalind. Twenty years ago, people had similar concerns about artificial intelligence taking over the world. Now, we cannot live without that technology. This is the same thing."

Harris glanced at her watch. "Well, it's nearly twelve thirty, so that's good timing. Lunch is available in the canteen. That was an interesting session. I propose we meet here daily at nine o'clock for a fifteen-minute stand-up, so that everybody can keep abreast of progress. Every Monday morning, we will hold a longer meeting like this. With your wide-ranging expertise, I anticipate a fruitful collaboration. Together we're going to beat this virus once and for all."

Rosalind pushed back her chair and rose to her feet with the others. As she trailed after her fellow scientists, a hand landed on her forearm. She whirled around to meet Christine Harris's stern gaze.

"If you wouldn't mind staying behind for a moment, Mrs Baxter," the professor said. "I'd like a quiet word." She waited until the other attendees had left, then pushed the door closed.

Rosalind pulled up the nearest seat. Harris crossed to the opposite side of the table and followed suit.

"What can I do for you, Christine?"

For many years, the two women had maintained a professional rivalry. Over that time, they had met at several conferences and often found themselves on the same expert panel. On more than one occasion, they had argued about the best way to approach the pandemic.

Harris leant forwards with a slight frown on her face. "Before I say anything else, I want to make it clear it wasn't my idea to include you in this project. I have been instructed to utilise every resource at my disposal, but your presence here is not something I asked for. As I mentioned earlier, Dr Kubar is one of your biggest supporters. I am not alone in believing you should remain in prison for what you did."

Rosalind met the woman's gaze. "Well, it's nice to receive a vote of confidence. They offered me a choice between staying in my cell or returning to this place. I chose to come here, but it was a close-run decision."

Harris's frown deepened. "If I must have you on-site, I want you to assume a role acting across all the different research teams. Despite my objections to your being here, I still value your scientific opinion. Make sure you keep up to date with what's happening."

"Fine."

"Oh, one last thing. If you cause any trouble, or I feel you aren't making a significant contribution to the work we're doing, I'll request your immediate removal from the team."

Sunday 29th March 2037
Ilithyia Biotechnology, Northstowe

Antimone shuddered as she rolled through the entrance to the Ilithyia Biotechnology facility. The last time she came this way, she had been trying to rescue her son. It all turned out well in the end, but she, Jason and Jason's father, Daniel Floyd, had come within moments of losing their lives, and the place still gave her the creeps.

The building had a different look and feel about it from what she remembered. For a start, the foyer was far quieter. Five years ago, the bustle of patients and scientists had filled the space with noise. Now, most of the people present were security staff. The curved reception desk had gone, replaced by a ten-foot-high barricade incorporating a pair of barriers, one side for entry, the other for exit. Antimone's gaze focused on the two unsmiling men in pale-blue uniforms, who stood guard beside the electronically operated gates, blocking access to the area beyond.

She gave a start as Jason's hand landed on her shoulder.

"Are you okay?" he asked.

"Yeah, fine," she replied in a flat monotone.

He glanced down at Paul, whose tiny fingers intertwined with his father's. "And how about you, buddy?"

"Why does it smell funny in here, Dad?"

The air carried the strong odour of disinfectant.

"Oh, it's only the stuff they use to keep this place clean," Jason said.

Antimone twisted in her wheelchair and directed her attention to Derek Walker. The man assigned to their security over the last few months approached the two guards, and they conducted a conversation in low voices.

After a few seconds, Walker beckoned them forwards. "They're expecting us. You'll have to pass through a scanner to check for concealed weapons. Once we're inside, they'll show you to your rooms. They're just waiting for somebody called Nick Butler to turn up. Apparently, he's in charge of site security."

"Is this the only way in and out?" Antimone asked. "Will we be safe here?"

"From what I understand, there's a goods entrance as well, but that's equally secure. There's absolutely no chance the press, or anybody else for that matter, is getting in without permission. You saw the barrier across the road when we came in. And if that isn't enough, there's also the electric fence around the building. This place is locked down tighter than a duck's arse."

"Right. Do you think we'll be allowed to go outside?"

"You'll have to discuss that with Mr Butler."

A man with short-cropped grey hair stepped through the exit barrier. "Did I hear somebody mention my name?" he asked.

Walker and Butler introduced themselves. Knuckles cracked as they shook hands, but neither signalled weakness by displaying any discomfort. The former was three inches taller than the latter, but Butler's heavily muscled frame more than compensated for his lack of height. Antimone watched on as the two men sized each other up. If it came to a fight between the pair, she couldn't decide who she would put her money on.

The person responsible for ensuring their security from this point on passed from one member of the family to another, crushing their fingers in his powerful grip.

When he got to Paul, he patted him on the head. "Hello, big boy."

"Hello, little man," the four-year-old replied with a cheeky grin.

Butler raised an eyebrow, unsure how to respond.

Walker maintained a deadpan expression. "I'll say my goodbyes now," he said, turning to Jason and Antimone. "It's been a pleasure working with you." He spun on his heel and headed back to the exit without a backwards glance.

Butler waited for their former protector to depart through the rotating doors. He gestured towards the entrance gate. "Good afternoon, everybody. If you'd like to go through, we'll run through a brief induction session."

Butler went first, followed by Jason and Paul, then Antimone. As each of the adults passed through the barrier, one of the uniformed guards handed them a laminated card bearing a 3D hologram of the holder and instructed them to hang it around their neck. Antimone studied the image on her badge. Judging by the background, the camera must have taken the picture as she entered the building. The people running this place were definitely leaving nothing to chance.

"But I want one too," Paul said.

"Perhaps when you're a bit bigger," Butler replied.

Antimone slipped hers over her son's head. "You can wear mine for now." The plastic rectangle dwarfed Paul's body.

Butler flashed an irritated glance at her. He clasped his hands behind his back and addressed the family of three. "Welcome to the Ilithyia facility. When you are on-site, you must keep your identity card on show at all times.

Please do not leave your rooms without it. It gives you access to all the areas you are permitted to visit and will operate lifts and doors as appropriate, including entry to your room. There is a canteen, which remains open twenty-four hours a day. We have a gymnasium with all the latest equipment for those of you who want to exercise. The laboratories are off-limits to everybody apart from the scientific staff.

"All the rooms are well equipped with state-of-the-art entertainment systems. The building provides free Wi-Fi access, but I need to warn you that we monitor all network links. Maid service will come in every morning between ten and eleven o'clock. Please hang a sign on your door handle if you don't want to be disturbed. Now, are there any questions?"

"Can we go outside?" Antimone asked.

"I'd rather you didn't, but if you're determined to leave the building, then one or more of my men will escort you at all times."

"What about leaving the site?"

Butler chuckled. "You've only recently arrived, and you want to go already? Look, the reason for transferring you here is to keep you safe. We can't spare the resources to protect you outside the fence. If you can find somebody else to guarantee your safety, then I don't see why not, but it's not something my team is able to support. The scientists operate under the same restrictions. They all live on site too."

"I heard that Mrs Baxter is staying here," Jason said. "Is that true?"

Butler's forehead creased in a frown. "I suppose you'll find out for yourselves pretty soon anyway, so there's no point denying it. Yes, she's helping out the research teams."

"Will we be allowed to visit her?"

Butler stared at him with an incredulous expression. When he saw Jason wasn't joking, he said, "You can't go in her room, and nor can she enter yours. However, if you wish, you may meet up in the canteen. Just be aware, a member of the security staff will be sitting close by all the time. Now, if there are no more questions, I'll leave you here, and one of my team will take you to your accommodation."

The three new arrivals trailed after the man in the pale-blue uniform, who had been assigned to their group. The card around his neck identified him as John Griffin. He led them across the foyer and prodded the call button when they reached the lifts. Moments later, the elevator doors parted. The others moved forwards to enter, but Antimone froze. A sudden sense of déjà vu overwhelmed her. For the past four years, she had tried to forget what had happened here, but now the memories of her failed escape attempt and the subsequent mistreatment came crashing back into her mind.

"What's wrong?" Jason asked, turning around and inserting a foot into the gap to prevent the panels from closing.

"I... I'm... It's nothing." She forced her hands to keep the wheelchair moving forwards. She closed her eyes and held her breath until the swish of the opening doors signalled their arrival. With trembling arms, she backed out into the corridor.

"This looks familiar," Jason said, lowering his voice. "This used to be where my mother had her office."

"I wouldn't know," Antimone snapped. "They kept me in the basement where they could study me like a lab rat."

"I'm sorry. This must be hard for you."

"Yeah. I would probably have died down there if you hadn't rescued me."

Jason had freed her using knockout gas grenades that his father, Daniel Floyd, obtained through a former prison cellmate.

Jason took her hand and squeezed it. They followed the guard in the blue uniform down the corridor until he stopped outside a door. He pulled a mobile device from his pocket and studied the screen. "Miss Lessing, Mr Floyd and your son are in here," he said. "Just hold your card to the reader to get in." He pointed at a small box mounted to the wall. "There's a fire escape that way, and the main stairs are over there."

"Thanks. Who's next door?" Jason asked.

"We've put some of the scientists on this floor."

"What are their names?"

The man shuffled uncertainly from foot to foot but didn't answer.

"Oh well, I suppose we'll find out soon enough," Jason continued.

"All right. That side is Mrs Baxter and the other room is Professor Fischer's. If you're worried about Mrs Baxter, you're perfectly safe. She can't come or go without one of the security team to open the door."

Jason's and Antimone's eyes locked for a moment. Jason shrugged. "Fine. Thanks for letting us know."

"I'll leave you to it," the guard said. "You can come and go as you please. Just remember to make sure your identity badges are visible at all times."

Jason held up his card. A green light flashed, accompanied by the click of the lock. He went first, holding the door open for Antimone and Paul. The overhead lighting immediately came on, illuminating a short hallway.

"I think this was Nigel Perrin's old office," he said. He stuck his head in the doorway on the right. "Bathroom," he announced. "This is where his secretary used to sit." He carried on down the narrow passageway, opening the pair of slatted doors. "Built-in wardrobe." He pushed through into the bedroom. "Oh, this is different."

The beds took up the floor space along the back wall. A bedside table separated a child's bed from a full-sized double, both covered with matching, brightly coloured covers. The person responsible for the room's decor had crammed in several items of wooden furniture, including two chests of drawers and a desk. A pair of armchairs sat beside the large window at the far end.

Antimone pushed herself forwards and looked out onto the gardens below, bordered by an electric fence. A man held a massive German Shepherd on a tight leash as he patrolled the perimeter.

She turned back to Jason. "It's comfortable enough here, but it still feels like a prison."

He stood beside her and stared down. "Maybe, but nobody's getting in with all that security. At least we'll be safe here."

Once again, a strong feeling of déjà vu descended on Antimone.

"I certainly hope so," she replied.

Sunday 5th April 2037
27 Boxworth Road, Northstowe

Max Perrin paced backwards and forwards. "So, now we know Baxter and Kubar are at the old Ilithyia building," he said.

The three-man team had moved into the rented house a week earlier. The two-bedroom semi-detached property provided a far superior base of operations, well away from the prying eyes of the landlady at the guest house. It also had the advantage of a long-distance view across the fields to where the aforementioned targets were staying. Max had a bedroom to himself, while his two colleagues shared a room.

"What about the others?" he asked. "Do we have any idea where they've gone?"

Mohammed Abadi glanced up from the screen. "I am still looking for them. There are some rumours on the net they may be in the same place."

"What?" Max moved over and stood behind him. "Show me."

The diminutive North African reached out a hand and dragged a window to the front. "Here. The information on this forum is usually fairly reliable."

Max lowered his head and studied the posts. "It would certainly make life easier if they were all together. We still have to figure out a way to get to them. The place is bound to be heavily guarded."

Omar Hijazi looked up from the virtual reality computer game he was playing. "As I said before, we should just go in and shoot them all."

Max rolled his eyes. "There are only three of us. We wouldn't even get inside the building, let alone any further than that. And getting the sort of weapons we'd need to complete the job would be difficult to organise."

A support team in The Republic of North Africa had been set up to supply them with any equipment they requested for the mission. Their handlers dealt with a list of local suppliers who arranged delivery and asked no questions about the intended purpose of the items they provided.

"Yes," Mo agreed. "And they use dogs. Look." He flicked his wrist and brought up a picture of the security fence surrounding the facility. In the photograph a man stood beside the meshed barrier, leading a huge black and tan dog. "The fencing is probably also electrified," he added.

Omar shook his head. "The British police do not carry guns. They will have no defence if we shoot them."

"I wouldn't be so sure," Max replied. "They won't be using ordinary policemen to guard somewhere like that. I'm not ready to sacrifice my life for this."

"That is where we are different. I would gladly die if I could take those traitors with me."

"I want them dead as much as you, but there has to be a better way. There are some important people on site, so they're bound to have some fairly serious protection. This requires a more subtle approach. We need to prepare properly."

"Okay," Omar said, returning to his game. "You are the boss. I am sure you know best."

"Before we proceed, we must confirm who's in there."

Mo flicked the picture off the screen. "Leave it with me. I am already on it."

"What about those microbots you brought with you? Can't you get one of those past the fence?"

"Perhaps, but I think they will have radio detection and EM blocking," Mo replied.

The tiny robots carried a camera and could be remotely controlled, but if electromagnetic interference blocked the signal to control them, as seemed likely, they were useless. As an added downside, if the guards discovered one of the machines within the grounds, that would raise the alert level, and the operation would become much more difficult.

"We've already set up long-range surveillance," Max said, referring to the telescope upstairs, targeted at the entrance. "Can't we use that?"

"The glass on the building is reflective. This is common to stop industrial espionage, so it is not possible to see inside. But if they come outside..."

"You're telling me there's no easy way to tell who's there, then?"

"Yes." Mo focused his attention back on the computer. After a few seconds, he turned around again. "Did you not say your father worked at Ilithyia?" he asked.

"Yeah, but that was four or five years ago. The company has changed ownership since then."

"But maybe the systems are the same?"

"What are you getting at, Mo?"

"I am thinking perhaps if you know your father's password, we can break into their computers."

"Unfortunately, I've no idea what it might've been."

"Oh, well. It was just a suggestion."

Max tapped his teeth. "Actually, now you mention it, my dad was useless at remembering details. He always wrote things like passwords down. He used to keep them in a notebook he kept locked in his desk drawer."

"If I could see that, I might be able to use the information to get inside their systems."

"Wouldn't the new owners just delete his account?"

"Yes, that is likely, but it is worth a try." Mo leant closer. "Do you know where this book is?"

"Yeah, I may have an idea. As long as my mother hasn't thrown it away, it's probably still at her house."

"Can you get it?"

The motors in Max's arm whined as he repeatedly clenched and unclenched the fingers of his artificial hand. "I haven't been in contact with her for many years. Let's just say we didn't part on the best of terms. She stole my father's inheritance from me. I've been meaning to pay her a visit for a while."

"Is there not a risk she will tell the British authorities she has seen you?"

Max's face took on a thoughtful expression. "No, I don't think so. She won't say a word."

Sunday 5th April 2037

Ilithyia Biotechnology, Northstowe

Rosalind Baxter read the label on the door: BioNEMS. The fact she had no idea what the letters stood for summed up her lack of knowledge when it came to nanomachines. She had arranged a two-hour meeting with the French leader of the team, Armand Allard, to rectify the situation.

She held her card to the reader. A red light glowed for a moment, then turned off. Clearly, they didn't trust her enough to permit access to the laboratory. She raised her hand and knocked.

A guard in the ubiquitous pale-blue uniform strolled down the corridor in her direction, glaring at her suspiciously. When he was still a few paces away, the door swung open.

"Ah, there you are," the rotund Frenchman said. "Please come in."

Rosalind followed him into a room fifteen metres long by ten wide. When she had been the CEO of the company, this was one of the operating theatres. Now computer workstations had replaced the surgical tables. Four people sat in front of the screens. None of them looked up at her entry.

"This isn't what I was expecting," Rosalind said.

"No," Allard replied, "but this is the future of medical research. We use nanomachines to do the work once performed by drugs. But somebody has to tell these machines what functions to perform. We do this using computers."

"Surely, you must still carry out tests and experiments."

"Yes, of course. We have small-scale production capabilities here. That happens in there." He pointed towards the room where the surgeons had once scrubbed up before an operation. "The researchers only go in when they want to run an experiment. We take precautions to ensure none of our creations can escape."

"Pardon my ignorance, but what do the letters on the door outside stand for?"

"You mean BioNEMS? Bio-nanoelectromechanical systems. Shall we sit down?"

Rosalind followed Allard to an unoccupied workstation. He grabbed an empty chair and pulled it up alongside the one already there. Both sat.

"Now," the Frenchman said, "what would you like to know?"

"I guess, the first thing to discuss is how you think these nanomachines could destroy the virus."

"Okay. Put simply, we can program them to latch onto particular molecular sequences. They have the means to travel through the body, but we must tell them when they are in the right place. There are several ways to do this, but the two principal methods are magnetic fields and light."

"So," Rosalind said, "if I understand you correctly, you can design them to home in on and attack a specific pattern of molecules."

"Yes, but they can also be used to build. For example, one area of research for this technology is the reconstruction of severed nerves, such as those that occur in spinal cord injuries. However, this is not the focus of our work here."

"How do you program them?" Rosalind asked.

Allard spent the next hour taking her through the process of design and manufacture. The subject changed to the application of the technology for another thirty minutes. When he had finished, he turned to Rosalind. "Well, what do you think?"

She leant back and steepled her fingers. "If everything you've told me is right, I agree this could be the future of medicine. The biggest problem will be in convincing the public and scientific community that it's safe."

"I know this. It is so frustrating. I blame Eric Drexler."

"Who?"

"Many regard him as one of the main pioneers of nanotechnology. He wrote a book called the Engines of Creation in the nineteen-eighties. Over fifty years have passed since then, but still, people talk about grey goo. I have already told you all the precautions we take to prevent such a scenario from happening.

"I worry that the ignorant and the uneducated will always hold this technology back. The press love to sell fear, and it is a good theme for science fiction writers. Scientists have the capability to manufacture biological organisms today that are far more dangerous than anything I can create with my machines. In fact, the Orestes virus itself was artificially created."

Rosalind stiffened. "It was an accident."

Allard raised his hands apologetically. "I am sorry. I was not trying to say..."

"Let's move on. I'd rather not talk about it. An experiment went badly wrong, that's all."

"Fine. Do you have any ideas about how we can apply nanomachines to this question?"

Rosalind ran her fingers through her hair. She described the techniques they had used to prevent the activation of the virus. "The big problem," she added after finishing her explanation, "is that the approach I've just gone through doesn't address the underlying latent infection. Every living person already has this viral material inside their cells."

"I agree. We need to target both the lytic and the latent phases."

"Ideally, yes."

"And how do you propose we do that?"

"Well," Rosalind replied, "that's the billion-dollar question. Let me have a think about it. I have a meeting with one of the other teams now."

Allard rose from his chair and shook her hand. "That was a very interesting discussion. I look forward to working with you."

"The same here. I'm sure this technology will help us find a solution. That is, if it doesn't turn everybody into grey goo first."

The slightest hint of a humourless smile persisted on the French scientist's face as Rosalind left the room.

Sunday 6th April 2037
23 Daffodil Drive, Northstowe

Max Perrin pushed through the narrow gate and approached the house he had lived in for the first sixteen years of his life. He knelt and picked up a rock from the ornamental feature to the left of the front door. He turned it over and pressed with his thumb. The hidden lid sprung open. Some things never changed. After all this time, his mother still kept a spare key in the same place.

He removed the key from its hiding spot and slid it into the door lock. With a final surreptitious glance behind, he let himself in. Where was she? Her car occupied its normal position in front of the double garage, so the chances were she was somewhere inside. He stood still and held his breath, listening for a clue to her whereabouts.

The faint sound of voices carried from the living room. He crept down the hall. It seemed she had splashed out on a new carpet. The expensive weave in a shade of dark-green muffled his footsteps. He stopped and placed his ear against the door. A sudden burst of clapping emanated from the other side: a daytime chat show.

"What do you want?"

Max spun around at his mother's tense voice. The blade of a large kitchen knife glinted in her hand.

Her mouth dropped open in shock as recognition dawned. "Max?"

"Hello, Mum."

She placed the makeshift weapon on the hall table. "What are you doing here? I thought you'd disappeared off the face of the planet. Where have you been all this time?"

"That's a lot of questions," Max said. "I've been abroad. Shall we go through and sit down?"

As he reached for the doorknob, her gaze settled on his arm. "Did something happen to—"

"Yes, I lost it... in an accident. But they've done a good job with this prosthetic, don't you agree?"

Max stepped through the doorway into the lounge. More new carpets. His mother bustled in after him, snatched up the remote control and switched off the television. He studied her more carefully in the light streaming through the windows from the tidily kept garden. Her hair had turned totally grey, and her waistline had filled out a little. She wore a loose-fitting pair of cream trousers and a chequered shirt. She lowered herself into an armchair.

"Why didn't you ring the doorbell?" she asked.

Max sat on the sofa, perching on the edge. "I wanted to surprise you."

"Well, you certainly did that. I thought you were a burglar. You're lucky I didn't stab you."

"You really shouldn't leave the key in the fake rock."

"To be honest, I'd totally forgotten about it. So, you say you've been abroad? Where?"

"It doesn't matter."

"What was this accident?"

Max shook his head but remained silent.

"The police came here asking about you."

Max frowned. "When did this happen? What did they want?"

"It must have been nine months ago, maybe a year. They just asked me whether I knew where you were. I told them I had no idea. Do you know what that was about?"

"Yes."

Max's mother waited for him to expand on his answer. When he didn't, she continued. "So, what've you been up to for the last four years? An email or a phone call to tell me you were okay would've been nice."

"I was working because you wouldn't give me the money Dad left me in his will."

"It was for your own good. You were too young to have that sort of cash. I'm sure I can let you have some now if you need it."

"It's too late for that," Max said. "Did you keep Dad's things?"

"I gave away most of his clothes. I didn't think they were really your style."

Max remained impassive at his mother's failed attempt at humour. "What about his desk?"

Her face clouded in confusion. "I got rid of the medical books in his study, but I've left everything else as it was."

"So, you haven't been through the drawers?"

"No. Why are you asking?"

"I need a notebook Dad kept in the top drawer. Did you know, the day he died he called me and told me to pack a bag. We were going to leave together. This was before that bitch, Rosalind Baxter, killed him."

His mother lifted a hand to her mouth. "What are you talking about?"

144

"You thought he was the victim of a freak accident at work. They spun you some story about how he was holding a pen when an explosion sent it flying into his brain. But that was all a lie. Baxter stabbed him in the eye."

"Max, why would you say such a thing? I realise it affected you badly at the time, but—"

"You don't know the half of it. They made me sign the Official Secrets Act. They threatened to send me to prison if I ever spoke about what really happened. The Prime Minister himself was in on it."

"I don't believe you."

Max's face flushed. "For Christ's sake, listen to me, you stupid cow. Dad wasn't the man you thought he was. He was a mass murderer. Between them, Rosalind Baxter and my father created the Orestes virus. He's no longer with us, but it doesn't change the facts."

"I was married to him for over twenty years. He may have spent all his time at that damned company, neglecting his family, but I know what he was capable of, and he could never kill anybody."

"Well, you're wrong on that count. Unlike you, I was there. He was about to confess when she rammed a pen into his eye to prevent him from saying more. But I got my revenge on her. I broke into her house and slipped a mind control drug into her drink. Then I forced her to do the same thing to herself. I even used one of Dad's old pens. I should've stayed to watch until the end because somehow she regained enough willpower to stop."

"What happened to you, Max? What's made you like this? Your father didn't create the virus; he died in a terrible accident. If he was responsible, why would they allow us to keep the money when they sold the company?"

"Do I really have to explain? Rosalind Baxter pressured them into a deal—she agreed to complete development of the drug if they kept it all quiet and let her go. She also had to give up ninety percent of her stock. They could hardly hang on to Dad's shares without telling you why. You received all that cash because the woman who killed my father blackmailed the Prime Minister of this country into a pardon for her crimes."

"I'm sorry. I don't believe any of this. You need help, Max."

"That's why I've come back."

His mother shot him a puzzled look before continuing. "You were always a difficult child. Nothing made you happy. You never smiled as a baby. Just a few weeks after you were born, your father had to work on an urgent problem at the company and didn't return home for a few days. You cried day and night. You nearly drove me mad. The doctors examined you but couldn't find anything physically wrong with you.

"You became worse as you got older. They banned you from kindergarten for continually biting the other children. You almost killed another boy in primary school. The child psychologist told us afterwards that you lacked empathy. Your father thought having a pet might help. The gerbil lasted less than a week. I can still remember the blood coming out of its mouth. You crushed it to death in your hand because it nipped you.

"We spent thousands on counselling. They warned us you might suffer from mental health issues later in life. Things got better when you went to Oakington Manor. We thought we'd seen the back of your problems, but now this. I don't know where you've been for the last few years, whether you've been taking drugs or something, but it's clearly caused some sort of—"

"Stop." The quiet tone of Max's voice was more chilling than if he had shouted. "I didn't come here to listen to you list my faults. Do you still use CommsHub?"

"CommsHub? Why on earth are you asking about that?"

Max stood. "Just answer the question."

"Yes. I post the occasional status update."

"Can you log in?"

"I... I don't understand."

Max turned and spotted the tablet computer on the coffee table. He strode across, picked it up and handed it to his mother in silence. She stared at him for a moment, then held it up to her face as the iris scanner did its work. "There."

The familiar logo filled the 3D screen. Max flicked his finger and scrolled through her recent posts.

"What're you doing? You're frightening me."

Max tapped at the keyboard floating above the display. A few moments later, he clicked the off button. "Thanks." He tossed the device onto the sofa.

"What did you just type?" she asked.

"Oh, I posted an update to your account, saying you were planning to go away for a few weeks and that you wouldn't be able to log in."

"But I'm not going anywhere."

"I know."

"Um... how long are you staying?" His mother's voice trembled with fear.

"I'll be leaving shortly. But it's time to say goodbye now."

Max stood over her armchair and stared down at her. She leant forwards to rise, but he pushed her back. Then he clambered on top of her and wrapped his fingers around her throat. She tried to bat him away, but he avoided her feeble attempts with ease. The motors in his left arm whirred as he tightened his grip. Within moments, the light faded from her eyes, and her struggles stopped.

He pulled his mobile from his back pocket and dialled a number from contacts. "It's done. Make sure nobody sees you coming in."

The other team members were waiting at a kid's playground half a mile away. He turned and headed for the hall. Other than the mostly empty bookshelves, his father's study looked the same as when he had last been here four years earlier. He rounded the large wooden desk and lowered himself into the leather office chair. He tugged at the drawer on the right side. *Damn! Locked.*

A quick inspection of the room didn't reveal a matching key. The solution would require brute force. A pot containing pens and other items sat on one of the shelves. He got up and emptied it onto the desk's surface. A sturdy, brass letter opener spilt out along with the assorted writing implements. Max snatched it up and forced the shaft into the gap. A sharp jerk and the drawer shifted with a splintering sound.

Max rummaged inside and discovered a small leather-bound notebook hidden beneath various items of paperwork. He flipped the cover open. His father's neat handwriting filled the page with usernames and passwords.

He scooped up the pens and returned them to the pot except for one, which he placed in his shirt pocket. After a final check of the room, he closed the door behind him. Moments later, a light tapping sound came from the front door. He peered through the peephole and twisted the latch, stepping back to allow the other two members of the team to enter.

"She's in there," he said, pointing. "You'll find tools in the shed outside. Take her out through the patio doors, then bury her in the flower bed. It's a private garden so the neighbours won't see you."

"What are you doing, boss?" Mo asked.

"I just want one last look around this place," Max replied. He removed the pen and clicked the tip in and out a few times. "Thanks, Dad," he said, glancing down at the notebook.

Monday 7th April 2037
Ilithyia Biotechnology, Northstowe

Rosalind sat alone in the cafeteria. A burst of laughter came from the other side of the room. She stared across at the family of three. The boy she had raised—a man now—held a spoon to his son's lips in what appeared to be a game to get the child to eat. Judging by the state of Paul's face, more food had landed on the table than in his mouth. Surely, at four years old, he could feed himself.

She cast her mind back, trying to remember how Jason compared at the same age. The memories all blurred into one another. It had been a hectic period, and in those days, she spent most of her time in the office. The live-in nanny probably had a better recollection than she did.

As she dredged the recesses of her brain, she recalled an occasion—it must have been at a weekend—when they visited the seaside at Hunstanton. Jason was three, maybe four, and managed to get ice cream all over his face, his clothes and even in his hair. It took an entire pack of tissues to clean him up, and for weeks afterwards, the car seats remained sticky. Like father, like son.

Perhaps sensing the weight of her stare, Jason turned his head towards her. He flashed a brief smile. She raised a hand in return, then quickly lowered it again. Despite the promise to visit her after she had saved his son's life in Tripoli, he and his partner had only met up with her twice in the last two months. Like almost everybody else in this place, they kept her at arm's length, although the restrictions imposed on her movements didn't help when it came to arranging time together.

She twisted in her seat. Sure enough, the ever-present security guard occupied the next table over, half-watching her with a disinterested expression. Whenever she left the laboratories, somebody always accompanied her. What did they expect her to do? Make a bid for freedom? She would have to circumvent at least two checkpoints and numerous patrols to reach as far as the fence surrounding the compound. And what would she do then? Anybody who hadn't been living under a stone for the past year would recognise her immediately.

This was the best she could hope for from now on. The conditions of her confinement were massively better than the cell at Bronzefield Women's Prison, but nonetheless, she remained an inmate. At the end of every workday after eating her evening meal, one of the security team escorted her back to her former office. The other residents had free access to the on-site facilities, but she had no such opportunities. She spent more time between the four walls of her room than anywhere else.

The babble of voices dragged her from her thoughts. A group of scientists entered the canteen, the tall figure of Rachel Miller towering over the others. The French tones of Armand Allard rose above the rest as he shared a joke with Martin Hendrick. Christine Harris glanced across at Rosalind, then quickly looked away. The senior members of the leadership team queued at the serving hatch. When Naeem Kubar spotted her, he waved. A few moments later, he pulled up a chair on the opposite side of the table, a huge grin on his face.

"Hello, Rosalind. How are you?"

"Fine, Naeem. And you?"

"Good. Good. That was a very interesting meeting. I thought you would have attended."

"Nobody invited me," Rosalind replied in a monotone voice.

The doctor's cheerful demeanour lost some of its shine. "Oh, I am sorry. I did not know."

The majority of the scientists treated Rosalind with suspicion and shunned her company. Meetings often took place without her receiving an invitation, despite her official position as a cross-functional coordinator.

By contrast, Martin Hendrick had seemingly integrated into his role with little problem. He spent much of his time with Armand Allard and his microscopic machines but also mingled with the other researchers. Whenever she asked to become more involved, the French professor and his team found a convenient excuse to deny her request.

Dr Kubar was one of the few who went out of his way to keep her in the loop.

"What did you talk about?" Rosalind said.

"The nanotechnology research is going extremely well. They are making excellent progress."

Rosalind's interest perked up. "Yeah, it's got real potential to make a difference. They've developed an exciting technology if they can work out how to apply it to this problem."

"That is true. It is a shame the others waste time at meetings with Professor Allard. It is like a game. Whenever they mention grey goo, he always responds. They think it is a big joke when he becomes excited on this matter."

Rosalind stifled a smile. She had observed that the other team leaders loved to wind up the Frenchman. "Yes, I've noticed he's a bit sensitive about the whole subject, isn't he? So, what's new?"

Kubar tore off a piece of bread and popped it in his mouth. He took a sip of water before replying. "Dr Hendrick works most of the time with the nanotechnology group. He has presented some useful ideas on how to target the virus. They have set him up with a workstation in their laboratory."

"Well, he's certainly an expert in virology and a very gifted scientist. If anybody can cross the divide between the two disciplines, it's him."

"I had not heard of him before coming here. Did you know him in the past?"

Rosalind hesitated a moment before replying. "Yes, we worked together about twenty years ago."

"It is strange. He has not talked about this."

"No."

Kubar waited for her to say more. When it became clear she had nothing to add, he continued. "I will try to make sure they invite you to more meetings. We collaborated well before, and I know you have much to contribute. They should not waste your talents. I will send you the reports they presented at today's session."

"Thanks, I appreciate it." The security team had severely restricted Rosalind's online access. They prevented all outgoing links, including ones from the entertainment system in her room. With little else to occupy her time, she spent long hours reading through the technical papers written by the on-site scientists. If she wanted to read an external paper, she had to ask one of the other researchers to send her a copy. Plenty of good ideas occurred to her, if only somebody would listen.

Kubar's attention returned to the food on his plate, and the pair ate in silence. When he finished, he pushed the chair back and stood. "Well, it was nice to talk to you, Rosalind. Good evening."

"Yeah, you too."

She turned and stared at the security guard. He made a point of studying the face of his watch. When she left the canteen, he would accompany her to her room, where she would remain until morning.

Was this her future, spending her remaining years as a prisoner, if not here, then behind bars, but constantly under somebody else's control? Even if they allowed her to go free, she would always be looking over her shoulder. What was there to look forwards to?

For the first time in her life, she questioned whether she had made the right choices.

Wednesday 8th April 2037
27 Boxworth Road, Northstowe

Mo flung himself back in his chair. "Yes!" he yelled.

Max Perrin peered over his fellow conspirator's shoulder. "What is it?" he asked. "Have you found a way in?"

The North African hacker's fingers twitched and jerked above the surface of the desk. The focused ultrasonic waves generated by the advanced haptic technology created the sensation of tapping physical keys, but only he could see the keyboard floating in mid-air.

Mo stopped typing and twisted around, a wide grin on his face. "There is some good news. I have just received confirmation that Jason Floyd, Antimone Lessing and their son are staying at the Ilithyia building."

"Excellent. So, they're all together. That makes life—or perhaps I should say death—easier. What about gaining access?"

"Nothing so far. The systems where they keep the medical research all seem very secure."

"So, we wasted our time getting the book from my mother's house?"

Mo's grin faded. "It is too soon to say. I still have much to try."

"All right. Well, don't give up."

The diminutive figure refocused his attention on the computer. He picked up the notebook that had once belonged to Max's father and turned the page.

Omar looked up from the sofa, where he was playing a shooting game on a handheld console. "Is it time for guns yet?"

"No, we're not quite at that stage," Max replied. "You just keep practicing." He flashed his team member a slight smile.

"Fine, but I would rather shoot real people."

Max headed out of the lounge and up the stairs. He opened the window, drew the curtains together and pressed the button to power up the telescope. He pulled up a wooden chair and squinted into the twin lenses of the eyepiece. A three-dimensional boot message hung before his eyes. He could have used any screen in the house to view the images and orientate the instrument, but he preferred the immediacy of using the built-in display. A picture of the Ilithyia car park filled his vision. He tapped the control box and adjusted the direction until the fence surrounding the building came into focus. The image was crystal clear despite the two-mile range to the target. As he zoomed in, he discovered he could read the letters on the manufacturer's sign affixed to the barrier.

He widened the viewing angle and pressed a button to select the identification mode. After a few seconds, a thin red line appeared around the outline of a man and the large dog who patrolled beside him. He panned across the area in front of the building. Another guard rounded the corner, highlighted by the instrument's target acquisition system in the same way.

Once again, Max narrowed the field of view, focusing on the man's face. The guard's mouth moved as he called out a greeting to his colleague. The sharpness of the images made it seem as if the men were standing just a few feet away. Despite the distance, the advanced video technology allowed an observer to read the speaker's lips. Max's jaw muscles tightened in frustration; he knew the approximate location of the targets, but there was no way to get to them. Everything depended on the hacker.

As if responding to his thoughts, Mo's excited voice called out from downstairs. "Come. Come quick."

Max rose and hurried down the stairs. He arrived in the lounge to discover Mo pointing at the screen. Omar stood behind him. They exchanged a few words in their native Arabic. When the muscular soldier spotted Max's approach, he stepped back. "I do not understand any of this."

Max drew up a chair and settled beside Mo. "What've you got?"

"I have a way in."

"So, you can get into their systems?"

"Um, no. Not all of them. Only one. As I said earlier, the areas where they store research data and other important information are well secured."

"Okay, so what can you access?"

"It is the system that controls building maintenance. There is a single admin user. They must log into this account for all tasks. The software is at least fifteen years old. It is not tied to their directory services."

"And how does that help us?" Max asked.

Mo hesitated a moment before replying. "We can control things like the heating."

"Is that it?"

"Perhaps I could access the other systems from there."

"Won't that raise alarms or something?"

Mo bobbed his head in agreement like a small bird pecking a worm. "Yes, that may happen."

"So, you're saying you have the ability to adjust the temperature, and that's about it."

"I must do more work to see what is possible."

"What if you made it too hot for them?" Omar said from his position on the sofa.

Max let out a sigh of frustration. "What difference would that make? It's not as if... Wait a minute. If we get the heating controller to pump out so much heat that it becomes too uncomfortable in the building, they'll have to come outside."

"Yes, and then we shoot them."

"Actually, for once, that's not a bad idea."

Omar blinked in surprise at Max's response. "Really?"

"See what else you can discover about this system, Mo. And be careful. We don't want to trigger any alarms."

The North African hacker turned back to the computer.

Max paced across the carpet, deep in thought. A moment later, he stopped. "You mentioned the software is around fifteen years old. I find it hard to believe no parts have worn out in all that time."

"I do not know," Mo replied. "Why do you ask?"

"What if we make it appear like something has failed, then disguise ourselves as the maintenance team that's come to fix it?"

"Let me check the settings," Mo said. Once again, his fingers whirled over an invisible keyboard. Max resumed his pacing while the hacker worked.

Two minutes later, Mo twisted around, a satisfied grin on his face. "Yes, it is possible to set the temperatures inside the building remotely."

"So, you can make it look like there's a problem?"

"I think so."

"Won't that leave a trail behind?"

Mo shook his head. "It is easy to delete the logs, but if I do this, they can tell. Maybe I change the password. If I do that, they cannot see what is happening. They will probably call the maintenance company. The contact details are stored on the system."

"And after that, we pretend to be the engineers coming to fix the problem," Max said excitedly.

"But how do we stop them from sending their own people?"

"Ring them back immediately afterwards and tell them it's a false alarm. This might work."

Omar rose from the sofa. "Good. I am tired of waiting. But please explain the plan again."

Max ran his fingers through his hair. "Okay. Mo goes into the controller and adjusts the temperature settings inside the building to make it uncomfortably hot—or cold for that matter. At the same time, he changes any passwords on the control system so nobody else can access it. Somebody at Ilithyia will contact the maintenance company to ask them to fix the issue.

We know who the firm is, so we wait a bit, then place another call, pretending to be from Ilithyia, and cancel the job. We turn up dressed as the repair engineers, and they let us in."

"Then we shoot the targets?" Omar asked hopefully.

"We have to find out where they are in the building, but yes. Quietly if possible. I, for one, don't want to get caught. We'll also need uniforms, identity cards and a vehicle."

"I can print the identity cards," Mo said. "That is easy."

"We could steal a van and the uniforms," Omar added.

"Actually, I'm not sure that's such a good idea," Max replied. "We can't afford to raise any suspicions ahead of time. It's better if we make replicas. I suspect they'll have scanners to detect explosives and hidden weapons, so we'll also have to find a way to conceal anything we bring in with us. I'll contact our handlers and get them to put together everything we need."

The room buzzed with renewed enthusiasm.

Max draped an arm around the shoulders of his two colleagues. "Well done, guys. I think this'll work."

Friday 10th April 2037
Ilithyia Biotechnology, Northstowe

Martin Hendrick scrolled through the scientific paper with a flick of his finger. The more he read on the subject, the more convinced he became that nanotechnology was the way forward for medicine. Fusing together the worlds of computing and biochemistry, the possibilities were endless.

He glanced at his watch: just after eight-fifteen. His stomach rumbled. Maybe he should grab a bite to eat. The others had left ninety minutes earlier, so he was alone in the laboratory. He stood and stretched out his arms, working out the kinks from a long day staring at a computer screen.

"You are here late, I see," a voice said behind him.

He whirled around to discover Professor Allard standing by the door with a slight smile on his face.

"Yes, I was just thinking about heading to the canteen. I might come back later... if that's all right with you."

"Of course. I wish the rest of my team demonstrated the same levels of enthusiasm. So, what do you think of our little machines?"

Hendrick sat again. "They show a great deal of potential. While you're here, do you mind if I ask a few questions?"

"Be my guest," Allard replied, pulling up a seat.

"I understand what the technology is capable of, but not how you go about programming them."

"Well, let me explain. Each nanomachine has a set of instructions. We create those instructions with a computer. It is not like a microprocessor, which interprets code to decide what to do next. Once we have manufactured these devices, their function cannot be changed. It is fixed. The software compiles our designs into a format the manufacturing machines understand."

"I've had a play with the models generated by your group. We've had a few discussions about how to adapt the nanomachines to target the virus."

"Yes, I am told your input has been extremely useful."

"Thanks. If possible, I'd like to learn more about the programming side."

Allard patted Hendrick on the arm. "I will ask one of my team to show you."

"How do you design in the safety features?"

Allard's smile vanished. His shoulders tensed. "I hope you are not going to mention grey goo."

"No... It's not that. I just want to understand how the functions are built in."

The professor relaxed. "I am sorry if I seem overly sensitive. Whenever I discuss the technology, there is always someone who mentions ecophagy. It drives me mad. There is so much potential, but everybody only sees the negatives. I cannot remember the last time I spoke at a conference and somebody did not ask me about this. The audience think they are so clever, as if we have never even considered the dangers. But to answer your question, we created a standard platform on which we build the functions we require. This is common to all our designs."

"So, you can't edit this core?"

"No, and nor would we wish to. It is what we term a library component. Technically, it is possible to change the base model, but we would never do this. Why do you ask?"

"I was just curious. So, how do you manufacture the machines?"

"As I have already said, the compiler translates the instructions to a format understood by the manufacturing units. These use a combination of lithography and what we call molecular tweezers to manipulate individual atoms. In the same way that software engineers do not need to know how computers are manufactured to create code, most of my group have little knowledge of this side of the process and work on the application of these nanomachines rather than the production."

"Fascinating. I wonder if it would be possible for me to try out some of my own ideas."

"Of course," Allard replied. "But you already have access to all the tools for simulation."

"Yes, thanks for that. As I mentioned earlier, I've been having a play with the simulators, and I'm really impressed. But I was thinking about trialling something on some cell cultures."

"I will arrange for somebody to have a discussion with you about your suggestions. I am sure we can manufacture some samples for you."

"Actually, I'd prefer to operate alone."

"Hmm," the professor said. "We are not here to take credit or score points. We have come together to cooperate. What belongs to one belongs to all."

Hendrick nodded in agreement. "Yes, I understand that. It's just... well, I suppose my brain works slightly differently to other peoples'. If I have to stop to explain what I'm doing to somebody else, I find the thought often fades away. I guess you could say I'm easily distracted. I'm at my most productive when I'm in the groove."

Allard pondered the request for a moment. "Fine. I will allow you to do this, but I expect a weekly report on your progress. And any findings belong to the entire team. We need Christine's approval. If she is happy, I will set up the required privileges to access the manufacturing process. I trust you to be careful and adhere to all safety guidelines."

"What's different about the precautions for nanomachines?"

Allard's lips compressed into a thin smile. "Must I really go over this again? The other teams do not have anything like this level of scrutiny, even though this terrible disease came out of a laboratory."

"Oh, I see. No problem. You don't need to worry about that."

"May I ask you a question now?"

"Feel free," Hendrick replied.

"Where did you work before this? I thought I knew everybody in this business, but I am sorry to say I had not heard of you."

"I spent many years in Norway at the Oslo Medical Research Centre. Our group didn't publish a lot of papers. My particular area of study was cross-species viral transmission. The Orestes virus has had a terrible impact on human reproduction, but if it ever jumped to other species, the results would be catastrophic. Imagine a world where all creatures died when they gave birth. The majority would become extinct within a generation or two. Humans consume vast quantities of meat and dairy. If farm animals became susceptible to this virus, millions across the planet would starve."

"Frightening indeed," Allard said. "This is clearly a vitally important area of study, so why did you choose to come here?"

"I guess I wanted a change of scenery. I also enjoy a challenge. When I heard about this project, I jumped at the chance. Luckily, they accepted me."

"Well, from my point of view, you are a very valuable addition. I look forward to hearing more of your ideas."

"Thank you," Hendrick replied. "I am sure we'll achieve our goals together."

Monday 13th April 2037
Ilithyia Biotechnology, Northstowe

Max Perrin tried on the blue coveralls. The fit was a little tight across the shoulders, but they would do the job. He sat on the bed and slipped his feet into the safety shoes. Just the right size. He strolled to the adjacent bedroom, pushing open the door without knocking.

Mo and Omar stood together, buttoning up the front of their identical overalls.

Max cast a critical eye over the replicated uniforms. "Are they okay?"

"Good," Omar replied. "Now we look like British workmen. You have explained how we get into the building. But what happens after?"

"We repair the heating system," Max said. "By that, I mean we restore the original settings."

Mo frowned in puzzlement. "I do not understand. We create a problem then fix it?"

"We have at least four targets: Baxter, Kubar, the wheelchair girl and her partner. I want all of them. We'll only get the one chance once we show our hand, so we have to prepare properly. We don't know where they are inside the building, which means we have to track them down before anything else. Think of it as a scouting mission."

"So, we find out their location, then we complete the operation?"

"Exactly. During the first visit, we'll be unarmed. I want to get a good look at their security systems before we make a move. After that, we return with weapons and finish the job. If everything's ready at this end, Mo, access the system and set the temperature really high. Change the password, so they can't adjust it back. When we see people coming outside, we can safely assume somebody at Ilithyia has placed the call. That's when I contact the maintenance company. I tell them a junior trainee accidentally modified the settings and cancel the callout. At the same time, we jump in the van, turn up at the building, then restore everything to how it was. They'll think we fixed it."

"I will get on it right away," Mo said, hurrying out of the room.

"Finally, we are doing something," Omar added. "I am tired of all this waiting."

Max moved across to where the telescope poked out between the curtains and lowered himself into the chair. He could have watched from any computer screen in the house, but somehow it gave him a sense of greater involvement to observe the Ilithyia building through the control unit.

A few moments later, Mo ascended the stairs. "It is done."

"Make sure you put the ID badge around your neck. We're leaving as soon as people start coming out."

Max stared at the image of the chrome and glass structure. Several minutes passed with no change. The only signs of movement behind the fence came from the routine patrols of guards and their canine companions. Suddenly, a group of three white-coated scientists emerged through the rotating door. The trickle turned into a surge as more people hurried through the exit and gathered in front of the building.

"That's it. Let's go," Max called. He grabbed his mobile and selected the number he had stored in the contacts. The ringing tone echoed in his ear.

After a few seconds, a woman's voice answered. "Beechwood Environmental Systems. Please state the nature of your call, and I'll put you through."

"Um, yes, this is Nick Butler at Ilithyia Biotechnology." He had checked the name of Ilithyia's site manager the previous night. "I'm just calling up to let you know the callout from our building was a mistake. One of our trainees was messing with the heating system and adjusted the settings by accident. Sorry for any inconvenience. If you need to contact me again for any reason, you can reach me on this number."

"No worries," the woman replied. "I'll make sure our maintenance team gets the message. Thanks for contacting Beechwood."

Max ended the call and strode towards the front door, where his companions waited. The group of three left the house and hurried down the quiet residential road. They had parked the van fifty metres away. The distinctive Beechwood logo of a green tree adorned the sides. Max jumped into the driver's seat and pressed the start button. The support team had disengaged the vehicle's navigation system before delivering it two days earlier. They had also tinkered with the wiring of the onboard transponder to make it appear like it had become accidentally disconnected.

Max swung the wheel and pulled out. The roads were quiet, and it took less than five minutes before they slowed at the gates to the Ilithyia site. A smattering of journalists waited outside on the pavement. The arrival of the van generated some initial excitement, but their interest soon waned when the sign on the side panel became apparent.

Two men emerged from a booth to the left of the barrier. One held a large black and tan Rottweiler on a tight leash. The other approached the driver's door. Max wound down the window.

"What are you doing here, gentlemen?" the guard asked, peering inside.

"We're from Beechwood Environmental Systems. We've just received an urgent callout," Max replied. "Apparently, the heating system is on the blink."

The man stepped back and held a phone to his ear. He spoke for a few seconds, then beckoned them forwards. "Fine, they're expecting you."

Max breathed a sigh of relief as he drove the vehicle beneath the raised barrier. Moments later, they drew up outside the building. He snatched the baseball cap off the dashboard and pulled it down low over his eyes. At the van's arrival, a muted cheer rose from the group of people milling about beside the entrance.

Keeping his head lowered, Max got out, moved to the back of the van and grabbed the toolbox. He handed it to Omar. "Here, you carry this."

The large North African accepted the heavy metal box in silence. The three men approached the rotating door and pushed through, accompanied by a smattering of applause. As soon as they stepped inside, a wave of heat washed over them.

"What did you set the temperature to?" Max whispered to Mo.

"Thirty-five degrees," the diminutive hacker replied.

"Maybe not so high next time. Remember we've got to work here for a while."

Sweat already beaded on Max's forehead. He strode to the barricade, where a stressed-looking guard waited.

Dark patches stained the underarms of the man's pale-blue uniform. "I'm certainly glad to see you guys," he said with a grin. "It's like a furnace in here."

"We'll sort out the problem as quickly as we can," Max replied.

"I need to put your toolbox through the scanners if you don't mind." The man reached out a hand and grabbed the handle of the metal case. He passed it to a colleague, who appeared equally flustered in the intense heat. "Please step through the gate."

Max stood back and beckoned his two men to go first. His eyes surveyed the foyer for cameras while he waited. As he stepped through the arch, a shrill beeping sound rang out.

The guard's friendly expression vanished in an instant. He lowered his hand to a beige plastic device clipped to his belt. "Please stand still with your arms outstretched."

From the corner of his eye, Max noticed Omar's shoulders tense. "That'll be my prosthetic arm," he said loudly, following the man's instructions. "I should have mentioned it earlier. I lost it a few years ago in an industrial accident."

The second man approached, carrying a portable scanning device approximately the same size as an empty toilet roll. He ran it over Max's body. The scanner emitted a loud beep as it passed across his left arm.

The two men relaxed. "Sorry about that," the first said. "There're a lot of important stuff going on here, so we can't be too careful. Here are your security passes. Please wear them at all times. I'll let you get to work."

"Where's the heating control system?" Max asked.

The guard frowned. "Don't you guys know where it is?"

Max offered the man an apologetic smile. "We've only recently started at the company," he said. "Our manager told us you'd show us where to go."

"Fine. I'll ask my colleague to take you. I hope you know what you're doing."

"Yeah, no problem. We've all done training on this type of system. It's just that none of us has been here before."

Moments later, the man who had used the portable scanner led them across the foyer. He raised the card hanging around his neck to a reader. A light on the wall changed from red to green, and the electronic lock clicked.

Before the guard's hand reached the handle, the door swung open. Three people waited in the doorway: a man, a woman and a young boy. The woman sat in a wheelchair with the child perched on her lap. The Lessing girl, Floyd and their brat.

Max looked away, averting his face. Had they recognised him?

The guard stepped back and gestured for the group to come through. The family moved past, showing no signs of recognition. Max's gaze followed them as they headed towards the barrier across the foyer. Just as they reached the checkpoint, the boy turned and peered over his mother's shoulder.

Max quickly raised his hand to the brim of his cap.

"Are you coming, then?" the guard asked.

Max jerked his head around, realising that the others were waiting for him. "Sorry," he said. "I was miles away. By the way, do our cards open the doors too?"

"Yeah," the man replied. "They'll let you in anywhere you need to go."

"What if we find there's a problem elsewhere?"

"Come back to reception, and I'll get somebody to escort you. Right, we're here. That's the control room. I'd really appreciate it if you could sort the issue out as quickly as you can. Everybody's melting, and they won't allow us security guys to leave the building."

"We'll do our best."

"The canteen's that way if you need any refreshments."

"Thanks."

Max pushed open the door. A light flickered on, illuminating a five-metre square area containing an old-fashioned flatscreen terminal and an assortment of other equipment scattered around the walls. Although slightly cooler than the corridor outside, oppressively warm air enveloped the three men as they entered.

"What now?" Mo asked.

"Before we do anything else," Max snapped, "you can start by lowering the bloody temperature."

Monday 13th April 2037
Ilithyia Biotechnology, Northstowe

A tap came from the corridor outside the room.

"That'll be Paul," Antimone said. "Would you mind letting him in, Jason?"

The young family had been staying at the Ilithyia building for a fortnight and had quickly settled into a routine, which for Paul comprised five hours of education per day at the on-site kindergarten.

During the first week, the scientists took blood samples from Antimone and Jason, but the reason for Antimone's survival four years earlier—her body contained both male and female DNA resulting from the fusing of two foetuses in her mother's womb—was already common knowledge. The sight of needles terrified their son, and he resisted every attempt to draw blood. As Andrew Jacobs had promised, the science team didn't press the issue.

"Pause TV," Jason said. The highlights of the football match on the large three-dimensional screen stopped in mid-action. He swung his legs off the bed and padded across the carpet in bare feet. He twisted the handle and pulled the door open.

"Look what I did, Daddy," his son said, proudly holding up a rectangle of paper splattered with several blobs of brightly coloured paint.

"That's very good. What is it?"

Paul giggled. "It's a dog, silly."

"Why don't you show it to mummy?" The four-year-old skipped past him. "Thanks for bringing him up here," he said, addressing the guard. Most days, somebody called the parents when it was time to collect their offspring, but if the security guards weren't overly busy, they sometimes accompanied the children back to their rooms.

The man smiled. "No problem. You're lucky. He's a cute kid. My wife and I are trying for one of our own."

"Well, um... good luck."

"I'll see you around then."

Paul was the eldest child in his class of five by nearly a year. The other pupils had parents who worked as part of the science or security teams. Every weekday morning, a local preschool schoolteacher came in to educate the children. Paul had become attached to the woman. She reminded Jason a little of the old photographs he had seen of his biological mother with her dark hair and heart-shaped face.

Earlier that day, the teacher had been forced to abandon her lessons when the heating system failed, causing the temperature inside the building to rocket. The security team contacted the parents, advising them to collect their children and evacuate the facility while the maintenance company fixed the problem. Within an hour, the energy-sapping heat dissipated sufficiently to allow Paul to return to his classroom.

Jason closed the door and followed his son back into the room. Paul perched on Antimone's lap, explaining the features of his artwork.

"And there's his collar. Look, he's got a big pink tongue."

"You're an excellent artist," Antimone said. "I'm really proud of you. We'll have to stick it up on the wall. So, what have you been doing at school today other than painting?"

Paul climbed off her legs and hopped onto his bed, his eyes lifting to the television screen. "I want to watch cartoons."

"Fine, but I'd like you to tell me about your day first."

Paul shook his head.

Jason lowered himself onto the mattress beside his son. "Come on, buddy. What else did you do in school?"

The boy turned to his father. "I had a hundred babies today," he said.

Jason flashed a grin at Antimone. "Really? I thought only girls could have babies."

"No, boys can too," Paul replied confidently.

"If you say so. Did you learn any other interesting things?"

"We watched a programme about penguins. I want to be a penguin when I grow up."

Jason stifled a laugh. "You'd look good in black and white, but penguins live at the North Pole, and it's really cold up there."

"I don't mind. I like it in the snow. Can I watch cartoons now?"

"All right. TV, show me a list of cartoon programmes suitable for a child of four."

They had configured the entertainment system so that it listened only to the adults' voices. The built-in software monitored the amount of screen time every day. If left to Paul's whims, the device would have been displaying a constant stream of children's material from dawn until dusk.

"I want Peppa Pig," Paul announced

"Just for a few minutes," Antimone said. The ancient cartoon was her son's favourite programme. She could remember watching the same thing as

164

a child, although in those days, the animated images had been flat instead of the more recent three-dimensional technology.

After two episodes, Antimone instructed the television to turn off.

"Another one," Paul said, jutting out his chin.

"If you're going to be like that, young man, you won't get to watch TV at all in future. Now, tell me what else happened in school today."

The four-year-old jiggled his leg. "It was very hot. We went outside."

"Yeah, I know. We came to collect you if you remember."

"I saw the bad man."

"The bad man?" Jason asked, putting down the book he had been reading. "Yes."

"Which bad man?"

"He was with us."

"What do you mean? Where?"

"In that nasty place."

Antimone and Jason exchanged a confused look.

She reached forwards and placed her hand on Paul's back. "Are you talking about Africa?"

Paul didn't answer. He jumped off the bed and moved to the window, where he stood, staring down at the well-kept gardens bordered by the metal fence.

They hadn't really discussed the events of the previous year with their son. A group from the Republic of North Africa had kidnapped the family of three, together with Rosalind Baxter, after setting off a series of bombs at the Olympic stadium in Glasgow. The terrorists, led by a general in the North African military, transported them to a hospital in Tripoli where a team of scientists studied their biology, in the hope of developing a cure for a mutation of the Orestes virus that was killing children.

General Shaladi soon found himself held prisoner with the other captives, along with his daughter, Aya. They only escaped when Rosalind Baxter got a message out to one of the general's former colleagues, who mounted a rescue operation. This was the first time Paul had mentioned anything relating to their abduction. The child psychologists had advised Jason and Antimone not to mention their experiences unless their son raised the topic.

"Do you mean the place we went on the boat, buddy?" Jason asked.

Paul nodded silently.

Antimone steered her wheelchair over, stopping alongside him. "You're not talking about Dr Kubar, are you? He was with us in Africa, but he's not a bad man. He helped us all to get home."

Paul placed his hands against the glass.

Jason rose from the bed and squatted down beside his son. "What did this bad man look like?"

165

Paul shrugged.

"What colour was he wearing?"

"Blue."

"What, like the guards?"

Paul shook his head again.

"You don't need to worry about any bad men," Jason said. "We're safe here."

He stood and shot a puzzled glance at Antimone. He stepped away from the window and waited for her to join him.

"Who do you think he's talking about?" he asked in a whisper.

"I've no idea," Antimone replied. "I can't see how anybody from North Africa could be over here apart from Dr Kubar, and Paul has seen him loads of times since we arrived."

"Maybe he just saw somebody who reminded him of a person we met over there."

"He's really into his stories at the moment. Remember he told us a few minutes ago that he had a hundred babies today."

Jason let out a laugh. "Yeah, there is that. It's probably nothing. Who knows how the mind of a four-year-old works?"

"I'm worried though. He's never said anything like this before. I know we're all praying that what happened over there hasn't affected him too badly, but what if it's a delayed reaction?"

Jason placed a hand on her shoulder. "Let's wait and see. If he mentions it again, we'll contact the child psychologists."

"I suppose."

A shiver ran through Antimone's body. Despite Jason's assurances, something didn't feel right.

"Okay," Jason said, clapping his hands. "Who's hungry?"

Tuesday 14th April 2037
Ilithyia Biotechnology, Northstowe

"Come on," Max Perrin said with a leer. "You know you want to go out with me, don't you, trike queen?" He held a gun. The unwavering barrel pointed at her chest.

Antimone reached down to the hand rings of her wheelchair and tried to move backwards. No matter how hard she pushed, the wheels refused to turn.

"Mummy, are you coming?"

She turned and stared at her son. He stood beside her and seemed to be oblivious to the danger.

"Run!" she screamed, but no sound came out.

Paul tugged at her elbow. "I want to go now, Mummy."

She attempted to position herself between her son's body and the gun, but once again, she couldn't shift the wheelchair. Perrin took another step closer. Smoke rose from his arm as his flesh puckered, turned black and dripped on the floor. He swung the pistol to point at Paul's head.

"No, please," she begged.

Her gaze focused on Perrin's finger as, in exaggerated slow motion, he squeezed the trigger.

"No!"

Antimone jerked awake, the cry still fading in her throat. Her heart hammered in her chest. The white T-shirt she wore for sleeping clung damply to her skin. She reached for the bedside light, wincing at the sudden increase in brightness. Beside her, Jason groaned and rolled over to face the other way. Using her elbows, she levered her body up from the mattress. Paul lay asleep in the adjacent single bed, his head and shoulders protruding from the covers. With a sigh of relief, she sank back into the pillow and tapped the base of the lamp.

"Thank God," she whispered into the darkness.

Nearly a year had passed since the events that triggered her recurring nightmare. Even after all this time, the memories of the blackening skin on Max Perrin's arm and the accompanying inhuman screams escaping from his throat were never far from her thoughts. After several late-night discussions with Jason, they had agreed she should arrange some sessions with a psychiatrist.

The man had been sympathetic, but she found herself unable to tell him what truly happened in the Tripoli hospital. How could she confess to killing a man by injecting him with concentrated sulphuric acid?

After diagnosing her with Post-Traumatic Stress Disorder, the doctor had taught her a range of techniques to manage her anxiety and help her relax. Despite his best efforts, the burden of maintaining her secret prevented her from gaining maximum benefit from the treatment. On several occasions she came close to confessing what she had done but always held back from revealing the full story.

She reached out an arm in the darkness and felt for the reassuring warmth of Jason's body. He stirred at her touch and rolled to face her.

"Is everything all right?" he asked, his voice heavy with sleep.

"Just a nightmare," she replied.

"Oh. First Paul this afternoon and now you."

"I keep seeing him." She didn't have to explain to whom she was referring.

"Do you think we should arrange more sessions with the shrink?"

Antimone held her breath for a moment before replying. "I'm not sure it'll help."

In the silence, the sheets rustled as Jason adjusted his position. "We both need to be doing something constructive with our time. I've offered to assist in the labs, but none of the scientists seem interested. I suspect it's related to my mother; nobody really trusts her. Dr Kubar would let me join him, but he doesn't have a team of his own. He suggested distance learning, so I'm thinking about starting an Open University degree. Have you thought about returning to education? It might take your mind off things."

The administrators at King's College in London, where he had been studying biochemistry before being abducted by the terrorists from The Republic of North African, had agreed to defer his course for a year, but without a security team to watch over him, it seemed unlikely he would be able to accept their offer.

"There's only one thing I want to do," Antimone said, "and you know what that is. I really miss my wheelchair racing."

"Why don't you ask Butler? He's bound to complain, but I'm sure he can spare some of his men to keep an eye on you at the athletics track for an hour or two. It would do you good to get out of here."

"You could come with me and practice your javelin throwing."

"What about Paul?"

"We could go while he's at his lessons."

Jason remained silent as he considered her suggestion. "All right then. Let's ask him. If he says yes, you should give John Marshall a call. I'm sure he'd be delighted to see you."

"That's not a bad idea. I might just do that."

Part Four: Activation

Wednesday 6th April 2016
Ilithyia Biotechnology, Cambridge Science Park
Twenty-one years ago

A week had gone by since Martin Hendrick first identified the woman they were detaining in the newly created space behind the storeroom. He hadn't spoken to anybody about his discovery.

He could hardly ask the CEO and Chief Scientist why they had taken the drastic move to imprison an employee. How would that conversation go? If he contacted the police, the investigation was bound to focus on the reasons for her incarceration. When they questioned her, Eileen Floyd was sure to reveal the reason for her abduction.

His work would play a pivotal role in the subsequent inquiry just as his project was nearing completion. What's more, he would certainly lose his job when the company folded, as it was certain to do when the courts convicted the two co-owners of false imprisonment.

Hendrick quickly deduced what must have happened. He already knew about her complaint concerning the viral research he was performing. No doubt, Rosalind Baxter and Nigel Perrin had tried to talk her out of becoming a whistleblower. When she refused, they took the unthinkable step of taking her prisoner. Her husband, Daniel Floyd, was now in prison, serving a life sentence for her murder. Clearly, somebody had framed him, and there was only one person Hendrick could think of who might possess that particular skillset: the third partner in the conspiracy, Anders Grolby.

If the trio were prepared to go that far to protect the company, the primary unanswered question was why she remained alive. If they ever released her, she would quickly report them to the authorities. Something else had to be going on. He could think of no rational reason for allowing her to live.

Hendrick had spent several sleepless nights pondering what to do next. Whatever course he chose would have negative consequences. He would have to play this carefully. It seemed certain they would monitor her through CCTV. If he tried to establish communications with her, there was a good chance the three conspirators would learn of his actions. And that would place him firmly in their sights. There had to be a better way.

Finally, he had come up with a plan. It certainly contained elements of risk, but it had the potential to resolve all his problems. Now was the time to put the first phase into action. He sat at his workstation, his legs jiggling with tension.

Footsteps echoed down the corridor. At long last, somebody was coming. Hendrick glanced at his watch: 20:03. Rising to his feet, he waited for the person to pass, then inched open the door and spotted Dr Perrin's departing back as he headed to the storeroom. It seemed it was the Chief Scientist's turn to feed the prisoner that night.

The Belgian researcher returned to his seat. Five minutes passed until the sound of shoes scuffing on the floor resumed, travelling in the opposite direction. A knock from outside the laboratory. He hurried across the room and pulled the handle.

"It looks like you're the last one again tonight," Perrin said. "You're certainly putting in the hours. I found the preliminary research very interesting. I'm looking forward to seeing the results and reading the final report on this little project of yours."

"It's nearly ready," Hendrick replied. "Just a week or two more."

"Good. Would you mind locking up this evening?"

"No problem."

"Well, don't work too late."

"I'll probably only hang around for another half an hour. Goodnight, Nigel."

"Yeah, see you in the morning, Martin."

Hendrick waited until his boss reached the exit leading to the reception area, then returned to his workstation. Grabbing a pad of paper and a pen, he chewed the end as he thought about what to write. He scrunched up the first two attempts after a few words and stuffed them in his trouser pocket. He couldn't afford to leave clues lying around to be discovered later. The third version turned out more successful.

Somebody will unlock your room three nights from now one hour after they bring food. Make no attempt to open the door before then. You will find a key to the building in the first lab on the right. Under no circumstances tell anybody about my involvement. Do not let them see you reading this note. When you have read this, destroy it. Chew and swallow it. If this doesn't work, I will try again, but it is vital you do not mention that you received help.

Good luck,

A friend.

Hendrick scanned the words a second time. It wasn't perfect, but it would have to do. He folded the paper in half and placed it in his shirt pocket. In three days, it would be a Saturday. If they followed the same pattern as before, somebody would come to feed her around eight in the evening. By then, hopefully the building and the science park would be deserted.

Before proceeding with the plan, he needed to retrieve the key from Dr Perrin's office. He headed out of his laboratory towards the reception area. *Good.* The floor above lay shrouded in darkness. He climbed the stairs and flicked on the master switch. The lights flickered into life as he made his way down the corridor.

The door to the Chief Scientist's room stood open. He moved to the desk, opened the draw and retrieved the keys from the jar of paperclips. A sudden thought crossed his mind; what if Perrin started locking his office at night? Ideally, he would have preferred to get a replica set made, but the doctor might notice their absence. No, he had no option but to hope for the best and return the keys to their storage place after delivering the note.

He retraced his steps and headed back to the storeroom. By now, he knew which key to use. He let himself in and turned on the light. The familiar scratching sounds penetrated through the closed door on the far side. He hurried past the shelves stacked with chemicals and pushed his way into the cramped room beyond. The frantic scrabbling of startled animals set the bars of the cages ringing. As before, the stink of the rodents permeated the confined space. He approached the spyhole, placed his eye to the glass and peered inside.

Eileen Floyd lay on the bed, reading a paperback. She wore a white T-shirt and black leggings. Feeling like a peeping Tom, Hendrick studied the woman. Something seemed different about her. Maybe it was her casual attire or her unkempt hair. Perhaps sensing his eyes upon her, she lowered the book. That was when he noticed the rounded bump of her stomach. Christ, she was pregnant.

He stepped back. This changed everything. His mind spun as he considered the options. *No, the plan would still work.* He withdrew the note with trembling fingers. The key turned in the lock, and he opened the door a fraction. He crouched, slipping the folded paper in the narrow crack. Before she had time to react, he shut the door again. He rose and placed his eye against the peephole. Her forehead creased in a frown. She stared at the floor and swung her feet off the bed. Satisfied she had spotted his message, Hendrick backed away.

He retraced his route, turning off the light and locking the storeroom behind him. Two minutes later, he had returned the keys to the drawer in Nigel Perrin's office and stood beside the alarm panel by the entrance to the building, ready to arm the system.

There was no going back now. The wheels were in motion.

Saturday 9th April 2016
Ilithyia Biotechnology, Cambridge Science Park
Twenty-one years ago

Martin Hendrick glanced at his watch: 18:21. He had wedged the door to his laboratory open with a bin shortly after arriving that morning. Now, the distant sound of somebody entering the reception area echoed down the corridor. Whoever had just arrived was an hour and a half earlier than he had expected. He crossed the room and shoved the makeshift doorstop with his foot, allowing the gap to close.

He picked up a journal and flicked through the pages while he waited. After a few minutes, somebody hurried past his laboratory. A short while later, the person returned, coming in the opposite direction. A light tap broke the silence. Hendrick opened the door.

Nigel Perrin stood in the corridor. "I saw your car was still outside," he said. "I hope you're not working too hard. Is everything okay?"

"Yeah, fine, thanks. I'm just about to pack up for the evening. Actually, while you're here, I wonder if you could arrange for somebody to take a look at the light." He pointed to the fluorescent strip running along the ceiling. "It took ages to come on this morning. I think the starter must be on the way out."

"I'll try to remember, but remind me again on Monday."

"Right. I'll do that."

"Well, I thought I'd just finish off some paperwork," Perrin said. "I can lock up for a change tonight if you like."

Hendrick's stomach lurched. "No, it's fine. I don't mind doing it."

Perrin studied him curiously. "I'll be in my office. I'll let you know when I leave if you're still here."

"Likewise." Hendrick cursed inwardly. The clock was already ticking.

"Okay, catch you—"

The shrill tone of Perrin's mobile phone blared from his jacket pocket. He pulled it out and rolled his eyes. He stepped away and spoke in a low voice.

"Yes, darling. What is it?"

"... I'm sure it's nothing."

"... No, I can leave now.

"... Fine, I'll be home in a few minutes."

He turned back to the Belgian researcher and smiled apologetically. "Sorry. Change of plan. The baby won't stop crying, and my wife is worried. He kept us up most of last night as well. I've got to go. Is it okay if you lock up after all?"

A surge of relief flowed through Hendrick's body. "No problem."

"Thanks. Have a good weekend."

Hendrick blew out his cheeks. He still had much to do. He waited a moment before following Perrin's steps to the end of the corridor, where he remained, peering through the rectangle of glass into the reception area. A few seconds later, the Chief Scientist reappeared, emerging from the doorway to the upstairs offices. He hurried across the foyer and out into the car park, locking the outside door behind him.

Hendrick stayed where he was in case Perrin returned, then, deciding he had left it long enough, headed towards the stairs. He didn't bother to turn on the lights; the overcast evening sky, penetrating through the open doors, provided all the illumination he needed. When he reached Perrin's office, he opened the drawer and retrieved the keys. A quick glance at his watch confirmed twenty-five minutes had already passed since the woman had received her second and final meal of the day.

He jogged down the steps and along the corridor to the storeroom, where he let himself in. After unlocking the next door, he stood outside the woman's cell. He lowered his eye to the peephole and peered inside. Eileen Floyd paced across the narrow width of the room, the pre-packed sandwich and soft drink resting untouched on the bed.

Hendrick slid the key carefully into the lock. He twisted the head. Despite his attempts at stealth, the mechanism clicked. Cursing his clumsiness, he completed the revolution. For a second time, he studied her through the fish-eye lens. The woman stood still, staring back at him as if she could see right through the reinforced barrier. Would she follow his instructions and wait the full hour before attempting to leave?

After a few seconds, she sat on the bed and placed her face in her hands. Hendrick breathed a sigh of relief. He turned and retraced his footsteps through the storage room.

Saturday 9th April 2016
Ilithyia Biotechnology, Cambridge Science Park
Twenty-one years ago

E ileen Floyd took the three paces to cross the room. She spun about and returned to her starting point. She maintained a count in her head with every step. *Wait one hour*, the note had said. How was she supposed to do that without a watch? She had no idea of the time of day. She assumed it was sometime in the evening.

Two weeks earlier, Dr Perrin had brought her meal. Normally, he emptied the contents and used the empty bag to store the waste from the previous night. On this occasion, he was clearly in a hurry and simply deposited the thin plastic bag on the floor before beating a hasty retreat. Inside was not only the food but also a petrol station receipt. The slip of paper contained details of the amount paid together with the date, and more significantly, the time of the transaction—six twenty in the evening.

Forty-seven minutes. One second, two second. *This is ridiculous. What am I waiting for?* Surely, she had left it long enough. She stopped and glanced up at the camera, out of reach on the ceiling in the corner above the bed. *Is anybody watching? Is this some cruel trick?*

Eileen halted when she reached the wall and stood still. She inhaled deeply. Hiding the camera's view with her back, she extended a hand and pulled the handle gently towards her. It moved. Her mysterious helper had come through for her. With a final backward glance, she hauled the door open the rest of the way and darted through the doorway.

The stack of animal cages greeted her. She rushed past without a glance. Her heart sank at the sight of the closed door to her left. She approached and twisted the latch, expecting to find it locked. To her relief, the mechanism turned. The band of illumination coming from behind her cast long shadows on the shelves of the unlit storeroom. The only way out lay on the opposite wall. That was where her previous escape attempt had ended. She rushed across to the far side. Panic engulfed her as the wedge of light narrowed and disappeared altogether, plunging the room into darkness.

The inky blackness pressed in on her like a physical force. She could barely breathe. Her hands felt along the rough wall until she touched a large area of smooth plastic. She clawed desperately for the mechanism. Finally, her fingertips brushed against something cold and metallic. She twisted the knob and stumbled out.

In the dim twilight penetrating through the small window at the end of the corridor, she recognised her surroundings. Her old laboratory lay to the left. In the other direction was the exit to reception, but she would need the front door key to get out—or to shatter the glass. She recalled the words from the note; *You will find a key to the building in the first lab on the right.*

That had been Dr Hendrick's workspace. A stab of pain shot through her stomach. *No, please, not now.* She waited for the spasm to abate, then staggered the short distance to the next doorway, using her hand to support herself against the wall. She pushed inside and reached for the light switch. Nothing happened. Apart from the occasional abrupt click accompanying the flickering of the fluorescent tube, the room remained in near darkness. As she drew a ragged breath, a pungent chemical smell registered on her senses.

Her eyes picked out a waste bin by the open door. She wedged it in the gap and edged forwards. The further in she moved, the worse the stench became. Broken glass crunched beneath her feet. She almost tripped over the computer base unit lying on the floor. What the hell was going on? Somebody had trashed the place. But why? She ran her hands over the top of the work surface but came up empty. She cursed in frustration. Where was the damned key?

She would just have to find another way out of the building. Maybe she could call Daniel from reception. But no, she remembered Grolby boasting about how he had framed her husband. The ex-soldier wouldn't be quite so smug when she escaped, and they arrested him for her abduction. Perhaps she should phone the emergency services. Whatever option she chose, she couldn't afford to stay here.

Using the dim wedge of light to guide her, she retraced her steps. She followed the corridor and pushed through into the foyer. Immediately, more signs of damage drew her gaze. A beige computer unit and matching monitor, the display screen fractured in a criss-cross pattern, lay strewn across the floor beside the receptionist's desk. The fragmented parts of a two-piece telephone rested nearby. A breath of cool air dragged her attention to the entrance. The lower pane was missing. Fragments of glass glinted in the overcast twilight.

What should she do? Somebody had apparently broken into the building, leaving a trail of destruction behind them. Should she try to find a different phone? The nearest was probably in the boardroom, just a short distance up the stairs.

Surely, the intruder had set off the alarm, so why wasn't it sounding? She vaguely recalled her manager telling her that the system stayed silent for ten minutes before triggering the siren in the building to allow time for backup to get there and apprehend the criminals. That meant the break-in must have occurred very recently. Somebody would be along soon. Perhaps she should sit tight and wait for help to arrive. But what if the intruders hadn't left and remained on the premises? Worse still, what if her captors were the ones to respond to the alert?

No, she had to leave. She would flag down a car or find a building where someone was working late and try to catch their attention. She hurried to the front door and crouched down to clamber through the broken frame. Had she not been pregnant, she would have fitted through the gap with ease, but the bulge in her stomach made it hard to fold her body small enough. As she twisted sideways, her shoulder caught on a shard protruding from the top edge. She cried out in pain.

Tears welled in her eyes. She had to keep going, if not for herself, then for her unborn child. She tried again, earning another gash on the upper arm for her trouble. Finally, she rose on unsteady legs beneath an overcast sky and considered her next course of action. Her heart almost stopped in fright at the sudden wail of the siren on the side of the building above her head.

Eileen set off across the car park at a half jog. Lack of exercise and the advanced stage of her pregnancy meant she had to stop every few paces to regain her breath. The ear-splitting screech of the alarm cut through the evening air and trailed her to the pavement. She stopped and considered her options. To the right lay the main road leading out of the science park. There, she could flag down a car. If she turned left, it would lead her deeper into the maze of industrial units. That route offered the greater chance of discovering somebody working late in one of the adjacent buildings.

She stood still, caught in a moment of uncertainty. The headlights approaching from the right decided for her. She staggered into the road, waving her arms above her head.

"Help!" she screamed, silhouetted by the twin beams.

The car slowed and stopped. A deep sob escaped her throat. Her sense of relief lasted just long enough for the driver to open the door of the battered white Saab and step out onto the tarmac.

"Planning on going somewhere, Eileen?" he asked.

Saturday 9th April 2016
Ilithyia Biotechnology, Cambridge Science Park
Twenty-one years ago

Anders Grolby tapped the button to end the call. He muttered a curse under his breath. Martin Hendrick had just called to let him know about two suspicious men he had seen loitering outside the Ilithyia premises after locking up for the night. It seemed the scientist's suspicions were well-founded because only five minutes earlier, Grolby had received an automated intruder alert from the building's alarm system.

Now he was on his way there to check the place out. More often than not, such call-outs were false alarms. Most likely, the idiot scientist had forgotten to close a door properly, but in his role as head of security, he couldn't afford to take the chance. For the life of him, he didn't understand why the owners allowed Martin Hendrick to work in the building alone when his laboratory was mere metres from the room in which they were holding their secret prisoner.

Grolby was particularly irritated because the call from the alarm system had interrupted the World War II movie he was watching on the huge 3D television in his flat. The story had been entertaining enough, but he found the fighting scenes somewhat unrealistic. In his experience, warfare was much dirtier and far more violent than the action portrayed on the silver screen.

Still, it could have been worse. At this time of night on a weekend, he could cover the five miles to Ilithyia in less than ten minutes. As he turned into the science park, the faint screech of a siren penetrated the old Saab's interior. If that was the alarm on the side of the building, any intruders would be long gone. He just hoped they hadn't caused too much damage. He really didn't want to hang around for hours while he waited for the maintenance company to arrive and board up any broken windows.

As he rounded a left-hand bend, a woman wearing a white T-shirt and black leggings leapt out into the road, waving her arms above her head. He jammed on the brakes and slowed to a halt. It was a bit early for the usual half-dressed Saturday night partygoers to be staggering about on the street, and she was more than a little off the beaten track. Still, nothing surprised him these days.

This girl seemed to be carrying a lot of excess weight. Or perhaps she was pregnant. *Shit!* With a jolt of recognition, he identified the figure as Eileen Floyd. What the hell was she doing here? He flung open the door and levered himself out of the leather driver's seat.

"Planning on going somewhere, Eileen?" he called.

Immediately, she turned and ran down the centre of the road in the opposite direction. Within ten paces, he caught up to her. He put an arm around her neck and hauled her back.

"Come on, now. We can't have you roaming the streets in your condition, can we?"

"Get off me!" she screamed. "Help!"

He clamped a hand over her mouth and frogmarched her to his car. After a quick scan of his surroundings, he opened the boot, lifted her and bundled her inside.

"No!"

Her cry cut off as the lid slammed shut. Grolby breathed a sigh of relief. Two minutes later and she would have been clean away. He navigated the short distance to the Ilithyia building and parked beside the entrance. This close, the screech of the siren was deafening. It would take real balls to stay around with that racket blaring in the background, but he should check anyway before returning her to the cell.

He got out of the car. *Damn.* It would be a long night after all; the bitch had smashed the lower pane of the front door to escape. Or had she? Most fragments lay inside, implying somebody had shattered the glass from the outside. The large rock, lying by the wall a few feet away, confirmed his hypothesis.

He selected the key for the building and let himself in. His first action was to silence the alarm. His next step was to open the flick knife he kept in his trouser pocket. He advanced cautiously, blade extended, towards the reception desk. As he drew nearer, he spotted the broken computer equipment on the floor. Had she done this or the intruder?

Should he check upstairs or downstairs first? He pondered for a moment, then headed for the steps. All the lights remained off. In the darkness, he pushed through the door to the boardroom and reached for the spot where he knew the light switch resided. The sudden brightness revealed nothing out of the ordinary.

He moved along to the toilets, checking the gents first, and then the ladies. Both empty. The open-plan office proved equally undisturbed, as did the offices of the two bosses, Nigel Perrin and Rosalind Baxter. The last place he checked was his own domain, the server room. A wash of cool air passed over him as he stepped inside, but like everywhere else, there was no trace of an intruder.

He retraced his steps and descended the stairs. At the bottom, he navigated around the damaged equipment and turned left towards the laboratories. Broken glassware and another wrecked computer greeted him in the first laboratory. When it came to Martin Hendrick's space, a bin jammed the door open. He flicked the switch, but the light refused to come on. With knife drawn, he slid inside and waited for his eyes to acclimatise to the darkness. The powerful stench of chemicals washed over him. As the room slowly took shape, he spotted the pile of shattered glass, the toppled chair and the computer base unit lying on the floor. When he was sure nobody lurked in the shadows, he moved on.

He twisted the handle to the storeroom. It turned without the use of a key. His hand reached inside and flicked on the lights. There was no sign of a disturbance. He crossed the room and tried the next door. Also open. The lab animals scuttled in their cages as he stepped through the doorway. Light flooded out of Eileen Floyd's cell. How the hell had she got out? Somebody must have helped her.

Unless... Dr Perrin had been on feeding duty that night. Could he have forgotten to lock up behind him? That didn't explain the destruction and the broken glass inside the reception area. He planned to have a quiet chat with the woman when she was safely back in her cell.

There were still a few places to check. He retraced his route to the corridor and inspected both male and female toilets, coming up empty on both counts. The laboratory at the end, where Floyd had worked months earlier, also seemed undisturbed. Time to get her in the building and ask a few questions.

When Grolby returned to the car, a series of muffled screams emerged from inside the boot. He slammed his palm down three times on the top before opening it.

"If you make another sound, I'll hurt you," he growled. "Is that clear?"

Tear-stained eyes glared up at him.

"Good, let's get you into your little room." Grolby reached down and helped Eileen out. He wrapped an arm around her waist and steered her across the lobby. "Looks like you've picked up some nasty cuts there," he said, studying the rips in her T-shirt and the lacerations to her shoulder beneath.

As they passed through the reception area, she pulled away. "Just let me go," she pleaded. "Please. I won't say a word to anyone."

"I'll think about it if you explain how you escaped."

"There was a noise outside the room. I tried the door, and it opened. I didn't break anything. The glass at the entrance was already broken by the time I got there."

Grolby studied the discoloured stains on her trainers. "Why did you go in the laboratories, then? There's no point denying it. The chemicals are all over your shoes. I can smell them from here. If you didn't smash all that stuff, who did?"

"I don't know, but it wasn't me. I thought I might be able to find a key in there to get out."

"Hmm, I'm not sure I buy that. You expect me to believe somebody entered the building, caused all that damage, and it had nothing at all to do with your escape."

"Yes, I swear that's the truth."

"Fine. We'll talk about this again in the morning."

"No, no, no. You said—"

The slap across the face stopped Eileen in mid-sentence. She tried to pull away, but Grolby's rough hold tightened around her upper arm as he dragged her along the corridor. When they reached the storeroom, he relaxed his grip to put the key in the lock.

Halfway through the door, she staggered and grasped the frame for support. She stopped and glanced down; a puddle expanded around her feet.

"What—?" The question died in Grolby's throat as he took in the damp patch on her leggings.

She squatted on her haunches. "But it isn't due for another two weeks."

"Let's get you inside," Grolby said, once again taking her by the arm. He guided her to the small room, where she sank onto the bed. "I'll make a call. Try to remain calm."

He removed the mobile from his pocket and dialled the first number on speed dial.

"We had a close thing tonight," he replied after receiving a peremptory greeting. "The woman nearly escaped, and she almost certainly had help."

He listened patiently to the barrage of questions, then spoke again.

"Before I answer any of that, there's something else you should know; her waters have broken. You better come in straight away."

Sunday 10th April 2016

Ilithyia Biotechnology, Cambridge Science Park
Twenty-one years ago

Rosalind Baxter sank into the chair as exhaustion crept up on her. She lowered her eyes and stared down at the front of the once white laboratory coat, now stained a dark, almost black, shade of red. So much blood. She raised her sleeve with trembling fingers and studied the dial of her watch: 3:34. She clamped her right hand with the left.

On the opposite side sat Nigel Perrin, his face deathly pale. Anders Grolby stood by the door. Even the Swedish ex-soldier looked shaken.

"What the hell just happened?" Rosalind said, lifting her head.

Neither of the other two replied.

"I've never seen anything like it," she continued. "Everything seemed to be going well..." Her voice trailed off into silence.

"What do you want to do with the body?" Grolby asked.

"I never wanted to kill her," Perrin said in a dull monotone.

"Technically, we didn't," Rosalind snapped. "But to answer Anders's question, in my opinion we should perform a post mortem before deciding what to do next."

Perrin removed a pen from his pocket and clicked the tip in and out. "Why? What's the point? She's dead now, and there's nothing we can do about it."

"Well, apart from anything else," Rosalind replied, "we need to know if whatever killed her is infectious." She gestured to the brightly coloured box on the floor, and the tiny face that peeked through the blankets. "We also have the child to consider."

The lightweight plastic container was the best solution they could improvise at short notice.

"He's not our problem," Grolby said. "We can leave him somewhere safe, and I'll call the police on an unregistered phone to tell them I heard a baby crying."

"You think she might have infected us?" Perrin asked, his face creased in alarm.

Rosalind sighed. "I really have no idea. The symptoms she exhibited had all the hallmarks of a haemorrhagic fever or something similar."

"Christ!" Perrin exclaimed. "You mean like Ebola or Marburg? If that's the case, we should stay well away from the body."

"Don't you think it's a little late for that?" Rosalind replied, pointing at the stains on her white coat. "Whatever she had, if it's infectious, we've already got it by now. What's weird is that she seemed okay right up to the point she gave birth. Normally, with those types of disease, the patient suffers aches and pains before progressing to the later stages over the course of several days. You'd expect to see diarrhoea and vomiting too, but she never complained about anything like that. The symptoms developed extremely rapidly. If we do a post mortem, we might learn more about what this is."

"How would she catch this illness?" Grolby asked. "The only three people she came into contact with over the past few months are in this room."

"We should go to a hospital," Perrin said. "Get them to check us over."

Rosalind rolled her eyes. "Don't be ridiculous, Nigel," she snorted. "You can hardly wander in to A&E and say, 'I think I may have contracted a haemorrhagic fever'. The first question they'd ask would be why you suspected that to be the case. It's not as if you've been abroad recently."

"I'm not single like you two. There's more at stake for me. I have a son of my own and a wife. I can't take the risk I might pass something on to them."

"Look, it's highly unlikely to be Ebola. If any of us start exhibiting symptoms, that's a different story, but for now, the one thing we need to do is learn what we're dealing with. If you're worried, tell your family you can't come home because you have to attend to some urgent business. Then self-isolate somewhere. You could make yourself useful by staying here and looking after the baby."

"I'm not going to stay in the same room she died in."

"Okay, just relax. All of us have been in regular contact with her. I don't know about you two, but I certainly haven't suffered any fever-like symptoms."

"So, what do we do now?" Grolby asked.

"I suggest Nigel and I examine the body while you clean up the mess," Rosalind replied.

"We aren't equipped for this," Perrin said. "We don't have any of the right protective gear."

She pushed back the chair, stood and leant forwards. She slammed her fist down on the table. "For crying out loud, will you stop whining and pull yourself together? If she died of something transmissible, it's likely we're already infected. We can't change that. Let's just get this done, and then we can decide on our next course of action."

"Fine," Perrin muttered.

"Anders, any chance you could find some of those large black bin liners?"

"Yeah, I know where they're stored."

"When everything's finished, we'll wrap the body up. We'll need to do a thorough clean of the room afterwards to sterilise it and remove any signs she was there. How are you going to dispose of her?"

"I've already given that some thought," Grolby replied. "There are some lakes just off the A14, near St Ives. I bought an inflatable dinghy; it's in the boot of my car. I'll row out to the middle, weigh her down with stones, then dump her. There are no houses nearby, so I shouldn't be disturbed."

"Good. While we're busy, I suggest you start cleaning up the two labs."

"Who's going to look after the baby?"

"When he wakes, we'll have to feed him. There's formula milk in her room. Nigel and I will take him with us now. We need to get a move on. It may be the weekend, but everything has to be finished by the morning in case Martin comes in to work on his pet project."

Armed with a roll of bin bags, Rosalind entered the small cell. Both she and Perrin wore facemasks and thin plastic gloves. Eileen Floyd's body lay on the bed where she had died. A mass of red stained the bedding. Rosalind placed a towel over the dead woman's face.

"We don't have the right tools for this," Perrin said.

"I agree, but let's do the best we can. We should be able to examine the internal organs at least."

The pair worked in silence for several minutes.

Rosalind blew out a deep breath. "Take a look at this. The kidneys and liver are both liquified. It's no wonder she died so quickly." She removed the towel. "Check out her eyes. See these burst blood vessels."

"It definitely looks like a haemorrhagic disease. What the hell could've caused this?"

"I've no idea. I suggest we keep some tissue samples. After we've done that, we'll bag the rest." She glanced at her watch. "It's too late to dispose of the body today. It'll be light soon. Anders can do it tonight."

"My wife will wonder what I've been up to," Perrin said.

"Tell her about the break in. Say we had to clean up afterwards."

"What excuse do I give her for not going home?"

"Maybe explain that the intruders spilled some dangerous chemicals. You're staying here to keep your family safe. I mean, it's half true, isn't it?"

"I never wanted any of this, Rosalind."

"That may be the case, Nigel, but we can't go back now."

Sunday 10th April 2016

Ilithyia Biotechnology, Cambridge Science Park
Twenty-one years ago

Rosalind Baxter drummed her fingers on the boardroom table. On the opposite side, Nigel Perrin clicked a pen in and out. Both glanced up as the door opened, and Anders Grolby entered.

It had taken until after nine o'clock to clean up all the mess and remove all traces of Eileen Floyd's presence. Her body, together with the bedding, lay in bin bags in the boot of Grolby's car. They had fed the baby twice already. He remained in his makeshift crib on the floor of the room in which his mother had died. The failed light in Martin Hendrick's area hadn't made Grolby's task any easier. In the end, after clearing the adjacent laboratory, the Swede borrowed the fluorescent tube starter from there and replaced the faulty one.

"Is everybody still feeling all right?" Rosalind asked.

"Yeah," Grolby replied. "Just a bit tired."

"I'm okay," Perrin said.

Rosalind ran a hand over her face. "We haven't yet discussed how she got out. What do you think happened?"

"She couldn't have opened the door by herself," Grolby said, stifling a yawn. "That leaves two possibilities." His gaze fixed on Perrin. "Either Nigel forgot to lock up, or somebody else released her."

"I'm sure I didn't leave her room open," Perrin protested. "I definitely remember turning the key before I left."

"You mentioned receiving a call last night from your wife, asking you to come home. Is it possible you were distracted?"

"That came after I'd already locked her up. I was in Martin Hendrick's lab at the time. I was going to finish up some work in my office, so I offered to lock the building."

"Well, if it wasn't you, she must have received outside help."

"What about the break in?" Rosalind asked.

"Yes," Grolby said. "That's puzzling. Somebody apparently smashed the front door, came in, caused a load of damage, then left without taking anything. If they were intent on smashing stuff, why only target two laboratories and not the third?"

Rosalind shrugged. "Perhaps they planned to trash that too, but the sound of the siren disturbed them."

"Or maybe Eileen Floyd did it," Perrin added.

"So, somehow she gets out of her room and hangs around wrecking things instead of escaping or calling for help," Grolby replied. "Sorry, but that doesn't seem likely to me. I checked the time of the alarm. Martin called me five minutes after the silent alert had already gone off. He told me he saw a pair of suspicious men on the road outside."

"What if the intruders let her out?" Rosalind asked.

"Again, that seems pretty unlikely. How would they know she was there? Where did they get the keys from? She claimed she didn't see who released her. Why didn't they talk to her after opening the door?"

"Perhaps they expected the building to be empty," Perrin said. "If they broke in, they'd worry she might be able to identify them later."

"But that still doesn't explain the other two points."

"Could it have been Martin?" Rosalind asked.

Silence descended on the room. After a few seconds, Grolby spoke. "We have to consider the possibility. He spends a lot of time here, working by himself. His laboratory is a short distance down the corridor from the storeroom. Perhaps he found out about her."

"Christ, that's all we need," Perrin muttered.

"It still doesn't make sense. If it was him, why smash up his own area? Why not just contact the police? They haven't come knocking, so we have to assume he didn't call anybody. And if he was going to release her, he could've done it at any time. Where did he get the key to open her door?"

"I keep mine on me at all times," Rosalind said.

"Me too," Grolby added. "Nigel?"

"I hide a set in my office, in the desk drawer."

Grolby folded his arms. "Could somebody have borrowed them to let her out?"

Perrin shook his head. "How would they know where to look? Anyway, if the intruders were criminals, they'd probably have the expertise to pick a lock."

"This is getting us nowhere," Rosalind said. "So, what do we do now?"

"I suggest we call Martin Hendrick in and have a chat with him," Grolby replied.

"What?" Perrin's forehead creased in confusion. "We can't ask whether he was the one to release her."

"I don't plan to, but I'd like to question him about the two men he spotted outside. He might be able to provide additional information."

188

"If we're infected, there's a chance we could pass it on to him."

"When I asked a minute ago, you both told me you're feeling fine," Rosalind said. "We've all had regular contact with her, and none of us is showing any symptoms. I reckon the risk is low." She stood and retrieved the phone from her bag. "If past performance is anything to go by, he's probably planning to come in today anyway, but I'll call him now." She stepped into the corridor and spoke in a hushed voice. Moments later, she returned. "He'll be here in twenty minutes."

"What are you going to say to him?" Perrin asked.

"I'll tell him about the break in," Grolby replied, "then get him to describe the men. I also want to clear up the sequence of events around the time he left."

"How will we find out whether he knew about the girl?"

"Well, obviously we can't ask him directly. Leave the questions to me."

"I'll be in my office," Rosalind said. "Call me when he gets here."

She strolled down the corridor, sank into the leather executive chair and placed her face in her hands. *What a mess.* Eileen Floyd's unexpected death had saved them from one unpleasant task, even though they still had to dispose of her body. But if Grolby had arrived a minute or two later, she would have got away, and all three of them would be facing a long jail term. There were too many coincidences; Martin Hendrick had to be involved somehow, but she could hardly accuse him outright.

The financial situation at Ilithyia was far stronger than when she had agreed to support his pet project. Several major contracts had landed in the last six months. Whilst the rewards of Hendrick's research were potentially huge, everything was at risk if anybody ever found out about the work he was performing. He had yet to demonstrate any meaningful progress. Maybe it was time to pull the plug.

She logged into her computer and sighed at the long list of emails in her inbox. She scrolled down the page, deleting all of them unread, apart from three sent by important clients. Her vision shimmered as she tried to focus on the screen. A headache pulsed just behind her eyes. Unable to concentrate, she signed out. They would have to wait for a response until Monday.

She stood and stared out of the window. When she had founded the business with Nigel Perrin, she had imagined developing Ilithyia into a global pharmaceutical company. The struggle to make ends meet and the constant battle to find new customers were factors she hadn't really considered.

After three tension-filled years, all they had to show for the long hours and continual stress was contained within these four walls, and even then, they didn't own the building. She had invested too much time and money to fail now. Whatever it took, she wouldn't allow anybody to take away her life's work.

The arrival of a red Ford Focus in the car park below dragged her back from her thoughts. She strode out of her office and down the stairs. She arrived at the bottom just as Martin Hendrick came through the entrance.

"Hello, Rosalind. What happened here?" he asked, pointing at the empty lower pane in the door.

"Somebody broke in last night. I've spent most of the time since then cleaning up the mess they made."

"Oh. I called Anders about a pair of men behaving suspiciously outside. He said the alarm had gone off. I offered to come back, but he told me to go home. Did they take anything?"

"No, but there was considerable damage in two of the laboratories, including yours."

"What sort of damage?"

"They emptied the contents of the refrigerator onto the floor and smashed up your computer."

"Shit!"

Rosalind followed the scientist as he jogged towards his workspace. If he was the instigator of the events that had taken place over the previous night, he was doing a good job of disguising his involvement. She stepped through the doorway to discover Hendrick staring at the bare shelves of the fridge.

"What did you do with it all?" he asked, turning as she entered.

"They broke everything. We bagged it and threw it into the industrial waste bin."

"What about the metal flasks?"

"Empty. Why?"

"That's where I kept the virus samples I was working on."

Alarm bells went off in Rosalind's head. "What? I didn't see any biohazard labels. We would have taken more precautions if we'd known."

"You asked me to keep anything like that out of sight."

Rosalind clenched her fists and took a deep breath. "Is there any risk of infection?"

"No, it's perfectly safe. There's nothing to worry about."

"Right. Where did you store the data?"

"I backed up all my regular work to the network, but I kept the stuff for the other project on the hard drive. If you remember, you told me not to put it on the file servers."

"You better see if it still works."

Hendrick crossed to his workstation. The beige unit exhibited several dents and scratches. He pressed the power switch. After a short beep, followed by the manufacturer's logo, a line of white text appeared on a black background.

DISK BOOT FAILURE - INSERT SYSTEM DISK AND PRESS ENTER

He tried a second time with the same result. He turned to Rosalind, his face pale. "It looks like it's gone. There aren't any backups. Everything was on there."

She studied him for a moment before speaking. "I'll get Anders to take a look and see if he can fix it. He wants to talk to you, anyway."

Hendrick trailed her up the stairs and into the boardroom. Perrin and Grolby already sat on the far side of the table.

"Hello, Martin," the Swede said when everyone was seated. "You called me last night about two men you spotted outside the building."

"Yeah, they were standing on the pavement by the main road just past the entrance. I thought they looked suspicious."

"What makes you say that?"

"They didn't seem to be going anywhere, and they turned away from me as I drove by."

"Can you describe them?"

"No, sorry. Like I said, I didn't get a look at their faces."

"What were they wearing?" Grolby asked.

"Oh, uh... dark clothes, I think. I can't really remember. One of them wore white trainers. I should've mentioned it last night, but I heard some strange sounds outside just before locking up."

Rosalind's gaze met Perrin's. "What sort of sounds?" she asked, focusing back on Hendrick.

"Um... banging. There was also some shouting. It sounded like kids. It seemed to be coming from the rear of the building."

"Let's return to these men you saw," Grolby said. "Why did you wait until you were nearly home before calling me?"

"I didn't want to disturb you unnecessarily. Then I thought about it some more and decided to phone you."

"You set the alarm last night."

"Yes, as I do most nights."

"I checked the logs. The silent alert went off two minutes after it was armed. How do you explain that?"

Hendrick scowled at the Swede. "What? Are you suggesting I had something to do with this?"

"I didn't say that. I'm just trying to find out what happened."

"Well, obviously you believe I am involved, otherwise you wouldn't be asking these questions. Why would I smash up my own lab? I've spent months on this project. What possible reason could I have for destroying my research?"

"This work of yours," Rosalind said. "Is there any way it could cause disease?"

"Of course not. You know what the goals were—to provide a vaccination for Chlamydia. Why do you ask?"

"Just curious."

"So, back to the break in. Was it you?" Grolby asked.

Hendrick slammed his palms down on the desk. "Seriously?"

Perrin raised his hand in a placating gesture "Calm down, Martin."

"Why should I?" He poked a finger first at Rosalind, then at Perrin. "After all the unpaid overtime I put into this company, you sit there and let him accuse me of something like this. Well, I've had enough. If that's the way you want to play it, you can have my immediate resignation. The only reason I stayed here these past few months was to finish this work, and now it's all gone, destroyed by some mindless vandals. I'm really not interested in any of the other crap jobs you give me."

Stunned silence greeted Hendrick's outburst.

"Look, Martin..." Perrin began.

"No, I've had enough. You never wanted me to take on this project in the first place."

"Actually, I—"

"I trust you'll at least have the decency to pay my wages up to today. I'm leaving right now."

Hendrick pushed back his chair and strode through the door, slamming it behind him.

"That went well," Rosalind said, drily.

Saturday 23rd April 2016
North Middlesex University Hospital, London
Twenty-one years ago

"**B**reathe," the man said.

"As opposed to what?" his wife replied through clenched teeth.

"Remember the techniques they talked about at the NCT sessions."

"Oh, piss off, will you?"

He reached over to brush aside a strand of sweaty hair that had fallen across her face.

She slapped his hand away. "Don't touch me."

He glanced at the door. Where the hell was the midwife? Just before departing, she had told them his wife's cervix was nearly at the full ten centimetres dilation. The woman had received a call on her pager and promised to return soon after helping with the final stages of another birth. That had been fifteen minutes ago.

A piercing scream echoed through the thin walls from the adjacent room. The man winced. *Was that normal?*

As if in sympathy with the other expectant mother, his wife clenched her fist, digging her fingers into his palm. He tried to pull away, but she tightened her grip.

"Ow, you're hurting me," he said.

"Good, you bastard," she replied, her face twisting in agony.

A moment later, the contraction ended and the pressure on his hand relaxed.

"I need more gas," she mumbled between short pants of breath.

He lifted the transparent facemask, which was attached to the wall via a white tube, and handed it to her. "The midwife said not to overdo it."

His wife ignored him and continued to breathe deeply. After twenty seconds, her arm dropped to the side. Her grip loosened on the mask, and he gently removed it from her hand before replacing it on the stand beside the hospital bed.

"Why didn't you get back sooner?" she whispered.

"Sorry, but I got the first flight I could," he replied. "I drove here straight from the airport."

"You should've told them you couldn't go. It was your second trip this week."

"It's part of the job, but I've booked a fortnight off now, so I can stay at home and look after you and the baby."

She pushed herself up on her elbows as another contraction surged through her body. Thirty seconds later, she sank back onto the pillows, her face beaded with sweat. "Where is that bloody woman?"

"Shall I try to find her?"

"Yes, but be quick. I don't want to go through this by myself."

The man rose and let himself out of the door. As he stepped into the corridor, a white-coated doctor jogged towards him.

"Excuse me."

The medic ignored him, ran past and barged into the adjacent room. Moments later, a woman in similar attire rounded the corner and rushed in the same direction.

"My wife is—"

"Somebody will be with you shortly," she interrupted without breaking stride.

The man stood in bewilderment. After a few seconds, the midwife, who had been assisting with the birth of their child until she was called away, emerged from the adjacent delivery room.

Finally. "Ah, Marie..."

His voice trailed off as he took in the dark crimson stains splashed across her uniform, contrasting with the paleness of her face. She staggered and leant against the wall for support.

"Is everything all right?"

She shook her head.

"Can I do anything? Only, my wife—"

"Give me a minute to clean up, Mr Gowan," she said.

"Is the woman in there okay?"

"I'm sorry, I can't talk about it." She turned away and headed in the opposite direction.

The man returned to his wife's room. A shiver of apprehension ran through him. Something bad must have happened to cause that much blood.

His wife lay on the pillows, her hair straggled in damp clumps. "Is the midwife coming?" she asked in a hoarse voice.

"Yeah, she'll be here shortly," he replied, lowering himself into the chair beside the bed. He didn't want to alarm her by telling her what he had seen. He took her hand in his own. "It'll soon be over."

"I can feel another contraction on the way."

"Breathe in through your nose and sigh out through your mouth."

His wife scowled. "I don't need you to tell me that. I was at the course—ah." Her teeth clamped together, and her hands grasped her stomach. "More gas," she groaned.

She snatched the mask out of his hand as he offered it to her.

At that moment, the door opened, and the midwife burst in. She had changed into a fresh uniform. "Sorry to leave you like that, Sarah. How are we doing?" She raised the maternity gown. "You're crowning. I can see the baby's head. Not long to go now."

Minutes went by, and the intensity of the contractions increased.

"One final push," the midwife urged. "The baby's almost out."

His wife groaned. All her muscles seemed to tense at the same time. The man watched as the midwife's hands caught the slippery bundle. She placed the child on a clean towel and wiped the blood and mucus from the tiny body. A reedy wail filled the room.

"It's a boy. Would you like to cut the umbilical cord, Mark?"

He glanced nervously at the twisted white tube and grasped the offered surgical scissors. "Here?" he asked.

"Yes, just by the clamp."

The razor-sharp blades severed the coiled link with little effort.

The new mother accepted the bundled child and clasped him to her chest. Her lips curved in an exhausted smile as her husband gently touched her cheek. "He's..."

A look of confusion clouded her face. Her right hand moved to her throat as a wet cough shook her body. The midwife snatched up the baby and deposited him in a cot at the end of the bed.

"What's wrong?" the man asked.

The coughing intensified. His wife hacked up a gobbet of bloody fluid. Her lips bared, revealing bloodstained teeth as she opened her mouth to scream. A patchwork of broken blood vessels discoloured the once white sclera of her eyes.

"What's happening?" the man shouted.

"No, not another one," the midwife muttered. She rushed to the wall and pressed the large red emergency button.

Moments later, the sound of urgent footsteps echoed down the corridor outside the room. The doctor, who had hurried past a few minutes earlier, burst through the door. His gaze immediately focused on the patient. "Status?" he asked.

"She's haemorrhaging," the midwife replied, "just like the other two."

Choking sounds emerged from the new mother's throat. Convulsions shook her body. Her stomach heaved, and a thick, dark-red fluid spouted from her mouth, leaving a Rorschach ink blot pattern splattered over the doctor's white coat. With a final gasp, the woman's movements ceased, and she lay still.

The doctor placed a finger to her neck and frowned with concentration. A moment later, he raised his eyes and met the man's desperate gaze. "I'm sorry," he murmured.

The new father shoved him out of the way. "This can't be happening." He leant over and shook his wife's shoulders. "Come on, Sarah, please wake up."

The midwife's hand landed gently on his back. "There's nothing we can do for her. She's gone, Mark."

Unseen by the grieving husband, the female doctor entered the room. She took in the scene with a single glance. Her male colleague gave a surreptitious shake of the head.

"That's the third today," she said, her grim expression hidden by a surgical mask. "It has to be more than a coincidence. I'm afraid we're going to have to quarantine the building. We have a nightmare scenario on our hands."

Monday 25th April 2016
Ilithyia Biotechnology, Cambridge Science Park
Twenty-one years ago

Rosalind Baxter knocked on the door. For once, she waited for a reply before striding into Nigel Perrin's office. She carried a newspaper beneath her arm. Perrin glanced up from behind his desk.

"Good morning, Rosalind. How's the boy doing?"

"Fine. The nanny is costing me a bloody fortune though."

"You're using a company, aren't you? What did you tell them?"

"I said he belongs to a niece who's still at school. Her family wants to keep the birth quiet, so I offered to look after him. The agency claims to be discreet. Let's just hope they're true to their word."

"He's not showing any symptoms, then?"

"No. And by the way, his name is Jason."

Perrin peered over his glasses. "You're not growing attached to him, are you?"

"No, but we all agreed it was a good idea to keep an eye on him. I can hardly do that as well as running the company. His mother told me that's what she wanted to call him. I didn't see the harm in following her wishes."

"I understand. Anyway, I'm assuming you haven't popped in for a social chat. What can I do for you?"

"I take it you've seen this," she said, dropping the folded newspaper on his desk.

Perrin opened out the front page and read the headline.

New Virus Strikes Recent Mothers. In-Depth Feature Inside.

"Yes, I've been following the news reports."

"And?"

"And what?"

"Doesn't any of it sound familiar?" Rosalind asked. She snatched up the paper and rustled through the pages. "Here," she said, jabbing a finger at the newsprint. "Victims die within minutes of giving birth."

"Right."

"And here. Doctors say the symptoms are similar to those seen in patients suffering from haemorrhagic fevers, such as Ebola. That sounds exactly like what Eileen Floyd died from."

Perrin removed his glasses and peered at the page. "Well, I'll admit there are similarities."

"No, Nigel, it's more than that. The cases are identical. And it's not just a few. I checked Yahoo News on the Internet this morning. There have been numerous deaths across the world. It says here, the first reported case was a week ago. I'm sure I don't need to remind you that Eileen Floyd died two weeks ago."

Grolby's disposal of Eileen's body had gone as planned. Her final resting place was the bottom of a lake near St Ives.

"So, you really think she had this disease?" Perrin said.

"I do," Rosalind replied.

"What are the newspapers calling it? The Orestes virus?"

"Yeah, apparently Orestes was some character from Greek Mythology who killed his mother when he discovered she had murdered his father. It was something to do with the Trojan War. Anyway, it doesn't matter what the press have called it. I read this morning that the medical authorities have quarantined a number of maternity units across the world, including one in north London. The report said there have been several deaths at the site."

"But you can't possibly think it started here."

"For Christ's sake, Nigel, open your eyes. Eileen Floyd suffered exactly the same symptoms a week before anybody else. The evidence is staring us in the face."

"But if she did contract this virus, how did she get infected?"

"That's the million-dollar question. As I see it, there are only two possibilities; either you, me or Anders gave it to her or..."

"Or what?"

"Anders mentioned that she went into one of the labs after she escaped from her room. She had chemical stains on her trainers. She told him afterwards that she was looking for keys to open the front door to the building. What if she picked up the infection in there?"

"How could that happen?" Perrin asked.

"Let's face it, neither of us really has a clue what Martin Hendrick was working on. We know it was based on the flu virus, but that's all. We don't have any notes from his research; the contents of his computer were destroyed during the break-in. Anders was only able to retrieve a few file fragments. It gives us some clues, but it's not enough.

"The intruders also smashed everything in his refrigerator. He told us he was storing the organisms he was working on in unmarked containers. Is it

198

possible that when all that material got mixed together, it somehow combined into a new strain?"

Perrin's face turned pale. He snatched up the pen from his desk and began clicking. "Shit. I hadn't thought of that. So, what do we do next?"

"I guess the first step is to try to get hold of Martin."

"If he'll even talk to us. I have his personal mobile number on record. But what do I say to him?"

"I suggest you grovel a bit and ask him to come in for a chat."

"And if he refuses?"

Rosalind chewed a fingernail. "I don't know. We've still got the autopsy samples."

"I suppose we could send them off for analysis, but that might raise a few unwanted questions. Look, I'll try him now."

Rosalind paced while Perrin tapped the keys of his phone. He held the device to his ear. Moments later, he lowered it again. "I'm getting number unobtainable."

"I assume you have his address. Why don't we pay him a visit?"

"What, right this minute?"

"Well, I'd say this is more important than anything else we've got on at the moment."

"Fine. Your car or mine?"

"We'll take mine," Rosalind replied. She marched along the corridor, down the stairs and past the reception desk, ignoring the receptionist's greeting as she passed. Perrin trailed behind her, hurrying to keep up.

Twenty minutes later, after riding in silence, they drew up outside the address they held on record.

"That's the one," Perrin said, pointing at the small semi-detached house. A large to-let sign dominated the front garden. The two business partners emerged from the car and approached the bright-red front door. Nobody responded to the ringing of the bell. A stack of post lay on the doormat.

Rosalind pointed at the pile of unopened mail. "It looks like we might be too late. Why don't you call the letting agent and try to find out where he's gone?"

Perrin read the number off the board and tapped in the digits. He spoke for a few minutes, then clicked the button to disconnect. "She said he moved out two days ago. They don't have a forwarding address."

Rosalind returned to the car. When her partner had buckled himself in, she turned sideways in the driver's seat. "Somehow, I don't think we're going to be having that chat with Martin Hendrick after all."

Friday 20th May 2016
33 Apple Tree Drive, Cambridge
Twenty-one years ago

A groan of pain came from inside the room. Dominic Lessing placed his hands against the wood panelling. His wife, Helen, had gone into labour five hours earlier.

"Are you all right?" he asked from the other side of the bedroom door. "What's going on?"

"The last two contractions were two minutes apart," she replied in a shaky voice. "I think I'm getting close."

Despite the barrier between them, Dominic still wore a surgical facemask. "Are you sure you don't want me in there to help?"

"No, we can't take the risk. I'll manage."

He desperately wanted to sit by his wife and support her as she gave birth, but ever since news broke of the Orestes virus and its devastating effect on recent mothers, Helen had isolated herself in the master en-suite bedroom of their home. Stacked against the wall with her were a pile of disinfectant wipes and several bottles of hand sanitiser.

Over the same period, Dominic had instigated a similar isolation policy, confining himself to the house throughout. He booked all his annual vacation allowance in one go, so he didn't have to leave the building. He ordered all food and groceries online, wiping down anything that would come into contact with his wife.

Despite all the precautions, there was no guarantee Helen would survive the birth of their child. After numerous deaths, maternity wards across the country had closed. Blanket television coverage encouraged expectant mothers to self-isolate, but many succumbed to the desire to be with loved ones or medical staff when the baby was born—resulting in a near one-hundred per cent mortality rate.

There was still no test yet to determine whether a woman had contracted the Orestes virus. Those who were infected died without exception. The scientists had determined that provided the mother survived the first few minutes after severing the umbilical cord, the chances of dying reduced to practically zero.

Another cry of pain came through the door, followed by the sound of several short, sharp breaths. Dominic sank down with his back to the wall and buried his face in his hands. A feeling of helplessness washed over him. Giving birth was supposed to be one of life's greatest moments for a parent, but a surge of dread ran through him. Could she do this alone? Would she survive long enough to hold her baby? The ultrasound scans had confirmed it would be a girl; he had wanted to wait to discover the gender when the child was born, but Helen preferred to know in advance.

They had spent many hours discussing a name. They agreed it should be something unique that would stand out but without being too alternative. After much deliberation, they settled on Antimone. *Like the metal*, he had joked. Four syllables: in some ways similar to the main female character in the Harry Potter books, Hermione Granger.

Another scream jolted him from his memories.

"Is everything okay?"

Several seconds of silence passed. What was happening?

Then his wife's voice. "I think it's—"

Her words morphed into a long shriek of agony.

"Helen, please talk to me."

The cry ceased, sending an icy shiver of apprehension racing through his body.

"Helen!" he yelled, pressing his face against the door.

Nothing.

He was about to barge in despite their previous agreement when his wife spoke in a weak voice. "I'm holding her. She's beautiful. I'm going to cut the cord."

A thin, reedy wail penetrated from inside the room.

"Please tell me what's happening," Dominic called.

"It's done."

"Keep talking. Describe her to me."

"She has wispy brown hair. Her eyes are dark, almost black. Her face is..."

"What is it?" He tried to hide the note of desperation in his voice, but it came through loud and clear.

His wife continued in little more than a whisper. He pressed his ear against the cold wood to hear. "Her face is all scrunched up. She's definitely not happy." The wailing sound intensified.

Dominic exhaled the breath he had been holding. "Can I come in yet?"

"Just give it a while longer. She's started feeding. She seems to be hungry."

Each second seemed like an hour as he waited. Finally, she said, "I think it's probably safe by now."

Dominic turned the handle and pushed open the door. His wife lay on the floor in the centre of the room. She greeted him with an exhausted smile, clutching a small bundle to her breast.

"Come and meet your daughter," she whispered.

His gaze lowered to the blood-soaked towels beneath her. The glint of the surgical scissors caught his attention.

"Is everything okay?" he asked, crouching beside her. "Are you all right?"

Helen glanced down at their child, then met his eyes. "I'm tired, and I hurt like hell, but apart from that, I'm fine."

Dominic placed his little finger against his daughter's tiny palm. Her fingers closed around his. "I promise I won't let anything bad happen to you," he murmured in Antimone's ear.

Part Five: Revelation

Tuesday 21ˢᵗ April 2037
23 Daffodil Drive, Northstowe

The two North Africans sat on the sofa. Max Perrin paced backwards and forwards, holding a thin metal object. He rotated the sealed tube and examined it carefully.

"It doesn't look anything special, does it?" he said.

Omar held out a hand. "Let me see."

"Don't open it, will you?"

The muscled soldier rolled his eyes. "Do not worry. I am not stupid." He raised it to the light. "I cannot detect a join." He passed the item to Mo.

The diminutive hacker studied the cylinder for a moment before handing it back to Max. "No. It should not appear out of place in a toolbox."

Two days earlier, Max had requested a supply of firearms from their handlers. The metal object contained one of the components, which, when combined with the other pieces, would form a gun. It was designed to pass through the scanners at the Ilithyia entrance without triggering an alert. The weapons dealer had sent through a demonstration video showing the assembly process and a test-firing of the assembled item. After thoroughly cleaning the exterior surfaces of all gunshot residue that might trigger the sensitive sensors, the anonymous supplier had shipped the parts using three different couriers.

"So," Max said, "we know we can get inside by adjusting the thermostat setting. We have a gun. That leaves one remaining issue; how to locate our four targets. None of them ever leave the building, but we must reach them all without being discovered."

"If we raise the temperature high enough," Mo said, "they will come outside again. Yes, we have asked for a handgun, but maybe we could use a sniper rifle to shoot them from distance."

"No, that would never work. We're too far away. As soon as the first one went down, the rest would all scatter. Anyway, I want them to know who's pulling the trigger. I want to look them in the eyes when I do it."

"The last time we adjusted the temperature, they all waited by the entrance," Omar said. "So, we turn up the heat inside, arrive in the van and shoot them at close range."

"I didn't sign up for a suicide mission. Anyway, what about the guards?"

"I did not see one gun. They carry only non-lethal weapons."

"Too risky," Max replied. "Even if they aren't carrying guns, there are too many of them. They'd quickly disable us if we just opened fire. And don't forget the dogs."

"So, you want to do this inside," Mo said. "How do we find the traitors and kill them?"

"Okay, what about this? We start by reassembling the weapon in the control room. Then we take a member of the security team prisoner and force him to reveal their location. Those guys should know where everybody is in the building."

"Yes, this could work," Omar said. "The best time to do this is at night. Our targets will be in their rooms, and we can kill them quietly one by one without raising the alarm."

Max nodded. "Good suggestion. We can't leave it too late in the day, though. We'll stand out too much if we're wandering about when all the people who live there are tucked up in bed. I suggest we access their system and raise the temperature sometime in the early evening, then hang around out of sight in the control room pretending to fix the problem until later. That will allow everybody time to get back inside. When we're ready, we grab a guard and force him to take us to the targets. If anybody asks what we're doing, we tell them the sensors are giving out faulty readings, and we need to replace them. That should enable us to go where we want."

"This sounds a good plan," Omar said. "How do you say? It is like shooting fish in a box."

"You mean a barrel," Max replied with a slight smile.

"Right. When do we do this?"

"Why not today? It's just after eleven o'clock now. Let's do it this evening. Is everything else ready?"

"Let me check I can still access the system," Mo said. He rose and sat in front of the computer screen. His fingers moved in a blur of motion. After a few seconds, he turned around with a grin on his face. "Yes, it all works well."

Max placed the metal tube in the toolbox, which lay open on the floor. "Excellent. At four o'clock, I want you to raise the temperature again. I'll call their site manager, Nick Butler, at ten past, telling him we've been monitoring the system and have spotted a problem. As soon as I've done that, we'll head over there.

"When we arrive, we go to the control room and lower the setting to normal. Then, we just hang around for three or four hours, pretending to be working on a fix. When the place is quiet enough, we grab the guard and find out where they're keeping the traitors. If necessary, we get him to open the doors to their rooms. Once we've killed them all, I call Mr Butler, inform him the problem's fixed, and we leave. By the time they discover the bodies, we'll be long gone and on our way back to Tripoli."

"How will we travel?" Mo asked.

"There's too much security at the airports," Max replied. "I'll book us some train tickets. We can't sit together because it might draw attention. It's less than an hour from Cambridge to London and a little longer from there to Paris. We can decide on the rest later. If all goes well, we should be home in a couple of days."

"Good," Omar said. "I hate this miserable country. I will be glad to return to the desert."

"Right. Before we go, we have to remove all evidence of our presence here. We need to ensure we leave nothing for the police to find. Let's get to work."

Tuesday 21ˢᵗ April 2037
Ilithyia Biotechnology, Northstowe

Antimone pulled the door shut behind her and propelled herself towards the lift. Moments earlier, she had received the call that Paul was ready to be picked up from his classes. It was half an hour before the usual five o'clock finish, but the flustered sounding receptionist had offered no explanation. Whatever the reason, it seemed no members of the security staff were available to escort him back to his room, so the responsibility fell to his parents.

She pushed the button. As she waited, she allowed her mind to wander. Jason had suggested she restart her athletics training. Two days ago, she had followed her partner's advice and called her former coach, John Marshall. The conversation was awkward at first, but in the end, he agreed to an initial trial session after she promised to answer his questions concerning the events surrounding the previous summer's Olympic wheelchair final. Now, all she had to do was persuade the security team to let her leave the building.

She shivered slightly at the thought of the agony she would have to endure to get back to her former fitness level, but if she wanted to compete again, there was no alternative. As her coach was fond of saying, *no pain, no gain.* The prospect of appearing in public now that everybody knew the details of her past filled her with trepidation. Some still blamed her for not revealing the facts following the birth of her son. But what did they expect her to do?

The ding of the bell drew her back to the present. The doors slid apart, and she wheeled herself inside. Moments later, a wall of warm air swept over her as she emerged into the foyer. Surely the heating system wasn't on the blink again? She hadn't noticed any significant temperature rise in the room, but here the heat was oppressive. That would explain the early finish to Paul's day.

A few people milled about, mostly scientists judging by the white medical coats. A group of security staff stood in a huddle by the scanners, deep in conversation. She turned right and headed towards the classroom. She arrived moments later to find the teacher, Mrs Prendergast, waiting with the last two of her students.

"Sorry," the woman said at Antimone's arrival. "We had to wrap up early because it was getting too hot for the children. One of the other parents mentioned that at least the maintenance engineers have already arrived to fix the problem. You'd think with all the money they spend on this place, they could sort out the heating system."

"How's he doing?" Antimone asked.

"Oh, he's a little star. Have you got your drawing to show your mum, Paul?"

The four-year-old placed the paper he was holding in his hand on the table. Antimone's smile faded slightly as her gaze took in her son's artwork. The picture depicted a crude stick man, drawn in blue crayon. The face comprised two wonky eyes and a disproportionately large downturned mouth. Dark hair rose in jagged lines from the top of the head. The figure oozed menace.

"Um, no, I meant the painting you did earlier," the teacher said. She turned to Antimone. "We let them draw while they're waiting."

Paul placed a second sheet over the first. This one showed several trees and what appeared to be an animal in front.

"It's a dog," he announced. "Can we get a dog, Mummy?"

The two women exchanged a glance.

"Maybe when you're a bit older," Antimone replied. "We can't really keep a pet here, though." She reached out a hand and uncovered the second picture. "Who's this then?"

"It's the bad man."

A shiver ran through Antimone's body despite the temperature. "Which bad man?"

"The one in blue."

"Have you seen him?"

Paul nodded.

Mrs Prendergast shrugged. "I'm not sure where that could have been. Nobody else has been in the classroom all day."

"I saw him when I went for a wee-wee."

The teacher shot Antimone a worried look. "We let the older ones go to the toilet by themselves. It's just down the hall. I have to say Paul has an especially well-developed imagination. It's probably nothing."

"He mentioned the same thing a few days ago," Antimone said, frowning. "Paul, have you seen this man before?"

"Yes."

"You mean while we've been here?"

Another nod.

"Was he alone?"

"No."

"How many were there?"

Paul pondered the question for a moment. "A hundred."

The teacher squatted beside the boy. "Remember, we've done counting. What comes after one?"

"Two."

"Good."

"Three, four, five, six..."

"That's excellent, Paul. So, can you tell us how many men you saw?"

A look of concentration occupied Paul's face. "Three," he announced, proudly.

Mrs Prendergast straightened her legs. "I wouldn't worry about it. Like I said, I'm sure it's nothing."

"Yeah," Antimone replied, a frown creasing her forehead. "Paul, this is important. Are you saying you've seen one of these men before when we were in that place in Africa, you know, after we went on the sailing boat?"

"Can we go now, Mummy?"

"Did you recognise the man from our time in the hospital, Paul?"

"I'm hot. I want to watch television."

Antimone shrugged at the other woman. "Fine. Would you like a ride?"

Paul clambered onto his mother's lap with no hesitation.

"Say goodbye to Mrs Prendergast," Antimone said.

"Bye."

"See you tomorrow," the teacher replied.

Antimone steered her wheelchair through the doorway, then stopped. "Where were the men when you saw them?"

Paul pointed a finger. "Just there."

"What were they doing?"

"I don't know. Can we go and watch Peppa Pig now?"

"You said these people were wearing blue?"

"Please, Mummy."

Antimone shook her head. "Fine, but only for a few minutes. Then we need to take you down for tea."

Tuesday 21ˢᵗ April 2037
Ilithyia Biotechnology, Northstowe

Max Perrin glanced at the band on his wrist: a few minutes before six o'clock. The site manager, Nick Butler, had greeted them upon arrival and expressed his displeasure at the second disruption to the facility in a week. Max promised to resolve the issue that day, no matter how long it took. Mo had already adjusted the temperature back to the regular setting. Now, they just had to sit tight, pretending to fix the underlying problem, until the time came to carry out the next stage of the mission.

"I am bored," Omar said, inspecting the assembled weapon he held in his hands. "How much longer do we need to wait?"

"We've already been over this," Max replied. "We have to stay here for another two hours at least."

"But I hate waiting. Also, I am hungry."

"Bloody hell. It's like babysitting a bunch of children. You knew the plan, and I reminded you to bring food with you."

"Yes," Omar said sulkily, "but it is all gone. The man told us we could eat in the canteen."

When they had arrived, Nick Butler offered them use of the building amenities and handed them a card, which they could use to order meals.

Max shrugged his shoulders in resignation. "All right. If you must, but I'm staying here. There are too many people about who might recognise me. Don't be long. And for God's sake, don't do anything to attract attention."

Omar grinned and placed the reassembled pistol in the toolbox. "Good. Are you coming, Mo?"

"No, I am not hungry."

The muscular North African crossed to the door. "Fine. I will be back soon."

"I do not know how he can eat at a time like this," Mo said when his colleague had left.

"Yeah." Max rose from his seat and bent down to pick up the weapon. He turned it in his hands. It looked totally unlike a conventional gun, but the purpose was clear from the shiny barrel and simple trigger mechanism.

Although only a single-shot pistol, it was deadly at close quarters. Re-arming required the user to unscrew the parts before inserting a new bullet. Another metal tube held a supply of ammunition.

"What do you plan to do after the mission is over and we have reached Paris?" Mo asked.

"I don't know. I haven't really given it much thought. One thing's for sure; I can't stay here. Maybe I'll spend some time on a beach. How about you?"

"Oh, I will return to my family. They live in Tripoli."

The conversation lapsed into silence. Neither man had anything in common with the other. Mo returned to the computer screen and navigated the menu options for the heating system. Max paced across the room with the gun in his hand. Both men spun around at a sound from the door.

The handle turned, and Nick Butler entered. Despite the heat, he still wore a suit. The acrid scent of body odour followed him inside. He loosened the red tie at his neck, then ran his fingers through his short, grey hair.

"How's it going?" he asked. "The temperature seems to be returning to normal, so I assume you're making progress."

Max moved against the wall, hiding the pistol behind his back. "We're still not quite to the bottom of things," he replied. "We suspect there could be a sensor fault, so we may need to track the faulty part down. But don't worry, we'll get it done tonight."

"Good. We can't afford any more disruption." Butler's attention settled on the screen. "Could you show me where to find the readings on the system in case this happens again?"

Mo shifted uneasily on his seat. "Um..."

"We're pretty busy just at the moment," Max said. "Perhaps we can run you through it when we've finished."

"Oh." A frown developed on the site manager's forehead. "I suppose so. I'll catch you later." His gaze tracked to Max's right arm. He turned away, then seemed to reconsider his decision. "Actually, do you mind if I ask what you're holding behind your back?"

Max withdrew his hidden hand and pointed the pistol barrel at the man's chest. "You probably shouldn't have asked that."

Butler's face turned pale. "Is that a...?"

"Yes, it's a gun. It doesn't look like a conventional weapon because we had to disguise the parts to get it through the scanners."

"But, what—?"

"I'm sorry," Max said in little more than a whisper. He squeezed the trigger.

The bang wasn't as loud as he had expected. Even so, Butler staggered backwards. A crimson stain expanded rapidly across his white shirt on the left side of his chest. He coughed, and a trickle of blood dribbled from his mouth. He extended his right arm, then toppled silently onto the floor and lay still.

Mo leapt back from his chair. "What are you doing?"

"We can't afford to take a prisoner now," Max replied.

"I... I thought that was the plan."

"Yes, but there are only the two of us. If somebody else came in, we wouldn't be able to control the situation."

"What if someone heard the bang?"

"Hopefully nobody noticed. I guess we'll find out soon enough."

"But they may look for him when he does not return."

"That's a risk we're going to have to take. Help me move the body."

Mo stared at Max wordlessly for a moment, then moved to the side of the dead man. "Where shall we put him?"

"We need to get him out of sight. Can we shift that cabinet?"

"Yes, but it will not hide him for long."

"I'm aware of that," Max snapped. "We just have to make sure he's not visible to anyone coming in."

The pair manoeuvred the heavy metal unit away from the wall. Between them, they dragged Butler's corpse across the floor, leaving a streak of red behind in their path.

"What about that?" Mo asked, pointing at the bloodstain.

"There are some rags in the toolbox. You clean up the mess while I reload the gun."

The hacker looked like he was about to argue, but after a moment's deliberation, he followed the instructions.

Max grabbed the shiny cylinder and unscrewed the end. The metal cap escaped his grip and bounced across the floor in a series of metallic tings. With trembling fingers, he extracted a bullet from the tube, removed the barrel and reloaded the weapon.

As he reassembled the final part, the rattle of the handle drew his attention. Both men in the room froze as the door swung open.

Omar appeared in the doorway, a wide grin on his face. "I feel better now," he said. "Did I miss anything?"

Tuesday 21ˢᵗ April 2037
Ilithyia Biotechnology, Northstowe

Paul skipped ahead of Antimone into the canteen. She had allowed him to watch two episodes of Peppa Pig in their room, but now it was time for him to eat. A variety of tantalising food smells set her stomach rumbling as she followed her son through the swing doors.

At a quarter past six, the canteen was mostly empty. Most people at the site ate their evening meal later. A handful of scientists in white coats congregated around one table, engaged in a vigorous conversation. A security guard, identifiable from his pale-blue uniform, occupied another by himself. He picked at the contents of his plate while he stared into the screen of a mobile device. The schoolteacher, Mrs Prendergast, also sat alone. Paul hadn't spotted her yet, or he would have rushed up to greet her.

Antimone followed her son to the serving area. "What do you fancy tonight?" she asked.

"Turkey dinosaurs and chips," he replied.

"You had that yesterday. How about the beef stew?"

"But I don't like stew. I want ketchup too."

Antimone debated with herself whether to hold her ground or concede. Getting Paul to eat healthily was a constant battle. Jason was far better at persuading their son to vary his diet, but her partner wasn't here.

"All right," she said after a short pause. "But tomorrow you have to try something else."

The woman behind the counter flashed her a sympathetic look. "Is there anything in particular you'd like us to get in? I'm on this shift for the rest of the week. I can probably arrange for the chef to make a special meal for you."

Antimone's mind went blank for a moment. Every food her son enjoyed seemed to have some unhealthy aspect. "Um, I don't know. Actually, he likes macaroni cheese."

"No problem. I'm sure we can manage that."

"Thanks."

"And what about you? What would you like?"

"Oh, nothing, thank you. My partner and I will be eating later."

"Right, see you then."

Antimone placed the payment card against the reader, perched the tray on her knees and steered herself towards an empty table.

At that moment, Paul spotted his teacher. "Can we sit with Mrs Prendergast?"

Antimone tried to steer him away. "We don't really want to bother her. You've been with her all day. I'm sure she needs some time alone. You can see her again tomorrow."

The woman turned in her seat and flashed a smile. "It's all right. I don't mind."

Paul ran over and perched on the edge of a chair. "I watched Peppa Pig," he announced.

"That sounds exciting."

"Peppa made a friend. It was a cat."

Antimone placed the food in front of him. He reached out a hand. "Knife and fork, please," she said.

The teacher sipped from her drink, then put the glass down. "Thank goodness the place has cooled down."

Antimone helped her son to hold the cutlery. "Yeah," she replied. "It's ironic that with all this advanced technology and all these scientists on site, they still can't manage to keep the temperature under control."

Mrs Prendergast hesitated a moment before speaking. "You mentioned a trip on a boat to Africa earlier. Do you mind if I ask what that was about? Paul has talked about bad men a few times. It seems whatever happened had a big impact on him."

The rescue of four British citizens from Tripoli had been front-page news for many weeks, but most of the details concerning the abduction from the Glasgow Olympics stadium and the subsequent journey by ship stayed out of the press.

Antimone pondered how to reply. Paul spent several hours a day with this woman. If her son's experiences were having a bearing on his behaviour, his teacher deserved to know the basic facts.

Antimone leant forwards and lowered her voice. "You must have heard that I'm Paul's birth mother. Despite what you may have read, Anna Mayfield wasn't actually the first to survive childbirth. I was."

"Yes, I already knew that."

"Well, it seems some other people found out before it became public knowledge. They kidnapped the three of us and transferred us by boat to Tripoli so they could study our biological makeup. They would be the bad men Paul talks about."

"Did they hurt him?"

214

"They extracted blood and tissue samples. He's terrified of needles now. They also deliberately infected him with the modified strain of the Orestes virus."

"I can't imagine what that must have been like."

"Most people have the new variant, so that's no longer such a big deal. What affected him—and me—most was when they separated us. They took him away from me and planned to put him in a room with a pregnant woman. They were trying to coerce members of our group into developing a cure."

"You mean Mrs Baxter?" the teacher asked.

"Correct."

"It must have been awful."

"It was."

"I've seen her in here a few times," Mrs Prendergast said. "I don't understand why she isn't rotting in prison. She caused this whole thing."

"Yes, I'm certainly not a fan of hers, but she did save Paul's life. Luckily, she and Dr Kubar came up with a drug that protected my son from the virus. She's working here with the other scientists to develop a cure, but a guard escorts her everywhere, and they lock her up every night. By the way, she claims the original outbreak was an accident."

"Even if that's true, she still kept quiet about it. As far as I'm concerned, they should put her behind bars and throw away the key."

Paul continued to eat his food, resorting to fingers now that his mother was distracted by the conversation. He looked up as another person entered the canteen.

"A blue man," he announced.

The two women twisted in their seats and stared at the new arrival. The newcomer wore a set of dark-blue, one-piece overalls. Standing at over six feet tall, the fabric of his uniform stretched tightly around his upper body. The tanned skin of his clean-shaven scalp glistened under the bright ceiling lights.

"Is he the bad man you saw earlier?" Antimone asked, watching as the workman approached the counter.

"No, silly," Paul replied.

"Oh." Antimone turned back to Mrs Prendergast. "Well, I've never seen him before."

"Me neither," the teacher said.

"He has the tree logo on his chest. That's Beechwood, the maintenance company, isn't it? I remember seeing the van outside the first time it got too hot. He must be one of the engineers who've come to fix the heating system."

"You're right. He does look like he might be from North Africa though."

Antimone twisted her neck and surreptitiously studied the engineer. "Yeah, possibly."

Paul lifted a chip to his mouth and wiped his fingers on his T-shirt. Patches of tomato ketchup stained his face.

"The bad man was with him," he said, pointing.

Tuesday 21St April 2037
Ilithyia Biotechnology, Northstowe

Paul chattered away as he finished his meal. Most evenings, Antimone would have chivvied him along, telling him to spend less time talking and more time eating, but she sat in distracted silence, mulling over what her son had said about the bad man. Soon, the teacher, Mrs Prendergast, made her excuses and departed. Every few seconds, Antimone glanced over at the workman in the blue coveralls. He seemed oblivious to her scrutiny as he worked his way through a mounded plate of food.

"I'm finished."

Antimone dragged her attention back to her son and pointed at the last half-eaten turkey dinosaur. "Aren't you going to eat that?"

"No."

"So, you don't want anything else?"

"I'm hungry for jelly and ice-cream."

"So, you're too full to finish your main course, but you can still fit in some pudding?"

"Please."

"Fine." Some battles just weren't worth fighting.

Antimone steered her wheelchair to the counter and returned moments later carrying a small bowl. Paul rapidly consumed the contents, although a fair proportion landed on the tabletop. She wiped his mouth, despite her son's vigorous attempts to avoid the paper napkin. When her attention shifted back to the maintenance man, he was no longer sitting at the table. She glimpsed a flash of blue as the doors swung closed.

"Come on, we're going now," she said. "Jump on."

Paul needed no second invitation. He scrambled onto his mother's lap. With a pang of guilt, Antimone headed to the exit. On any other occasion, she would have followed the notice on the wall and taken the dirty crockery to the return station, but she wanted to see where the man went.

She emerged from the canteen and spotted the distinctive uniform thirty metres away to her left. She pushed down on the hand rim and accelerated after the departing figure. He rounded a corner as Antimone hurried to catch up. She reached the point where he had disappeared from view and stopped. Other than a group of three security guards standing by a water cooler further down the corridor, the place was empty. Where had he gone?

A slight movement drew her gaze as a door set in the wall to her right clicked shut. The man must have entered the room beyond. What should she do? She was probably worrying unnecessarily. As Mrs Prendergast had said, Paul possessed a vivid imagination. More than likely, the man's appearance had reminded her son of somebody he had seen during their time in North Africa. But she had to be sure.

She glanced across to the pale-blue uniforms, gathered approximately forty metres away. If she discovered anything untoward, she could always call for help. Her heart rate crept up as she wheeled herself nearer. Should she knock or just go in?

"Can I watch television when we get back?" Paul asked, shifting his position.

"We'll see," Antimone replied, distractedly. "I want to have a peek in here."

Her son's presence cemented her decision. She would open the door, take a quick look, then shout to the security guards if necessary. She reached out a hand and turned the handle. A wave of cooler air washed over her, tainted by a faint oily smell. The gap widened to reveal a control room of some sort, with metal cabinets containing electrical equipment lining the walls. Three male figures stood together, all wearing dark-blue coveralls embossed with the Beechwood logo. The men stared at her in surprise.

Antimone's gaze darted from one to the next. Her mouth gaped as her eyes locked onto the third maintenance man with the paler skin.

"Max?" she croaked.

Paul's arms wrapped tightly around her neck. "Mummy, it's the bad man. I'm scared."

Antimone glanced down at her son. A scrabble of movement from inside the room snapped her attention back. When she looked up, the burly, shaven-headed workman she had followed from the canteen was pointing a shiny metallic cylinder at her face.

"Don't," Max barked.

The barrel of the weapon wavered in the other man's hand for a moment.

"If you make a sound, both you and your son will die," Max continued in a quieter tone. "Come in slowly and pull the door closed behind you."

The maintenance man holding the pistol scowled at Antimone. "We should just shoot her," he said.

"Not now," Max hissed. "Not with the door open. There are probably security guards out there. They'd be onto us in a flash."

Every muscle in Antimone's body froze. "But I thought you were—"

"I won't ask you again," Max interrupted. "It may not look like much, but believe me, that gun is deadly at close range. And my colleague here is more than willing to use it."

Antimone edged forwards. How could she have been so stupid? A swirl of conflicting emotions spun through her brain. For months, she had believed herself to be a murderess, but here was her victim, alive and well. But what the hell was he doing in this building? What would they do if she called for help?

The cold eyes glaring back at her left her in no doubt that the man holding the weapon would shoot if ordered to do so. She moved into the room and pulled the door closed behind her.

"Good," Max said. "Much as I'd enjoy watching you die here and now, it would jeopardise the rest of our mission."

"But your arm..." Antimone's gaze locked onto the spot where she had inserted the needle. "The acid..."

"Yes, this is all artificial thanks to what you did to me." The fingers of his right hand tapped his left shoulder with a solid sounding clunk. The low whir of motors accompanied the movement as he rotated the prosthetic limb.

"I never meant... How did you survive?"

"Luckily, they have some decent doctors in Tripoli. They tell me it was touch and go, but I'm still alive."

"But what are you doing here?"

"Enough with the questions. If you don't do what you're told, the boy will be the first to suffer. Now, move over there away from the door."

Antimone could barely tear her eyes from Max's left arm as she navigated across the room—until her gaze lowered to the faint streaks of blood on the tiled floor and tracked them to their destination. A leg protruded from behind the cabinet. She gasped and held her hand to her mouth. "Is he—?"

"Yes, he's dead."

"Who is it?"

"Somebody who didn't do what he was told."

Antimone clutched her son tightly to her chest. "Please don't hurt us."

"That depends upon whether you follow my instructions."

"What do you want?"

"You can start by telling me where the others are."

"Which others?" Antimone's voice quivered as she asked the question.

"You know exactly who I mean. Kubar, Baxter and that arsehole boyfriend of yours."

"What are you going to do to them?"

"Let me worry about that. Now, where are they?"

"I don't—"

"Shoot the boy."

The barrel of the pistol moved. Antimone tried to wrap her arms around her son to cover his body. "No, please. I'll tell you."

Max directed a slight shake of the head to his subordinate. "Go on, then."

"The rooms are all along the corridor on the second floor. Jason said the one we're in is where his mother used to have her office."

"You better not be lying."

"I'm not, I swear. But they keep Mrs Baxter's room locked. Nobody can get in or out without a key."

"That figures. The bitch should be behind bars. Will she be there now?"

"I don't know. Most of the scientists will already have finished for the day, but she's probably still working. We were going to eat with her tonight, but that's not until eight o'clock."

"Quite the happy family. I can't believe either of you has anything to do with her. If the police hadn't turned up when they did four years ago, she would've incinerated both of you."

"I don't want to spend time with her, but Jason agreed to let her be part of our lives if she saved Paul when we were in Tripoli."

"You'll take us to her workplace. If anybody asks, you're showing us the way so we can repair the sensors for the heating system. If you make any attempt to raise the alarm, I'll shoot your boy first."

"Please. Leave him out of this. He's only four years old for God's sake."

"No, he's coming with us. Omar, you take the gun. As for you, trike queen, if anything goes wrong, you'll watch your son die. Then it'll be your turn. Is that clear?"

Antimone stifled a sob. "Yes."

"Right. Let's go."

Tuesday 21ˢᵗ April 2037
Ilithyia Biotechnology, Northstowe

Max opened the door to the control room. He surveyed the area outside before beckoning Antimone forward. "Remember, if you do anything to alert the guards, well... you know what will happen."

Paul clung tightly around her neck. She sensed the trembling of his body as he buried his face against her chest. She clasped him to her and lowered her lips to his ear. "It'll be all right," she murmured.

Max trailed behind her, his hands resting on the back of her wheelchair. The big man she had followed from the canteen stood to the side, carrying a toolbox. She had watched as he placed the pistol on top of the other tools. The smallest of the three brought up the rear.

As soon as they emerged into the corridor, Antimone's gaze settled on the group of guards, still standing by the water cooler. One of them said something to his colleagues, and a peal of laughter carried across. They paid no attention to the workmen in the blue coveralls or their reluctant companions.

"Which way is it?" Max whispered.

She turned away from her potential rescuers and pointed. "The labs are down there."

"Lead on, then."

Antimone reached down to the hand rings and propelled herself to the left. Thoughts of escape rattled through her brain. If she accelerated at top speed, could she put enough distance between them before the big North African retrieved the gun from the toolbox and took a shot? Had she been alone, she might have taken the chance, but having her son on her lap made it too risky. No, she would wait for a better opportunity.

"Don't even think about it," Max said from behind as if reading her mind. She felt a vibration through her back as he grabbed the handles. They followed the corridor to a pair of swing doors. Max stepped forwards and placed his card against the reader. A red light shone briefly, accompanied by a buzzer. He tried a second time with the same result.

"What's going on? Why won't it open?"

"You obviously don't have the correct access rights," Antimone snapped.

"What about yours?"

Before she could reply, Max ripped the laminated rectangle from around her neck and repeated the process. Once again, the lock refused to release.

"If you'd bothered to ask," Antimone said, "I could've told you mine wouldn't work either. Only the scientists can get through here."

"So, how…?"

Max's voice trailed off as a security guard turned the corner and strode towards them. The man drew nearer, a scowl on his face. He was of medium build with short brown hair. The pale-blue uniform was at least one size too large for him. Antimone hadn't seen him before. His hand reached down to a plastic object on his belt.

To her left, she watched as the muscular North African placed the toolbox on the ground.

"What's going on here?" the guard asked.

"We're from Beechwood Environmental Systems," Max replied. "We're here to repair the heating system."

"But why are you trying to get through this door? The control room's back that way."

"Yeah, we know. The computer's telling us there's a faulty sensor in one of the laboratories. I thought the card we were given would allow us in."

"Right. Well, clearly it doesn't. And what's this young lady doing with you? She should be aware access to this area is restricted."

Antimone's wheelchair jolted slightly as somebody gently kicked a wheel from behind. The man Max had referred to as Omar crouched over the toolbox with his hand on the lid. Their eyes met.

"Um…" she said. "They asked me where the labs were, so I was just showing them the way."

"Wait a sec," the guard said, his face lighting up with excitement. "You're that wheelchair racer, Antimone something, aren't you? I was watching the Olympic final on the television. I couldn't believe what happened when the bombs went off and everything. You were definitely going to win though."

"Yeah."

"Hey, would you mind signing an autograph for me?"

"Actually, we're in a bit of a hurry," Max said. "It's late, and we're already on overtime. The boss won't be pleased if this takes too long. He's a real cheapskate. Time is money and all that."

"Oh, sure," the guard replied, his face falling in disappointment. "I'll catch you later, Antimone. I haven't got a pen or paper on me at the moment, anyway. Perhaps you could sign something when I'm on duty again

222

tomorrow. Hang on a sec, sir, and I'll get the office to update your pass. Can I just have the number?"

Max removed the rectangle of plastic from around his neck and handed it to the other man. The guard stepped a few paces away, unclipped the walkie talkie from his belt and spoke in a low voice.

"Right, that's sorted," he said a moment later, handing the card back. "You should be able to pass through all the doors leading to the laboratory area now, but you'll have to find a scientist to accompany you if you need to get inside any of the labs. Even the security guards aren't allowed in there alone. I'm afraid most of the science team have already knocked off for the night. I think Dr Hendrick is still working, though. He's normally one of the last to leave."

"What about Mrs Baxter?"

The guard shot Max a curious look. "Why are you asking about her?"

"It's just, um... somebody mentioned that she works in the same lab as the faulty sensor."

"Okay. I don't know if anyone's there now. If you find Dr Hendrick, he can let you into anywhere you need to go."

"Thanks," Max replied. "You've been a big help."

"No problem. Happy to be of assistance. I'll catch up with you for that autograph tomorrow, Antimone."

The guard returned in the direction from which he had come. He turned and threw a wave before turning the corner and disappearing out of sight.

"There, that wasn't too hard, was it?" Max said. "You're quite the celebrity, aren't you? And by the way, you just saved fan boy's life." His gaze flicked across to the burly North African, who straightened up and tapped the toolbox lid. Max held his pass against the reader. This time, the light flashed green, accompanied by a clunk as the lock released.

"Please," Antimone said, "let my son go. I did what you asked."

"Sorry, I can't do that," Max replied, his lips curling into a smirk. "We've barely started yet. Now, let's find that murderous bitch. I have a score to settle with her."

223

Tuesday 21St April 2037
Ilithyia Biotechnology, Northstowe

Martin Hendrick stretched out his arms and cracked his knuckles. He checked the time: 18:28. The other scientists left a quarter of an hour earlier, and once again, he was alone in the nanomachine laboratory. He hit save, navigated the menu options, then selected the compile command. It would take at least five minutes for the complex software to convert his program into a format understood by the manufacturing machines in the room next door.

He had studied his colleagues' creations and now felt competent enough to undertake his own. It had taken him a while to adapt to this new methodology, but the technology was hugely powerful and would definitely change the face of medical research. In a few minutes, all being well, he would be ready to perform the first trials on a tissue sample. His design was relatively simple and an order of magnitude larger in size than the machines the team were developing to treat the Orestes virus, but he was still excited to transfer a simulation from the computer screen to the real world.

As he waited for the compilation to finish, his thoughts returned to his final days at Ilithyia twenty years earlier. If he had stayed, he would have become immensely wealthy alongside the two founders of the company. He didn't regret the way things turned out. The science interested him far more than wealth or fame. When it all went wrong—as it had—celebrity could just as quickly switch to notoriety. He was lucky to have kept his name out of the headlines when the story about the company's involvement broke in the press nine months ago.

A beep from the terminal signalled the end of the job. Hendrick leant forwards to study the compilation report: no errors and only one warning. He reached out a finger and prodded the information button to provide more details. Apparently, he had omitted an initialisation, but it seemed the software was intelligent enough to substitute a default value.

Ever the perfectionist, Hendrick switched back to the development screen and corrected the issue. He waited impatiently for the process to complete a second time. When the message box appeared, he studied the display and sighed with satisfaction: no warnings at all on this pass.

The next step was to manufacture samples of his design. Professor Allard has asked him to ensure somebody peer-reviewed his work before the manufacturing stage, but nobody was around. He decided to proceed. If anybody queried his actions, he would claim he'd become so wrapped up in the excitement of the moment that the professor's instructions had slipped his mind.

Operating procedure required a full decontamination of the machine's assembly chamber before activation to prevent cross-contamination between samples. Hendrick knew the machine had remained inactive all day, so it was ready to accept his project. Afterwards, if he set the cleaning process in motion before leaving that night, the operation would complete long before the scientists arrived to start the following day's shift.

He pulled up the manufacturing screen and loaded the job. The software worked through a list of questions, starting with the quantity to manufacture. Hendrick selected five grammes. That would be more than enough to prove out this initial batch. Finally, a message box popped up, informing him the operation would take fifty-four minutes to complete. He clicked the accept button. A timer appeared, the digits counting down every second.

He knew there would be little to see, but he wanted to witness the birth of his first creation with this technology. Rising from his workstation, he rolled his neck. He strolled across the room to the archway separating the manufacturing area from the rest of the laboratory.

A prominent sign on the wall warned about the presence of high-strength magnetic fields that remained energised at all times. Professor Allard had explained that the purpose of the field was to deactivate any nanomachines that might accidentally transfer from within on a worker's body or clothing. The devices were so small that even a gentle breeze could carry them in the air like dust. A red glow shone around the doorframe, serving as a secondary warning.

Hendrick felt no discernible difference as he strolled inside. The overhead strip light flickered on, bathing the room in harsh illumination. A hulking, obsidian-black machine occupied the whole of the back wall. A series of winking multi-coloured lights broke up the flat surfaces on the front. Set in the centre was a display panel. It showed the number of his job and the estimated time remaining: 52:04.

As Hendrick approached the mechanism, he picked up a low humming noise. He stretched out a hand and touched the matt surface. A faint vibration ran through his fingertips. A sudden feeling of déjà vu flashed through his mind. He recalled the same sense of fascination when, as a young man, he had spent hours studying his 3D printer as it built up his creations, one wafer-thin layer at a time. He imagined the inner workings of this machine putting together his design in a similar way but at a significantly smaller scale.

After watching the countdown for a few minutes, he tore himself away. There was still much to do if he intended to perform the initial tests of his work that night. He grabbed a pair of disposable gloves from the dispenser mounted on the wall, slipped his fingers inside, then crossed to the refrigerator, where he had placed the thin sections of defrosted skin cells a few hours earlier.

Picking up the plastic case, he carried it to the workbench on which the biocontainment unit rested. The sealed, glass-fronted cabinet allowed researchers to work without fear of contamination from whatever they were testing.

Unlike his previous time at Ilithyia, he had no intention of cutting corners and taking risks. He removed a pre-prepared slide from the box and mounted it inside the unit. After sealing the exterior, he manoeuvred the sample beneath the high-power microscope and adjusted the focus until the regular pattern of the cells showed up clearly.

Satisfied with his preparations, Hendrick strolled over to the manufacturing machine. Still just over ten minutes to go. He paced the width of the room as the timer counted down to zero. After what seemed an age, a loud beep emerged. The screen displayed a *Job Complete* message. He slid back the hatch and removed a glass vial. A tiny printed label on the side indicated the batch number, date of manufacture and a bright yellow biohazard symbol. He held it up to the light and studied the contents; the thin layer of grey powder at the bottom of the tube looked unremarkable in the harsh glare.

His heart beat faster as he returned to the biocontainment cabinet and slotted the vial into the sliding drawer. Now to activate the nanomachines. He pressed the button to switch on the ultraviolet light. Everything inside the sealed box took on a purple-blue tinge. After a few seconds, the lamp turned off.

He placed his hands in the two slots and confirmed the robotic actuators followed his exact movements. With great care, he unscrewed the vial and inserted a plastic rod until the tip touched the contents. It would take only a tiny amount of the substance to prove its operation.

He moved the stick to the sample and dabbed the end against the wafer-thin layer of cells, then dropped it inside the yellow biohazard bin in the corner of the cabinet. The maintenance team would remove the container later and pass it through an array of high-strength magnets before a furnace incinerated the contents.

He resealed the vial and opened the drawer in the side of the unit. He retrieved the glass tube and fitted it into the foam insert inside the small metal box he had placed on the bench earlier, then slipped it into his pocket.

Turning back to the microscope controls, he performed a few minor adjustments until the screen displayed a razor-sharp image of the test sample. Ten seconds passed. Nothing appeared to be happening. Twenty seconds. Still no activity. What had he done wrong? He tweaked the knobs to adjust the horizontal position of the lens. As the view moved sideways, all the cells seemed perfectly normal.

Then a movement at the edge of the display caught his eye. The regular shape of the cell wall collapsed into a thin oval. An adjacent cell did the same, followed by several more. When he peered closely, he spotted a handful of tiny black dots, barely visible even under maximum magnification, drifting across the image ahead of the wave of destruction.

"Yes," he murmured in triumph, as the pattern radiated outwards. He continued to watch until every circle had collapsed. He stood and rotated his shoulders to ease out the kinks. The experiment was a success, but now came the clean-up.

He re-inserted his hands in the slots at the front of the cabinet and directed the robotic fingers to deposit the test sample into the disposal bin. The next task was to set the manufacturing machine to a decontamination cycle. He strode to the control screen and selected the command. A few seconds later, a low hum emerged from deep inside the mechanism, accompanied by a countdown timer on the display.

Satisfied with his day's work, he crossed the room and stepped through the glowing red doorframe into the outer part of the laboratory. Sensing his presence, the overhead lights, which had turned off due to a lack of activity, burst into life, throwing a bright illumination over the workstations.

One job remained. Hendrick returned to his seat and entered his login credentials into the system. At that moment, the sound of knocking on the outside door disturbed the silence. The other scientists who worked in the laboratory would use their access card to enter. That meant the visitor had to be somebody without the necessary permissions. He debated whether to respond. Unfortunately, the lighting gave away his presence.

If he failed to answer, there was a good chance the person might think the occupant had suffered an accident and raise the alarm. And that would entail answering some awkward questions.

"Just a minute," he called.

He hurriedly navigated through the menu options until he found the setting he wanted. A few clicks later, he finished the task and logged out.

The knock repeated.

Tuesday 21ˢᵗ April 2037
Ilithyia Biotechnology, Northstowe

Antimone steered the wheelchair behind the two North Africans. Paul had stopped trembling, but his arms still clung to her like a limpet to a rock. Max brought up the rear, his hands resting on the back of Antimone's seat. The group progressed without talking, the silence broken only by the click of footsteps and the low hiss of wheels on the tiled floor. They approached another sealed door.

Max strolled forwards and used his card to let them through. A long corridor stretched ahead. Doors lay at regular intervals along both walls, each carrying a sign with white letters on a black background. Frosted glass obstructed a view of the interior of each laboratory, but the darkness from behind the windows of all but one suggested the majority of scientists had already left for the day.

Max strode towards the only brightly lit area and studied the label: BioNEMS.

"What the hell does that stand for?" he said.

Nobody answered.

He glowered at Antimone. "I asked you a question."

She stared back at him for a moment before replying. "I've no idea, but Dr Hendrick is focusing on nanomachines or something like that."

"Who's Dr Hendrick?"

"He's one of the scientists. From what Jason told me, he used to work for Rosalind Baxter, so he must have worked with your father, too. The guard we spoke to earlier mentioned he'd probably be working late."

"So, this guy had a job at Ilithyia?"

"Isn't that what I just said?"

Max scowled at Antimone. "Which lab would Baxter be in?"

"I don't know. I've never been in this part of the building before."

"What do we do next, boss?" the thin North African asked.

"I'm thinking, Mo," Max replied. After a moment, he continued. "Right. Get the gun out. We knock on the door. When he opens it, we force our way in. You've got the tie wraps in the toolbox, haven't you, Omar? Then we ask him where that bitch is."

"What if he doesn't know?"

"Well, if she isn't here, she'll probably be in her room." He turned to Antimone. "What time did you say you were eating with her?"

"Eight o'clock," she said.

"That's twenty-five minutes from now. Let's find out if she's still working first."

Max waited for Omar to retrieve the gun, then approached the door. He knocked.

After a short delay, a muffled male voice responded from inside. "Just a minute."

Max shifted impatiently from foot to foot as several seconds ticked by. He repeated the action, knocking a little louder the second time.

A few seconds later, a figure moved behind the frosted glass. A gap opened, revealing a man with thinning sandy hair and wearing a white medical coat. He stared at the three men in blue uniforms for a moment, then lowered his eyes to Antimone and her son.

"Yes, what can I do for you?"

Omar raised the pistol, aimed it at the man's chest with his right hand and pushed him back into the room with his left.

The scientist turned pale at the sight of the weapon. "What do you want?"

The other members of the group followed the pair inside. Max closed the door behind them. "I could tell you we've come to fix the heating system, but that would be a lie."

Hendrick's gaze settled on the Oaktree logo, then returned to Max's face. "Sorry, I don't understand."

"We're looking for someone. Do you know where Mrs Baxter is?"

"I haven't seen her all day."

"Doesn't she work in here?"

"Sometimes, but not today. Who are you?"

"That's not important."

"This is Max Perrin," Antimone interjected. "You probably knew his father."

"What?" Hendrick said. "Not Nigel Perrin's boy? It must be over two decades since I last saw him."

"Well," Max replied, "he's been dead for four years, so you've missed your chance. Anyway, we're not here to catch up on old times. Where would I find the bitch?"

"Like I said, I haven't seen her. If she's not in one of the other labs, she'll be in the canteen or back in her room."

"This is the only lab with the lights still on. Whereabouts is her room?"

"It's on the second floor."

"Didn't I just tell you that?" Antimone said, scowling.

Max glared at her. "It doesn't hurt to be sure." He turned to Omar. "Secure his wrists and gag him."

"Wait. What're you going to do to me?"

"If you keep quiet, nothing will happen to you. But if you make a noise or try to escape... well, all you really need to know is that my friend here is an expert in causing pain."

Max waited as Omar restrained their prisoner, then beckoned his men towards him.

"What now?" Mo asked.

"People will be eating. We should sit tight for an hour or two until they're all back in their rooms."

Omar scratched the thin layer of stubble on his scalp. "What if a guard comes in?"

"Didn't you hear what the other guy said? They can't get inside the labs. If we turn off the lights, nobody will know we're here."

The North African scanned the wall beside the door. "I do not see a switch."

"They must be automatic," Max said. "Look for a master switch." He spotted a likely candidate above a workbench. "Here we are." The laboratory plunged into darkness, lit only by the red glow of the archway leading into the manufacturing area. Another click and the brightness returned to its previous level. "Good. That's sorted."

"What about the body of the man you shot?" Omar asked.

"They won't find him unless they go in the control room."

"But will somebody not look for the wheelchair girl and her son?"

"Maybe, but there's nothing we can do about that."

"Okay," Mo said. "So, we wait in the dark, then we come out and finish the mission. When do we kill her?"

"I'll deal with her after the others," Max replied. "I want to save the best for last."

Tuesday 21ˢᵗ April 2037
Ilithyia Biotechnology, Northstowe

Jason paced backwards and forwards across the bedroom. Where were Antimone and Paul? The site administration manager had provided him with a desk and a computer in one of the offices for the day so he could prepare his application for the Open University. He had expected to find his partner and son waiting for him when he returned to their room an hour earlier, but nobody was there. He performed a brief search but didn't uncover a note.

They were due to eat with Rosalind Baxter that night. Most of the other people on site shunned the company of the person universally blamed for the release of the Orestes virus. He knew Antimone would prefer to be among that majority, but he had made a promise eight months ago in Tripoli; he agreed to visit his adoptive mother if she saved Paul's life by developing a drug to protect his son against a new strain of the disease that was attacking children. It had been touch and go, but the woman who had raised him for sixteen years succeeded in achieving that goal with the help of Dr Kubar.

The first tendrils of worry burrowed through his stomach. It was unlike Antimone not to contact him or leave a message. They had planned to feed Paul early, but when Jason had checked the canteen half an hour earlier, there were no signs of either mother or son. The serving staff remembered them coming in but knew nothing about their movements afterwards.

He whirled around as somebody knocked at the door. Had Antimone and Paul returned? But if that was the case, why didn't they use the key card? He rushed across the room and twisted the lock without checking through the peephole. A security guard stood beside Rosalind Baxter.

"Are you ready?" she asked.

Jason failed to hide the disappointment on his face. "Um... no. Sorry, but we're going to have to reschedule. Antimone and Paul seem to have vanished. You haven't seen them around, have you?"

"No, I'm afraid not. But it's not as if they can go far. I guess I'll have to eat alone—again."

"Look, if they turn up, we'll come down and join you later."

"Fine." Rosalind turned to the man standing beside her. "I suppose you better take me down then."

Jason watched as the pair headed to the lifts. What should he do? He couldn't just wait in the room. Grabbing a pen, he scrawled a quick note and left it on the bed. He stepped into the corridor, allowing the door to close behind him. But where to start? He had already checked the canteen, but it wouldn't hurt to check again. He jogged in the direction his mother had taken, but the numbers above the lift signalled that both cars were on the ground floor.

Unwilling to wait, he descended the stairs two at a time and emerged into the foyer area. A quick survey confirmed no sign of Antimone or Paul. Fifty yards ahead, Rosalind and the guard disappeared through a pair of swing doors. Jason followed them. The hubbub of raised voices and clinking cutlery greeted his ears as he shoved through and rushed to catch up.

His mother turned in surprise as they reached the entrance at the same instant.

"I thought you weren't going to join me."

"Yeah, I just wanted to make sure they're not waiting here."

Rosalind joined Jason in inspecting the diners. "Well, I can't see them."

"No, neither can I."

"Why don't you contact the security team?"

Jason addressed the guard, who was standing a few feet away. "Excuse me. Have you seen my partner this evening? She goes around in a wheelchair."

The man shook his head. "Sorry. I only started my shift half an hour ago. You'd be better asking somebody over by the front of the building. Do you want me to call them on the radio?"

"No, it's all right. I'll go there now and talk to them."

He said goodbye to his mother and jogged back the way he had come. Moments later, he arrived at the row of barriers by the entrance. Still out of breath, he approached one of the two men on duty.

"Sorry to bother you, but I'm looking for my partner. She and my son have disappeared. She's in a wheelchair."

"Yeah, I know who you're talking about," the man replied. "I'm afraid I haven't seen her. What about you, Dave?"

The second guard scratched his head for a moment, then his face brightened. "You mean the girl with the young child? I remember seeing her earlier with those maintenance men."

Jason frowned. "Which maintenance men?"

"The crew who are here to fix the heating system."

"What was she doing with them?"

"I've no idea. I just saw them walking together. There was a boy of about three or four sitting on her lap. They went through that door over there."

"Do you know where they were going?"

"Sorry, no."

Something Paul had said a few days earlier tugged at Jason's unconscious. What was it? *That's right.* His son talked about seeing a bad man.

"What were they wearing?" Jason asked.

"Who are we talking about now?" the guard called Dave replied with a puzzled expression.

"The maintenance men."

"Oh, they work for Beechwood. They wear dark-blue coveralls with a tree logo on the front."

Paul told them the bad man wore the same colour. Was it a coincidence?

"Are they still here?" Jason asked.

"I haven't seen them."

"Can you check the visitor log?"

"Why?"

"It's something my boy said a day or two back. Are these maintenance men the same ones who visited earlier in the week?"

"I'm afraid the visitor log is confidential, sir."

"Okay. Will you at least tell me whether they've checked out tonight? And while you're at it, could you please confirm that my partner and our son haven't left the site? She's called Antimone Lessing."

The two men moved away and conversed in low voices. One of them removed an electronic device from his pocket and tapped at the screen. After a few moments, both returned.

"There's no record of Miss Lessing or your son leaving the building," the guard said. "The maintenance team are still on the premises, and I can confirm they're the same guys who visited earlier. What was it your boy said that's got you so worried?"

"He told us he'd seen the bad man. He's only four and has a vivid imagination, so we thought it was just a story or something. When we asked him what he meant, he said this person was in Tripoli with us. And he was wearing blue."

"Tripoli? You and your partner were mixed up in that whole bomb thing at the Olympics, weren't you?"

"Yeah."

"So, you think these guys might be linked back to that?"

"It's possible."

"All right," the guard said. "I'll put out an alert on the radio to let us know if anybody spots either the maintenance men or Miss Lessing. I'll also

233

arrange a quick sweep of the building. We'll call you if anything comes up. I suggest you go and wait in your room until you hear from us or in case she turns up."

"Okay, thanks."

Jason turned away. What he had learned in the last few seconds had transformed his initial worries into gut-wrenching fear.

Tuesday 21ˢᵗ April 2037
Ilithyia Biotechnology, Northstowe

Max glanced at his watch band again in the red glow cast by the archway. Just after nine o'clock. His two men sat on the floor, conversing in low voices. Beside them, the scientist lay curled on his side, his arms bound behind his back. The girl was still in her wheelchair, holding her son. The irritating brat had nearly revealed their presence when a guard came down the corridor outside the room an hour earlier. Only the threat of violence had persuaded her to silence her child. Even now, he clung to his mother, making small sniffling sounds.

Max rose to his feet, yawned and stretched his arms. The lack of activity after the initial surge of adrenaline, combined with the muted lighting, had made him feel sleepy. But the time had come for the mission to continue. He strolled over to his two colleagues and kicked the larger man's shoe.

"Let's get going."

The men stood. "Where do we go first?" Omar asked.

Max replied in a low voice. "From what she's told us, their rooms are all together. We'll start with Baxter, then Kubar and finally, her boyfriend. Somebody will have to remain here to guard the scientist."

The North Africans exchanged a glance. "I'll come with you," Omar said.

Max narrowed his eyes in thought. "No, I'm sorry, but you should stay. If anybody discovers you here, I'd rate your chances higher than Mo's in unarmed combat. We'll take the gun and the girl."

Omar glared at his boss. "We should have brought more guns."

"That would have increased the risk of discovery when they scanned the toolbox. Anyway, we can't do anything about it now."

"We could just kill the scientist, then we can all go."

Max considered the suggestion for a moment, then shook his head. "No, we may need a hostage later. We keep him alive for the time being."

"What about her boy?" Mo asked.

"He's the only reason she's doing what we tell her. If she sees a chance, she'll try to escape with him. We should leave him here."

"But he will make much noise."

"If he won't stay quiet, we gag him."

"She will not like that."

"So what? We're the ones in charge. Right, let's do it."

Max strolled across to Antimone. Her eyes glinted in the red glow of the archway as she stared up at him.

"It's time for you to take us to Baxter's room," Max said. "Your son stays here."

"No way. You're not separating us."

"I give the orders. Do you want me to hurt him?"

"If you—"

The sound of Paul's shrill crying interrupted her words.

"Shut him up," Max barked.

"He's four years old, for Christ's sake. What do you expect me to do?"

The wailing grew louder.

"I swear, if he doesn't keep quiet, I'll silence him myself."

A flurry of movement on the floor drew Max's attention. The scientist made several muffled grunts through the gag.

Max crouched by the prisoner and lowered the damp cloth from the man's mouth. "What the hell do you want?"

"I'll show you the way to Mrs Baxter's room," Hendrick said, his voice cracking. He directed his gaze at Antimone. "She can stay here."

Max stared at him for a moment before replying. "All right." He turned back to Antimone. "We'll take him instead. But if you cause any trouble at all, the kid dies. Got it?"

A slight nod signalled Antimone's agreement. She murmured into her son's ear and stroked his head. Paul's cries reduced to a series of muted sniffles.

Max stretched upright. "Mo, get the toolbox. Omar, grab whatever you want to keep as a weapon and untie Dr Hendrick. He's coming with us. If she doesn't follow your instructions, you have my permission to hurt both of them."

Moments later, the three men stood by the door.

"We'll be back soon," Max said. "If anything happens, contact me by phone."

A dishevelled Martin Hendrick followed him through the doorway, rubbing his wrists as he tried to restore circulation. The skinny North African came last, carrying the toolbox.

"Um... How do you plan to get into her room?" the doctor asked.

"What do you mean?" Max replied.

"She's under house arrest. The only people who can open her door are the guards. She can't do it by herself."

"We'll worry about that later. Which way do we go?"

"Follow me."

Hendrick started moving, but Max placed a restraining hand on his shoulder and spun him around. "Not so fast. Just in case you've forgotten, my colleague is armed. Make any attempt to alert somebody and you'll be the first to die, but the girl and her brat will be next. If anyone stops us, we're trying to track down a faulty sensor for the heating system. We asked for directions, and you're showing us where to go."

The scientist nodded. "Yes, I understand."

"Right. Let's get going."

Hendrick turned left and used his card to open the door at the end of the corridor. Mo trailed behind, toolbox in hand. Max brought up the rear. They passed by several more darkened laboratories until eventually they emerged into the brightly lit foyer area. A few people milled about. On the far side, a couple of guards stood, deep in discussion, facing the opposite way. Nobody paid any attention to the group of three as they headed towards the lifts.

Hendrick reached out a hand to press the call button. The leftmost doors slid apart almost immediately.

Max glanced nervously behind him. "No, let's take the stairs. We can't be sure who might be there when we get out."

"Suit yourself," Hendrick replied. "The staircase is just over here."

They climbed the carpeted steps in silence. At the second floor, Max held out an arm. "Hang on. Which room is Kubar in?"

"Dr Kubar? Why do you want to know that? I thought we were going to pay Mrs Baxter a visit."

Max's artificial left hand shot out, and his fingers closed around the scientist's throat. "Just answer the question," he growled.

Hendrick tried in vain to prise the grip loose. He drew a deep, gasping breath when Max released him a second later. "It's four down on the right. I'm not sure what the number is. Actually, it's two oh nine, I think."

"Okay. That wasn't so hard. Now, do the doors have peepholes to check visitors or anything like that?"

"Yeah, they do."

"This is what's going to happen. You knock. We'll stand to the side so he can't see us. When he opens the door, we all go inside. And remember, any attempt to raise the alarm, you, the girl and her son all die. Clear?"

"Understood."

"Good."

Max eased the door open and stuck his head through the gap. The corridor beyond was deserted. He stepped through the doorway and headed to the right, counting off the rooms as he went. The thick carpeting muffled their footsteps. He stopped outside the fourth. The sign on the wall matched the number Hendrick had provided.

"You're sure this is the one?" Max asked.

The scientist swallowed hard. "Yes."

Mo placed the toolbox on the floor and retrieved the assembled pistol. His eyes met Max's, then he handed the weapon over to his team leader.

The two men stood, one on either side of the frame.

Max pointed at Hendrick. "Go ahead and knock," he whispered.

Hendrick's first attempt was barely audible. The second was louder. A muffled call, followed by a rattling sound, came from inside. The door swung inwards. Immediately, Max barged through and shoved Kubar hard in the chest with his left hand.

The North African doctor stumbled, lost his balance and fell backwards in the narrow passageway leading to the main part of the room. When he looked up in shock at the intruders, the barrel of a gun pointed at his head. He opened his mouth, but no words came out.

"Well, well," Max said, his lips twisting in a malicious grin. "Finally, we meet again."

"What... what do you want?" Kubar stammered.

"We'll come to that. What's through there?"

Kubar scrambled back on all fours as Max advanced towards him. "It is the bedroom."

"Go in, sit on the bed and shut up."

Mo pushed Hendrick forwards as all three followed Kubar into the room. The African doctor's eyes remained fixed on the pistol as he lowered himself to the mattress.

Max turned to Hendrick and gestured to an armchair by the darkened window. "Over there. If you move, you'll be next." He refocused his attention on Kubar. "A nice place you have here. Much better than that shit hole in Tripoli they kept us in."

"I... I thought you were dead. The acid..."

"Well, I lost the arm, but as you can see, I'm still alive—unfortunately for you."

"Traitor," Mo spat. He muttered a curse in Arabic.

"They would never have shared the work," Kubar said, his voice quivering with fear. "Many more children would have died without the drug I created."

"I don't care about any of that," Max replied. "You helped the prisoners to escape. You used that damned stun baton on me. When I woke up, the Baxter bitch had me tied down. You knew she intended to inject the acid into my eye, didn't you? There's no way I could've survived something like that."

"I had nothing to do with it. Anyway, you were going to shoot them."

"Maybe, but you're still the main reason I lost my arm."

"If I had stayed, they would have executed me," Kubar protested.

"You deserved it," Mo added. "You betrayed your country."

"They planned to kill all the Western hostages when they had a cure," the North African doctor said, "including you." His gaze flicked to the gun barrel and back to Max's face. "And they lied to me about my daughter. They told me she was still alive, even though they knew she was dead. Those bearded fanatics do not care about anybody but themselves. Can you not see that?"

"All I see is a traitor who deserves to die," Mo snarled.

"Enough," Max said. "It's time to end this. Do you want to do the honours, Mo?"

Nationalistic pride glinted in the diminutive hacker's eyes as he reached out to accept the weapon. "It would be my pleasure."

Kubar raised his hands. "No, please. Do not—"

The subdued pop stopped the doctor in mid-sentence. His body slammed backwards onto the mattress. A small round hole lay in the centre of his forehead. He stared sightlessly at the ceiling.

A crimson stain expanded from behind the dead man's head, darkening the floral-patterned bed cover.

Tuesday 21ˢᵗ April 2037
Ilithyia Biotechnology, Northstowe

Jason put his eyes to the peephole. The knock a few seconds earlier had startled him. A guard in a pale-blue uniform stood in the corridor. Jason's pulse raced. Something was badly wrong. Where could Antimone and Paul have got to? By now they had been missing for nearly two hours. Why was a member of the security team here?

He yanked on the handle and pulled the door open. "What is it? Have you found them?"

"May I come in, sir?" the man asked. Acne scars disfigured both his cheeks and his forehead. He looked little older than Jason.

"Yeah, sure. Is there any news?"

"Not at the moment, but I wanted to ask you a few questions."

Jason ran a hand through his hair. "Fine." He led the way past the bathroom into the bedroom and plonked himself on Paul's bed. He gestured towards the other bed, and the guard settled down opposite.

"So, what's this about?"

"First of all, I want you to know we're taking this very seriously."

"Good."

"When did you last see your partner and your boy?"

"We met up for lunch, but I haven't seen them since. My son has been in school all afternoon."

"Yes, we checked all that," the man said. "We confirmed that they visited the canteen after lessons finished, and they were spotted a short while later with the guys from Beechwood Maintenance. They were heading to the laboratory area. When one of our team asked what they were doing, they told him they were looking for a faulty sensor. Unfortunately, there's no sign of them there, although I should say we can't actually get into any of the labs."

"What? You're saying that even in a situation like this, you aren't allowed in to perform a search?"

"The site manager, Nick Butler, has the authority, but he seems to have disappeared as well. Nobody else in the building is senior enough to override the regulations. We're trying to track down Christine Harris, but she's apparently eating out in Cambridge tonight. Unfortunately, we haven't been able to find out which restaurant she's at, and she isn't answering her phone."

Jason's face screwed up in puzzlement. "But any of the scientists could let you in. They all have key cards."

"In theory, yes, but most can only access their own areas. We'd also need permission first or at least evidence that something serious has happened. Some of the work that goes on here is top secret, and that's not to mention the dangerous bugs they're working on, so security is very tight."

Jason blew out his cheeks. "Bloody hell, my partner and son are missing. Isn't that serious enough for you?"

"I'm sorry, sir, but they're very strict on process."

"And you're absolutely positive they haven't left the building?"

"That seems highly unlikely. The only ways in and out are through the checkpoints, and everybody is logged as they come in and leave."

"So, you're saying they're here somewhere, but you don't know where?"

"As I mentioned earlier, we're doing our best to find them. There was something else I needed to discuss with you."

"What's that?" Jason replied.

The man shifted uncomfortably. "Look, we're supposed to keep the visitor logs confidential, but in the circumstances... The guys you talked to downstairs said you suspected your son might have recognised somebody on the Beechwood team. Would you mind checking out their photos to see if you can identify any of them?"

"Yeah, no problem."

The guard handed over a portable device. "Just swipe to the left to move onto the next picture. There are three of them."

Jason scanned the first image. It showed the head and upper body of a well-built man with broad shoulders. The man's face expressed no emotion. The bright overhead lighting reflected off his shaved scalp. His skin tone matched that of the people he had come across in The Republic of North Africa. Jason could see why Paul might think he had seen this person before, but he was certain they had never met.

"Not him."

He moved onto the next photo. If the first man was muscular, the second had almost the exact opposite body shape. The only similarity was in the Mediterranean cast to the man's skin. His shoulders hunched slightly, and his face seemed pinched with worry.

Jason shook his head. "No."

He swiped to the third image. His heart leapt into his throat, and he dropped the device on the carpet. "Max," he whispered.

The guard leant forwards and inspected the screen. "You recognise this man?"

Jason stared straight ahead without answering. He reached out a trembling hand. "Let me see." He studied the picture for a second time. There was no doubt. "Yeah, I do. His name is Max Perrin. He was in Tripoli with us, but we left him behind when we escaped. We thought he was dead. He tried to shoot me."

"Do you have any idea what he might be doing here?"

"His father used to be a co-owner of this place, but if he's inside the building now, it's certainly nothing good. If I had to guess, I'd say he's here to get revenge on a few people. That includes Mrs Baxter, Antimone and me. Oh, and maybe Dr Kubar too."

The guard jumped to his feet, a panicked look etched on his face. "Shit, all their rooms are on this floor. I better go check them out. Stay here, and don't let anybody in unless it's somebody you know."

The man jogged towards the door, slamming it shut behind him.

Jason put his head in his hands. A sense of dread ate through his chest. Max Perrin: how the hell had he survived? Jason had been unconscious, suffering from a gunshot wound, but Antimone told him later how, in a fit of uncontrolled rage, she had emptied a syringe of concentrated sulphuric acid into Max's upper arm. Now she was missing along with their son, and the victim of her actions was somewhere in the same building. The two events had to be related.

"Please God, let them be safe," he whispered.

Tuesday 21ˢᵗ April 2037

Ilithyia Biotechnology, Northstowe

Max was the first out of the door. Martin Hendrick came next, followed by Mo. Max's heart thundered in his chest. Finally, he was getting payback for what they had done to him in Tripoli. But how could he get to Rosalind Baxter?

"Where do we go now?" Mo asked.

"I'm thinking." Max turned to Hendrick. "You're saying there's no way into Baxter's room without a special key card? So, she can't open the door from the inside?"

"Yeah, that's correct."

"And only the security guards have access?"

"Yes."

"Maybe we should kill Floyd first," Mo said.

"Which room is he in?" Max asked.

Hendrick shook his head.

Max grabbed the gun off his partner and jammed it under Hendrick's chin. "Do you want to die right here? Now, I won't ask again. Which one is Floyd's room?"

"Will you let me go if I help you?"

"You have my word. I don't have any quarrel with you."

Hendrick stared into Max's face for a second, as if his gaze could pierce through to his captor's thoughts and determine his true intentions. He swallowed hard and dropped his eyes to the deep carpet. "All right," he said, quietly. "It's that one." He pointed to a door on the opposite side of the corridor.

Max lowered the gun. "Good. I want you to do the same thing you did before. Knock until he lets us in."

"Okay."

Max pushed Hendrick forwards. At that moment, a rattle followed by the click of a lock broke the silence. "Wait," he hissed.

A guard emerged from Jason's room. The man spoke into a radio. "Yeah, it's Sam. I've just spoken to him and showed him the photos from when the

Beechwood team checked in." His eyes rose. He blinked in surprise as he took in the three men standing ten feet away.

Max immediately identified the topic of the conversation. He raised the gun and pointed the barrel at the guard's torso. In four quick paces, he was at the man's side. "If you want to live past the next second," he whispered, "tell them he didn't recognise any of us."

"Say again, Sam," the voice at the other end said. "I missed that. Has he seen any of them before?"

"Ah... no. He thinks his son mistook one of them for somebody they met in North Africa."

"Well, it was worth a go. We should still try to find them. Get back down here as soon as you can."

"Okay."

Max gestured for the man to hand over the radio. "Give me your key card and any weapons you're carrying too."

The guard withdrew the rectangle of plastic from his shirt pocket, his eyes never leaving the pistol directed at his chest. Next, he unclipped a grey, cylindrical object from his belt.

Max took the item and studied it. Two buttons protruded from the side. A rectangular slot occupied one end of the cylinder. "What does this do?"

"It's a non-lethal stun weapon."

"You mean like a taser?"

"Yeah, except it uses a small dart instead of wires."

"How does it work?"

"Press and hold the red button to arm it. The green one makes it fire."

"Is it single shot?"

"Yes."

Max pocketed the device. "You," he said, turning to Hendrick. "Come over here and stand next to him." He stepped a few paces away from the two prisoners and beckoned his partner closer.

"Who do we do first, Baxter or Floyd?" he whispered.

"If this man has spoken to the boy, he will know we are here. We may not have much time. Who do you wish to see dead more?"

"That's easy: Baxter, of course. That bitch murdered my father and tried to kill me too."

"Well then, you have your answer."

"What do we do with him?" Max gestured towards the guard, who stared fearfully back, clearly aware that he was the subject of the discussion but too far away to decipher the words.

"We do not need another hostage, and there is only one gun."

"Two, if you count this," Max replied, removing the object from his pocket. "Take it. Did you hear what he said about how it works?"

"Yes. Red to arm, green to shoot."

"But you still think we should get rid of him?"

"That is what I would do, but you are the boss."

"Okay. I'll let us into her room. You go at the back. As soon as we're inside, use that to incapacitate him. We can't leave him lying in the corridor for the other guards to find, and I don't want to have to drag him anywhere."

Mo nodded. "Fine."

"I've been waiting a long time for this. Let's not mess it up." He returned to the captives. "Right. Which room is Baxter in?"

Hendrick pointed to the next door down. "That one."

"Good," Max said. There's been a slight change of plan. We're going to pay her a surprise visit first. I'll lead, you two follow. My colleague will be at the back. If either of you tries anything, you'll die too. Got that?"

Both men's heads bobbed in acknowledgement.

Max strode forwards and raised the stolen key card. The lock clicked, and he pushed his way in. An overhead light automatically switched on, illuminating a narrow passageway. The open doorway to the right led into a white-tiled bathroom. A floral scent of female toiletries drifted out. He progressed to the closed door straight ahead, his feet scuffing through the deep pile of the carpet. He turned and waited until the others were out of the corridor before turning the handle.

Extending the gun in front of him, he eased into the main part of the room. A sense of déjà vu washed over him. The décor was different, but the wide window looking down onto the gardens and car park outside awoke memories of the times he had visited his father's office.

He whirled around at the sudden cry of pain behind him. The guard writhed on the floor. Mo stood over the prostrate man, holding the grey plastic object in the palm of his hand. As Max turned back, a rapid movement at the periphery of his vision caught his eye. A picture frame spiralled through the air, striking his upper arm. The weapon flew from his grip, hit the wall and landed six feet away.

A lamp followed immediately afterwards, glancing off his skull. He raised his arms to ward off the barrage of objects raining down on him and advanced into the room. Rosalind Baxter stood beside the bed, her face twisted in fury. A drawer from the bedside cabinet arced towards him. He ducked at the last moment as the sharp edges sailed past his head and smashed harmlessly into the wall.

Max took another pace, his lips drawn back in a savage grin. Rosalind's eyes cast about, searching for more ammunition. In desperation, she lifted the empty unit from beside the bed and tossed it in his direction. It fell short but tumbled over the thick carpet and caught him on the shin. He let out a grunt of pain, but it didn't stop his advance.

Rosalind scrambled over the bed to escape. Max lunged after her, grabbing at her legs. A shoe came away in his hand. She lashed out and struck his cheekbone with the sole of her bare foot. Momentarily dazed by the blow, he rolled off the mattress and landed on all fours. Another kick smashed into his stomach, winding him.

Slowly, he rose to his feet. "I'm going to enjoy killing you," he growled.

Rosalind backed away. "I should have finished the job in Tripoli when I had the chance."

With a scream of fury, Max leapt forwards and swung his left arm in a vicious arc. The clang of metal on the bone of her skull reverberated through the room. She staggered backwards, blood already welling from the cut on her temple. Her feet tripped over each other, and she fell to the floor in an undignified tumble.

Max stood over her, his breath coming thick and fast. "I lost my left arm because of you," he said, tapping his shoulder. "And now I'm going to make you pay."

"Stop!" a voice yelled from a few metres away.

Max turned slowly. Martin Hendrick held the pistol. The barrel pointed at Max's chest.

"Stop," the doctor repeated, quietly.

Max's gaze slid across to where Mo stood in the open doorway, the useless weapon still clutched in his hand. Behind him, the unconscious guard lay sprawled on the carpet.

Hendrick's aim alternated between the two men in the dark-blue overalls.

"You can't shoot both of us," Max said.

"But I can take one of you. Who's going to try first?"

Rosalind pushed her upper body upright. A bruised knee protruded from the rip in her cream trousers.

"You piece of shit," she snarled, glaring at Max. "How come you're still alive? Did you plan all this just to get your revenge?"

"You killed my father, and you came within an inch of killing me. And that's not to mention the millions of women who died because of what you did. Somebody should've put you down ages ago."

Rosalind let out a bark of laughter. "Don't forget, your dear departed daddy was as much to blame as me. We were in it together. Anyway, it looks like you failed, doesn't it?" She reached out a hand to the edge of the bed to steady herself as she prepared to stand.

"No, stay down there," Hendrick said, transferring his aim.

"Oh, come on, Martin. You're not listening to what he says, are you? I mean, you were there back then. It was an accident. We didn't intend for it to turn out like that."

"Yes, I was, Rosalind. By the way, I know about Eileen Floyd. Who do you think let her out?"

Rosalind's eyes locked onto her former employee. "What? That was you?"

"I called Grolby a few minutes later to tell him that she'd escaped."

"What the hell's going on here?" Max asked. "What are you two talking about?"

"I don't understand," Rosalind said, ignoring Max's question. "You freed her, but then you phoned Anders Grolby?"

"Never mind," Hendrick replied. "It all happened a long time ago." He stepped forwards, extended his arm and handed the pistol to Max. "This is yours, I believe."

"What the hell are you doing?" Rosalind yelled.

Max accepted the gun. His fingers closed around the grip. "Does it still work?"

Hendrick shrugged. "I haven't done anything to it, so I expect it does."

"Right... thanks." Max's forehead creased in a puzzled frown. He turned back towards Rosalind. "I made a big error four years ago when I left before you were dead. I won't make the same mistake a second time."

He raised his arm and aimed the barrel at her head.

Saturday 9ᵗʰ April 2016
Ilithyia Biotechnology, Northstowe
Twenty-one years ago

Martin Hendrick studied Eileen Floyd through the fisheye lens. He had just twisted the key to unlock her room. She must have heard him because she stopped pacing and stared at the door as if she could see him standing on the other side. A moment later, she sat on the bed and placed her face in her hands. It seemed she would follow his instructions to wait an hour, after all. He turned and sprinted back to his laboratory, where he once again wedged the door open.

He had spent the earlier part of the day backing up the data on his hard disk to a USB stick. After a final check, he shut the computer down. Next, he removed the side from the base unit and ran the powerful magnet he had retrieved from his pocket over the thin casing of the internal drive before replacing the cover. Nobody would retrieve anything useful from this machine.

He replaced the side panel, raised the metal-sided box above his head and hurled it downwards with all his strength. It hit the ground with a clatter as something inside broke loose. He moved to the refrigerator. Hauling open the door, he swept the contents of the top shelf onto the hard flooring. The glassware smashed with a satisfying crash. Within seconds, the acrid stink of chemicals filled the air. He turned his attention to the lower shelves, removed the lids from the unmarked steel flasks and emptied out the liquid. The empty containers landed on the floor with a reverberating clang.

After a final survey of his destruction, he moved a chair to the centre of the room, then stood precariously balanced on the seat. His fingers grasped the small white cylinder of the starter in the light fitting and removed it. The laboratory plunged immediately into darkness, lit only by the narrow band of brightness penetrating from the corridor. He reached into his pocket, grabbed the faulty replacement part he had brought with him and twisted it into the slot.

The fluorescent tube clicked intermittently but, other than the occasional flicker, provided no illumination. He returned the chair to its original spot and tipped it over on its side. Grabbing the notebook off his desk, he raced back towards the reception area. He hesitated by the door to the adjacent laboratory. Time was short, but it would arouse suspicion if his room was the only one targeted. He dropped the book, barged inside and flicked on the light. After a moment's thought, he emptied the fridge contents onto the floor and shoved the nearest computer off the work surface. That would have to do.

He retrieved his notebook, rushed up the stairs to Nigel Perrin's office and returned the storeroom keys to their hiding place in the desk drawer. He descended the staircase at a more sedate pace and strode towards the alarm panel. There, he tapped in the arming code, followed by the button labelled with a green tick. The shrill warning tone rang out, transitioning to a series of rapid beeps as the timer ran down.

Finally, the sound stopped. Hendrick studied the face of his watch: 19:01. It had been forty minutes since Perrin had brought the woman her meal. He didn't expect her to wait the full hour, but she would surely take action when she heard the siren. Now was the time to leave. Before he did so, he returned to the door leading to the laboratories and pulled it open. After a few seconds, he let it swing shut. A final thought occurred to him as he surveyed the reception area. He marched to the receptionist's desk and shoved the contents, including the computer monitor, base unit and telephone, onto the tiled floor.

Satisfied that he hadn't missed anything, he crossed to the entrance. A brief inspection of the alarm panel confirmed a flashing icon, signalling the countdown of the silent alert. He let himself out and locked the door behind him.

He stood in the cool evening air and inhaled deeply. One more task remained. He strode to the side of the building and picked up the large stone he had left there upon arriving that morning. After a surreptitious examination of his surroundings to make sure nobody was watching, he angled his head away and swung the rock at the glass panel. It took three further blows to clear the shards from the lower half of the frame.

The red Ford Focus chirped as he pressed the unlock button. He sank into the driver's seat and started the engine. He couldn't be here when the next stage of his plan unfolded, but he wanted to observe. The spot he had identified earlier was in the car park for the industrial unit on the opposite side of the road. He navigated the short distance and sighed with relief when he found all the spaces empty. He parked in a space invisible from the Ilithyia building and retrieved his phone. The ringing tone sounded once before a male voice answered.

"Hi, Anders, it's Martin Hendrick."

"I'm in the car. What can I do for you?"

"When I locked up tonight, there were a couple of suspicious men on the pavement outside. It's probably nothing, but I thought I should let you know just in case."

"Actually, I'm on the way to the office right now. The silent alarm went off about five minutes ago. Where are you?"

"Oh, sorry, Anders. I should have called you sooner. I'm nearly home."

"Okay, don't worry about it. I'll be there in a minute or two, anyway."

"Do you want me to come back in?"

"No, it'll be fine. I'll ring you if I need you. Goodnight."

Hendrick ended the call and got out of his car. He moved behind the cover of a bush and waited for the action to start.

Tuesday 21ˢᵗ April 2037
Ilithyia Biotechnology, Northstowe

Max opened the door and stuck his head into the corridor. *Good.* Nobody was about. He strode through the doorway and waited for the others to emerge behind him. He tried to calm his rapid breathing. Two down, two to go. Despite achieving the goal he had dreamed about for the past four years, a sense of satisfaction still eluded him. So many times, he had pictured how it would end, but now it was over, he felt nothing. Rosalind Baxter was dead.

He tried to examine his feelings. Perhaps it was the way she had stared back at him. She seemed resigned to her fate. There was no sign of fear in her eyes. She didn't beg for her life. In fact, she actively encouraged him to finish the job. "Go on. Do it then." Her final words still reverberated inside his skull. He had expected a buzz of euphoria as he pulled the trigger, but instead, the completion of his goal left him feeling strangely empty.

Perhaps he had enjoyed the thrill of the chase more than the achievement of his ambition. Now that his nemesis lay dead on the floor, what came next? The girl and her boyfriend remained alive. She was the person who had destroyed his arm, even if the woman whom he had recently murdered was the instigator. It seemed that Antimone regretted injecting him with concentrated acid. Had he seen a look of relief on her face when she first recognised him?

Maybe it was time to leave while he still had the chance. The North Africans would be satisfied with the execution of the traitor, Kubar. They didn't really care about the three Westerners. Was it worth risking his freedom to gain his revenge?

He cast his mind back to the beginning. Everything had started at the athletics track. If he was being honest with himself, he *had* overreacted a little. Perhaps she hadn't intentionally tripped him after all. What irked him most though, was the disrespect they demonstrated afterwards when they showed him up in front of his friends.

He could forgive an accident, but they had humiliated him. To add insult to injury, her boyfriend had assaulted him. He couldn't allow that to pass. He shook his head. No, he had promised himself he would get payback. He would only regret it if he backed down and let them live. Now was not the time for weakness.

But one mystery still remained; why did the scientist hand him the pistol? After Max shot Baxter, the man had stayed stationary, watching on impassively while he reloaded the weapon.

Max beckoned Hendrick closer. "Why did you do it?"

The researcher shrugged. "You promised you would let me go. I decided to trust you."

"But you had the gun. Why didn't you ask her to call security?"

"Are you saying you'd rather I had you arrested than hand it back?"

"No, I'm just curious. And what about that stuff with Eileen Floyd?"

"As I mentioned earlier, it all happened a long time ago—twenty years, if I'm not mistaken. Mrs Baxter, Mrs Floyd, your father and I all worked for the same company. Mrs Floyd threatened to become a whistleblower, so Mrs Baxter kidnapped her and held her prisoner, even though she was pregnant. I found out and released her, although Mrs Baxter didn't learn about that until just now."

"Wait. I've heard this before."

"I doubt it, Hendrick," replied. "Nobody else knows I was the one to release her."

"No, not that; I meant the whistleblower part. You must be talking about Jason's mother."

"Yes."

Max scratched the ridge of skin between his forefinger and thumb. "You mentioned something about Grolby too."

"Yeah, he was the head of security."

"I know who he was, but you said you phoned him when Eileen Floyd escaped."

Hendrick folded his arms but didn't reply.

Max's gaze settled on the clear surgical gloves covering Hendrick's hands. "Why are you wearing those?"

"Oh, I had them on when you came into the lab. I never took them off."

Max scowled at the scientist. "I'm sure I would've remembered that."

"I thought you mentioned you were running short of time."

"Right. Wait there."

Max stepped a few paces away and gestured for Mo to join him. The North African stood nervously, shifting from foot to foot. He carried the toolbox in his hand.

"Are you ready for the next one?" Max asked.

Mo responded with a silent nod.

"We're nearly done," Max said. "Only two more, and then we can leave."

Mo leant forwards and spoke in a hushed voice. "I do not understand why he gave you the gun."

"Well, I'm not about to complain."

"Something is wrong. Why did he help us? I do not trust him."

"From what I can tell, there was prior history between him and Baxter. But it worked out for us, didn't it?"

"I suppose so, but it is still very strange."

"Right. Let's do this. We'll make this one a quick in and out. I'll use the card to open the door. Once I'm inside, I'll locate him and put a bullet in him. After that we'll go down to Omar, finish off the girl, and then we can all get out of here. You wait here with Hendrick. I don't think he'll cause you any trouble."

"Fine."

Max strode a few paces down the corridor and raised the rectangle of plastic. The lock released with a click.

Tuesday 21St April 2037

Ilithyia Biotechnology, Northstowe

Jason sat on the edge of the bed, tapping his knees. Max Perrin was in the building and nobody had seen Antimone and Paul for hours. Surely, it was no coincidence; the two events had to be related in some way.

Only five minutes had passed since the guard left. The man had told him to remain in this room and not to open the door to anybody he didn't know. But waiting here by himself was sheer torture. Perhaps he should call security and ask whether they had tracked down the intruders yet. No, they would be busy enough as it was without added distractions. There was nothing he could do to help but wait.

A thud reverberated through the wall from next door. His mother occupied that room. Neither he nor Antimone had ever heard any disturbance from her before. Jason held his breath and cocked his head to listen. Another bump. He leapt to his feet and placed his palms against the coolness of the plaster. What the hell was going on? More banging sounds followed.

The noise stopped as abruptly as it had started. He strained his ears to pick up any repetition of the previous commotion. Silence. His eyes strayed to the telephone on the bedside table. Should he alert the security team? He turned his head sideways and placed his ear against the partition. Were those voices? The sounds were too faint to work out who was talking and what was being said.

Jason's heart stopped pumping as a muffled pop penetrated from the other side. Had somebody fired a shot? Who was the target? Were the walls thick enough to stop a bullet? He ducked down and crouched behind the bed. A flurry of hundred-mile-an-hour thoughts rattled through his brain. Was his mother still alive? Should he run or hide? Should he call security now or wait until he had reached a safe place first?

If Max Perrin and his two accomplices were in the adjoining room, they would probably come here next. And if that was the case, he needed to get out as soon as possible. Staying low, Jason scrambled across to the passageway leading past the bathroom to the door. The overhead light clicked on automatically. He crept towards the peephole and raised his eye to the spyhole.

The lens restricted his view to a narrow band, but from what he could see, the corridor seemed empty. He passed this way every day, but in the stress of the moment, he struggled to remember the layout of the floor. How far was it to the staircase? How long would it take him to cover the distance? His hand reached for the handle. A sound penetrated from outside.

Jason froze. He shifted his head to the side and tried to identify the source. A shape moved at the periphery of his vision. The murmur of low voices came from the same direction. A figure in dark-blue overalls crossed into the edge of the frame, the outline distorted by the curvature of the glass.

Shit! There was no way to escape now without being spotted. If they had managed to get into his mother's room, they would certainly be able to enter his. He turned. His eyes darted frantically along the narrow passageway, searching for somewhere to hide.

The bathroom? No, he would be far too exposed.

The bedroom? Perhaps he should take cover on the opposite side of the bed, out of sight from anybody entering the room. But if they did come in, they would spot him almost immediately.

The blood rushed in his ears. Seconds remained.

The in-built wardrobe to his right? It might work. He yanked it open and eased his way in. If he crouched a little, he could just about fit inside. His fingertips scrabbled against the smooth surface as he desperately attempted to close it from within. After a moment of panic, his nails snagged a seam with sufficient purchase to pull the door closed. The clothes hangers clinked gently as they swayed around his head. In the confined space, the scent of Antimone's deodorant tickled his nostrils.

A muffled click came from outside. Somebody had let themselves in. Jason tried to slow his rapid breathing. He fought the desperate urge to release his bladder. The floor vibrated slightly as the intruder moved, then stopped. He tensed every muscle, ready to burst out at the slightest hint the person had discovered his hiding place.

The door to the wardrobe shifted and tapped against its frame, disturbed by the airflow from the main part of the room. Jason prayed it wouldn't swing open. The seconds crawled past. After what seemed an age, the footsteps returned.

"Did you kill him?" The speaker's words carried a slight Arabic accent.

"No, he's not there." Jason immediately recognised Max Perrin's voice. "We'll have to leave him. Let's go and deal with the girl, then we can get out of here."

Jason breathed a huge sigh of relief; Antimone was still alive. Moments later, another click signalled Perrin and the other man had left. He remained in his hiding place for a few seconds longer, then emerged.

He rushed back into the bedroom and snatched up the phone. His hands shook as he tapped the zero key and waited impatiently for somebody to answer. A female voice spoke. "Hello, reception. How may I—?"

Before she could complete the sentence, he gabbled out his message.

"This is Jason Floyd. There are at least three intruders on site. They're wearing dark-blue uniforms and are disguised as maintenance men. They have weapons. One of them is Max Perrin. I overheard them talking, and they're holding my partner, Antimone Lessing, and my son hostage. They plan to kill her. I need you to call security. I'm going after them. Did you get all that?"

"Um... is this a joke?"

"No, I'm deadly serious. Tell them Max Perrin is here, and he's armed. They'll know who I mean. I'll try to make contact again when I find out where they're keeping my family."

"Well, I..."

"Please just do it." Jason slammed the handset down. He didn't have time to argue. Hopefully, the receptionist would pass the information on to the security guards. He rushed back to the peephole and stared out. Satisfied nobody lingered outside, he eased into the corridor. Which way had they gone? A quick glance at the panel above the lifts confirmed both were still on this floor, so they must have taken the stairs. The door to his mother's room was closed, and he had no means to let himself in and check on her status. For now, his first priority was to find Antimone and their son.

He rushed to the staircase in a few strides. The distant click of footsteps reached his ears from below. He slipped off his shoes, leaving them where they fell, and set off in pursuit. His bare feet made barely any noise as he dashed down the steps. He arrived at the bottom, already panting from the exertion. It seemed unlikely they would cross the foyer, especially if they suspected the guards were searching for them. Only two choices remained: right or left.

The doorway on the left led past rows of offices to the entrance, the one on the right to more offices and towards the wing containing the laboratories. He selected the latter and peered through the glass panel. Fifty yards away, three people strode down the corridor. Two wore dark-blue overalls, the third a white doctor's coat.

Jason waited for them to pass through the next set of doors, then followed at a jog.

Tuesday 21st April 2037
Ilithyia Biotechnology, Northstowe

Max Perrin hurried along the corridor. The clock was ticking down. Somebody might have heard the shots that killed Kubar and Baxter. The weapon was designed to make minimal noise, but the sound was still loud enough to carry through the walls. It was clear from the guard's overheard radio conversation that the security team already harboured suspicions about the identities of Max and his two men. It was only a matter of time before someone either found the bodies or called the maintenance company and discovered the truth.

Max increased his pace. This route would take longer, but it avoided the foyer, where somebody was sure to spot them. It was a shame he had failed to kill Jason Floyd. The only consolation was that his former classmate would still suffer from the loss of his precious girlfriend. Perhaps he should shoot the kid too. That would really screw Floyd up.

They reached a set of swing doors. Max barged through and waited for the others to join him. Hendrick came last. The doctor hunched forwards with his hands on his knees as he gasped for breath. "Sorry," he puffed between breaths, "I'm not as fit as I once was."

"We can't stop," Max said. "How much farther is it?"

Hendrick gulped a lungful of air before replying. "Just down there and to the left."

"Let's get going then. You go first."

Hendrick straightened up and set off at a fast walk. Mo trailed a pace behind. The toolbox clanked with every step.

Max transferred the gun to his pocket and scratched distractedly at the ball of his right thumb. The itch was getting worse. He rubbed his palm on the trousers of his overalls, then jogged to catch up. At this time of night, the corridor was deserted, and they reached the sealed door to the laboratory area without encountering another person.

"Give your card to Mo," Max said to Hendrick.

"I thought they gave you one."

"They did, but if they're suspicious about us, they might be tracking its usage or maybe even have disabled it by now."

Hendrick fumbled in the breast pocket of his shirt and handed over the rectangle of plastic to the small North African. A green light flashed, and the lock clicked.

Max followed as Hendrick and Mo passed through the doorway. The ceiling lights sprang into life, illuminating a corridor with darkened laboratories on both sides. "Which way is it?" he asked.

Hendrick pointed. "It's the third on the left. We're coming at it from the opposite direction to when we set off."

"Okay."

Max strode forwards. He reached the door labelled *BioNEMS* and let them in.

A muffled scream emerged from the corner. As Max's eyes adjusted to the gloomy red glow, he picked out the form of Antimone Lessing sitting in a wheelchair with her child clinging to her neck. A muscular figure crouched behind them. A blade glinted in the dim light.

"It's all right, Omar. We're back."

The burly North African rose to his feet and lowered the knife. "You have been gone a long time. Did you kill the traitors?"

"Yeah. I shot Kubar and Baxter. They're both dead."

"Good."

"What happened to Jason?" Antimone's voice trembled with fear.

Max hesitated a moment before replying. His mouth twisted in a thin-lipped smile. "I killed him too."

Silence settled over the room. He stared at her, trying to gauge her reaction.

"You're lying," Antimone whispered.

"Why would I lie?"

Antimone's words grew in strength. "You mentioned Dr Kubar and Mrs Baxter straight away, but you only said something about Jason when I asked."

"I missed by a millimetre or two in Tripoli, but this time, the bullet ended up here." Max tapped the centre of his forehead.

"I don't believe you."

"I don't care whether you believe me or not. It's your turn now. Any last words?"

"Screw you."

"Not the most eloquent I've ever heard. Omar, grab the child."

Paul screamed as the man peeled him off his mother and carried him under his arm.

"Close your eyes, Paul," Antimone shouted to her son. "Don't watch."

Max raised the pistol and aimed at Antimone's head.

Tuesday 21ˢᵗ April 2037
Ilithyia Biotechnology, Northstowe

Jason stopped at the door leading to the laboratory area. He peered through the square of glass but could see no signs of the three men he trailed here. At one point, he got so close he could hear them talking on the other side of the swing doors. From the brief conversation he overheard, he identified the man in the white doctor's coat as Dr Hendrick. Realising it would only take a single unlucky glance for them to spot him, he held back after that. But where had they gone now?

The overhead lights were on, signalling that they must have passed this way a short time earlier. He raised his key card and let himself in. The security staff had given him access to this part of the building when he was helping some of the scientists with their administrative work, but his privileges didn't extend to permitting entry into any of the laboratories.

All the frosted windows on both sides lay in darkness. He crept down the corridor, straining his ears to pick up any clue to his targets' whereabouts. He stopped outside the first doorway he came to. One of the virology labs. No sounds emanated from within. He moved on to the adjacent laboratory. Also silent. This was taking too long.

He continued forwards in a low shuffle, crouching to keep his body below the level of the glass. He crossed to the opposite side to listen at the next door on the right. A click. His head snapped around as he picked up a sudden movement at the periphery of his vision. A group of five men, wearing the pale-blue security uniform, filed through behind him.

The leader of the group pointed the barrel of what, at first glance, looked like an oversized water pistol at Jason's torso.

Jason shook his head and raised a finger to his lips. The guard shot him a puzzled stare, then edged closer.

"Who are you?" the man whispered when he was close enough. He kept his weapon up.

"I'm Jason Floyd. I take it the receptionist contacted you. They must be in here somewhere. I followed them this far, but I didn't see where they went after that."

"We got your message and tracked your key card. The system also reported that Dr Hendrick's card opened the door to the nanotechnology lab a minute ago, but the lights are off, so we think they're probably hiding out in there. Do you know who might be with them?"

"My partner, Antimone Lessing, and our son, Paul. I saw Dr Hendrick with them, so it seems they must be holding him hostage as well. We've got to hurry."

"Were they carrying any weapons?"

"Max Perrin had what looked like a gun in his hand. I heard a gunshot earlier."

"Right, sir. I need you to move back." The man beckoned his colleagues closer.

"How are you going to get in?" Jason asked. "The guard I spoke to before said your guys didn't have access to the labs."

"They finally tracked down where Dr Harris was eating, and she elevated our privilege levels. Now, please sir, move back and let us do our job."

A child's piercing scream broke the stillness.

Jason's heart lurched in his chest: Paul.

The group of guards hurtled towards the door. The leader raised a card to the lock mechanism. Antimone's voice rose above the sounds of movement. "Close your eyes, Paul. Don't watch."

The men surged through the opening. Several low thuds reverberated from within. A single gunshot rang out. Then silence.

Jason didn't wait for the all-clear. He jumped up from his crouch and sprinted towards the open doorway. At first glance, his brain couldn't make sense of what his eyes were telling him. A dim red glow illuminated what appeared to be a collection of grotesque statues.

As he entered, somebody flicked on the master light switch. The three men in dark-blue overalls stood draped in what appeared to be loops of grey foam. Judging by the grunts and straining muscles, they were trying to escape, but the tubular folds of material held them tight. The gun lay on the floor at Max's feet. He attempted to move his leg, but a brief squirt from the nozzle of the nearest guard's weapon cemented his foot in place.

Jason's gaze immediately transferred to Antimone. He rushed to her side. "Are you all right?"

"Yes. He missed."

"Thank God for that. Where's Paul?"

Antimone pointed at the tiny figure, cowering in the corner. Jason stepped forwards and scooped up his son.

"It's over. I've got you," he murmured into the four-year-old's ear, clutching him tightly to his chest.

Dr Hendrick stood to the side, a blank look on his face. Suddenly, his mouth curved in a smile. He took a pace towards Antimone and patted her wrist. "I'm so glad you're okay." He turned to the security guards. "Thank you so much for saving us. I thought they were going to kill us. Let me shake your hands." The bemused men accepted his outstretched palm as Hendrick moved from one to the next.

A cry of agony brought an abrupt end to the celebrations. All the occupants of the room, who still retained the ability to move, turned to stare at Max Perrin. He squirmed in the grey material's embrace.

"My hand," he screamed.

Jason winced in shock as he stepped closer to study the reason for Max's anguished cries.

Blood dripped from a deep hole of exposed, weeping flesh, forming a ring in the centre of his former schoolmate's right palm.

Tuesday 21ˢᵗ April 2037
Ilithyia Biotechnology, Northstowe

"What's wrong with him?" Antimone asked. "Is it the foam?"

The guard standing beside her shrugged. "He won't be able to move until somebody sprays him with the release agent, but that's all it does."

"So, why's he complaining so much?"

The man didn't answer. Instead, he stepped closer to Max and studied the dripping wound. His face crinkled in confusion. "Something is eating away at his hand."

Max stared in horror at what remained of his palm. His gaze swung to the doctor. "He did this to me. It was him."

"Who?" the guard asked.

"Hendrick."

The scientist raised his eyebrows. "I've no idea what he's talking about."

"I dropped the pistol, but he gave it back to me." Max let out a groan of agony. "He could've stopped us, but he didn't. It made no sense. He must have put something on the grip. You've got to help me."

Antimone rolled nearer to the smallest of the three restrained intruders. "You were with them. Is he telling the truth?"

"Yes, it is true," Mo said. "He picked up the gun and returned it. Why is he wearing those gloves?"

Hendrick thrust his hands into the pockets of the white lab coat. "They took me prisoner. They told me if I failed to do what they asked, they'd kill me. And you too." He angled his head towards Antimone. "You were there. You heard them."

Antimone folded her arms. "They did threaten us, but that doesn't explain why you've still got the gloves on. Or what's happening to him."

Hendrick frowned. "Look, this has been a very stressful evening. Why would you listen to them? You can't believe a word they say. I've done nothing wrong. I'm a victim of all this, just like you. As for the gloves, I was wearing them when these terrorists burst in here and took me hostage. I have no idea what's affecting his hand, and frankly, I don't much care. He forced me to watch as he murdered two people in cold blood. He deserves to suffer after what he did. It's probably an allergic reaction or something. You seem to have the situation well under control, so I'm going back to my room now. If you have any questions, you can ask them in the morning."

He turned and strode towards the door. The guards exchanged glances but didn't move to stop him. As Hendrick reached for the exit button, an anguished cry erupted from behind him. Every eye in the laboratory locked onto Max Perrin. His index finger dangled by a thread of skin, then dropped to the floor, followed moments later by his thumb. The bones of his hand showed through the exposed flesh. The drips developed into a steady flow. A red pool expanded around his feet.

The parts of his body that could move writhed against the bonds of the solidified foam. Suddenly, a jet arced from Max's wrist and splattered the white wall with blood. The tendons in his neck thickened into tight bands as his lips drew back from his teeth in a shriek of agony. The shocked guards took a hurried step backwards to avoid being splashed.

Jason clutched Paul tightly to his chest, blocking his son's view.

A thin trail of smoke accompanied the whine of the electric motor as Max's left arm fought against his bindings. With a splintering crack, he wrenched it free. The limb gyrated in wild circles. The artificial fingers sliced through the material of his overalls and gouged a deep wound in his leg, adding to the haemorrhage.

"Help me!" he screamed.

Antimone tore her focus away from the horrific sight. She scratched absentmindedly at an itch on her wrist. She glanced down and spotted a band of inflamed skin. The patch of redness spread over the same area where the scientist had patted her moments earlier.

Her gaze settled on Martin Hendrick. He stood watching like the rest of them. She couldn't read his expression—somewhere between fascination and... something else. Satisfaction maybe.

He turned his head towards her. Their eyes met. A slight smile played at his lips. He tapped the button, and the lock released with a click.

"Stop him!" Antimone yelled.

The two nearest guards whirled around in surprise, weapons raised.

"Perrin was telling the truth," she said. "Dr Hendrick has infected us all with something. I've got a rash where he touched me."

The men flashed a glance towards the writhing figure. Max's features had become much paler, and his struggles seemed to be waning. One guard lifted his hand. He gasped as he took in the inflamed skin of his palm. "It's true. Stay right there and don't move."

Hendrick slowly raised his hands, revealing the thin white gloves he still wore. "It must be something you touched in here. I had nothing to do with this."

Fear was etched into the faces of the security team. "They make those tiny machines in this lab," the nearest man said. "What the hell have you done to us?"

"I just told you. It wasn't me. I'm the victim here."

Max Perrin groaned, and his head slumped onto his chest. The flow of blood had reduced to a trickle. All attention switched from his limp body to the scientist in the white coat.

"He is lying," the smaller of the two North Africans babbled, panic lacing his voice. His eyes flicked to the fingers of his right hand.

"Shut up," the guard beside him snapped, "unless you want another shot of this stuff in your face."

"No, let him speak," Jason said, clutching Paul tightly to his chest. "What's your name?"

"Mohammed Abadi, but people call me Mo. First, he handed over the gun that killed Mrs Baxter. He gave me his key card to open the door. Where I touched it, my fingers are burning."

"Why are you listening to this terrorist?" Hendrick asked, glaring at his former captor.

"He knew Mrs Baxter from before," Mo continued. "She was very surprised when he said he set free a person called Eileen."

"You're not talking about Eileen Floyd, are you?"

"Yes, yes. This man here worked with Mrs Baxter many years ago. He told her he released this Floyd woman. Then he made a call to somebody else. I cannot remember the name. Gral—"

"Anders Grolby?" Jason asked.

"Yes. That is right."

"But my biological mother was the first to die of the virus. My mother— I mean Mrs Baxter—always claimed it was an accident. If he was the one to let her go... But why tell Grolby? He handled security."

"Yes, I admit I was a researcher at Ilithyia," Hendrick said, "but I left before the pandemic started. I worked with Eileen Floyd. She threatened to become a whistleblower. It would've destroyed the company, so they kidnapped her and kept her in a cell behind the storeroom. The courts convicted her husband for killing her. I only found out about the kidnapping later when I heard a noise from the place where they were keeping her locked up, so I tried to help her escape."

"Why didn't you just call the police when you discovered what they were doing?"

"It was complicated."

"I don't see... Oh, I get it. You were involved in developing the virus."

Hendrick stared at Jason. His forehead creased in a scowl. "I'm leaving now."

"It was you, wasn't it? You were the one performing the dangerous research. You couldn't allow my biological mother to escape because she would've implicated you, so you told Grolby. But why let her go in the first place? It doesn't make sense unless... My God. You wanted her to spread the virus."

"That's all conjecture," Hendrick said. "You can't prove any of it."

"Maybe, but there's plenty of evidence of what you've done here. What is this stuff?"

Hendrick's gaze fixed on Jason as he contemplated his response. After a moment, he shook his head. "Not so bright after all, are you? You're in a nanotechnology lab. What do you think it is?"

"But why?"

"Don't you see that humanity is causing the annihilation of the planet? We rape and pillage the natural world for resources. Humans worry about new viruses and pandemics, but *we* are the disease. *We* are the ones killing the earth. Mankind is the greatest threat to the future of life. Do you know how many species we have driven to extinction? It's well over a million and still counting. If we keep going like this, soon nothing will remain."

A pious light lit up Hendrick's eyes. "Yes, I created the Orestes virus, and the irony is, Mrs Baxter and his father..." He pointed at Max Perrin's now limp body. "... funded my research. I designed it to save the world. When I discovered they were holding your mother, it provided an excellent opportunity to initiate the pandemic and deflect blame all in one go.

"I had no inkling how successful my plan would be. I always thought somebody would find a cure within the first few months, but as time went by and the virus kept mutating, I realised I'd created the perfect solution to curb mankind's destruction. No woman in their right mind would get pregnant, knowing it would cause their own death. The global population has been declining for over twenty years, and nature is finally making a recovery.

"When the opportunity to join this research effort came up, I jumped at the chance. I wanted to learn what the brightest minds in the world were working on. The old methods of antivirals are doomed to failure, but nanotechnology has the potential to cure all human diseases. I couldn't let that happen and destroy all my previous good work.

"Ironically, it was Professor Allard who sowed the first seeds of an idea. He can't stop talking about grey goo. What better way to put an end to this area of research than to turn his worst nightmare into reality? Yes, I placed a small quantity of these nanomachines on my gloves. They're designed to attack human tissue. I've touched most of you. They'll also transfer to anybody who touches a surface I've come into contact with.

"Before you worry too much about them spreading across the world and killing everybody on earth, that's not my intention. I only want to prevent this technology from becoming widely adopted and undoing my previous efforts. Their power source will run out of juice after a few hours. By then it'll be far too late for any of you. But if you allow me to go, I'll tell you how to stop them."

Stunned silence greeted Hendrick's confession.

"So, you were just going to leave and let us die?" Jason said.

"That's no longer necessary. The authorities won't be able to cover this up. Once word gets out about the real-world dangers of nanotechnology, the public will complain so loudly that they'll have no option but to stop all development."

"How much time have we got?" a guard asked, studying the reddening skin on his palm

"Not long. I'd say about ten or fifteen minutes before it starts getting really painful."

The man frantically rubbed his hand against the trousers of his uniform.

"I wouldn't do that if I were you," Hendrick said. "You'll only drive them in deeper. Oh, and by now, soap and water will have no effect. They've already worked their way below the surface of the skin. They're remarkable little machines."

"If we do let you go," another guard asked, "how do we know you'll keep your word?"

"Well, you don't, I suppose. You have no alternative but to trust me."

"I'm sure Professor Allard knows how to stop them," Antimone said.

"Perhaps eventually, but not in time to save any of you I've touched. The only way to deactivate these little critters is by using the magnetic field built into the archway over there." He gestured towards the section of the lab where the manufacturing machine sat. "I deactivated the magnetic field earlier tonight and changed the code. Not even the professor will be able to bypass my changes before it's too late. I'm leaving now. I'll call in a few minutes with instructions on how to reactivate it. It's been nice meeting you all, but I really must dash before the police arrive."

Tuesday 21ˢᵗ April 2037
Ilithyia Biotechnology, Northstowe

The five guards remained motionless, watching as Hendrick strode through the open doorway. Jason placed Paul on Antimone's lap.

"What are you doing?" she asked, her face creased in concern.

He lowered his lips to her ear and whispered, "Saving your life, I hope."

She held their son in an awkward embrace as she tried to prevent the inflamed patch of skin on her wrist from touching him.

Jason dashed after the scientist. "Wait!" he yelled.

Hendrick flashed a backward glance, and his pace quickened from a fast walk to a jog.

Jason broke into a sprint. His hand landed on the fugitive's shoulder and spun him around.

"If you don't let me go, they'll all die," Hendrick said between deep breaths.

"I'm guessing you have no intention of telling us how to stop the machines, so the chances are all of them will die, anyway."

"Well, you'll just have to trust me."

"Rosalind Baxter was vilified for the deaths of all those millions of women, but it was you all along. Why should I believe anything a mass murderer has to say?"

Hendrick's face twisted into a grin. "You really have little choice. Now, back off unless you want me to touch you too." He raised a gloved hand.

Rather than backing away, Jason lunged forwards. He seized both of Hendrick's hands in his own. The thin latex felt cool beneath his fingers.

Hendrick frowned in confusion. "What the hell are you doing?"

"This," Jason replied, releasing his grip and sliding a palm down each side of the scientist's face. Next, he spun the bewildered man around and forced his right arm behind his back.

Hendrick yelped in pain. "You're hurting me."

Jason ignored the doctor's protestations and, grabbing him by the neck, frogmarched him to the laboratory. Neither had a key card on their person that would permit entry, so he rapped a knuckle on the smooth surface.

Moments later, the door slid open, revealing Antimone's worried face. He shoved the scientist inside.

"Do those guns still work?" Jason asked the nearest guard.

"Um... yes," the man replied.

"Well, what are you waiting for? Shoot him. Make sure you immobilise his hands and legs."

Jason stepped back from his prisoner, and a squirt of grey material jetted from the nozzle of the guard's gun. Within a second, Hendrick could no longer move, locked in place by several loops of foam.

"Right," Jason said. "As I see it, you have two choices; you can either explain how to deactivate the nanomachines, or you can die with us."

"I told you earlier, release me and I'll let you know what to do."

"No deal. I should think your cheeks might be starting to itch a bit by now. They do look a little red."

Antimone shot Jason a questioning glance.

"The good doctor has some of his own creations on his face," he said.

"But how did you...?"

Jason held up his hands. "It's possible I accidentally touched his gloves and smeared a few nanomachines over his skin."

Antimone stared at him incredulously. "That means you're infected too."

"Yes, we're all in the same boat now. I imagine it might turn more than a little messy as they munch through to his brain."

Hendrick's eyes widened in panic as he tried to pull his arm free. "If you release me and promise to let me go afterwards," he said, "I'll tell you what to do."

"I don't think so," Jason said.

"This is blackmail."

"Call it what you like." Jason stepped closer to Hendrick and placed his hand on the man's forehead. "Oh, you're feeling warm. Oops, I may have spread a few more by doing that."

"All right," Hendrick gabbled. "I'll tell you how to disable the nanomachines, but you have to put me through first."

"Okay," Jason replied.

"Log in to my account on that computer over there. The username is M dot Hendrick, and the password is *save the earth* but using numbers for the S and E."

"What do you mean?"

"For Christ's sake. Five, lower case A, lower case V, three, capital T..."

"Oh, I get it."

Jason moved to the terminal and tapped the keys, floating in mid-air before his eyes. "Right, I'm in. What next?"

Hendrick navigated him through the options to access the controls for the powerful electromagnets built into the archway. After several more entries, a message box appeared: *Settings Updated.*

"Is that it?"

"Yes."

The red glow around the arch seemed unchanged. "Are you sure?" Jason asked, doubtfully.

"Of course I'm sure. Please hurry."

"Okay. Who's first?"

"Wait," Hendrick yelled. "You promised it would be me."

"Sorry, I forgot. Just walk through when you're ready."

The man struggled ineffectually against the grey loops of material.

"Oh dear. It looks like you missed your turn."

Hendrick screamed in rage. "You lied to me."

Jason ignored the increasingly vociferous protests and stood aside to allow the five guards to file through the glowing archway, one after the other. Antimone waited at the back of the line with Paul on her knee, shielding him from the grisly sight of Max Perrin's body. The four-year-old buried his face against her chest. She kept her wrist outstretched to prevent herself from transferring the nanomachines to her son.

"Come on, buddy," Jason said. "I need you to be a big boy and walk through by yourself." After a moment's more cajoling, Paul released his grip and stepped through to the adjacent room.

Jason leant over and picked up Antimone. "There's a strong magnetic field, so it's probably best not to go through in your wheelchair."

"What are we going to do about them?" she asked, nodding towards the three remaining live captives.

"We'll call for a decontamination team in a second, but quite frankly, I'm not in any great hurry. Let them sweat for a while. They deserve everything they get."

Jason shuffled sideways through the archway. "This reminds me of that time on the beach in Hunstanton."

"Could you assist me to the ground, sir knight?" Antimone said with a smile.

"Yes, my lady."

"But perhaps you would do me the honour of a kiss first."

Their lips met as they clung to each other for a brief moment, then he knelt on one knee and lowered her gently to the floor.

Epilogue

Tuesday 23rd June 2037
The Royal Palace of Tripoli, Tripoli, North Africa
Six months later

The aroma of spicy food drifted on the steamy air. Pots and saucepans clanged in a frenzy of activity as the army of cooks scurried about preparing the feast. The meal would feed fifty times the number of people who would actually be in attendance. Most would be wasted despite a significant proportion of the population in The Republic of North Africa suffering from malnutrition.

The cook bowed to his supervisor. "I am very sorry, sir, but I need to go to the toilet."

"Well, do not take too long about it," the sous-chef snapped. "We still have much work to do. Everything must be perfect for Mullah Awad. Only ten minutes remain until we must start serving. And make sure you wash your hands before returning."

"I will be as quick as I can, sir," the cook replied.

He turned and hurried from the kitchen. As he pushed through the doors into the men's washroom, the stench of faeces and stale urine provided a stomach-churning contrast to the enticing smells of cooking. The cook covered his face with his elbow and breathed through his mouth. He passed down the row of stalls, looking for one with clear water in the bowl of the stained white porcelain.

Finally, he settled on a cubicle marginally cleaner than the others. There was no toilet paper on the roll, but he wouldn't be needing any. He locked the door behind him and dropped the lid before settling down on the plastic cover. His pulse raced as he lowered his head to the floor to confirm the absence of any fellow workers. No, he was alone.

He removed his left shoe and turned it over, wrinkling his nose in distaste at the ingrained dirt staining the sole. His fingers grasped the heel and twisted. The bottom ten millimetres rotated with a click, revealing a tiny circuit board fitted with a small pushbutton at the centre. His handler had assured him the device was undetectable by the scanners used to check the workers before they were allowed in the vicinity of the ruling elite. So far, the promise had held true.

The mullah's movements were a closely guarded secret. This was the sixth time the cook had worked in the kitchens, preparing food for important dignitaries, but the first occasion the leader of the country had attended in person. The calls from the agency always came at short notice. The humourless security staff confiscated all electronic devices before they even allowed the workers on the bus to take them to the venue.

They paid him barely enough to survive, but he had little to live for after his wife and teenage daughter had died within the space of a few months of each other. The authorities forced the two most important people in his life to bear children to replenish the population lost to the Orestes virus. And of course, without the drugs to protect them, death followed moments after the multiple births. They hadn't even allowed him to see his twin daughters or four granddaughters before the bearded men in dark robes whisked them away to be raised by the state.

The operative had approached the cook when he left the hospital for the second time as a recently created widower with no surviving dependents. The agent kept his face covered. He offered to create the paperwork to get the cook to neighbouring Algeria and pay him enough money to live out the rest of his days in comfort. All he had to do in return was press the button when Mullah Awad was somewhere nearby.

He didn't know what would happen after that. The agent had promised that the people he worked for would spare him from any attack, provided he maintained a distance of at least fifty metres from the intended target. The cook didn't care whether he lived or died. All that mattered was that the man responsible for the deaths of his wife and daughter paid the price for his actions.

A satisfied smile occupied the cook's face as he pressed the button. Nothing happened, but he didn't expect it to. At least, not immediately. He planned to stay where he was for the next few minutes. If they came looking for him, he would claim he was suffering from diarrhoea. Judging by the foul stench lingering in the air and the state of the toilet bowls, he wasn't the only one.

He sat on the toilet seat, waiting for retribution.

***

Across the border in Algeria, an automated listening post picked up the radio signal. Within two minutes, a dozen human operators pored over a map, studying the location of the source. They pulled up satellite imagery and soon spotted the dark outlines of the heavily armoured vehicles used to transport the mullah and his entourage. The Reponan military frequently used decoys to mask the mullah's movements, but this was a confirmed sighting.

Next, they checked the name of the operative and confirmed he was a cook. There were several spots inside the recently restored Royal Palace where the ruler of The Republic of North Africa might be dining. But that didn't matter. After a short confirmatory phone call, the British Prime Minister and the American President gave their approvals for the mission to proceed.

Thirty-six thousand kilometres overhead, the geostationary satellite released three of its array of kinetic bombardment weapons. The dart-shaped projectiles fell towards the surface of the earth. With nothing to oppose the force of gravity, they accelerated rapidly to a speed of eight kilometres per second. At a height of four hundred kilometres, the fins on the exterior began to interact with the thin atmosphere, guiding the warheads to their target. As the air grew thicker, the resistance increased, slowing the rate of descent. The noses of the bombs punched through the troposphere, glowing a bright cherry red.

A few seconds later, they carved through the sky above the Royal Palace in Tripoli. The metre-long tungsten rods carried no explosive charge, but they didn't need to. The kinetic energy they carried, as they neared the earth's surface, was equivalent to that contained in many times their weight of conventional explosives.

A sonic boom trailed behind the weapons, but if their targets registered the sound, it was far too late to react. The warheads were still travelling at over three kilometres per second when they reached the ground. They hit almost simultaneously, instantly vaporising everything within the immediate vicinity. The bodies of Mullah Awad and his entourage disintegrated into their constituent atoms in less time than it took to blink an eye.

Afterwards, the intelligence reports confirmed the deaths of over seventy people. Among the few survivors was a cook who had the good fortune to leave the kitchens due to a bout of diarrhoea moments before the bombardment began.

Saturday 7th July 2040
New York Olympic Stadium, USA
Three years later

Antimone rounded the final bend onto the home straight. She risked a quick backward glance. Her nearest competitor trailed by at least thirty metres. She drove down hard against the shiny hand rings of her wheelchair to accelerate towards the finish.

She tuned out the deafening roar of the crowd as she neared the end of the race. Almost every person in the stadium chanted her name. Five metres short of the finishing line, she allowed herself the luxury of raising her arms. That raised an even louder cheer from the enthusiastic spectators.

Out of instinct, she lifted her eyes to the electronic scoreboard to check her time: half a second outside the world record, but that didn't matter. She already held the achievement of being the fastest woman ever to cover fifteen hundred metres in a wheelchair. There would be plenty of opportunity in the future to improve upon her lifetime best.

The most significant factor in this race was that she had smashed the field, leading from start to finish, and had finally achieved her goal of winning a gold medal at the Olympics. The letters 'OR' after the time signalled another major accomplishment: a new Olympic record.

She cruised to a halt. Shielding her eyes from the blazing sun with her left hand, she completed a three-hundred-and-sixty-degree rotation, waving to the packed arena with her right. Every seat seemed to be occupied, and not one facemask in sight. The recent rapid advances in nanotechnology had all but eradicated the Orestes virus, rendering protective face coverings a thing of the past. Strict guidelines regulated the use of the new miracle technology, but by now, few diseases remained that the tiny machines couldn't cure.

A figure jumped over the barrier at the edge of the track. Immediately, half a dozen law enforcement officers raised their weapons. They relaxed when they spotted the security badge hanging on the lanyard around the man's neck.

"It's all right, guys," the man called. "I'm her trainer."

John Marshall jogged over, his craggy face cracking in a wide grin. He draped a Union Jack flag over Antimone's shoulders. "I always knew you'd do it. Congratulations."

"Thanks, Coach," Antimone replied. "I couldn't have done it without you."

"Enjoy the occasion. You've earned it. I'll catch up with you afterwards." Her gaze followed him as he retraced his steps.

She looked up to the giant screens mounted between the four stands. Every corner of the stadium showed three-dimensional images of the last few seconds of the race. The shot changed to one of her family. Her parents sat side by side at the centre of a group of people wearing the red, white and blue colours of the British flag. Her father hugged her mother as both wiped tears of happiness from their cheeks. The three adjacent seats were empty.

Where was Jason? Her eyes tracked down the rows of seating to where the cheering crowd parted to allow somebody to descend the steps. Then she saw him. One hand grasped their son, Paul, now seven years old. The other arm held their fifteen-month-old daughter, Eileen. Antimone and Jason had married shortly after their last brush with death. The three surviving men who had threatened their lives, including the notorious creator of the Orestes virus, Martin Hendrick, were all serving life sentences without hope of parole. Max Perrin had suffered too much blood loss by the time the medical team arrived and was beyond help. Rosalind Baxter, Naeem Kubar and Nick Butler were also pronounced dead at the scene.

None of the leaders in The Republic of North Africa responsible for instigating the plot had survived the aerial bombardment of the Royal Palace in Tripoli. In the leadership vacuum following the bombing, free elections took place for the first time in over a decade. Under pressure from the world's superpowers, the new government adopted a more moderate stance. They no longer forced women to bear children and benefitted from the subsequent influx of medical aid.

Behind the three members of her family stood Antimone's onetime competitor, Aya Shaladi. The North African woman had applied for permission to remain in Britain after being released from the asylum centre. The authorities had believed her when she told them she was coerced by her government, under fear of death, into assisting her father in the attack at the 2034 Olympics in Glasgow. Antimone had agreed to speak on her behalf, and Aya's assistance in helping the Westerners escape from Tripoli counted in her favour at the adjudication.

Aya had become an unlikely friend and was now Antimone's main training partner. In a few months' time, she planned to apply for British citizenship, which would enable her to compete for her new country.

Antimone attributed much of her recent success to the friendly competition offered by her former rival.

Antimone guided her wheelchair to the side of the track. Jason passed Paul over the barrier, then handed Eileen to Aya before clambering over himself. He accepted his daughter back and leant down to kiss his wife. Raucous cheers, interspersed with several oohs and ahs, greeted the embrace. Paul ran up to his mother and wrapped his arms around her neck. He held her for a moment, then released his grip and grabbed his father's hand.

The girl who survived the Orestes virus waved to the crowd as the three most important people in her life accompanied her on a lap of honour.

The End

Author's Notes

Dear Reader,

This marks the end of not only this book but also the whole series. First of all, thank you for spending your hard-earned cash. If you bought all the books in the Decimation trilogy and made it this far, you have now read approximately three-hundred-thousand words.

I sincerely hope you enjoyed reading Annihilation and its predecessors, Decimation and Termination. Writing is a solitary activity, and it takes several hundred hours of effort to complete a novel. What makes it all worthwhile for me (and I suspect almost all other writers) is when people enjoy what I have written. If that is the case, I would be immensely grateful if you could spread the word by leaving a review on Amazon, Goodreads or preferably both. Good reviews are a significant factor when readers are searching for their next book and are especially important for independent authors, who often struggle to raise awareness of their work in a crowded market. I pay particular attention to all review comments and use them to improve my writing.

I want to express my gratitude to my advance readers: Marika Dworzak, Fergus Belcher, Mark Potter, Brian Baker and fellow authors, Ross Greenwood, Shaun Griffiths and Terry Marchion. This small group has supported me through the whole trilogy, and for that I'm totally in their debt. Between them they spotted several issues, including a character who mysteriously changed first name halfway through this book. This novel has undergone thorough review, but those typos can be hard to spot and occasionally sneak through undetected. Please let me know if you find one so that other readers benefit from your sharp-eyed attention. The best ways are to leave a comment on my website or email me at readers@rjne.uk.

As ever, my wife, Judith and daughter, Emily, deserve a special mention for putting up with the endless discussions about plot and characters. Thanks also to Hampton Lamoureux, who designed the covers for all the books in the series. Having tried my hand at cover design in the past (with somewhat mixed results I might add), I am in awe of his skills and now leave such matters to the professionals.

Finally, I receive a lot of support from members of the Facebook author community through various writing groups. The administrators of The Book Club and its spinoff, The Book Club Reviewer Group, deserve special mention for their tireless help in bringing together readers and writers.

Little did I know when I started work on Decimation in 2016, and the sequel, Termination, in 2019, that we would soon be living in a world where viruses play such a huge part in peoples' lives. When I first wrote about the fictional Orestes virus, nobody had even heard of COVID-19. I lost my mother to this dreadful disease. I can only hope that fact follows fiction, and scientists discover ways to prevent this and other, as yet unknown, illnesses in the future.

Nanomachines are still a long way from being the universal panacea described within the closing pages of this book. However, many nanotechnology research labs have recently directed their efforts towards the development of a vaccine for the treatment of COVID-19. Whether they provide a step-change in how medical professionals treat illnesses remains to be seen.

The "grey goo" scenario, the mention of which upsets Professor Allard in this novel, has been covered before in fiction. Blood Music by Greg Bear is a fine example of the genre, and despite being written over thirty-five years ago, is still well worth a read. But don't worry too much; self-replicating machines at the nanoscale remain a long way from becoming reality.

The non-lethal weapons described in Annihilation are all in development or exist already. For example, guns that shoot sticky foam were used in Somalia to assist in the withdrawal of peacekeepers. Tasers have been in widespread use for many years, but it is possible to buy a weapon today that shoots a projectile to incapacitate the target through electrocution without using wires.

Unfortunately, the lethal variety have also become easier to manufacture. One such weapon is the Liberator, a 3D-printable single shot handgun, similar to that used by Max and his team.

If you enjoyed this book, you might like to try some of my other standalone novels including The Rage, The Colour of the Soul and Assassin's Web.

Finally, I have several ideas bubbling away for future books, so if you want to keep up to date with what's coming next, please sign up to my mailing list at www.rjne.uk. Updates are only every few weeks, and I promise not to spam you! I would also be delighted to hear from you through the comments section of my website or via email (readers@rjne.uk).

Thanks for reading.

Richard T. Burke
August 2021

To read the author's blog and to see news of upcoming books, please visit www.rjne.uk or follow him on Twitter (@RTBurkeAuthor) or Facebook (https://www.facebook.com/RichardTBurkeBooks).

Printed in Great Britain
by Amazon